"WHEN WE LEAVE HERE IN A COUPLE OF DAYS YOU'RE GOING TO LEAD ME TO THAT VALLEY. UNDERSTAND?"

"You can't make me do anything," Anabeth challenged him.

"Can't I?" Jake stood and in the same movement grabbed Anabeth's hand and yanked her out of the chair. She came flying toward him, stopped only by contact with his broad chest. One of his hands caught a handful of her hair and arched her head back at a painful angle so she had no choice except to look at him. His other arm circled her hips, pinning her against his thighs.

Jake felt the heat in his loins and cursed. "You'll do what I say, Kid, or I'll—"

Anabeth opened her mouth to argue, and Jake closed it in the most efficient way possible—with his own.

Dell Books by Joan Johnston

After the Kiss
The Barefoot Bride
The Bodyguard
The Bridegroom
Captive
The Cowboy
The Inheritance
Kid Calhoun
Maverick Heart
Outlaw's Bride
Sweetwater Seduction
The Loner
The Texan
Frontier Woman
Comanche Woman

Kid Calhoun

Joan Johnston

A DELL BOOK

Published by
Dell Publishing
a division of
Random House, Inc.
1540 Broadway
New York, New York 10036

The trademark Dell® is registered in the U.S. Patent and Trademark Office.

ISBN: 0-440-21280-4

Printed in the United States of America

Published simultaneously in Canada

March 1993

11 10 9 8 7 6

OPM

This book is dedicated to
two women who have
encouraged, emboldened, and exhorted me
always to do my best—
and believe that I will.

My sincere thanks to
my editor Damaris Rowland
and
my agent Denise Marcil.

1

"You cheated!"

Kid Calhoun admitted to a few vices—drinking, smoking, and swearing among them—but he never cheated at cards. The Kid's mouth flattened and his eyes narrowed at the accusation being flung across the table.

"You cheated! Nobody could have that kind of luck!" the cowboy ranted.

"Those are fighting words, mister," the Kid said in a quiet, whiskey-laced voice.

The cowboy seemed to realize suddenly how quiet the saloon had become. He glanced around and saw his friend at the bar gesturing frantically, but he had no idea what had his compadre so upset. He looked back at the whelp sitting across the table from him. The stripling was rail thin and had a face as smooth as a baby's behind. The Kid's extreme youth rankled. Bluffed by a brat who was still wet behind the ears! It was humiliating. He wasn't going to stand for it.

The Kid pulled the coins in the center of the table toward him, but his eyes stayed on the grizzled-looking cowboy. Smoke curled lazily from a cigarette caught at the corner of the Kid's mouth. A sweat-stained hat with a silver concho band was pulled low on his forehead, shadowing his eyes. "I don't cheat," the Kid said. "Since I'm in a good mood, I'd be willing to accept an apology for the insult. Assuming you're man enough to own up to being a bad loser."

"Why you—"

The cowboy surged out of his chair and grabbed for his gun. He stopped with his fingertips brushing leather and stared, for the Kid already held the barrel of a Colt aimed at his belly. The Kid was fast. Faster than fast. The cowboy swallowed hard. Sweat beaded on his upper lip. Ever so slowly, he moved his hand away from his side.

"I'm waiting for that apology," the Kid said.

"Figure it was my bad luck did me in," the cowboy conceded.

The Kid's lip curled in the semblance of a smile. "Luck's like that sometimes." The Kid holstered his gun and reached for the whiskey in front of him. There was a slight movement from the cowboy, and the Kid said, "Don't."

The cowboy froze.

"You're thinking that you'll be able to draw on me." The Kid's eyes left the cowboy and returned to the pile of coins in front of him, as though the cowboy were not standing across from him, waiting for a chance to shoot him down. "I wouldn't bet on it. Your luck hasn't been running too good lately."

It was plain the cowboy wanted to draw his gun. And just as plain that the Kid wasn't particularly worried about the prospect. The Kid continued holding the whiskey glass in his gun hand, while his other hand sorted through the pot on the table. Could the Kid really beat him to the draw under those circumstances?

The men in the saloon remained silent, waiting to see whether the cowboy would call the Kid's bluff.

"What's going on here? Everything all right, Kid?"

The tall man standing at the batwing doors to the saloon bore a striking resemblance to the Kid, having the same crow-wing black hair and blue eyes. But the man showed the promise of the boy. He was broad-shouldered and lean-hipped, with a voice an octave lower and a strong jaw shadowed by a day's beard.

"No problem, Uncle Booth. Everything's fine," the Kid answered.

The cowboy welcomed the interruption like a long-lost brother. "Just a difference of opinion," he said to the tall man. Now that the Kid had reinforcements, he could retreat without losing any more of his pride. He turned and headed for the bar where his friend was standing.

"Do you know who you was callin' a cheat?" his friend hissed. "That was Kid Calhoun. Fast as greased lightning. He ain't never killed a man, but it's only a matter of time.

"Always has lots of money to spend, but nobody knows where he gets it. Says he's got a mine down south a ways, but all you have to do is see his hands to know he ain't workin' no claim.

"There's them that say the Calhouns—the Kid and his uncle—have been robbin' stagecoaches from here to Texas. But ain't never been nobody could peg 'em for sure. You was damned lucky to get off with a whole skin!"

The cowboy called for a rye and downed it in a gulp. He had been luckier than he'd thought.

"It's time we were leaving, Kid," the man at the door said. "Gather up your winnings, and I'll meet you at the hotel."

The Kid nodded his agreement. He finished his whiskey and dropped the coins from the table into his calfskin vest pocket as though he were in no hurry to leave. Then he stood and crossed to the door. At first, his hands hung down easily at his sides. The men in the saloon shifted uneasily when halfway to the door he slowly curled them into fists.

Little did they know the Kid had done it to hide the fact his hands were trembling. The Kid shoved his way through the batwing doors and stalked down the Santa Fe boardwalk to a boot and saddle shop halfway between the saloon and the hotel. To anyone who passed by, it appeared as though he was admiring a black saddle decorated with silver conchos displayed in the window. For a moment, he did.

Then his gaze slipped to the dressmaker's shop next door. To the fashionable Wedgwood blue silk taffeta dress, with its frog trim decorating the fitted waist and long sleeves, and eighteen cloth-covered buttons down the front. Kid Calhoun took a deep, shuddery breath and let it out. This time things had almost gone too far. This time, he had almost had to kill a man. The day was bound to come when he wouldn't be able to bluff his way free. Then there would be no turning back. All his hopes and dreams for the future would be lost forever.

The Kid hung his head for a moment. This charade had to stop. It had been Uncle Booth's idea, and it had been a good one at the time, but the situation had gotten out of hand. Imagine how angry that cowboy would have been if he had realized it was not a young man who had backed him down, but a young woman! Imagine his wrath if he had realized that the Kid's real name was Anabeth Calhoun!

Anabeth looked longingly at the stylish dress from beneath lowered lashes. She had never worn a dress, at least not that she could remember. From the age of six, Anabeth had lived in a stone house in an isolated, hidden valley southwest of Santa Fe. She had been raised by her father and her uncle, who had headed west from their farm in Pennsylvania the year her mother died. The two men had discovered Treasure

Valley while prospecting for gold shortly after they arrived in New Mexico thirteen years ago.

The grassy valley, with its wealth of fresh water, had been a treasure, all right, but it was the only one they had found. The valley was a vast oval of land surrounded by impenetrable rock walls, totally invisible from the outside, and only barely accessible to humans. To this day, none of her uncle Booth's outlaw gang knew where it was. It had provided a haven from marauding Apaches and, lately, a refuge from the law.

But her father hadn't found much joy of it. He had been crippled in a mine cave-in when she was nine. Her uncle Booth had supposedly continued working in the Two Brothers Mine, located several miles west of the valley, eking out enough to support them. Meanwhile, she had nursed her invalid father, raised vegetables in a garden, and studied from books that Booth brought her from Santa Fe.

It wasn't until her father's death of pneumonia when she was sixteen that Anabeth had learned the truth about where Booth had gotten the money to support them. Her uncle hadn't dug all that gold from the Two Brothers Mine with backbreaking labor. He had stolen it from other people. While he was supposedly off working in the mine, he had been playing cards and living the high life in Santa Fe.

In hindsight, Anabeth saw how the outlaw trail must have appealed to her uncle. As a younger brother, he had always depended on her father to lead the way—and do the bulk of the work. Booth was a dreamer and used to getting what he wanted by his wits and his charm, rather than by working for it. He had been much indulged by Anabeth's father, who was a full fifteen years older and used to smoothing Booth's path in life for him.

Anabeth could remember a long-ago day when her

father had labored with a pick-ax while Booth sat on
a stone in the shade nearby and created marvelously
accurate drawings of his brother at work. Then Booth
had busied himself creating truly lifelike creatures
carved from wood. By the end of the day, her father
had dug out a scant ounce of gold, and Anabeth had
added a burro to her collection of wooden animals.

When her father had been crippled, the responsibility for supporting the three of them had fallen
squarely on Booth's shoulders. To his credit, Booth
hadn't shirked his duty. He had simply found an easier way of providing for them that didn't require the
sweat of his brow.

When Anabeth had learned the truth about Uncle
Booth three years ago, she had been appalled. It was
hard to think of her charming, fun-loving uncle as an
outlaw. But at the age of sixteen she had been well
aware of Booth's penchant for doing things the easy
way. And being an outlaw was apparently easier than
working to earn a living.

The way Booth described it, he was simply reliev-
ing people of gold who had more than they needed.
Her uncle made it sound like he was some sort of
Robin Hood—only he was the poor soul who ended
up with the rich man's gold. To Anabeth, the outlaw
life appeared both daring and romantic. So much so,
that she had begged Booth to let her come along and
see for herself.

It was because her uncle had indulged her, that
Anabeth was in this fix now. Because when she had
insisted that Booth take her along on one of his hold-
ups—for the adventure it promised—he hadn't been
sensible enough to deny her.

Booth had come up with the idea of dressing her as
a boy and passing her off as his nephew. She had
braided her long black hair and tucked it up under a
battered Stetson. To the members of Booth's gang—

Whiskey, Reed, Solano, Grier, Snake, and Teague—
she was "The Kid."

The hardened outlaws had treated her like the troublesome, if entertaining, brat she often was. Indiffer-
ently. Irascibly. And downright inhospitably. Booth
had taught her how to shoot to protect herself, and
along the way she had acquired a few vices that
added to her disguise.

It hadn't taken long riding with Booth's gang before Anabeth realized that she didn't want to spend
her life as an outlaw. As far as she was concerned, the
rewards were never as great as the fear of getting
killed—or of having to kill someone.

Anabeth should have quit riding with the gang. But
she was too anxious about Booth's safety when he
rode off alone. She was a better shot than he was, and
she paid more attention to the details that kept them
safe, both during the robberies and afterward.

Anabeth had soon realized that if anyone was going
to do something to put them back on the right side of
the law, it was going to have to be her. So she had
begun asking for a portion of Booth's share of the loot
to save toward the day when they could leave the outlaw trade. Booth had laughed at her, but he had given
her what she asked for.

It hadn't been easy saving. Booth spent his share of
the spoils on whiskey and women, and it never
seemed to last very long. Anabeth always ended up
giving her uncle a part of her savings to delay the
necessity of having to hold up another stage.

Despite her uncle's faults, Anabeth loved him
dearly. She lived in dread of the day when all her
carefully laid plans to go straight would go awry.
What if Booth were shot and killed? Or they got
caught? Unfortunately, her dream of saving enough
money to buy a ranch in Colorado—where Booth had
never robbed a stage—was a long way from being

realized. Sometimes she felt as though she were fighting a losing battle.

Only it was a battle she couldn't afford to lose. Because Anabeth didn't want to spend the rest of her life masquerading as a man, either. She wanted to see what it was like to dress and act like a woman. She had watched the ladies stroll the boardwalk in Santa Fe, so she knew a lot about how to walk with small, delicate steps, how to smile flirtatiously and twirl a parasol. But she had never had the chance to try it out.

Anabeth knew from seeing her uncle with Sierra Starr at the Town House Saloon that there was also a physical side to being female. But she had no inclination to rut with a man. Her lack of desire shouldn't have bothered her, but it did. She worried that there must be something wrong with her because, at nineteen, she didn't possess the more tender feelings a woman was supposed to display toward a man.

It was easy to excuse why she hadn't been attracted to any of the men in Booth's gang. For each one she could find a fault—too old, too drunk, too dirty, too mean. But there was another man who should have been attractive to her, for whom she should have been able to feel something, and hadn't.

Wolf.

She had met the Apache years ago when they were both children. Wolf had discovered the valley when he had trailed a deer there. Each of them had filled a void in the other's life, and they had become fast—if secret—friends.

In the years since they had met, Wolf had taught her all he knew of the Apache; she had taught him the white man's customs and tongue. More recently he had helped her capture wild mustangs and taught her how to tame them. The seven horses she had now

were the beginning of what she hoped would be a
herd she could someday take to Colorado.

Lately, she had noticed a change in Wolf's behavior
toward her. The last time she had seen him, just before she left the valley to come north to Santa Fe, she
had realized for the first time that he desired her as a
woman. Anabeth felt a knot in her stomach when she
remembered what had happened between them that
day.

It was the first time in nearly a month that she had
seen Wolf. They had been lying in the cool grass beside the deep, crystal clear pond that graced one end
of the valley, watching the clouds pass overhead. She
had been feeling especially restless, and the words
were out before she realized the meaning that could
be attached to them. "You were gone a long time. I
missed you."

"It has been a single moon since last I saw you," he
had teased.

"Where have you been?" she asked.

His smile was feral. "Hunting. Stealing horses.
Fighting soldiers."

"I wish you didn't enjoy it so much." She touched a
wound on his thigh that had barely healed. "And that
you would be more careful." She felt his flesh tense
under her touch.

"I am a warrior. It is my destiny to die in battle."

"Not too soon, I hope," she chided. "I would hate
to have to cut off all my hair."

"Would you mourn for me as a proper Apache
woman?" Wolf reached out and grasped a handful of
her hair.

Anabeth was surprised by the look in his eyes, by
the possessiveness of his touch. She didn't know what
to do about either, so she rose abruptly. He let her
waist-length hair slide through his fingers.

She turned and looked back at him over her shoulder. "I'll never have to mourn you, Wolf, because there will be no one to tell me you're gone." It was the truth. No one in his village knew Wolf came to the valley. No one would know to tell her he was dead.

Anabeth was wearing only an Apache breechclout, two strips of fringed buckskin that fell to the knees in front and the ankles in back, held at her hips with a cord of rawhide. It was the dress of an Apache brave. Even with Wolf, she had never acted the role of a woman. She had been too young when she met him to feel any modesty around him, and she had never felt uncomfortable with her breasts bared to his gaze. Until today.

Anabeth raised her arms and dived gracefully into the pond. When she came up for air, Wolf was dragging off his moccasins. For a second he stood in his breechclout on the grassy verge. He was a magnificent-looking man.

Her eyes drifted up his bronzed body, from his sinewy legs to his flat, taut stomach, then across his chest where the muscles rippled. His shoulder-length black hair was parted in the center and held off his face by a rawhide band. Her gaze roamed up his corded neck to his jutting jaw and strong cheekbones, until she finally met his dark, dark eyes.

Desire.

Anabeth had never seen that particular look directed at her before, but she recognized it all the same. It should have elated her. Instead, it frightened her. She turned and swam rapidly toward the opposite edge of the pool.

She should have known better. Wolf was a hunter. He responded instinctively to her flight by chasing her. She raced to elude him, but he grabbed her ankle. This was a familiar game, but there was something different about Wolf's hold on her. Anabeth kicked herself free, as she had in the past, but instead of letting her escape, Wolf caught her again at the waist.

"Let go!" she cajoled, breathless with excitement, anxious without knowing why. "I want to swim. I—"

Suddenly, with a shriek of delight, she lunged up out of the water and put the full force of her weight on his shoulders, forcing him underwater. By the time he came up again, spitting, spluttering, eyelashes dripping, she was already levering herself out of the water and onto the wide rock ledge on the opposite side of the pond that eventually rose into a sheer cliff.

She stretched out on the hot stone, her wet hair conforming to her shape like a shiny, form-fitting cloak. Ordinarily she would have urged Wolf to join her. This time she did not.

He swam over to the ledge anyway, and levered himself out in a single powerful move. He lay down beside her, close enough to make her feel uncomfortable. She started to edge away, but he put a hand on her hip to keep her still.

Slowly, deliberately, Wolf's hand stroked down the naked length of her thigh where her breechclout had fallen away.

Anabeth shivered at the ticklish touch. She watched Wolf with wary eyes. He had never touched her this way. She felt confused and unsure of what he wanted from her. Surely not to couple. But she did not know how else to explain Wolf's strange behavior.

His eyes were heavy-lidded, his lips full, his jaw taut. Every muscle in his body seemed tense. The pulse in his throat beat fast. Anabeth reached out to touch it, and he actually recoiled from her.

Suddenly he was on his feet pacing back and forth before her. She leaped up to confront him, fists on hips. "What's the matter with you?" she demanded. "What is it you want from me?"

"What a man wants from a woman," he said in a low, guttural voice. "To hold you. To lie with you."

Anabeth drew a sharp breath. She had never thought of Wolf as a man, with a man's desire. Her eyes dropped to the ground. Her bare toes traced a wet pattern on the rock. She looked back up at Wolf with curious eyes. Maybe she would feel something for him if she let him touch her. Maybe all that was needed to awaken her feminine nature was to let him make love to her.

"All right," she said at last.

Wolf stared suspiciously at her, as though he expected her to pull some trick on him, as she had in the pond. At last he stepped close enough to slip an arm around her waist. Slowly, surely, he pulled her into his embrace.

Anabeth felt Wolf's shudder as their two bodies aligned. His flesh felt warm against hers. Tentatively, she rested her cheek against his shoulder. His body had a distinct scent, a musky fragrance that she found pleasant because she associated it with the boy who had grown to manhood as her friend.

Anabeth traced his collarbone and the hollow above it. Her eyes widened with surprise when she felt his body tighten beneath her fingertips.

Wolf's hand left her shoulder and smoothed over her hair, all the way down to her hips. It felt good. Comforting.

"Do that again," she murmured.

He did as she asked, then slipped his hand under her hair and caressed the length of her back, from the dimples in her buttocks up her backbone, until he finally circled her nape with his hand.

Anabeth shivered. "Don't stop."

Wolf's hand skimmed the length of her again, and Anabeth couldn't help the soft sound of pleasure that escaped her. She was jarred when Wolf put both hands on her hips and pushed her away.

"Why did you stop?" she asked. "That felt good. Will you do it again?"

Abruptly, he turned his back on her.

"What's wrong?" She reached out to touch his shoulder, but he flinched away from her.

"You do not want me," he said in a curt voice.

"What?"

He turned to face her, and she saw the frustration in his dark eyes. "I do not see a woman's passion when I look into your eyes."

"What?" She had known for some time that she didn't react as other women did to a man, but it was still a shock to hear Wolf say the words aloud.

"You do not desire me."

He sounded so unhappy that for a moment Anabeth was tempted to lie. But she met his brooding gaze and knew he would see the truth in her eyes. "No," she admitted. "I don't."

His lips flattened in dissatisfaction.

Her temper flared. "Did you want me to lie?"

"No. There has always been truth between us. So I will tell you this. I want you for my woman. And I will have you."

"But that's ridiculous. I don't desire you! I can't—"

"Enough!" His voice was sharp. "There is nothing more to be said now."

Anabeth was angry. "We'll talk about this right now! I don't think—"

"Helllllooooooo! Anabeeeetttthhh. Where are yooooooou?"

Anabeth had whirled at the sound of her uncle's voice echoing down the valley. "It's Uncle Booth! You'd better go now. I—"

When she had turned around, Wolf was gone. He had disappeared as though he were never there. It

was something every Apache learned from birth, as
hunted beasts do, because moving quickly and silently meant the difference between life and death.
Wolf had taught Anabeth how it was done, though she
was not nearly so good at it as he was.

As she loosened the breechclout and let it fall to the
stone beneath her, she felt a sense of frustration, of
things left unfinished. She pulled on long johns,
socks, shirt, jeans, and boots, all the while remembering the look on Wolf's face before he had left her. The
hardness and the determination had been very unsettling.

She stuffed the wet buckskins into a hidden crevice
in the rocks by the pond where her uncle wouldn't
find them. Later, when Booth was not around, she
would come back and lay them out to dry. She was
frowning when she headed for the entrance to the
valley. If she hadn't known Wolf, trusted him as she
did, she might even have been afraid of him after
what had just happened.

Above all, she was left with the feeling of having
failed somehow as a woman. She had been tempted
to speak to Booth about the problem, but there was
no way she could do so without bringing Wolf into the
conversation. She could not betray the Apache's existence without endangering his life.

Anabeth had done her best to ignore what had happened, or rather, *not* happened, between her and
Wolf. Maybe she wasn't a whole woman. That didn't
keep her from wanting the silk taffeta dress in the
next window, even though she could never wear it so
long as she remained Kid Calhoun.

Anabeth turned her feet in the direction of the hotel
and continued down the boardwalk. She kept her
eyes straight ahead, aware of the way men and
women both avoided her. The law in Santa Fe kept an
eye on Booth's gang, but none of them had ever been

arrested. So far, no victim of any of the robberies had ever positively identified anyone in the Calhoun Gang.

Anabeth intended to keep it that way. Which was why she had to talk Booth out of the robbery he had planned for the end of the week near Old Horse Springs.

She knocked before she entered Booth's hotel room. She had learned from experience that she might find Booth in an awkward situation. At least it was awkward for her. Neither Booth nor Sierra ever seemed to mind being seen in bed together.

"Come in."

She entered and wasn't surprised to discover Sierra Starr in the hotel room with Booth.

"I was just leaving," Sierra said. She was pulling on a pair of black kid gloves that completed an ensemble that could have come straight from *Harper's Bazar*. Sierra wore a plume-trimmed bonnet that did little to subdue her glorious head of naturally red curls.

In the green silk Polonaise gown, with its pristine white ruffle at the neck, the Soiled Dove from the Town House Saloon looked more a lady than most ladies Anabeth had seen in Santa Fe. Anabeth envied her because she was also a desirable—and desired—woman.

Not even Sierra knew the truth about the Kid being female. Booth had said, "It's best not to trust anybody." It was clear from the way Sierra teased Anabeth that, despite their bed-play, Booth had kept her secret from the other woman.

Sierra rubbed a gloved hand across Anabeth's baby-smooth cheek and said, "I have a lovely new girl who might interest you, Kid. Why don't you come by the saloon next time you're in town?"

Anabeth flushed scarlet. "I—I—"

Sierra laughed, a light, friendly sound that bubbled up from inside her. The look in her green eyes was kind, if teasing. "Her name is Bonnie. Tell her I said you should look her up."

Sierra turned from a flustered Anabeth and crossed back to the four-poster bed where Booth was stretched out fully dressed on top of the quilt with a sketch pad in hand. She leaned over him to see what he had drawn, and found herself looking every bit as ravishing on paper as she was in real life.

Sierra put her hands on either side of Booth's face and leaned down to kiss him tenderly on the mouth. "Take care of yourself."

Booth grinned. "I could say the same."

"Good-bye, Booth." Sierra said it as though she would never see him again. There was always the chance she wouldn't.

As many times as Anabeth had seen Booth and Sierra bid each other farewell, it still moved her to realize how much they seemed to care for each other. But Booth would never agree to live on what Sierra earned from her half of the Town House Saloon. And Sierra could never give up the security she had sacrificed so much to earn, only to be an outlaw's bride. They often met and made love, but they apparently were not destined to spend their lives together.

Once Sierra was gone Anabeth crossed and settled herself at the foot of the four-poster bed. She took out the makings from her vest pocket and concentrated on rolling a cigarette.

"I don't think we should do this job," she said.

"Why not?" Booth asked.

"Just a feeling I have."

"You'll have to do better than that if you want to change my mind."

Anabeth stuck the cigarette in the corner of her mouth. She raked a match across her jeans and squinted her eyes against the smoke as she took the first drag. "In the past you've always taken your time getting to know all about a man before you let him join the gang. What do you know about this new fellow, Wat Rankin?"

"He came to me with information about a rancher who'll be carrying more gold than any of us have ever seen at one time."

"Doesn't that sound the least bit suspicious to you? Why did Rankin share his information with us? Why not just steal the gold himself?"

Booth shrugged. "There's safety in numbers, I suppose."

Frustrated, Anabeth blew out a stream of smoke. "I don't like Rankin," she said flatly. "And I don't trust him. How do we know his information about this Sam Chandler being on the stage isn't just a ploy to set us up for the law?"

"I checked. Chandler is a rancher from around Old Horse Springs who recently drove a herd of cattle to Colorado for sale. According to Rankin, Chandler is returning on the stage, and he's carrying the gold on him."

"What else do you know about Rankin?"

"I admit I don't have much information on him. He doesn't seem to have many friends," Booth conceded.

"Doesn't that prove something?"

"Most outlaws don't," Booth pointed out reasonably.

Anabeth threw her cigarette on the floor and ground it out with the toe of her boot. "Dammit, Booth! I'm scared!"

Booth scooted down the bed and put an arm around Anabeth's shoulder. "Everything's going to be fine, Kid. I've got this holdup planned down to the last detail. If you don't feel comfortable, why don't you sit this one out?"

"I'd feel even worse not knowing what was going on," Anabeth confessed. "Please, Booth. Let's not do this job."

Booth's voice hardened. "Look, Kid. It's not just me who needs the money. There are six other men to think about."

"They'll listen to you," Anabeth cajoled. "If you tell them not to do it, they won't."

Booth shook his head. "It isn't that simple, Kid."

"Why the hell not?"

Booth stared down at strong hands that should have been callused from hard work—but weren't. "Rankin has been talking to the rest of the gang." He hesitated, then said, "And they're listening.

"You know how little the take has been this past year. Rankin told them that I was too chickenhearted to go after the really big money. Said I was too yellow-bellied to kill a man if I had to. Rankin even insinuated that the gang might be better off with someone besides me making decisions. I can't very well suggest that we don't pull this job."

"Dammit, Booth, it's *your* gang! Get rid of Rankin. Don't wait. Do it now!"

"I can't," Booth said. "My mind is made up, Kid. If you don't want to come, don't. It's up to you. I've got to leave now to get to the rendezvous on time." He visibly reined his temper. "You can always go back to the valley and wait for me."

"If you're going, I'm going!" Anabeth retorted. "Someone's got to keep an eye on you."

Booth's lip curled in a charming smile meant to appease her worry and cool her ire. "I knew I could count on you, Kid. I can't say I'll be sorry to have someone I trust at my back."

As Anabeth rode out of Santa Fe with Booth she had the feeling they were being watched. She looked

over her shoulder but couldn't find anything—or anyone—who looked suspicious.

Maybe this job would turn out to be a blessing in
disguise. If Sam Chandler was carrying as much gold
as Rankin had implied, Booth's share might be
enough to buy that ranch in Colorado. She hoped like
hell this was the last time she would be riding the
trail as Kid Calhoun.

2

Booth and Anabeth arrived around noon at the line shack near Old Horse Springs that was their rendez- vous site. The windows were broken out of the weatherbeaten wooden shack, and the porch sagged to one side like a horse canted on three legs. The rest of the gang was already there—except for Wat Rankin. The absence of the newest member of the Calhoun Gang made Anabeth even more uneasy about Rankin's intentions.

"Anybody know where Rankin is?" Anabeth asked as she stepped down from her horse at the front of the shack.

"Said he had some personal business to attend to, but he's gonna join us in plenty of time to do his part," Snake answered from his seat in a broken- down rocker on the porch.

Snake's tongue darted out to wet his lips before retreating inside his mouth, much as a snake's tongue might. It was a habit that had earned him the only name he had. The porch creaked as he kept the rocker moving with the toe of a worn-out boot. It had never ceased to amuse Anabeth that Snake's name fit his personality so well. Snake was a shifty, skulking snake-in-the-grass.

Anabeth exchanged a speaking look with Booth, who had also dismounted and was standing nearby. *Rankin is trouble*, she said with her eyes. When she would have spoken her thoughts, he shook his head to keep her silent. Anabeth's chin jutted mulishly, but she held her tongue.

Anabeth didn't like the six men in Booth's gang, and the best that could be said was that they tolerated the Kid. But until Booth had mentioned it, she hadn't been aware of any dissatisfaction with Booth's leadership. Now she suddenly realized she heard none of the raunchy jokes and sly talk that the gang normally exchanged when they got together just before a job. The air seemed somehow charged with tension.

Otis Grier and Clint Teague played cards on the rickety steps, blocking the way inside the shack. Grier reminded Anabeth of a grizzly. He had the size, and his frizzy brown hair and full beard made it look like he was covered with fur. If Grier looked like a bear, Teague smelled like one. To Anabeth's knowledge the man had never bathed. His buckskins were greasy, his hands grimy, his teeth rotten. Anabeth always stayed upwind of him.

"I will take your horses for you."

Anabeth turned to greet the one Mexican in the gang and its oldest member, Jaime Solano. *"Gracias,"* she said. "It's been a long time, Jaime. How have you been?"

The Mexican shrugged. "The days pass." Solano ran his hand down the neck of her dun-colored mustang. "This is a fine animal. Where did you buy him?"

"I caught him and trained him myself." With a little help from Wolf.

The Mexican nodded approvingly. "A good horse."

Solano was an expert on horseflesh—he had stolen more than a little of it in his day—so Anabeth took his compliment at face value. It gave her hope that she and Booth might someday end up raising horses instead of robbing stagecoaches.

The Mexican collected the reins for Anabeth's and Booth's horses and headed for the lean-to not far from the shack where the rest of the horses were stabled.

Anabeth watched Solano as he hobbled away. The Mexican wore a sombrero that revealed a fringe of salt and pepper hair that matched his mustache. He had fathomless eyes the color of black coffee. Because of his age, and his noticeable limp, he reminded Anabeth of her father. Except Solano had never done anything for which he did not expect to get something in return.

Anabeth feared and hated the man lounging against a post that held up the porch roof. A jug hung over his shoulder, held there by a forefinger. Whiskey was a mean drunk, and he was rarely sober. He had once picked a fight with the Kid, and Anabeth had drawn her gun on the outlaw before Booth showed up to settle the matter.

Anabeth had several times asked Booth why he didn't kick Whiskey out of the gang. Booth had merely said there were reasons why Whiskey drank, and pointed out that he wasn't mean unless he was bothered. Anabeth made it a point to avoid him whenever she could.

"Hey, Kid. How you doin'?"

Anabeth smiled at the young, handsome man hanging out of the broken window of the shack. "I'm fine, Reed. Meet any new range calico in Santa Fe?"

"Found a pretty little girl with yellow hair," Reed said with a grin. "Soft and fluffy as a goose-hair pillow. How 'bout you, Kid? Any luck?"

Anabeth managed a lopsided grin of her own. "If you're talking cards, I did fine." Well, that was true enough. No need to mention that the Kid had visions of becoming a lady, not seducing one. It had taken Anabeth a long time to realize that beneath Reed's charm lay the heart of a cold-blooded killer. She had once seen him pick a fight with a man and shoot him down without ever losing the smile on his face.

These men were a strange lot, but over the past three years that she had ridden with them, Anabeth had learned to endure their foibles and appreciate their good qualities. Few though they might be.

Reed's eyes skipped beyond Anabeth, and she turned to see what had attracted his attention. Wat Rankin. Rankin was of average height and weight, but he had a face that, once seen, was unforgettable. Anabeth perused the man as he rode up and tried to decide what it was about Rankin that made her dislike and distrust him.

His eyes. They had the slitted, too-close look of inbred Tennessee hill folk.

His mouth. It was so small that his toothy grin appeared almost ghoulish.

His chin. A deep cleft split it, making him look as though someone had hit him as a child, breaking his face in two.

His hair. Blond and baby fine, it was obviously a source of pride to the man. He kept an ivory comb in his pocket and used it often.

His voice. Too smooth, too confident. He sounded more like someone used to giving orders, not taking them. Which only added to Anabeth's anxiety. Why had he joined the gang? What did he really want?

"Sorry I'm late," Wat said with an ingratiating smile.

"If you want to stay a part of the Calhoun Gang, this had better be the last time," Booth warned.

Anabeth was surprised at the harshness of her uncle's voice. She watched Wat's mouth pinch shut, but he said, "Sure, Booth. Whatever you say."

"Now that you're here we can talk about who does what."

The gang gathered round as Booth knelt and picked up a stick to draw in the dirt. He outlined where each of the men was to wait for the stage, when the chase would begin, and how it would end.

"I don't want any killing," Booth said. "Pick your shots if you have to shoot at all." Anabeth realized that such an announcement had to be for Wat's benefit. The rest of the gang knew Booth's feelings. The law wasn't as likely to come after robbers as it was to come after killers. Consequently, Anabeth hadn't seen much blood shed over the past three years.

"Anybody got any questions?" Booth asked when he was done.

"I have one," Wat said.

"What?"

"After we get the gold, what happens then?"

"We meet back here and divide it up."

Anabeth was aware of a conscious shifting among the outlaws. They looked at each other and then at Wat, who nodded almost imperceptibly. Anabeth wondered if Booth had seen the same thing she had. *What's going on here?* she wondered.

"Fine," Wat said.

But it wasn't fine, Anabeth realized as she studied Rankin's face. Why was Wat lying? What had that surreptitious nod to the others meant?

"Let's get moving!" Booth said.

Once they were on horseback, Anabeth had a hard time getting close to Booth. One or the other of the outlaw gang always seemed to get in her way. Reed stopped her to tell her a story. Solano took time to admire her horse. Grier and Teague had an argument and involved her in it.

Anabeth began to feel frantic. Something was desperately wrong. She needed to speak privately with

Booth, to warn him of her suspicions. Before she knew it, they had topped a rise, and dust from the stage could be seen in the distance.

"Remember what you have to do," Booth said. He flashed a warning look at Anabeth and said, "Kid, you stay out of the line of fire."

"Booth, I need to talk to you—"

It was too late. Booth had already pulled his bandanna up to cover his face and kicked his horse into a gallop. Anabeth turned and sought out the newest member of the gang. She felt the hairs stand up on her neck. Her heart missed a beat.

Wat Rankin was wearing his ghoulish smile. And he held his Colt in his hand.

"Is that your wife?"

Sam Chandler looked up from the worn daguerreotype in his hand. His eyes narrowed as he studied the greenhorn sitting across from him on the stagecoach. A Western man would have known better than to ask questions of a stranger, but things had changed some in the years since the War Between the States. The West was rife with pilgrims seeking adventure. Sam's inborn courtesy prodded him to indulge the young man's curiosity. "Yes, it's my wife."

The Eastern gentleman reached for the photograph. "May I see it?"

Reluctantly, Sam relinquished the picture of Claire.

The young man had difficulty holding the picture steady in the swaying stagecoach but finally announced, "She's very beautiful. Have you been married long?"

Sam responded "Ten years" in his most forbidding voice. Unfortunately, the tinhorn wasn't deterred.

"Any children?" the man asked.

Sam swallowed over the sudden thickness in his throat. "A son."

"How old is he?"

The Easterner could have no idea what agony his questions conjured. Sam felt like doing violence to the man, but forced himself to answer, "Jeff will be— would be—nine next month." Then, in a snarl intended to silence the tinhorn once and for all, "He was stolen by Apaches three years ago."

The young man was more curious than ever but chary of offending the now dangerous-looking cowboy. He muttered to himself, "I thought that sort of thing only happened in storybooks."

Sam turned away to stare out the window. The memories were all too real. He had taken Jeff with him on the roundup, even though his six-year-old son was too young to be of much help. He and several cowhands had been working at the head of a box canyon branding cattle. Jeff had ridden his pony a short distance away, following the trail of a horned toad in the sand. The shrieking savages had appeared from nowhere and were gone just as suddenly. They had taken Jeff with them.

Sam hadn't been able to face Claire and tell her their son was a captive of the savages. They had both been witness to the recovery of another rancher's son, thirteen-year-old James Tripley, who had lived among the Apache for four years. During the time the white boy had been gone, he had become a savage himself.

The parents who had welcomed their long-lost son with tears of joy and open arms had been found the next morning murdered and scalped. The Tripley boy had disappeared. Claire had been one of the women who helped prepare the bodies for burial. He had never forgotten the ashen look on her face when she had stepped into his arms after coming out of the house.

So he had lied to her about what had happened to

Jeff. He had told her Jeff was dead. And hoped
against hope that he could recover the boy before Jeff
adopted the Apache way of life. If Sam had found Jeff
within the first few weeks or months of his capture,
he knew Claire would forgive him for the lie. And if
not . . . Their son was lost to them anyway.

Sam had never stopped looking for Jeff, but over
the past three years he had seen no sign of his son. As
far as Claire knew, Jeff was buried in that lonesome
canyon. Sam bore alone the burden of knowing that
his son—if he was still alive—was slowly but surely
becoming a bloodthirsty savage.

He and Claire had not grieved together, but they
had grieved. Were both still grieving, to tell the truth.
But not for much longer, if Sam had his way.

With the gold he had just received from the sale of
fifteen hundred head of prime Window Rock cattle
Sam hoped to take Claire north to Montana. There
they could make a new start in a place where there
were no painful memories. Maybe he could somehow, someday, erase the tragic look from her eyes.

The young man's voice intruded on Sam's
thoughts.

"The stories I've heard about the savages . . . are
they true?"

Sam's green eyes turned stony. "Don't know what
you've heard. Likely the truth is worse."

"Will I be safe out here?"

Sam snorted. "Safe as any greenhorn can be."

The young man puffed up instantly at this affront.
He pulled a shiny derringer from his vest pocket. "I'll
have you know I'm well prepared to defend myself."

"Put that away," Sam said. "Don't ever pull a gun
unless you intend to use it because, believe me, out
here the other gent will."

"Now look here, you—" The Easterner was thrown
back against the seat as the stage lurched forward,

tilting precariously as it suddenly accelerated over the bumpy trail. The driver shouted curses at the lagging team, and a thunderous boom sounded just over their heads.

The Easterner's eyes went wide with terror. "What was that? What's going on?" He started to lean out the window, but Sam yanked him back.

"Stick your nose out that window and you're liable to get it shot off."

"Do you mean to say we're being attacked?" The young man's face was frozen in a look of astonishment so absurd it made Sam laugh.

"Surely in one of those storybook novels you've read, a stage has been held up," Sam said with a wry twist of his mouth.

"Why, most certainly. But I never— That is I— Do you mean to say we're being held up?"

"Looks that way."

"We'll be killed!"

Sam's mouth flattened into a determined line. "Not if I can help it."

The tinhorn gaped when Sam unrolled the saddle blanket on the seat beside him to reveal a Colt .45 Peacemaker. Sam methodically checked the weapon to make sure it was loaded and added a sixth bullet to the chamber under the hammer that was usually left empty.

Then Sam took aim out the window at one of the pursuing outlaws and fired. He smiled grimly as the Easterner jumped a foot off the seat at the noise from the blast.

Sam hadn't time to comfort the terrified young man. He concentrated instead on firing at the gang of outlaws chasing them. His eyes narrowed with satisfaction as a heavy-set bearded man clutched his shoulder and abandoned the chase.

The outlaws fell back out of sight so that Sam

would have had to expose himself to be able to get a
good shot at them. The stage seemed to be pulling
away from the following horde. He felt a surge of excitement as he realized they were going to escape.

Suddenly he heard a warning shout from the
driver, and all hell broke loose. The stagecoach
careened sharply and Sam didn't have time to brace
himself before the coach began to roll. His head
slammed against the side panel, his foot caught under
the seat, and his shoulder bounced off the tinhorn's
back as the two of them were tossed and pitched like
marbles in the belly of the stagecoach.

When the coach stopped, it took Sam a moment to
get his bearings. The traces had broken when the
coach rolled, and the horses were long gone. The
stage had landed on its side, and the door was above
him. His shoulder felt bruised, but he didn't seem to
be seriously hurt. He leaned down to check on the
tinhorn and saw at once from its awkward angle that
the man's arm was broken.

"Can you move?" he asked.

The Easterner groaned. "I'm hurt."

"I know you're hurt. Can you move?"

To his credit, the tinhorn made an effort and,
though pasty-faced, managed to get to his feet. Sam
looked at the distance up to the door and worried
how he was going to get the injured man out of the
coach. Though it was questionable whether they
ought to get out. Sam heard horses approaching and
realized that he had lost his Colt in the tumble.

He made a quick search but hadn't located his gun
when he heard, "You inside the coach, come on out!"

"There's an injured man in here," Sam called back,
stalling for time and frantically looking for his gun.

An instant later someone pulled open the door of
the coach and stuck a shotgun inside. Finding his gun
suddenly lost its importance. Further resistance was

useless now. At this distance, a smart man didn't argue with buckshot.

When Snake peered over the edge of the coach, he was looking at two defenseless pigeons, ripe to be plucked. "Two men in here," the outlaw said. "Both unarmed."

Anabeth breathed a sigh of relief. At least there wasn't going to be any more gunplay. Already this holdup was something out of the ordinary. Teague was tending to Grier, who had been shot high in the shoulder. She was appalled at the carnage that had been wreaked when the stagecoach overturned. Fortunately the traces had broken and the horses had escaped uninjured.

But the driver lay sprawled on the ground facedown, his neck broken on impact. Nearby, Reed held a rifle aimed at the shotgun rider, whose nose was bleeding. Anabeth was amazed that anyone inside the shattered stagecoach could have survived. As the two men were dragged out of the coach she realized they hadn't escaped the ordeal unscathed.

The first man Snake and Whiskey pulled from the coach was obviously a greenhorn. Nobody else wore a vested suit, white collar and cuffs to travel out West. To be fair, the Easterner didn't make too much fuss as he was hauled up out of the coach, even though it was immediately clear that his arm was broken.

His face had paled considerably by the time the second man, much larger and dressed in Western gear, joined him beside the overturned stagecoach. The Western man must be Sam Chandler. He was the one Wat had said would be carrying the gold.

Anabeth remained on horseback, as did Booth, Wat Rankin, and Solano. Anabeth was slightly behind the other three, who faced the two men from the coach.

Wat gestured with his gun and said, "Hands up!"

The Western man obeyed, but the tinhorn moaned and said, "I can't. My arm's broken."

"Then raise your good hand," Rankin snarled, aiming his gun at the greenhorn.

The Easterner blanched.

Booth turned to Rankin and said, "Put your gun away." He waited until Rankin had holstered his weapon before turning back to the two men standing before him.

The tinhorn breathed a sigh of relief as he clutched his broken arm with his good hand.

For a man who was carrying as much money as Sam Chandler was supposed to have on him, Anabeth thought the rancher seemed particularly calm. It was more than that, she realized. Chandler seemed ready and willing to confront and defeat whatever challenge was presented to him. Anabeth hoped Booth would not underestimate him.

"You there," Booth said to Chandler, "unbutton your shirt, nice and easy, and hand over that money belt you're wearing."

Anabeth saw surprise and then anger in Chandler's face. Apparently he had been hoping the outlaws wouldn't know he was carrying gold.

In fact, Sam felt only a fleeting sense of loss for the new beginning that was being stolen from him. This theft meant he was going to have to ask for an extension on the loan he had made from a neighboring rancher. But he was sure Will Reardon would be accommodating. After all, Will had seemed happy enough to make him the loan in the first place. No amount of gold was worth dying for. With a shrug of resignation Sam began to do as he was told.

The mountain air was chilly in the early spring and Sam shivered as he pulled the tails of his wool shirt loose.

"Hurry up!" Rankin said.

Sam had both hands on the ties of the money belt when he looked up at the outlaw who had shouted at him to hurry. His eyes widened in recognition. At almost the same moment, Sam realized that the outlaw knew he had been identified. Before Sam could speak he saw movement out of the corner of his eye.

The tinhorn was reaching for his gun.

Sam lowered his raised right hand to grab for the tinhorn's wrist, to stop his foolhardy move. He only had time to shout "No!" before two gunshots exploded.

Anabeth saw the whole sequence of events as though it were happening in slow motion. As the Easterner's hand slipped inside his coat, she saw the rancher grab for the man's hand to stop him. She was unprepared for what happened next.

Wat Rankin had calmly, mercilessly, shot both men.

The tinhorn fell dead, a bullet between the eyes, the pitiful derringer lying exposed half in and half out of the striped satin vest pocket from which he had begun to pull it. The rancher didn't fall right away, but Anabeth was horrified at how quickly the splash of red grew on his chest. A moment later, he crumpled to the ground.

Anabeth was off her horse before she knew what she was doing. Chaos had erupted among the outlaws, a cacophony of shouting and yelling that made it sound like the world was coming to an end. Anabeth fell to her knees beside the rancher and lifted his head into her lap. Chandler wasn't dead, and his lips moved as though he were trying to speak.

"Please don't die," she begged. "Please don't die."

She was having trouble breathing and pulled the bandanna down off her face so she could suck air. Chandler's grasp on her sleeve surprised and horrified her. He was trying to pull her down toward him.

At first she resisted, but soon realized through her
haze of grief and regret that he could only speak in a
whisper. If she was going to hear his last words she
would have to lean down and put her ear near his
mouth.

"Stupid," he muttered.

She couldn't believe what she had heard. "What?"

"Stupid to try and save that idiot."

Chandler's eyes sank closed, and Anabeth was
afraid he was dead. But his mouth began to move
again, and she leaned closer so she could hear.

His last words were no more than a whisper. "I
love you, Claire. I'm sorry. So sorry about . . . Jeff."

Anabeth's throat constricted as she heard Sam
Chandler's dying words. Her stomach turned as she
realized the enormity of what had happened here. A
man had died in her arms, calling to his loved ones
with his last breath. Who was Claire? Who was Jeff?
It was appalling to think that this man had a family
somewhere who would never know that his last
thoughts had been of them.

"Son of a bitch!" she swore. "Dammit to hell!
Damn! Oh damn! This wasn't supposed to happen."

She looked up and met her uncle's eyes, now full of
regret—and anger. Her own eyes narrowed as they
slid to Wat Rankin. He didn't look the least bit repen-
tant.

Anabeth carefully laid Sam Chandler's head down
on the ground and stood to confront the man who
was the cause of this tragedy.

Wat Rankin.

She had known he was up to no good. Now look
what had happened! But she didn't have to flay the
man with words. Booth was already doing it for her.

"Damn you, Wat!" Booth said through gritted
teeth. "I told you no killing!"

"Was I supposed to let myself get shot by some

greenhorn?" Wat demanded. "He was goin' for his gun—"

Booth snorted. "He was a tinhorn with a broken arm. You could have taken that toy gun away from him before he had a chance to use it. There was no need for killing."

"Figured I was facin' harp music if I didn't do somethin'. You don't like it, too damn bad."

Booth clenched his teeth at Rankin's lack of remorse for the killing or regret for flouting orders. He turned to the Mexican on the horse to his left and said, "Get the money belt."

Wat jerked his head in the direction of the shotgun rider, the only person left alive of the four men who had been on the stagecoach. "What about him?"

"Tie him up," Booth told Reed, who was guarding the man.

"You leave him alive, and we'll end up garglin' on rope," Wat snarled.

"Our faces are covered," Booth said. "There's no way he can identify us."

"You just called me by name," Wat countered. "And in case you haven't noticed, the Kid ain't wearin' his bandanna."

Anabeth saw the shotgun rider looking right at her. Knowing the damage was already done, she pulled the bandanna back up anyway. Now, unless the man who had seen her was killed, there was finally someone who could identify one of the Calhoun Gang. If they caught her, it might very well lead them to Booth and the rest of the gang. But she couldn't justify shooting a man to ensure her own safety.

"Please, Booth," she said. "No more killing."

"Tie him up!" Booth snapped.

Reed looked from Booth to Wat and back again, apparently undecided about whom to obey. "But—"

"I'm giving the orders around here," Booth said, "and—"

"That can be changed," Wat muttered.

Every man-jack of them froze at Wat's open defiance.

Anabeth saw the way the outlaws looked from Booth to Wat, saw the ugly faces they made. They weren't happy with Booth's decision and appeared to side with Wat. At first she thought the gang might confront Booth here and now. But he stared them down, one at a time, like a lion tamer in a cage full of less intelligent, though vicious, beasts.

"I said there'll be no more killing," Booth said in a voice that could have cut glass. He stared until Reed began to sling rope around the shotgun rider's hands.

Booth didn't have time to say more before Solano was handing him the belt full of gold dust.

"Mucho dinero, señor," the Mexican said.

"Looks like your friend was right about Chandler carrying a lot of gold," Booth grudgingly conceded to Rankin. "Let's get out of here. We'll meet at the hideout."

"Hold on!" Wat said. "You takin' all that gold with you?"

"That's the way I run things," Booth replied in a hard voice. "If you don't like it—you're free to ride."

"You bastard. Who said you—"

Anabeth took a step toward Rankin. "Watch who you're calling a bastard, mister."

"Shut up, Kid!" Rankin snapped.

"You're an idiot and a fool!" Anabeth retorted.

Without warning, Rankin's fist swung out and caught Anabeth on the jaw. She went flying backward and landed in the dirt. There was a moment of stunned silence as the gang registered what had happened.

An instant later Booth's fist had connected with

Rankin's chin, and the newest member of the gang joined Anabeth on the ground. Booth stayed on his horse, his hand poised near his gun. "Just move an inch," Booth said to Rankin. "Give me an excuse to kill you."

Rankin stayed frozen where he was, a scowl of heroic proportions on his face.

"Are you all right, Kid?" Booth asked.

Anabeth's jaw felt like it was going to fall off, and she was still groggy as she pushed herself upright. "I'm fine."

"Get on your horse, Kid," Booth said. "We're getting out of here."

"What about the gold?" Rankin said. He started to stand, but Booth pinned him with a look that threatened murder.

"I'll meet you at the hideout next week like I promised. Are you ready, Kid?"

"I'm ready."

Booth kicked his big roan into a gallop and Anabeth quickly followed on her dun, leaving the other outlaws behind.

"Come, señor," Solano urged as he put a hand down to help Wat stand. "It is time to leave this place."

"Not quite yet," Wat said. He stalked over to where the shotgun rider was lying on the ground hog-tied. He pulled his gun and shot the man in the stomach, a wound guaranteed to result in a horrid, lingering death. "Now we can go!"

Solano raised an eyebrow, but neither he nor any of the rest of the gang protested what the outlaw had done. Wat Rankin was surely *loco*. Yet he was the one who had known about the gold dust. And he was promising even greater riches—a bigger share of the loot than they had been allowed in the past—if only they were willing to kill Booth Calhoun.

It was something Solano was seriously considering, along with the rest of the gang.

The plan was for the gang to ride in seven different directions that all converged in Santa Fe, so that no posse would be able to track them down. Then they would meet in a week at the old line shack to divide up the spoils.

"Before you leave," Wat said, "I want to know whether you're ready to admit that Booth Calhoun has to go."

"We been ridin' with him a lotta years," Whiskey said.

"And where are you now?" Rankin demanded. "When I caught up to you, you were all playing cards for the money to buy whiskey. You hadn't done a job in six months. If it hadn't been for my information you wouldn't have even known to rob this stage."

"Why do we have to kill him?" Snake demanded.

"Because it's the only way to make sure he doesn't get in the way later," Rankin said. "Either I'm leadin' this gang, or I'm not. So what's it gonna be?"

"When you wanta do it?" Reed asked.

Rankin smiled his ghoulish smile. "Next week. When he brings the gold." He rubbed his jaw and said, "We get rid of the Kid at the same time. That way, there's two less ways to split the take. Are we agreed?"

One by one Rankin made eye contact with Booth's gang. One by one they nodded their heads, like bells tolling a death knell.

When the outlaws had ridden away, Rankin kicked his horse and set off at a trot toward Old Horse Springs. Things were working out just as he had planned. It had been so easy to turn the gang against their leader. But then, he understood greed and ruthlessness. He was greedy and ruthless himself.

Wat intended to use the Calhoun Gang for his own

purposes, but as far as he was concerned, they were all expendable. After all, he didn't want anyone around later who could testify to the fact that the outlaw, Wat Rankin, and that respectable citizen and good neighbor, Will Reardon, were one and the same man.

3

Booth hadn't a thought to spare for the gang. His first concern as he and Anabeth galloped away was to make sure they weren't being followed. He had kept Treasure Valley a secret because he needed a place where Anabeth would be safe in her female guise. So he doubled back and sent their horses over the black lava beds known as malpais, where there would be no sign of their passing, before he headed for the valley again.

But his thoughts weren't really focused on hiding their trail. He was too busy worrying about what to do with Anabeth now that the gang had ended up killing two passengers, while leaving a witness alive to identify her—albeit as the boy, Kid Calhoun.

It changed everything.

The law would be after them now, and there would be no rest for any of them. Maybe the time had come at last to consider that ranch in Colorado Anabeth was always dreaming about.

By the time they rode down the cool, dark tunnel that led into Treasure Valley, Booth's mind was made up. Their days with the Calhoun Gang were at an end. With the gold from this holdup he and Anabeth could start over again. He might even stop by Santa Fe on the way to Colorado to see if Sierra wanted to come along. But first he had a score to settle with Wat Rankin.

As they rode out of the tunnel and into the valley Booth was momentarily blinded by the sun. As his vision returned he saw the stone house that he and his brother had built thirteen years ago. It was backed up against a fifty-foot-high cliff. Behind the house was a cave large enough to hold several horses. A seep in the cave provided a fresh water supply that could be reached without the necessity of being exposed to gunfire from anywhere in the valley.

Beyond the house, on the valley floor, Anabeth's wild mustangs stood knee-deep in lush grass. A stream that began under the rock wall on one side of the valley ended in a pond on the other side. It was the perfect hideout for an outlaw. He was going to miss it.

"I'm sorry, Booth. I should have paid more attention to what I was doing. I wasn't even aware of pulling my bandanna down like that."

Booth stepped off his horse and tied it at the hitching rail in front of the house. "It's done now."

Anabeth dismounted beside him. "And I should have kept my mouth shut around Rankin."

Booth's eyes were bleak as he reached out and cupped her jaw, which was already turning black and blue. "I don't think I realized before today just what kind of chances you've been taking all along. What if your hat had come off when Rankin hit you, Kid? What if the rest of them had found out you're a girl?"

"They didn't."

"Because you were lucky!"

"I know I should have cut my hair when I started riding with the gang. But—" How could she explain that cutting off her hair would have been like cutting away the last of what made her female. She hadn't been able to do it. Booth was right. It was sheer luck that she had managed to keep her secret for so long.

"What happens now?" she asked. "I mean, now that I can be identified." Anabeth had visions of being confined to the valley for the rest of her natural life.

"We go to Colorado."

Anabeth's eyes went wide. She was afraid to believe that her dream was finally coming true. "Really? No fooling, Booth?"

Booth put a hand on her shoulder. "Don't you want to go?"

"Of course I do! Do you?"

Booth grinned his charming grin. "Sure, Kid."

"When?"

"As soon as I meet with the gang one last time."

Anabeth's suspicions regarding Rankin were superseded by her excitement over the prospect of actually going to Colorado. She couldn't stop talking about it. Booth seemed every bit as enthusiastic as she did. The only cloud on her horizon was the knowledge that she would never see Wolf again.

That afternoon, she built a mound of stones on top of the cliffs that could be seen for miles, and which would alert Wolf that she wanted to talk to him. Two days later, while she was grooming her dun, he called out to her from where he was hiding along the stone cliffs.

"Stalking Deer. I am here."

Anabeth located Wolf from the sound of his voice and left the animal she was brushing to join him. "I'm so glad you've come! I was afraid you wouldn't get here before I had to leave for Colorado."

"You are leaving the valley?"

Anabeth nodded vigorously. She reached out and clutched Wolf's hands. "Booth has finally agreed to go to Colorado. We're going to have a ranch there. I won't be an outlaw anymore. We'll live like normal people, have friends and go to parties. I'll get to wear dresses and be a lady at last!"

"I do not want you to go," Wolf said.

Anabeth's joy was cut short by the harshness of Wolf's voice. "I have to go," she said. "There's a man who can identify me as one of the outlaws who robbed the stage. Some men were killed, and the law will be after me now. I don't have any choice."

"You can come live with me in my village."

She raised a disbelieving brow. "As your friend?"

"As my wife."

"I can't— I don't— No, Wolf. It would never work."

"Why not?"

Anabeth was blunt. "I don't wish to be your wife."

Wolf's lids lowered to hood his eyes so Anabeth couldn't see his reaction there to her rejection of his proposal. But his hands tightened painfully on hers.

"I won't ever forget you, Wolf. Not ever. You're the best friend I'll ever have."

Wolf stood there stoically while the one person who had ever truly valued him as a person explained why she could no longer be a part of his life. What flashed through his mind was their first meeting thirteen years ago. It was the day he had fought Growling Bear for the first time.

The two Apache youths had writhed on the ground, their sweaty flesh collecting a fine layer of dust, with first one, and then the other on top. Locked in mortal combat, they had gouged and kicked and bit each other in a battle that had no civilized rules. The five Apache boys surrounding the combatants had shouted guttural incantations, urging their favorite on to victory.

"Ho, Growling Bear!"

"He is yours, Growling Bear!"

"Use your teeth, Growling Bear!"

None were there to call Wolf's name. To give him encouragement. To hope he would win.

But Wolf had not spent fourteen years as an outcast among his own people without acquiring a hard shell that protected him from such slights and snubs. He did not need the cheers of others to urge him on. He looked inward and found the strength to conquer his foe.

It soon became apparent that Growling Bear, though two years older and both taller and heavier than his rival, was having the worst of it. Wolf was stronger, more agile, more fleet of foot. The crowd surrounding the two adversaries was stunned into silence when Wolf pinned Growling Bear. His wiry forearm sliced across the older boy's throat, in position to choke the life from him.

The two youths glared at each other, their teeth bared, their breathing ragged, their bodies bloodied with scrapes and scratches, bruised by their struggle on the rocky ground.

"Take it back," Wolf demanded.

"I will not! You *are* a brother to Coyote."

Wolf's breath hissed in sharply at this repeated insult. He cut off the other boy's air and watched with merciless black eyes as Growling Bear began to turn blue. Nor did Wolf release his hold when the older boy's body began to thrash in death throes beneath him.

Abruptly, Wolf was grabbed by the shoulders and yanked off the other boy. "Hold! What are you doing there?"

Wolf backed away, his face feral in its wildness, his body poised for defense.

But Growling Bear's father, Yellow Shirt, ignored Wolf. He pulled his son to his feet and said, "Come. It is time to go hunting."

Yellow Shirt turned to the five boys who had been

watching the fight and said, "Go to your wickiups.
Your fathers await you also to join the hunt."

Red-faced with shame at having been beaten by
Wolf, and still heaving air into starved lungs, Growling Bear brushed past the outcast, his eyes filled with
hatred. The other boys followed after him, with Yellow Shirt bringing up the rear.

Wolf was left standing alone. As he always had
been. As he feared he always would be. His mother,
Night Crawling, had slept with many men, so he had
no father to claim him as son. No father to teach him
what a boy must learn. How to make his weapons.
How to hunt. How to steal horses. How to kill his
enemy.

So Wolf had watched and listened and taught himself. He had become better, stronger, swifter, more
ruthless. Still it had not won him the acceptance he
craved. They had not invited him to come along on
the hunt. But he would go hunting anyway. Alone.
And he would come back with a bigger deer than any
of them.

Wolf collected his bow and arrow and his knife
from the wickiup where he lived by himself. He
passed by his mother's wickiup and said, "I am going
hunting. I will bring you meat for your cookpot tonight."

Night Crawling merely nodded. She was aware of
the battle her son fought for the respect of the tribe.
She did her part to help. She did not boast of her
son's prowess as a hunter. But she generously shared
the meat Wolf brought her as well as the skin and
horn and the other delicacies that were to be had
from the kill, with the other women whose husbands
or sons had not been as successful hunting.

Wolf mounted one of his ponies—he had already
stolen several from the white men—and rode off in
the opposite direction from the hunting party of fa-

thers and sons. As soon as he was beyond sight of the last wickiup, he kicked his pony into a lope and then let him run full out.

No matter how fast Wolf rode, he could not escape from who and what he was. Soon he pulled the flagging pony to a trot, and then to a walk. Almost immediately, he saw the tracks of a deer. It was a large one, and he reminded himself of his vow to return with the greatest prize from the hunt.

He focused all his attention on tracking the deer, which followed a narrow, rocky trail upward along a high cliff. The track narrowed so that Wolf's foot hung out over a sheer drop. His heart was pounding by the time the trail crested. He stopped short at what he had found.

The deer was forgotten. Below him and stretching out in a wide oval was a lush, grassy valley. From what he could see, it was completely surrounded by impossibly high walls of stone. He could detect no other way in or out of the valley other than the one he had found. Nor could he see any signs of habitation.

Here, then, would be his sanctuary. A place of his own where he would come and be alone and where the stigma of his birth could not intrude. He kicked his pony and began the descent down the narrow deer trail that led into the valley below.

To Wolf's delight, a stream ran the length of the valley. He followed the trail of sparkling water to where it ended in a large pond in the shadows of the cliff. It was there at the pond that he discovered his valley was not as uninhabited as he had thought. Someone was swimming there.

He kept himself out of sight and was chagrined to realize that it was a white child, a girl. His eyes quickly scanned the valley again. She would not be here alone. There would be other white men. He felt angry. He had already claimed the valley for his own,

only to discover someone else had claimed it before
him.

But that could be remedied.

The girl in the pond was a child of no more than six
or seven. Nevertheless, he approached her stealthily.
He did not want her to cry an alarm and warn the
others who must be here in this valley with her.

He could not help but admire her grace in the water and her abandon. He could hear her laughter even
from where he lay hidden in the rocks. He realized he
did not want to kill such a free spirit. But that left him
in a quandary.

Should he capture her and take her back to the
village? Usually, the Apache did not take female pris-
oners, as they were useless. This child would be especially so. With no clear plan in mind, he decided to
approach her.

To his amazement, the solitary girl left the water
the moment she saw him. She stood there dripping
wet, wearing only a pair of thin white trousers that
came to her knees, totally unafraid. She even spoke to
him in the white man's tongue.

"Hello. Who are you?" she asked.

Of course, he had no idea what she was saying. To
his further astonishment, she extended a hand in welcome. Uncertain, he hesitated.

She dropped her hand and spoke again. "My name
is Anabeth Calhoun. Are you an Apache? My uncle
Booth told me Apaches are mean. But you don't look
mean. Can you understand me?"

The girl apparently realized he didn't understand a
word she was saying, because she began to use gestures with her speech. She spread her arm to encom-
pass the valley and pointed to the far end, where he
could see, now that she pointed it out, a stone house
such as white men lived in.

"I live here in Treasure Valley with my father and

my uncle Booth. Pa is gone from the valley right now, working in the Two Brothers Mine. He's already found a little gold, but he's hoping to strike it rich someday. My uncle Booth is down at the house. He looks after me while Pa's working at the mine. Would you like to join us for dinner?''

When she reached for his hand, Wolf jerked it away. It was the first time anyone had ever reached out to him in friendship. He continued staring at her. And she continued talking.

"Do you live near here? Do you want to be friends? I would like to have a friend. Booth is fun sometimes, but he doesn't always want to play. Would you like to play a game now?''

She reached out again and, intrigued, Wolf let her grasp his hand. A second later she had tripped him and sent him flying into the pond.

He lunged up out of the water ready to kill—only to find her pointing at him and laughing.

"Booth taught me how to do that. Oh, it was funny to see you go flying!''

Wolf's dignity was sorely wounded in the fall, and he quickly looked around to make sure no one had seen this slight child lay him flat. He who had vanquished Growling Bear had been thrown by a mere child! He glared at the girl who had been the source of his humiliation.

She stood there grinning down at him, asking him with laughing blue eyes to join her in appreciation of the mischief she had wrought. Then she stretched out her hand to help him from the water.

Wolf found himself utterly charmed. Reluctantly, then wholeheartedly, he grinned back. In that moment, an irrevocable, unbreakable bond of friendship was born.

Wolf levered himself out of the pool and sat down cross-legged on the stone that edged the water, patting the ground beside him to indicate the girl should join him.

She quickly sat down beside him and began jabbering again. For the first time, he spoke to her in the Apache tongue.

"I will call you Stalking Deer, because that is what I was doing when I found you," he said. "I will be your friend. But you must not speak of me to those who live with you. And I will keep this secret also."

He wished he could tell someone about the valley. It was such a magnificent discovery! But it would be impossible to explain to his mother—or anyone—that he had made a white girl his friend. He suffered enough ridicule as it was. And he did not want anyone else to come here. This special place belonged to him and to the child he had befriended.

They talked until the sun began its descent, when the girl rose and tried once again to get him to come with her to the stone house at the other end of the valley.

"I cannot come, Stalking Deer. I must return to my village. But I will come again," Wolf promised.

By signs, by gestures, by the few words they had already taught each other, they did their best to show that they would meet here again another day. From farther down the valley someone called for the girl.

"Hellllooooo. Annabeettth. Where are youuuuuu?"

"I have to go," the girl said. "I'll be here tomorrow. Will you come again?"

"I will come."

When she was gone, Wolf mounted his pony and began the long ascent back up out of the valley.

That evening, when he returned to the village without any meat for his mother's cookpot, Wolf did not mind the jeers of Growling Bear. He did not even acknowledge the taunts of Growling Bear's friends.

He turned cold, dark eyes on them and dared them to do their worst.

Stalking Deer's unqualified acceptance had provided a much-needed solace for an oft-bruised heart. The village could treat him with disdain and keep him at a distance. Their scorn no longer held the same power over him. Because Wolf had known he was not alone anymore.

Only now Stalking Deer had told him she was planning to go away forever.

"You cannot leave this place, Stalking Deer." *You cannot leave* me.

"You can't stop me, Wolf."

"We shall see."

Anabeth heard the agitation in Wolf's voice—and the determination—but there were no words of comfort she could give him. "I'll miss you, Wolf."

"I will come again," he told her. "When I have had time to think on what you have said." When he had come up with a way to convince her to stay.

"I won't change my mind," she warned. "I'm going to leave. I have to leave. I don't have any choice!"

Anabeth stumbled away, unable to bear the stoic look on Wolf's face any longer. They had been friends long enough, and she knew enough about him, to understand that his feelings ran deep. He would be back. Wolf never said what he didn't mean.

During the next week, Anabeth couldn't shake the fear that something would happen to wrest away her dream of a new life with her uncle in Colorado. Which was when she recalled her suspicions about Wat Rankin. She woke on the morning Booth was to meet the outlaws with the sure knowledge that she couldn't let her uncle go back to face Rankin alone.

She called out to Booth from her bedroom, but he didn't answer. When she padded barefoot across the wooden-planked floor from room to room, she dis-

covered that Booth had already gone. He had left a
note for her.

Dear Kid,
I took a little gold for the gang and put the rest
somewhere safe. Will be back as soon as I can.
Don't follow me!

Booth

For all of two seconds Anabeth considered waiting
in the valley for Booth to return. Then she dressed as
quickly as she could, saddled her horse, and headed
for the line shack where Booth was meeting the outlaw gang. Her feelings of foreboding increased the
closer she got to the shack. Something bad was going
to happen. She just knew it. The dun was tired, but
she urged him to a faster run. Time was running out
on her dream.

As she approached the shack she could hear angry
voices. Oh, God. Please, let her not be too late!

Anabeth slipped off her horse and kept herself hidden from view in the rocky terrain that surrounded
the shack. All the members of the outlaw gang were
visible. Except Wat Rankin. Where the hell was he?

"What took you so long!" Snake was demanding of
Booth. "We been waitin' here for hours."

"Weren't no posse come lookin' for us," Teague
said. "Got away clean."

"Where's the gold?" Grier demanded.

"Rankin sure knew what he was talkin' about,"
Teague said, rubbing his hands together. "Good thing
we hooked up with him in Santa Fe."

"Where is Rankin?" Booth asked. "I've got something to say to him."

"Here." Rankin stepped into the doorway of the
shack, his thumbs tucked into his belt. His lips were
curved in a sneer. "Speak up, Booth. I'm listenin'."

"I said there'd be no killing. I meant it. Get your things, Rankin, and clear out."

There was a rumble of protest from the other six outlaws gathered around the front of the shack.

Booth stared them into silence. "Two men were shot and killed, and Rankin is responsible. As long as I'm boss, I'll give the orders, and you'll follow them."

"So maybe you shouldn't be boss anymore," Rankin said.

Booth felt the hairs stand up on his arms. His hands slipped down to his sides where his two pearl-handled guns were holstered. He looked from one to another of the men ranged before him. "Any of the rest of you feel that way?"

Grier and Teague looked belligerent. Snake's tongue slipped out to lick his lips. Whiskey took a drink from the jug on his shoulder. Reed coughed. Solano wouldn't meet his eyes.

Booth's gaze slid back to the yellow-haired man in the doorway. There was real danger here. He could feel it. Like wolves that turn on their own, he could be savaged by the same men who had ridden by his side.

"You planning to draw on me, Rankin?" Booth asked.

Wat held his right hand away from his revolver. "Wouldn't think of it, Booth. By the way, where's the Kid? Thought he'd be with you."

"It's none of your business where the Kid is," Booth retorted. He watched Rankin's eyes, but there was nothing to tell him one way or the other what the miscreant was thinking. If anything, he felt danger even more strongly.

"You gonna divvy up that gold now?" Whiskey demanded.

There was a look in Whiskey's eyes, just a flicker of bloodlust that warned Booth how much trouble he was in. "Just let me get the gold and—"

Booth turned his back casually, as though he
wasn't aware of the slobbering fangs of the beasts
that surrounded him. A movement at the corner of
the shack caught his eye and distracted him for an
instant.

Anabeth!

Booth grunted, shoved forward as a bullet
slammed into his back. He whipped his head around
and saw the gun in Rankin's hand.

He never got his Colts out of the holsters before he
was shot in the left arm by Snake and the right hand
by Solano. Before he could move his wounded limbs,
Grier and Teague plucked his pearl-handled guns
from their holsters and threw them off into the
bushes. He was totally at the gang's mercy now.

"Your days of leadin' this gang are over," Wat said.
"But if you wanta live, you better tell us where the
Kid is."

"Forget it."

"He's prob'ly in that secret valley," Reed volunteered.

Wat's yellow eyes narrowed. "Then maybe you better tell us where that valley is, Booth."

"No."

"Put a couple of bullets in his knees," Wat said to
Grier and Teague. "Maybe that'll show him we mean
business."

Anabeth recoiled with each gunshot, and bit her
lower lip until it bled to keep from crying out. Her
whole body trembled with outrage. Tears welled in
her eyes. Even if Booth lived now, he would most
likely be crippled and never walk again. The next
time she looked, her uncle was lying on his side on
the porch, gripping his legs above the knees. He
groaned once from the pain and then was silent.

Anabeth thought about jumping from the bushes
and fanning her hammer, sending bullets flying. She

was lightning fast with a gun, but could she get seven
of them before one of them got her? The answer to
that question was no. And getting herself killed
wasn't going to help Booth.

"Where's the Kid?" Wat demanded.

"Go to hell," Booth said. He stared at the outlaws
who had been his friends, but was met with merciless
eyes.

Rankin rested his boot on one of Booth's mangled
knees and said, "Talk."

"You're one yellow-bellied—"

Rankin put his weight on the injured knee, and
Booth screamed with pain.

"You got one last chance to talk," Rankin said.

"You can kill me, but the Kid's going to come after
you," Booth gasped. "I wouldn't give a plugged
nickel for what your lives are going to be worth when
he finds out what you've done."

Booth watched the outlaws shift anxiously, saw the
sweat break out as they nervously shuffled their feet.
He wished there was some way of telling Anabeth to
stay hidden. He was a dead man any way you looked
at it. There was no sense in her getting killed, too. He
hoped like hell she didn't take his talk about revenge
to heart. Those were words meant to keep the gang
from going after her long enough for her to make her
escape. He regretted not telling her exactly where the
gold was hidden. Maybe, with luck, she would find it
anyway and get herself to Colorado.

"Finish him off!" Rankin said.

Anabeth watched with horrified eyes as Reed and
Whiskey put two more bullets in Booth. It was clear
from Booth's grunts, and the way his body flattened,
that they were mortal blows.

Anabeth! Get the hell out of here! Run!

It was a warning shouted in Booth's head, one that

never found voice as the muscles in his bullet-riddled body eased and slackened on the ground.

Anabeth ducked back completely behind the shack. Her stomach clenched and spasmed. *Booth was dead!* There had been nothing she could do to save him.

She slid down and hugged her knees, hidden by the bushes at the base of the shack. Maybe if she hadn't come here her uncle would still be alive! She had distracted Booth with her appearance only moments before Wat Rankin had shot him in the back. Maybe if his attention had been on Rankin—

But Anabeth knew deep down that Booth hadn't had a chance against Rankin. There was no defense against the sort of yellow-bellied cur who shot a man in the back.

Maybe, in that first instant, if she had pulled her gun, she might have helped Booth shoot his way free. But shock and fear had kept her frozen until it was too late. Until reason told her she would only get herself killed if she tried to help him.

Anabeth felt a sob rising in her throat and choked it back. If she made any sound at all the outlaws would surely find her. She pressed her face to her knees and held her breath. And prayed they wouldn't discover her presence.

"Hey! He's not wearing the money belt," Snake said.

"Look in his saddlebags," Rankin said.

"There is only a little here, señor," Solano said, handing Booth's saddlebags to Rankin.

"What the hell?"

Anabeth heard the outlaws' disgust and dismay, their terrible outrage when they realized Booth had brought only a pittance of the stolen gold with him.

"We've got to find the Kid," Rankin said. "He'll know where the gold is."

But I don't! Anabeth realized.

"We don't know where to find the Kid," Whiskey admitted. "Booth took the secret of that valley with him to the grave."

Rankin swore again. "Then we'll have to spread out and hunt for it. Even if we can't find the valley, the Kid'll have to surface sooner or later. When he does, we'll be waitin' for him."

Anabeth hunched into as small a space as she could when the outlaws rode past her. They had been gone for several minutes before she could force her trembling legs to stand, and several minutes more before she could force herself to go to her uncle.

Booth was lying on the porch in a pool of blood. She put her hand over her mouth to force back the gag that threatened. She knelt beside him, afraid to touch him because he was wounded in so many places. "Booth."

Anabeth had been so certain her uncle was dead that she gasped when his eyes fluttered open. "Booth! You're alive!" Her heart leaped with joy that quickly turned to horror when she reached for his hand and encountered torn flesh instead.

"Booth, you need a doctor."

"No doctor," he rasped. "Too late for that."

"Don't say that!" Anabeth clasped Booth's good hand in hers and brought it to her cheek. Booth couldn't die! He was the only family she had left.

Anabeth saw the despair in her uncle's eyes, the knowledge that the end was near. Booth's face was ashen, his breathing shallow. Her uncle was right. It was too late for a doctor to do him any good now.

"I'm so sorry, Booth."

"For what?"

"For being where I wasn't supposed to be. If I hadn't distracted you—"

"It wasn't your fault, Kid. What happened was go-

ing to happen whether you were here or not." He saw
the disillusionment, the loss of innocence in her eyes.
"You take the gold and you go to Colorado. You hear
me? You get away from here as quick as you can."

His eyes dulled and Anabeth felt panic at the realization he hadn't long to live.

"Watch out for Rankin," Booth rasped.

The tears in her uncle's eyes frightened her. "I
promise you they'll suffer for what they've done to
you, Booth. Every single one of them. Especially
Rankin. I swear it, Booth. *I swear it!*"

"No, Kid! You have to get away!" A moan of pain
was torn from his throat.

"Booth? What can I do? How can I help?"

He grasped her arm and she leaned down, putting
her ear near his lips. He whispered something, words
that made no sense.

"What did you say? I don't understand."

He whispered them again. The same meaningless
words.

She wanted to shake him. It seemed so important
to him for her to understand, but he wasn't making
any sense. "Booth, I don't understand!"

"Kid . . ."

Anabeth stared at him for a moment before she realized he was dead. His eyes glazed. His thick black
eyelashes looked unreal. His chest no longer rose and
fell. His fingers went slack in hers.

"No." Anabeth denied his death. "Please, Booth."
She felt anguish too painful to bear. "Noooooo!"

Later Anabeth was never sure how she got through
the next several hours. She searched through the
bushes until she found Booth's two pearl-handled revolvers. She would use Booth's own guns to wreak
the vengeance she had sworn.

Somehow she managed to get Booth on his horse
and back to the valley. There she dug a hole behind

the stone house and buried her uncle beside her father, covering the grave with stones to mark it well.

She sat beside Booth's grave, refusing to give in to the grief, nursing the desire for revenge instead. Outlaw or not, her uncle hadn't deserved such a gruesome death. And for what? For a cache of gold that Anabeth hadn't been able to find in a very thorough search of the valley. The secret of Booth's horde had died with him.

Anabeth vowed that Wat Rankin and the rest of Booth's outlaw gang were going to pay for their treachery. She couldn't go to the law. The law would only be glad to be rid of one more outlaw. So she needed a strategy, some cunning plan to avenge her uncle's murder.

The answer came to her like a flash of lightning in a mountain thunderstorm. Crisply defined, overwhelming, and absolutely beautiful in its simplicity.

Booth's gang would be looking for Kid Calhoun. But they knew nothing about Anabeth. Finally, she was going to realize her dream of becoming a lady. She would hide out in Santa Fe as prim little Anabeth "Smith" and watch the gang's movements. Then, when they least suspected it, Kid Calhoun would swoop down and wreak awful vengeance for her uncle's death.

4

"Please let me pass."

Claire Chandler lifted her chin as she met the insolent gaze of the cowboy standing in the doorway to
Sullivan's Mercantile. She should have stayed at the
ranch until Jake arrived. She should have known better than to make the trip to Old Horse Springs alone.
But she had sent her desperate message to El Paso
over two weeks ago, and there was still no word from
her brother. She had made the wire concise and to
the point:

> Sam murdered. Gold stolen.
> Need help to save Window Rock.
>   Claire

Why hadn't Jake responded?

Claire wasn't going to be able to hold off men like
the one standing in her way for much longer on her
own.

"You'll be needin' help with that package, Miz
Chandler," the cowboy drawled, reaching out for it.

"I can manage." Claire tightly clutched the cloth
bag that contained five pounds of coffee, three tins of

peaches, and ten boxes of .45 caliber bullets. She was expecting trouble at Window Rock.

Claire didn't delude herself that any of the men who had approached a grieving widow with proposals of marriage were the least bit interested in her welfare. They wanted the ranch. Window Rock was a prime piece of land, located near some of the best water in western New Mexico.

Worst of them all was Will Reardon. How could she and Sam have been so wrong about the man! As their closest neighbor, Will had been among the first to come calling to pay his condolences on hearing of Sam's death. When she had turned her face up to Will seeking comfort, he had looked her in the eye and said he would be glad to marry her and forget about the loan due on Window Rock. She had avoided answering his proposal by pleading her grief. He had left, but Claire knew he would be back.

Claire swallowed over the lump of sorrow that lodged in her throat. She had hoped the vultures would wait a little longer before beginning to circle. She couldn't face the loss of Sam. She had scarcely recovered from the loss of her son.

Every single day she relived the memory of the last moments she had seen Jeffrey alive. Her son had been so pleased as he sat on his pony beside his father. A gap-toothed grin had split his face from ear to ear. He had been wearing a red-checked cotton shirt with pearl snaps, black jeans, and shiny black boots—all birthday presents.

Her tiny son, his white-blond hair tucked under a hat that was too big for him, had proudly ridden away with his father—and never come back.

Funny, how she could remember every detail of how Jeffrey had looked—and not one single thing about Sam's appearance the day he had left Window Rock for the last time.

Oh, God! If only she could have that day to live over again! *Sam, Sam! I did love you once. I'm sorry I didn't kiss you good-bye. I'm sorry I blamed you for losing Jeff. I'm sorry I turned my shoulder to you in bed. I'm sorry you died thinking I hated you. I'm so sorry!*

The bag nearly slipped out of Claire's hands. She grasped at it and caught it at her hip. The cowboy was quick to put his arms around it—and her. Claire worked to keep the desperation out of her voice as she said, "Let go of me."

"Seems you need a man's strong arms to help you out, little lady. There's some hard-lookin' desperados 'tween here and Window Rock. Bein' widowed and all, you ain't got a man no more to—"

"I'll be seeing the lady home."

The cowboy turned to cuss out whoever had been stupid enough to interrupt him and stepped back with an audible gasp. The size of the man standing there would have been enough to intimidate all by itself. The implacable look in the man's gray eyes boded ill for anyone crossing him. A narrow scar ran through his mouth, turning it down on one side, giving him a fierce, hard as whetstone appearance.

The cowboy tipped his hat to Claire and backed away until he was sure he was going to be allowed to leave. Then he turned and scurried—that was the precise word that came to Claire's mind—scurried away.

She turned to the man who had caused the cowboy to flee and asked, "Do you always have that effect on people?"

"Afraid so." His lips curled in disgust. "I've never gotten used to it."

"I'm glad you came, Jake."

"Did you think I wouldn't?"

"I was worried when I didn't hear from you."

"I was busy. Had some business to finish for the

Rangers. When I got your message I was already halfway up the Chihuahua Trail, so I decided to come
ahead rather than stop somewhere to wire I was on
my way.''

Claire noticed the five-point star hammered from a
Mexican *cinco peso* coin that was pinned to Jake's
shirt, half-hidden beneath his black leather vest. She
had never been so grateful that her brother was a
Texas Ranger as she was now. Jake would make certain that the man, or men, who had robbed and murdered Sam were brought to justice.

Claire longed to step into Jake's arms, to give comfort, and to receive it. Things weren't that easy with
her brother. She stood there feeling awkward, letting
her eyes say everything her lips didn't.

*Thank you for coming. I'm frightened. I need your
help.*

Jake realized Claire was slowly but surely dropping
the package in her arms. He took it from her and was
amazed at how heavy it was. "What's in here?"

Her smile accentuated the lines of grief on her face.
"Coffee and peaches. And bullets."

He raised a black brow. "Expecting a little trouble?"

"More than a little."

Jake was forced to put a hand around Claire's
shoulder or watch her fall. "Where can we get a cup
of coffee?"

She gestured toward the cantina and Jake headed
off in that direction past a row of one-story adobe and
wooden buildings. There was no sidewalk, and the
spring rains had left the street muddy. Claire's hem
gave mute evidence to the fact she had already done
some walking in town. Not that there was much to
the town, just two rows of facing buildings that had
grown up around the springs. It was enough to justify
a stop by the Overland Stage.

All eyes turned toward them when they entered the dingy adobe building. There was a decided hush as Jake walked all the way to the back of the cantina. He seated Claire at a round wooden table, then took a chair that put his back to the adobe wall. As soon as they were settled, the cantina erupted in whispered exchanges.

A withered Mexican woman came to wait on them, and Jake ended up ordering a steak, pinto beans, rice, and tortillas to go with his coffee. When the food arrived, he wolfed it down like a starving man and asked for a second helping.

Amused, Claire asked, "When was the last time you ate?"

"Don't remember," Jake managed between bites. "Must have been day before yesterday."

During the meal, Claire took advantage of the opportunity to tell Jake everything she knew about what had happened to Sam. It wasn't much.

"He had sold the cattle in Colorado and was on the last leg of his journey back home when the stagecoach was held up. They brought his body back to me."

Jake stared around the room rather than confront the despair in Claire's hazel eyes. He scowled when he realized several of the men in the cantina were surreptitiously ogling her.

He could hardly blame them. Even with reddened eyes and exhausted from lack of sleep, his sister was a beautiful woman. Even more enticing was the appearance of vulnerability caused by her huge, doelike eyes. Her upswept honey-colored hair had begun to fall down in wisps at her brow and nape. Though she had a woman's body, she was tiny enough to raise a man's protective urges.

She would have been a prize for any man, even without the ranch. Only, from what Claire had said,

the men who had come calling were a lot more interested in Window Rock.

"You wouldn't believe the proposals I've gotten,"
she told him. "Young and old, rich and poor. I think
I've had a visit from every man within a hundred
miles of here. A few of the offers I've received seem
sincere; most of them aren't. And then there's Will
Reardon."

"What's special about him?"

"Last fall Sam decided to buy out a rancher who
was heading back East, but he didn't have enough
money. So he borrowed from Reardon. He was sure
he could sell his cattle this spring and pay Reardon
back. Only all the gold Sam got for the cattle was
stolen when he was killed."

"And Reardon wants payment on the note anyway," Jake deduced.

Claire's eyelids lowered to conceal the bleak hope-
lessness she felt. "He said he's willing to marry me
and forget the note."

"Hell and the devil!" Jake muttered. "How much
do you need to pay him off?"

Claire mentioned a figure that was considerably
more than Jake made in a year with the Rangers.

She leaned forward in her chair and crossed her
arms on the scarred wooden table. "I don't want to
marry again, Jake, but I won't have any choice if I
can't come up with the cash to save the ranch any
other way."

"Have you thought about selling out?"

Claire's hands fisted. Her eyes flashed with anger.
Her voice was all the more intense because she struggled to keep it calm. "I never wanted to leave Texas
and come to New Mexico in the first place. I never
needed the ranch, Sam did. He planned for Jeff to
carry on after him."

Claire fought the emotion that threatened to choke

her into silence. "Now both of them are gone. Window Rock is all I have left. I'll be *damned* if I'll give it up without a fight!"

"If I can recover the gold, will that solve your problems?"

"It would be a good start," Claire replied.

"I've got some questions to ask at the Overland Stage office. Do you want to come with me?"

Claire shuddered, remembering how Sam had looked lying on the wooden-planked floor of the stage office. Blood had left rust-colored stains on his long johns surrounding the single bullet wound near his heart. "If you don't mind, I think I'll wait here for you."

The stationmaster stiffened when Jake's shadowed body appeared in the door to the stage office. He visibly relaxed when he spied the five-point star on Jake's chest. "Howdy, Ranger. What brings you to town?"

"What can you tell me about the holdup that killed Sam Chandler?" Jake asked.

The stationmaster took out a pocketknife and began sharpening his pencil. "Well, sir, that was a bad day for sure. Three men killed, one wounded." He clucked and shook his head at the tragedy. "Quite a miracle, that one man surviving," the stationmaster added. "Gus Hemp is one lucky fella."

"Oh?"

The man chortled. "All trussed up like a pig for the spit, he was. Supposed to be gutshot. But Gus was carryin' a Bible in his shirt. Bullet hit the Bible 'stead of his innards. Gus was bleedin' some, but rarin' to go when we found him."

"Did Gus see any of the robbers? Can he identify any of them?"

The stationmaster nodded vigorously. "By golly, he did! One of them, the one called Kid, pulled his bandanna down when Mr. Chandler was shot. Gus said he'd know that face anywhere.''

The stationmaster crossed to the wall and pulled down a piece of paper that was tacked there. "Here's a picture right here of the Kid, the one Gus saw. Stage company had it drawn up and posted with a thousand-dollar reward for the Kid's capture, dead or alive. Heard tell there's a kid rides with the Calhoun Gang. Don't know if this is the same one.''

Jake took the WANTED poster from the stationmaster and looked at the youthful face with the name Kid Calhoun below it. Jake whistled softly. The reward for the Kid's capture was nearly as much as Claire needed to pay the note. "Can I have this?''

"I guess so, seein's how you're going after the Kid. You are goin' after him, aren't you?''

"Yes. I am.''

Jake folded the poster and slid it into his vest pocket. "Did Gus say how many were in the gang that robbed the stage?''

"Eight. Plus the Kid. Nine in all. Gus said one of the robbers was wounded. Don't know how bad it was, though. He was still standin'.''

"Anything else you can tell me? Any idea which way they headed?''

The little man tapped the counter with a bony forefinger and leaned forward to speak confidentially. "Heard Booth Calhoun—he's the boss of the Calhoun Gang—has a kept woman in Santa Fe. You might start lookin' there.''

"What's her name?''

"Don't know for sure. You can ask in Santa Fe. Somebody's bound to know.''

"Thanks.''

Just before Jake stepped out the door, the stationmaster said, "You're a long way from Texas, Ranger. What's your interest in this?''

"Sam Chandler was a friend of mine."

"You plannin' to marry the widow? Mighty fine-lookin' woman, if I do say so myself. Heard tell she's—" The man quailed at the look on Jake's scarred face.

"Mrs. Chandler is my sister. Bear that in mind next time your tongue starts flapping before your brain starts working."

"Yessir. Mighty fine—that is—good churchgoing woman, Mrs. Chandler."

Jake shook his head as he turned and left. Men made awful fools of themselves over women. It was a trail he was determined never to travel.

He met up with Claire, and in no time they were out of town and on the meandering road that led to Window Rock. He drove Claire's buggy, his horse tied on behind. Jake found pleasure in sitting beside her even though scarcely a word passed between them. Claire occasionally pointed out a landmark or a cactus flower or a bad rut in the road.

Jake found the country they rode through remarkable for its variety. The grassy plains spread out before them spotted with sagebrush and yuccas. To the east a limestone mesa rose up from the grassland. Beyond that, mountains were stained dark green with fir and pine. It was a land of vibrant contrasts. The sun was warm, but the spring wind was crisp. Jake raised the collar of the fringed buckskin jacket he had donned to protect himself from the cold.

"We're being followed," Claire said.

Jake turned and looked where she pointed. A large black dog loped along the ridge, his tongue lolling, his bushy tail swinging with each step.

"He's been shadowing us, stops when we stop, starts when we start again," Claire said. She looked at Jake, who didn't seem at all surprised by the dog's presence. "Does he belong to you?"

"Dog doesn't belong to anyone. He pretty much goes where he wants, when he wants."

Like you, Claire thought. "Is he vicious?"

"He's never bitten anyone that I know of. But then, he never lets anyone get too close."

Like you, Claire thought. She put a hand up to shade her eyes so she could get a better look at the shaggy black animal. He had a ragged ear and a noticeable limp. "How'd he get torn up like that?"

Jake shrugged. "Been in a few fights, I guess."

Claire smiled inwardly. *Just like you.*

They rode in silence for another half hour before Claire said, "There's Window Rock."

Jake thought she was talking about the ranch, but when he looked where she pointed he spied an immense boulder with a rectangular hole weathered into it.

"Sam took one look at that rock and named the ranch after it," Claire said. "It's just as impressive every time I see it. The ranch house is over the hill."

The whitewashed adobe house lay nestled at the lip of a valley, its red tile roof shaded by the branches of a weeping willow. A nearby stream was bordered with birch and willow. A bunkhouse and barn had been built downhill—and downwind—from the house. There were several horses in a corral that was attached to the barn.

Jake saw the cowhands stop what they were doing and turn to stare at them as they drove up. Obviously they hadn't expected Claire to arrive accompanied by anyone. His eyes narrowed as one of the men pulled a Winchester from the boot on his saddle.

When they reached the yard, Jake found himself the target of numerous weapons. His badge would have relieved their fears, but it was hidden beneath his jacket. He kept his hands visible and made no quick moves. He didn't want to end up killing anyone

unnecessarily. It never occurred to him that he was
the one who might end up dead.

"You all right, Mrs. Chandler?" one of the men
asked.

"I'm fine, Tim. This is my brother, Jake Kearney.
He's come in response to my wire." She looked for
Dog to point him out to the hands so they wouldn't
accidentally shoot him thinking he was a wild dog
that might be a threat to the calves. But Dog had disappeared. She settled for saying, "Jake's dog is
around here somewhere. He's big and black and
looks a little like a wolf. Tell the hands to make sure
what they're aiming at before they shoot any
predators, will you?"

Tim nodded. "Yes, ma'am, I'll do that."

Jake watched the air heave out of a half-dozen sets
of lungs. Several of the men offered smiles that faded
when Jake didn't return them.

An older, gray-haired man with a slight paunch
over his belt came out of the barn and said, "You men
stop gaping like greenhorns and get back to work."

Jake's lip curled in pleasure at the sight of the
leathery old man. "I'll be damned." He came off the
seat of the buggy in a single graceful move. His hand
reached out and was caught in an iron grip. "It's
good to see you, Shug."

The Window Rock foreman nodded a welcome.
"You're a sight for sore eyes, Jake. Glad you showed
up. Bad business here."

"Nobody's going to force Claire into anything,
Shug. I'll see to that."

By then Claire had joined them. "Why don't you
two come inside where you can be comfortable and
talk over old times."

Suddenly both men went still. They were reminded
that it was Sam who had introduced his best friend,
Jake, to his uncle, Shug, and given them a common

thread upon which to weave a friendship. Then Sam
had swept Claire off her feet at sixteen and married
her, making them not only friends, but relations.
Now, just ten years later, Sam was dead. It would
have been too sorrowful to reminisce about days gone
by without him.

Shug shifted his feet and said, "Got work to do. By
the way, Claire, that Reardon fella came by to see
you."

"Where is he now?"

"I told him to make himself comfortable inside. See
you at supper." Then he was gone.

"Would you like come inside and meet Will Reardon?" Claire asked.

"I'd rather make my peace with Sam first."

Claire lifted her eyes and watched the sun setting.
It looked like a piece of orange stained glass in the
center of Window Rock. "I buried him up there. By
the rock." She turned and walked inside the house,
leaving Jake alone.

Jake untied his buckskin from behind the buggy
and stepped into the saddle leather. The rangy gelding made short work of the distance between the
house and the rock. The graveyard wasn't hard to
find. It had a white picket fence around it, and Claire
had planted wildflowers. Jake stepped over the fence
and walked up to the headstone. He took off his hat
and turned the brim in his hands. He thought of all
the rivers he had crossed with Sam.

Jake listened for the wind and heard Sam's laughter, looked for the lowering sun and felt Sam's friendship. And missed them both. Sam was the brother he
had never had. A special part of Jake had died along
with his friend.

It was Sam who had tried to convince him not to be
so cynical about women.

"Take your lead from me," Sam had said with an irreverent grin. "You're looking at a well-loved man."

"I'll forgive your arrogance because it's my sister you're bragging on," Jake had replied. "But I'd rather stake my life on a hand of poker than a pretty woman. The odds are better of coming out ahead."

"You just had a bad experience with that Mama of yours," Sam said.

Jake grimaced. "You ought not to pay too much mind to what a man says when he's full of tonsil varnish."

"Doesn't seem fair to let one woman spoil you for all the rest," Sam needled.

"I haven't heard any complaints."

Sam snickered. "You never hang around long enough to hear the caterwauling start."

"I only need one thing from a woman," Jake said. "And I'm willing to pay well for it."

"One of these days, you ornery bronc, some woman's gonna come along and tie you in tee-tiny knots. When that happens—and it will—I'm gonna be there grinning like a jackass eatin' cactus."

"You'll be burning in hell before I fall prey to some maneuvering female!" Jake had retorted.

It had been a running joke between them for years. Every time they saw each other Sam would ask, "You been hogtied yet?" Jake would laugh and answer, "Never gonna happen!"

Jake stared at Sam's grave. "Never gonna happen," he murmured. He slipped his hat back on and told Sam about the red-headed hussy in El Paso who had kept him up for twenty-four hours straight.

"It was the longest night of my life." He grinned in remembrance. "And a helluva good time. But, Sam, I have to tell you, I didn't have a bit of trouble tipping my hat to her. Just laid the cash on the bed and said so long.

"You were wrong, Sam, about there being a woman who can tie me up in knots. I just wish to hell you'd hung around a little bit longer to let me prove my point."

Jake stayed by Sam's graveside until the sun went down. In the half-light between day and night, tear-tracks dried by the blowing wind, Jake vowed to bring Sam's murderer to justice.

By the time Jake rode up to the house, no signs of his terrible grief remained. He let himself in but paused just beyond the door. The rough pine furniture and woven Indian rugs gave the room a feeling of home. He could imagine Sam and Claire there. And Jeff. It had been nearly three years since Sam had come home from the roundup and told Claire their son had been killed by Apaches, but it seemed like only yesterday. How could Claire live with all the memories in such a room?

Claire rose from her chair as soon as she spied Jake. "You just missed Will. I told him you'd be back soon, but he said he had some business at his ranch that couldn't wait."

Jake turned to Claire and said, "I only came in to let you know I'm leaving."

"You just got here!"

"The trail's already getting cold, Claire. I need to get to Santa Fe. Booth Calhoun has a woman there."

"Can't you even spend the night?"

Jake looked around the room, felt the warmth, and shook his head. "If you need to get in touch with me for any reason, send a letter to me general delivery in Santa Fe."

Claire came to him, wrapped her arms around his waist, and hugged him. "Take care of yourself," she said.

"I'll find the men who killed Sam. And I'll find the gold. Then I'll be back." He took comfort from her touch as he comforted her in return. Jake was surprised at how hard it was to turn his back on her and leave.

An hour later, he had forgotten Claire. Eight shod horses had crossed the trail to Santa Fe. One horse seemed to be walking ahead—or perhaps was being followed by—the others. The trail was unclear in the moonlight. Eight shod horses. Nine members in the Calhoun Gang. Could that wounded outlaw have been too badly hurt to ride? It was a trail worth following.

The hunt had begun.

He searched the dark with ruthless eyes. Jake wasn't adverse to bringing Sam's killer—or killers—back for trial. But there were no laws here in the wilderness. It was often kill or be killed. Jake had learned better than to show mercy. A long time ago a young man named Bobby Latham had taught him a lesson he had never forgotten.

And if, by some chance, the Kid and the gang he rode with lived long enough to be captured, Jake would make certain the outlaws ended up swinging from the business end of a rope.

5

Anabeth sought out the one female she knew in Santa Fe who might be able to help turn her into a lady. Sierra Starr wouldn't have been called a lady in polite society, of course, but Anabeth had nowhere else to turn.

Sierra had a room upstairs at the Town House Saloon. Anabeth came in the back way and slipped up to the room while Sierra was dealing faro in the bar. She sat in the dark waiting. Thinking. It wasn't until the early hours of the morning that Sierra joined her there.

Anabeth raised her hand to shield her eyes from the lantern in Sierra's hand.

"Who's there?" Sierra called.

"It's me."

"Kid?"

"Yes."

Sierra quickly crossed to the cushioned chair by the window where Anabeth sat. She set the lamp on a nearby table. "What are you doing here? Is Booth all right?"

"He's dead. Murdered."

"Murdered!" Sierra sank onto the foot of the big

brass bed that dominated the room. "How? The holdup?"

"Not during the holdup. After. It's a long story."

"Why did you come here, Kid? Did Booth give you a message for me before . . . before he died?"

For a moment Anabeth thought of making something up. She knew how much Sierra cared for her uncle, and she didn't want to hurt the other woman's feelings. "He . . . he was wounded so bad he could hardly talk." That was true enough.

"What happened?" Sierra asked.

Anabeth's jaw tightened. "It was that yellow-bellied, back-stabbing, desert lizard Wat Rankin. He turned the gang against Booth. And they shot him."

"Someone in his own gang shot him? Who?" Sierra asked.

"All of them. Every damn one of those lowdown sidewinders put a bullet in Booth."

Sierra cried out as though she were the one who had been shot and hid her face in her hands.

In retelling the story to Sierra Anabeth felt the same fury and frustration all over again. She could not comfort Sierra, because she was still so angry herself. She stared out the window at a world that was still going about its business as though Booth had never existed.

Sierra dropped her hands from her face and said in a fierce voice, "I won't mourn for him. He didn't even have a word to spare—" Sierra leaped up and paced the length of the room and back again. "Why are you here?" she demanded.

Anabeth turned to face her. "Because I need your help."

"Vengeance?"

"I intend to have it," Anabeth said baldly. "But I plan to handle that myself. What I need from you is something else entirely."

Sierra crossed her arms and waited.

"I . . . I don't know exactly how to tell you this. But I . . ."

"You want me to find a girl for you?"

"No!" Anabeth jumped up and confronted Sierra. "I guess there's no way to say this except to say it. I'm not a boy. I'm a girl. I mean a woman. Booth was my uncle, but I'm not his nephew—I'm his niece, Anabeth."

Anabeth pulled off her Stetson and waist-length braids fell across her shoulders. She waited with bated breath for Sierra's response. It wasn't long in coming.

Sierra laughed. And laughed. Until there were tears in her eyes. "Why are you telling me this now?"

"Because I have to hide from Booth's gang. They think I know where Booth hid the gold from the last holdup. I don't. But they're looking for me. I don't intend to let them find me until I'm good and ready.

"Also, the shotgun rider saw my face during the holdup—as the Kid, of course. I thought if I dressed like a woman, no one would recognize me."

"So you came to me for help with your disguise?"

Anabeth shrugged. "You're the only woman I know."

Sierra took Anabeth's chin in her hand and turned the younger woman's face into the lamplight.

"Somebody hit you." It was a statement, not a question.

"Wat Rankin."

Sierra's eyes narrowed as she looked for signs of Anabeth's femininity. "I can see it now that I know the truth." She hissed in a breath of air. "It's a wonder you weren't discovered."

Anabeth had the same piercing blue eyes and coal black hair as her uncle. The same sharp nose and wide, high cheekbones. The same strong, stubborn chin. Only all these features were softened in the girl. Though she was nearly as tall as Booth's six-foot height, where he had been lean and hard, she was lithe and supple.

"I suppose everyone was looking for a boy, so that's what they saw," Sierra murmured.

"Can you help me become a woman?" Anabeth asked.

"I can put you in a dress, but there's more to being a woman than wearing a skirt."

"I can learn!" Anabeth said.

"Are you willing to give up smoking? Drinking? Swearing? Playing cards?"

Anabeth eyed her from beneath lowered lashes. "Is that really necessary?"

Sierra shook her head at Anabeth's naïveté. "It is if you want to pass for a lady. If you'd rather work downstairs—"

"No!" Anabeth realized how that must have sounded to Sierra. She softened her voice and said, "No, I'd rather do some other kind of woman's work."

A furrow appeared on Sierra's brow. She tapped her chin with a gracefully curved fingernail. "Can you sew?"

"Not well."

"Cook?"

"Not much."

"Take care of children?"

"I wouldn't know the first thing about what to do with one."

Sierra grimaced. "What *can* you do?"

"I'm wonderful with horses."

"I hardly think you can remain anonymous if you put on a dress and go to work at the livery," Sierra said. "I've got it! Anyone can make a bed and sweep a floor. I know just the place where you can hide. Eulalie Schmidt's boardinghouse. Eulalie might even have an extra bedroom you can use. She won't be suspicious, either, since I've sent girls to her before that I didn't think were right for the work here."

Sierra walked in a circle around Anabeth. "There's a lot of work to be done."

Anabeth flushed. "I know I'm not much to look at—"

"Actually, your looks may be a problem," Sierra said. "You've got wonderful bones in your face. Put you in a dress and you're liable to be a little too pretty. No, we're going to have to make you look like less than you are. Let me think about it for a while."

"I guess I'd better leave so you can get some sleep," Anabeth said. "I'll be back early tomorrow."

"Where will you stay tonight?" Sierra asked.

"I'll find a place."

"Why not sleep here?"

"Here?" Anabeth looked around at the feminine room. "I couldn't."

"Why not?"

"Wat Rankin's sure to come here sooner or later looking for me. Or you."

"No one comes into my room who isn't invited," Sierra said in a hard voice.

"I only meant Rankin might think you know where the gold is or where I am," Anabeth said. "Nothing else."

"Except for Booth, I haven't had a man—" Sierra's voice broke.

Anabeth stood across from the other woman, feeling helpless to ease her pain. "You must have loved him very much," she murmured.

"It wasn't love," Sierra denied. "I know better than to fall in love with any man. He'll only break your heart. That's your first lesson as a woman, Anabeth. Learn it well."

* * *

Jake felt hot, dusty, and disgusted as he rode down Canyon Road in Santa Fe. Shortly after he had picked up the tracks of what he hoped was the outlaw gang, they had split up and gone in eight different directions. Since he was headed for Santa Fe himself, he had followed the set of tracks that led directly here.

And lost them just outside of town.

He turned down a side street and headed for a two-story white frame building. A small wooden sign with painted letters hanging from the porch rail in front said simply "Eulalie Schmidt."

Jake knocked on the door to the boardinghouse but didn't wait for an answer before he pushed his way inside. "Eulalie? Eulalie Schmidt!"

The effusive greeting Jake got from the white-haired woman who came running when he called left no doubt that the two knew each other. Frau Schmidt was a woman who enjoyed her sauerkraut and dumplings. Jake had discovered she had a heart as big as she was. The Widow Schmidt wore her hair pulled back in a bun at her nape, exposing the myriad lines on her forehead, the crow's feet at the edges of her eyes, and the trellis of lines over her lips that attested to a lifetime of trial and tribulation.

"Good to see you again, Jake. It's been, what, two years?"

"Nearly three."

"Been that long since your nephew was killed by them savages, eh?" Eulalie said.

Jake nodded. He had been feeling pretty low the first time he had come to Eulalie Schmidt's boardinghouse. He had gotten drunk and spilled his guts. Eulalie had dispensed advice with hot coffee, and the two of them had been friends ever since.

"Come on in and make yourself to home," Eulalie said. "How long are you staying?"

"That depends on how long it takes me to find what I'm looking for," Jake said.

Eulalie led Jake into the kitchen. When they got there a tall woman was standing with her back to them at the sink peeling potatoes. "This is my new hired girl, Anabeth," Eulalie said. "Anabeth, say hello to Jake Kearney."

Anabeth choked on a mouthful of smoke. She quickly doused her cigarette in the bowl of water she had on hand for the peeled potatoes.

Jake had a glimpse of eyes hidden by bottle-thick lenses and blue-black hair scraped back so tight it must have hurt. The girl swiveled her head and murmured, "Hello." Just as quickly, she turned back to her chore. From the rear, her blousy shirtwaist and full skirt made her appear totally shapeless. He dismissed her as quickly as she had greeted him.

"Girl's a bit shy," Eulalie said, "but a hard worker. Pour Jake some coffee, Anabeth."

Jake sat down at the table and watched as Eulalie went to cut some streusel for him. His eyes skipped to the girl when she yelped sharply. He thought he heard some other words that no young lady ought to know, but he wasn't sure.

"Are you all right?" he asked the girl.

"Just burned my hand on the coffeepot," she muttered.

Anabeth adjusted the spectacles downward so she could see over them to pick up the pot with a hot pad. She reached with her other hand and grabbed a coffee mug from the nearby hooks. Then she shoved the heavy lenses up again with a knuckle to resume her disguise. She crossed to the small wooden table, but the thick glass distorted her vision and she ended up running into the sharp edge of it with her hip.

"Damnation!" she muttered.

Jake frowned, thinking he couldn't have heard

what he'd just heard. He raised his hands to steady
the girl, who had lost her balance. To his surprise, the
waist beneath the bulky cloth was firm—and slim.
"Are you all right?"

Anabeth's wits scattered completely when Jake
grasped her waist. "I'm fine," she muttered. She set
down the mug, but again mistook the distance because the thick glass blinded her. It slammed hard
against the table. "Sorry," she mumbled.

Jake exchanged a look with Eulalie as though to
say, "Is she always this clumsy?"

He realized a moment later he should have been
keeping an eye on the girl, because she had reached
the top of the mug and was still pouring coffee.

"Hold on! That's plenty!"

Anabeth jerked when the man shouted at her, and a
splash of coffee from the pot caught him on the
cheek.

"Hell and the devil!" Jake swore. He swiped at his
cheek, but the hot liquid had already done its damage.

"I'm so sorry!" Anabeth tried to set the pot on the
table but missed. It fell off the edge and clattered to
the floor, spilling coffee across the varnished surface.
"Son of a bitch!" Anabeth said. She clapped a hand
over her mouth, but the words were already out.

Anabeth stared through the thick lenses at the irate
face of the man at the table. She wished she could see
him better. She had a feeling it was lucky she
couldn't. "I'll get a cool cloth for your face." She
turned back toward the pump but slipped on the
spilled coffee. Her arms flailed, and she caught Jake
with an elbow in the jaw as she fell backward into his
lap.

She sat there holding her breath, waiting to see if
the chaos had run its course.

Jake was aware of the weight of the young woman's

breasts on his forearm. Of the slight shifting of her fanny on his thighs. Of the honeysuckle smell of her hair. He was also aware of the throbbing burn on his cheek and the ache in his jaw. If he didn't know for a fact that she was a walking disaster, he might have found himself aroused by the young woman in his arms.

"Are you all right?" he asked for perhaps the third or fourth time. He had lost count.

"I'm fine," Anabeth said through gritted teeth. She tried to stand, but Jake was holding her fast.

"Maybe you'd better stay where you are for a moment until Eulalie can take care of that puddle on the floor."

"Jake's right," Eulalie said. She had been flabbergasted by the chain of events that had resulted in the pool of coffee on the kitchen floor. Perhaps it would be best if she took care of matters before Jake let Anabeth go at it again.

At first Anabeth sat absolutely still in Jake's lap. But she got impatient when Eulalie went to hunt for the mop. Anabeth wiggled her fanny a bit to get more comfortable. Then Eulalie decided to wash out the coffeepot and start a new brew. Anabeth sat up straighter, couldn't get comfortable, and slumped back down over Jake's arm again. Finally, Eulalie decided to wipe up the coffee Anabeth had spilled on the table as well.

When Eulalie finally gave the okay, Jake quickly stood Anabeth on her feet and wiped the sweat from his brow with his sleeve. All that shifting had left him needing a woman. He felt like a tomcat in an alley with a she-cat sitting on the fence out of reach. How could that clumsy, shapeless woman have turned him into a rutting beast? "You're a menace, woman!" he snarled.

Anabeth opened her mouth to make a retort and

snapped it shut again. She was supposed to be mousy, docile, Anabeth Smith. She had better act the part. Anabeth turned to face Jake Kearney, knuckled her spectacles up her nose, straightened her apron, and said, "It was nice meeting you, Mr. Kearney."

Jake laughed. He couldn't help it. He was grinning when he said, "It was . . . an experience . . . meeting you, too, Miss . . ."

"Smith," Anabeth supplied. She glared daggers at Jake, but the effect was lost through the bottle glass perched on her nose.

"Miss Smith." *And may we never meet again!*

"Would you go upstairs and check the northeast corner bedroom for me, Anabeth? I'd like to make sure it's made up for Jake."

"Certainly, Frau Schmidt."

When Anabeth was gone—she ran into the door-jamb with her shoulder on the way out of the room—Jake turned to Eulalie and raised a brow. "Are you sure the room will still be there when she's done?"

Eulalie clucked her tongue and shook her head. "Sierra sent her over from the saloon. Said she wasn't suited for work there."

Jake rolled his eyes. "Perish the thought. How long has she been working for you?"

"A couple of days. She's still learning."

"Not fast enough!" Jake muttered.

Eulalie poured Jake another cup of coffee, served his streusel, and joined him at the kitchen table. "Now, tell me what I can do for you."

Jake filled Eulalie in on everything that had happened to bring him north from Texas. He was in the middle of his explanation when Anabeth came back.

"Everything's fine upstairs," she said. "I'll just finish those potatoes." She crossed to the counter by the pump, picked up the paring knife, and began working with her back to Jake.

Jake purposefully ignored her. "I've got some evidence that the Calhoun Gang is responsible for the robbery that killed Sam," he told Eulalie.

"And you've been sent to bring them in?"

"I'm not here officially on behalf of the Rangers," Jake said. "But I intend to bring whoever is responsible for Sam's death to justice."

"Rangers?" Anabeth could have bitten her tongue. Jake looked annoyed at the interruption.

"Jake's a Texas Ranger," Eulalie explained.

Good grief, Anabeth thought. She had been sitting in the lap of the law! "Why aren't you wearing a badge?"

"I am." Jake pulled his vest aside and exposed the star.

Anabeth squinted through the bottled glass. "Oh, I see it now. Did I hear you say you're going after the Calhoun Gang?"

"I suspect that the Calhoun Gang murdered my brother-in-law, Sam Chandler, during their latest holdup. If my sister Claire doesn't get back the gold they stole from Sam, she's going to lose her ranch."

Anabeth felt an awful surge of guilt. "Oh." She wasn't likely to forget the man who had died in her arms. It made her feel even worse to meet someone who had cared about him and to hear the consequences of their larceny. Not once while riding with Booth had she allowed herself to think about what happened to the people they robbed. Jake was giving her an eye-opening education she would rather not have had.

"Jake followed what he thinks might be one of the gang members here to Santa Fe," Eulalie explained.

"Oh," Anabeth said again. Had he followed her here? Or was some other member of the gang in town? Either way, she must be on her guard.

"I was told Booth Calhoun has a woman here in

Santa Fe," Jake said. "I thought maybe she could give
me a lead where I might search for the gang. Also,"
Jake paused and pulled the WANTED poster from his
pocket, "I've got a drawing of one of the members of
the gang. He was identified by the shotgun rider on
the stage."

Anabeth turned and stood with potato and peeler in
hand to watch as Jake unfolded the drawing for Eulalie. She pulled the lenses down her nose so she
could see over them. It was a good likeness of her.
The mouth was a little too wide, and the eyes too
close together, but that was definitely a picture of Kid
Calhoun.

Anabeth felt a shiver of fear run down her spine
when she saw that a thousand-dollar reward was being offered for her capture—*dead or alive*! For that
amount of money there would be a lot of people willing to hunt her down. And damned few of them
would worry about bringing her back alive.

"Have you seen anybody who looks like this?" Jake
asked Eulalie.

The frau shook her head. "Can't say that I have."

Jake turned to show the picture to Anabeth, who
quickly shoved her spectacles back up her nose.
"Have you—"

"No," Anabeth interrupted. She quickly turned
back to face the counter.

Jake carefully folded up the poster and returned it
to his pocket. "Any idea who Booth's woman might
be?" he asked Eulalie.

"You might try Sierra Starr," Eulalie said.

"Any relation to the Sierra who sent Miss Anabeth
Smith here to work for you?" Jake asked.

"The same. Sierra works the faro table at the Town
House Saloon. From what I hear, she owns nearly
half the place."

Anabeth peeled a little faster. What if Sierra gave

her away? She would have to warn the other woman that a Texas Ranger was in town asking questions.

"Sierra Starr sounds like some special kind of woman," Jake mused.

Eulalie pulled at the single white hair growing from a mole on her chin. "Sierra's an unusual woman, all right. For a while she worked upstairs, but not anymore."

"Does she make exceptions?" Jake asked with a lurid grin.

Eulalie's eyes twinkled with mirth. "Jake, you naughty boy. Why are you asking a question like that with this girl standing right here? You got a hankering for some woman, you go ask where there are no little pitchers with big ears."

Jake took one look at Anabeth's pink cheeks and rose abruptly. "I didn't mean—that is—"

Eulalie stood and patted Jake on the shoulder. "You go on, Jake. I'll have supper waiting when you've taken care of business."

There was no mistaking the kind of "business" Eulalie had in mind. A muscle in Jake's jaw flexed as he bit down to keep from making the kind of retort that was too coarse for Anabeth Smith's tender ears. Besides, if Sierra Starr took his fancy, he would see for himself whether she made exceptions about working upstairs. Maybe then he could forget about the surprisingly lush body of the awkward young woman peeling potatoes in Eulalie Schmidt's kitchen.

Once Jake was gone, Anabeth felt Eulalie's sharp eyes assessing her. If she wasn't careful, she would give herself away to the frau. Her safety depended on her disguise. Especially now that she knew the gang, including Kid Calhoun, was being sought by the law —even if the law wasn't officially on the job.

She turned to the older woman and said, "I'm sorry, Frau Schmidt. I'm afraid I don't see very well.

When I'm not in a hurry, I do fine. I guess I got flustered."

Eulalie closed her lips on the sharp setdown she had been about to give. How could she criticize the girl for something that was not her fault? "Don't worry about it, Anabeth." But she made up her mind to keep the girl away from her other customers. Otherwise, Anabeth Smith might singlehandedly put her out of business.

To Anabeth's chagrin, Jake sent word to Eulalie that he wouldn't be back for supper. After the supper dishes were washed, Anabeth excused herself to go to her room, which was near the kitchen on the lower floor. If it wasn't already too late, she had to get a warning about Jake Kearney to Sierra.

But she couldn't go out in the evening as Anabeth Smith. She would have to become Kid Calhoun again, which posed its own set of dangers. How many of those posters with her likeness were out there in the hands of lawmen and bounty hunters?

It was a relief for Anabeth to put on a pair of pants. She hadn't realized how much like a fish out of water she felt in a skirt. Besides, the outfit she had been wearing was a far cry from the silk taffeta dress of her dreams. She rebraided her hair and stuffed it up under her hat, then buckled on Booth's gunbelt, with its twin, pearl-handled revolvers.

When the house was quiet, she left her room and snuck down the hall and out the back door. She used the back streets and alleys to get from the boardinghouse to Canyon Road. She could already see the lights from the Town House Saloon when she realized there was someone leaning against the building at the end of the alley that led where she wanted to go.

She had already begun her retreat when the man called out, "Somebody there?"

Anabeth remained frozen, her hands poised above her guns. She said nothing.

The man slowly stood and turned toward her, blocking what little light was coming into the alley. "Booth?" The voice was frankly disbelieving. "Booth, is that you?"

Anabeth remained silent. She realized that whoever it was must have recognized Booth's pearl-handled revolvers. She slowly, quietly, backed completely out of the light.

"You're dead," the man said. "We killed you."

At last Anabeth recognized the voice. Otis Grier. "You're a backstabbing coward," Anabeth said in a voice keyed like Booth's, an octave lower than her own. "I ought to shoot you where you stand."

Grier pulled his gun, and Anabeth realized he intended to shoot. She hadn't expected to be confronted with one of the gang so suddenly, or in such a deadly situation. In the seconds before Grier fired, she thought of Booth, of her vow of vengeance. Suddenly, it was as though someone else was standing there. Anabeth felt a tightening in her belly, a lump in her throat.

Then there wasn't time for thinking—or feeling.

Grier began firing blindly into the alley. Anabeth dropped to the ground as she pulled Booth's right hand gun and fired once at the man silhouetted in the light.

Grier let out a howl and dropped his gun.

Anabeth's finger was on the trigger. All she had to do was shoot again and one of her uncle's murderers would be dead. But her hand was shaking so badly she had trouble keeping it steady enough to aim.

Suddenly there was a commotion at Grier's end of the alley. She couldn't take a chance on being caught. Her face was on a WANTED poster now. She holstered the Colt and, flattening herself against the walls of the alley, quickly made her escape. She headed for the next alley and soon found herself in back of the Town House Saloon.

She stuffed her hands in her pants because she couldn't get them to stop shaking. It was one thing to vow vengeance. It was quite something else to shoot another human being. Anabeth took a deep breath and let it whoosh out. She leaned against the slatted wall of the saloon and let her head fall back against the wood.

I should have killed him. He shot Booth in the knee without a second thought. He's a treacherous murderer. He deserves to die.

Then why didn't you finish him off? a voice asked.

Because I lost my nerve.

Then you better find it. Or move on to Colorado.

It'll be easier next time.

You're lucky to have a next time. You'd better shoot first—and shoot to kill—from now on.

Anabeth took another deep breath and let it out. This was no game she was playing. The men she had set out to kill were killers themselves. If they caught her, they would show no mercy. If she wanted to survive, neither could she.

Anabeth straightened her head on her shoulders. She would do what had to be done. Next time she would shoot to kill.

Anabeth stepped inside the back door of the Town House Saloon but stayed in the shadows beyond the patchy lantern light. It was noisy and smoky, and she did nothing to draw attention to herself. She was as silent, as invisible, as any Apache in the wilderness. Only her eyes moved as she surveyed those present in the saloon.

The one person in the bar she recognized was Jake Kearney. Without her spectacles she could see Jake

clearly for the first time. The sight of him took her
breath away.

His features were hard-chiseled, a strong jaw, a
sharp blade of nose, blunt cheekbones, and thick-
lashed, wide-set eyes framed by dark brows. A small
scar slashed through his mouth, drawing it down on
one side. She felt a shiver of awareness and realized
that her body was responding merely to the sight of
him.

Anabeth let out a soft, soughing breath. *So this was
desire.* She hadn't expected it to be so powerful. Or so
indiscriminate. She didn't particularly like Jake Kearney. So why was she physically attracted to him?
Anabeth felt confused and a bit overwhelmed. She
was aware of strange stirrings in her body. She
slowly, imperceptibly moved to lay a hand on her
belly, but that didn't seem to help.

Anabeth's lips twisted at the irony of the situation.
Finally, she had found a man for whom she felt the
first stirrings of desire. Only she was an outlaw, and
Jake Kearney was a Texas Ranger. Even worse, he
knew her only as stumbling, bumbling Anabeth
Smith. He hadn't been able to get away from her fast
enough. This was not exactly a match made in
heaven.

Anabeth was turning to leave when Jake noticed
her. She stood frozen for a moment. Luckily his attention was distracted when Sierra sat down across from
him. Anabeth watched Jake smile at the other
woman. Watched him laugh and grin at something
Sierra said. Then she watched as Sierra left the table
and headed upstairs with Jake following after her.

At first, Anabeth was grateful to Sierra for distract-
ing Jake's attention from her. Then she realized it was
too late to give Sierra a warning about why Jake
Kearney had come to Santa Fe. Unless Anabeth

wanted to run, she had no choice except to trust Sierra not to give her away.

And Anabeth had no intention of running.

She was leaving when she saw Grier come into the bar. His arm was in a sling and a bloody bandage covered his wrist. He seemed agitated as he crossed to a table in the corner and spoke to a man whose back was to her.

Anabeth recognized the man as he turned around. It was Wat Rankin. She took a step forward to confront him, and realized she couldn't do that with Jake Kearney upstairs. Any gunplay and the Ranger was liable to come running. After he put his pants on, Anabeth thought with a cynical smile.

In the future she would carefully choose the time and place for any confrontations. Anabeth watched Wat Rankin and Otis Grier head toward the batwing doors of the saloon. She snuck out the back way and hurried down the alley after them.

From now on she would be the hunter, and they would be the hunted.

6

Wat shoved his way through the batwing doors and followed Otis Grier into the night. "I'm telling you the man who shot at you couldn't have been Booth Calhoun. Booth is dead!"

"It sounded like Booth. And you know Booth was gone when we went back to the shack to search again for the gold. I tell you it was him."

"And I say you're crazy," Wat said to the big man as he stepped into the saddle. "Even assuming he could have survived getting hit by seven bullets, Booth wouldn't be on his feet yet. Have you forgotten he was shot in both knees?"

"What about those pearl-handled Colts I saw in the alley? How do you explain that?" Grier asked as he slung his heavy weight onto his horse with surprising grace.

Wat was silent for the length of time it took them to get to the last lights of Santa Fe. "I figure the Kid came back and found Booth. He took the body and the guns. The man you met in that dark alley was the Kid. Which means he's somewhere in Santa Fe."

Grier grunted and scratched at his beard. "I suppose it coulda been the Kid. I didn't get a good look at him in the shadows."

"Where'd you leave the rest of the gang?"

"Camp's set up a couple miles south of town. We gotta warn 'em about the Kid," Grier said.

"Yeah, the Kid will have to be taken care of." This newest crisis made Wat wonder if he had made a mistake manipulating the Calhoun Gang instead of simply hiring someone to murder Sam Chandler.

Then he thought of the look in Chandler's eyes when he had recognized Will Reardon behind the outlaw's mask, and the expression on Chandler's face when he realized he was a dead man. No, it had been worth the risk to do the deed himself.

He had set up everything perfectly so that when he got possession of Window Rock, he would get Claire Chandler as well. Only there had been a few hurdles along the way. Booth Calhoun was one.

Booth hadn't wanted anyone killed during the gang's robberies, so Wat had been left with no choice except to get rid of him. The Kid was another problem altogether. The Kid would have to die, of course. But not until he had told them where Sam Chandler's gold was hidden.

Wat didn't mind the killing. He had gotten an early start at it, having shot his drunken father for beating him when he was only eight years old. At ten, he had stabbed to death the man who pimped for his mother. He had learned early that if he wanted something he had to get it for himself. And he had discovered that the easiest way to deal with an obstacle was to remove it.

Wat had never flinched from the dirty jobs that had to be done. Shooting Booth in the back hadn't given him a qualm. There was, after all, no honor among thieves. But he had made a serious miscalculation by not making sure Booth had all the gold with him before he ambushed him.

And he should have made sure the scoundrel was

dead. He was *almost* positive that the ghostly specter Otis Grier had seen was the Kid. Since he was hunting the Kid anyway, he planned to hang around Santa Fe long enough to be sure, one way or the other.

Wat would have an appropriate reception waiting no matter who showed up at the outlaws' campfire.

Jake went upstairs to Sierra's room with her because it was the one place she said they could talk without being disturbed. Sierra sat in a cushioned chair by the window. Jake stood by the door.

"All right, Ranger. Talk."

"I was told you know Booth Calhoun," Jake said.

"What if I do?"

"I'm hunting the Calhoun Gang. I hoped maybe you could tell me where to start looking for them." He took the poster out of his pocket and crossed to hand it to Sierra. "Have you seen this man?"

Sierra was shocked at how accurate a drawing it was of the Kid, but she kept her features even. She knew by sight all the members of Booth's gang. Except for Wat Rankin. For a moment she considered agreeing to point them out for the Ranger. At least that way Anabeth Calhoun would be safe. But a lifetime of hard lessons made her cautious. "Why should I help you?"

"Because these men are murderers. Because they need to be brought to justice."

What kind of justice would the law exact for Booth's death? Sierra was inclined to believe Anabeth Calhoun's justice would be more swift and sure. But she wasn't averse to having the law hound Booth's murderers, either. "I can tell you where they usually rendezvous when they come to Santa Fe," Sierra said at last.

Jake followed Sierra's directions to an isolated spot five miles south of Santa Fe. The fire beside the

waterhole at the bottom of the rocky trail was a sure
sign of human inhabitants. Ordinarily Jake might expect a welcome there and an offer to "Light and set."

But there was no one anywhere near the fire. The
camp looked deserted. Jake was certain it was not.
He suspected that some or all of the Calhoun Gang
were out there somewhere. They must have scattered
when they heard him coming.

But the danger below wasn't his only concern. Because ever since he had left Santa Fe, he hadn't been
able to shake the feeling that someone was watching
him—that he was somehow being pursued himself.
Jake shivered and blamed it on the cold. He nudged
his horse with his knees and headed down the slope
to the fire below.

The only way to spring the trap was to ride into it.

Jake felt the hairs prickle on his neck only an instant before he heard the first gunshot. He threw himself from the saddle, but the shot must have been
aimed low because the bullet hit him anyway. Jake's
leg crumpled under him as he collided with the
ground. A second shot tore a hole in his sleeve. A
third shot sent splinters of rock to blister his face, but
by then he was safely concealed in a shallow gully
lined with thick sagebrush.

He remained perfectly still, knowing that any
movement would give him away. Jake heard mur-
muring voices and knew the bushwhackers were de-
ciding how and when to make their move. He had
plenty of ammunition in his gunbelt. Of more concern
was his wound. His pants leg was soaked with blood.

Jake took off his bandanna and tied it around his
leg. It stemmed the bleeding, but didn't stop it. The
outlaws wouldn't have to shoot him. All they had to
do was keep him pinned here, and he would eventually bleed to death.

The hairs on Jake's neck prickled again, an instant

before he felt a hand on his shoulder. Jake brought his gun to bear as he rolled over. He never knew what kept him from firing, but a moment later he was glad he hadn't.

The lean man who was crouched on the ground beside Jake, the upper half of his face shadowed by his hat, had his finger to his lips, indicating the need for silence. He gestured for Jake to follow him, then began crawling along the gully away from the light of the fire.

Jake didn't know what to make of it. The stranger could easily have killed him. Apparently the man wasn't a part of the Calhoun Gang. But if not, then who was he, and what was he doing here? Hell, Jake thought, there would be time enough to find that out once he made good his escape—if he made good his escape.

Jake took one look back toward the fire and made his choice. He rolled over onto his belly and began to slither down the gully after the stranger.

The lean man moved like an Indian, swiftly and silently. Jake might have done a better job of emulating him if it hadn't been for his wounded leg. It wasn't cooperating. The distance between them grew larger, until Jake could no longer see the man who had come to rescue him.

Jake stopped for a moment, breathless from exertion and dizzy from loss of blood. He turned to look over his shoulder to see how far he had come from the fire and realized it was no longer visible on the horizon. Jake leaned his forehead on his hand. If he took a moment to catch his breath he would be all right. His eyes drifted closed.

"Well, now, what do we have here? Don't move an inch or I'll blow your head off."

Jake gladly played dead, but his mind was racing, searching for a way to avoid catastrophe.

"Hey! I found the Kid! He's over here!"

"Is that you, Grier?" one of the outlaws called.

"Yeah," Grier answered.

"Are you sure it's him?" someone shouted back.

Grier shoved Jake over with his boot so he could get a look at his face in the moonlight.

"Hey! It ain't him. It's somebody else."

"Kill him, and let's get out of here."

Jake shivered at the cold-bloodedness of the command. He knew if he was going to do something it had to be soon. His gun was in his hand at his side. The problem was how to shoot without getting shot first. What he needed was a distraction.

He got it when the stranger who had stopped to help him suddenly stood up in plain sight of the man holding the gun on Jake. The stranger also had a gun in his hand, and it was aimed at Grier.

Grier seemed rooted to the ground, stunned by the apparition that had appeared before him. "It's the Kid! Somebody *do* something!" Grier shrieked.

"I thought you said it wasn't him!" a voice shouted back.

"You have to pay for what you did," the stranger said to Grier. "I want you to think about the bullet that's going to kill you. First I'm going to shoot the gun out of your hand. Then I'm going to put a bullet in each of your knees, just like you did to Booth. But I'm not going to kill you. I'm going to let you live as a cripple."

"Shit. Shit," Grier muttered.

"If it is the Kid, don't shoot to kill!" someone shouted. "The Kid's the only lead we have to that gold! He's bound to know where his uncle buried it."

Jake heard pounding footsteps as the members of the gang converged on them. He didn't understand why the Calhoun Gang wanted to kill the Kid. But one thing was certain. The gang thought the Kid knew where Sam's gold could be found. Which meant Jake wanted the Kid alive, too.

He could see the big man torn between aiming his gun at his prisoner on the ground, and bringing it to bear on the Kid. It was as though he knew the instant he moved the Kid would shoot.

Grier's eyes were on the Kid, but his gun was on Jake. Jake figured he had an even chance of getting Grier before Grier could aim and fire at him. He had to do something to get free before the rest of the gang arrived on the scene.

"Grier!" Jake shouted.

Jake's gamble paid off. Grier made the mistake of swinging his head back around before pulling the trigger. The time it took him to find a target was all the time Jake needed to bring his gun to bear on the big man.

Jake's bullet hit Grier square in the chest. The outlaw turned his head and looked back at the Kid. "It was better this way, Kid," he said.

Jake heard the Kid say, "Son of a bitch." But when he raised himself on his elbows he could see nothing in the darkness. Where had the Kid gone?

Despite the shouts of one man exhorting the other gang members to finish Jake off, the outlaws mounted their horses and fled. Jake watched them race away as though the hounds of hell were chasing them. He turned to search for the man who had saved his life.

Only the Kid had disappeared.

Jake was confused. Was the stranger who had led him to safety really the Kid he was searching for? Why did Kid Calhoun know where the gold was, and not the other members of the gang? And what had the Kid meant, when he said Grier had to pay for what he had done to Booth? Exactly what had happened to Booth Calhoun?

Jake whistled for his horse and the buckskin geld-

ing came on the run. He used a stirrup to pull himself
upright and grabbed the horn to help him into the
saddle. Finding the Kid would have to wait until he
could get his leg patched up. Jake turned the buckskin north and headed back to Santa Fe.

It wasn't long before that same prickly feeling as-
saulted him again. He was being followed, which
wouldn't be difficult, considering the trail of blood he
was leaving on the rocky ground. But he never heard
a sound, nor saw so much as a blade of grass move
behind him. Whoever was on his trail was awful
damned invisible.

Jake felt himself slipping out of the saddle. Suddenly there was a hand on his shoulder to steady him.
When Jake recognized the figure beside him, he
frowned. "Who the hell are you?"

The stranger hesitated an instant, then said, "I'm
Kid Calhoun."

The young outlaw tensed, waiting to see whether
Jake would draw on him. It was hard for Jake to pull
his gun on a man who had just saved his life. He
resisted the urge and instead asked, "Why did you
help me?"

"I've got no use for the Calhoun Gang anymore."

"Why not?"

"They murdered my uncle, Booth Calhoun."

"Why did you follow me?"

The Kid shrugged. "I figured you might need some
help. I was right."

Jake reminded himself that although he had acted
the Good Samaritan, Kid Calhoun was also a wanted
man. "What do you know about Sam Chandler's
death?"

"I know that Wat Rankin killed him," the Kid said.

"You were there?"

The Kid looked down at white-knuckled hands,
then back up at Jake. "I was there."

"What about Sam's gold?"

"Booth hid it. He died without telling where."

Jake wondered whether he could believe such a tale. It made a very convenient lie.

There was a long silence. Finally the Kid said, "We'd better get to shelter. Storm's coming."

Jake still hadn't pulled a gun. But he didn't trust the Kid any farther than he could throw him. He had made the mistake once upon a time of trusting an outlaw's word and five innocent people had died. Never again.

Besides, he didn't intend to let the Kid out of his sight until he found out for sure whether the Kid knew where Sam's gold was hidden. "All right. Let's ride."

The wind sent tumbleweed blowing. Clouds darkened the moon. Lightning streaked through the sky in jagged patterns. Thunder rumbled down the rocky hills. The air smelled like rain.

The icy water came down first in fat drops. Soon it fell in thick sheets, rolling off Jake's hat and down the yellow slicker he had donned. Jake followed where the Kid led and was relieved when they entered a shallow cave. He slid off his horse, but his wounded leg wouldn't hold him. He would have fallen except the Kid slid an arm around him to keep him upright.

"Lean on me," the Kid said.

A flash of lightning lit the Kid's face and Jake was surprised at how young the outlaw was. But he knew as well as anyone that the looks of a man had little to do with what was on the inside. A clean scab could hide an ugly sore.

The Kid helped Jake to the rear of the cave well out of the wind and rain and settled him with his back to the rock wall. A ring of stones held brush and firewood that had been left ready so that only a match was needed to provide both heat and light. The Kid had obviously used this hideout in the past.

Jake watched as the Kid lit the fire, then unsaddled the horses and wiped them dry with handfuls of the grass that also had been left in the cave against a future need. Once the animals had been tended, the Kid turned to Jake.

The Kid didn't ask permission, simply knelt beside Jake and used a Bowie knife to cut away his pants leg, exposing the wound in Jake's thigh. He probed the gunshot with gentle hands.

"That bullet has to come out," the Kid said after he had finished his examination.

"Figured that." Jake winced as he tried to get more comfortable. "I'll wait for the doctor in Santa Fe."

The Kid looked at him askance. "You need to get that bleeding stopped."

"When the storm ends we'll be on our way."

Several hours later, with the storm still raging, it was apparent the Kid had been right. Jake felt himself growing weaker and knew it wouldn't be long before he lost consciousness. He hadn't felt like eating any of the beans the Kid had fixed, though he had managed to drink some coffee.

He was still trying to decide what kind of man stood by and watched cold-blooded murder being committed when he robbed a stage and then risked his life to save a perfect stranger on the trail.

Jake had taken a good look at Kid Calhoun, and he wasn't much impressed by what he found. The Kid was tall and rail thin, with cheeks that were almost gaunt, making his deep blue eyes seem even larger in his face. His skin was beardless, smooth as a brat's bottom. His black hair was tucked up under his hat, but strands hung every whichaway around his face and down over his collar.

His nose was small and straight, not taking up

much room on his face. On the other hand, his mouth
was wide, the lips not too thin. A cigarette hung from
the corner of his mouth. When he talked around it
Jake had noticed he had all his teeth. It was easy to
guess he had done his fighting with a gun, rather than
his fists.

Jake didn't think much of the Kid's grooming hab-
its, either. The jeans he wore were ripped at the knee,
and the gray flannel shirt was too big for him. All in
all, Kid Calhoun didn't fit his image of a heartless
killer. It was hard to believe someone so innocent-
looking had ridden with the outlaws who had shot
Sam down.

All Jake had to do was remember the past to know
that looks could be deceiving. Bobby Latham had also
looked innocent as a lamb. He'd been a wolverine in
sheep's clothing. The memory of what Bobby Latham
had done would be with him forever.

Before Jake lost his senses, he had to decide
whether or not to trust the Kid to take out the bullet.
In truth, he hadn't any choice at all.

"Guess you were right," Jake admitted. "That bullet has to come out." A wry smile twisted his lips before he continued, "Since either me or you has to do
it, I vote for you."

The Kid hesitated, then reached for the knife at his
belt. "All right. I'll do it." He put his knife in the fire
to burn it clean, then set it on a rock to let it cool.

Jake chose a stick from the pile near the fire. "Go
ahead. I'm ready." He put the wood between his teeth
and bit down against the pain to come.

The muscles corded in Jake's neck, and his hands
fisted at his sides as the Kid began to probe with his
knife. He hoped to hell the Kid knew what he was
doing—that he wasn't cutting tendon and sinew that
Jake would need later to walk.

"I'm done," the Kid said at last.

Jake looked into the outlaw's deep blue eyes and saw that the Kid had survived the ordeal on pride and stubbornness alone. "Thanks," Jake murmured.

The Kid rooted in Jake's saddlebags for something he could use as a bandage. He wrapped the wound with one of Jake's shirts, which he tore into strips for the purpose. Then he rose and began saddling his horse.

"Where do you think you're going?" Jake demanded.

"Out for some air."

Jake drew his Colt, which had gotten almost too heavy to hold, and pointed it at the Kid.

"Hold it there," he ordered. "You're not going anywhere."

The Kid turned and looked at him with steady eyes. His hand hovered over his Colt. "I don't think you'll shoot me. You owe me your life."

Jake's eyes narrowed, and a muscle jumped in his jaw. "Nevertheless, I'm taking you in."

The Kid's eyes looked troubled, and he gnawed on his lower lip, making him look even more like the kid he was. "I'm not who . . ." He seemed to change his mind about what he wanted to say. He thrust his chin out and said, "I give you my word I'll be back."

Jake's lip curled. "The word of an outlaw?"

"Even an outlaw can have honor."

"Not in my experience," Jake said bluntly.

"You're going to have to shoot me to keep me here," the Kid said.

"Don't think I won't," Jake warned.

The Kid apparently believed him, because he leaned against the wall of the cave and crossed his arms belligerently.

Beyond the fire, at the mouth of the cave, Dog suddenly appeared. He whined once, but didn't come inside. Jake focused his attention on the animal to try

and stay awake. He called to the animal, urging him
to come inside, to the warmth of the fire. But Dog
stayed where he was.

Jake felt cold and wondered whether it really was
chilly in the cave or if the feeling came from inside.
Jake's throat felt parched, and his leg ached. His eyes
were already half-closed when he realized he had almost fallen asleep. He tightened his hold on the Colt
in his hand and stared at the outlaw across the cave
from him.

The next thing Jake knew, the Kid had tugged the
gun free of his hand, leaving him unarmed. He was
helpless now. At the mercy of his enemy. Gentle fingers tested the pulse at his throat. Lean strength lifted
his head so he could drink.

Jake tried to hold onto consciousness. His life
might very well depend upon it. The darkness slipped
over him and sucked him down.

Anabeth let her eyes roam over the pale, chilled
man. Her feelings for him confused and annoyed her.
She had interrupted her trail of vengeance to help
him. But she couldn't for the life of her understand
why she had done it.

At first she had trailed Jake because he was following Wat Rankin. She had seen the trap and realized
she didn't want him killed. It had been a spur of the
moment decision to help him. And look what had
happened. Now she either had to stay here with Jake
until he got well enough to travel or figure out a way
to get him back to Santa Fe.

It was the latter solution she had finally decided
upon while she was waiting for Jake to lose consciousness. She would leave Jake Kearney on the
back steps of Eulalie Schmidt's boardinghouse where
Anabeth Smith could discover him when she went to
get kindling for the morning fire in the kitchen.

Anabeth admitted to herself with chagrin that she didn't want to let Jake Kearney out of her sight until she was sure he was well. She knew full well it was a mistake to get involved with the Ranger, but the man fascinated her. However forbidding his countenance —and with those steely gray eyes and that scar turning down his mouth it could be awesome—she found herself attracted to him, compelled to know more about him.

It had been downright reckless to reveal herself to the Texas Ranger as Kid Calhoun. He believed her to be a thief and a murderer. *He thought she was a man.*

Anabeth had no intention of correcting his mistake. Especially since Kid Calhoun was about to disappear again. Nor was she about to allow her inexplicable feelings for Jake Kearney to distract her from exacting vengeance for her uncle's death.

She thought back over the events of the past evening. She had wanted to make Grier suffer the way Booth had suffered. The outlaw had cheated her by choosing death instead of life as a cripple. But Grier's death was only the beginning. Her vengeance would not be complete until all the members of Booth's gang—especially Wat Rankin—had paid for their treachery.

Just before dawn she would take Jake Kearney into Santa Fe. Then Kid Calhoun would disappear again while sweet, submissive Anabeth Smith continued plotting the downfall of the Calhoun Gang.

7

Anabeth was dozing when she heard a stone turn at the mouth of the cave. She was fully awake in an instant, her gun in hand. What she saw in the firelight had her smiling in welcome relief. "Wolf! What are you doing here? How did you find me?"

"Who could not see the light from your fire, Stalking Deer?"

Stung by Wolf's censure, Anabeth stopped her movement toward the Apache. "I needed the light to—"

"Why are you here? I did not think to see you again."

Anabeth heard the longing in Wolf's voice. And the anger. Their parting had not been an easy one. Wolf had not yet forgotten or forgiven their argument. He had a right to ask why she had not left for Colorado as she had vowed she would.

Her explanation was equally painful. "Booth is dead. He was murdered—by his own gang! I couldn't go to Colorado—"

Wolf stiffened as he suddenly became aware of the figure lying in the shadows. "Who is there?"

Anabeth laid a hand on Wolf's forearm. It was taut as a bowstring. "His name is Jake Kearney. I've been

trying to tell you—I needed the light to watch over
him. He was ambushed and wounded by Booth's
gang. I removed a bullet from his leg, but he's lost a
lot of blood."

Anabeth left Wolf to kneel beside Jake. She put her
hand to his throat, seeking a pulse. The beat was
faint.

Wolf searched the face that was precious to him,
surprised by the concern he saw there for the
stranger. A sharp, uncomfortable feeling rose in his
breast.

Jealousy.

He told himself his feelings were unfounded. Nevertheless, within him rose the urge to kill the white
man. Wolf did not crush it, but he did not act on it,
either. The death of Stalking Deer's uncle changed
everything. Now there was no need for her to go
away. Now she could stay with him.

Then and there he made a vow to himself that he
would have Stalking Deer for his wife. She would
learn to love him. He was certain of it. As for the
white man, he could be killed if he became a threat to
Wolf's plans.

Anabeth's eyes begged for understanding from
Wolf. When her silent plea did nothing to move him
she explained, "I had to help him. I couldn't let him
die."

Wolf's lips flattened, but otherwise his face revealed
nothing of what he felt at this further proof of Stalking Deer's attachment to the other man.

The sound of voices dragged Jake back to consciousness. When he saw an Apache at the mouth of
the cave he grabbed for his gun—only it wasn't there.
Though his mind knew what he must do to save himself, his body refused to help him. When he tried to
move his hands, they lay there like lumps of clay. He

turned his head and discovered the Kid kneeling beside him.

"Apache!" The warning Jake shouted in his head came out in a whisper.

"Lie still."

Jake gritted his teeth at the fire in his leg when he tried to move. "Dammit! Get my gun!"

Anabeth laid the weight of her body across Jake's chest to keep him still. Weak as he was, it was still a struggle to subdue him. "Be still," she urged. "It's all right. He's a friend."

The Kid's reassurance echoed in Jake's ears as he succumbed once again to the blackness that wrapped itself around him.

"He's fainted," Anabeth said. She was more worried than she cared to admit. "The fever's getting worse."

Wolf reached across Anabeth's shoulder and caught her chin, turning her to face him. "Come away from here. You have done all you can."

"I can't leave him alone," she protested. "I have to get him back to Santa Fe."

"What is this man to you?"

Too quickly Anabeth replied, "Nothing!" She knew as she spoke that it was less than the truth. But how could she explain to Wolf what she didn't understand herself? "He needs my help." Her eyes searched Wolf's for some sign that he understood. "Would you leave one of your own kind who was in trouble?"

"An Apache would not want another to stand a death watch over him," Wolf countered.

"He's not going to die!" Anabeth broke away and stalked the length of the cave. "And I'm not leaving." She turned to face Wolf, her arms crossed in determination. "You're free to go."

Wolf considered taking her away by force. Pride kept him from admitting that such a thing was need-

ful. He did not have to lay his heart before her to be
trampled. Especially now that she was not leaving
right away for Colorado, he would have time to woo
her properly. He turned to depart but stopped when
Anabeth called to him.

"Wait! Won't you stay and talk with me?"

"What is there to say?"

"I . . ." She wanted to share with him everything
that had happened since she had seen him last. How
she was seeking vengeance for Booth's death. How
she had adopted the disguise of a woman in Santa Fe.
Most of all, she wanted to ask him about the strange
feelings she had for Jake Kearney.

She met his dark-eyed gaze and found no encouragement to share her thoughts and feelings. It was as
though Wolf had thrown up a stone wall between
them. The openness they had enjoyed since they were
children was gone as though it had never existed. Before her stood not her beloved friend, but a threatening stranger. A stranger who wanted her in a way she
could not handle.

Before Anabeth could find words to breach the un-
familiar chasm between them, Wolf was gone. She
suddenly realized how cold it was in the cave. She
built up the fire until it crackled and roared, filling up
the ominous silence.

While Jake slept, Anabeth cut some pine saplings
and used a blanket and rope to rig a travois. An hour
or so before dawn she shook the Ranger awake.

"You have to help me. You're too big for me to tote
by myself."

Anabeth coaxed, and Jake responded by moving
where she directed him. Once she had him tied down
on the travois she headed for Santa Fe. She had to get
to town before first light. She didn't want to be seen
by anybody who might ask for explanations she
would be hard-pressed to make. And she had to get

back inside the boardinghouse before Anabeth Smith's absence was discovered.

On the trip back to town Anabeth became conscious of something shadowing their movements. She feared reprisals from the gang, but the shadow turned out to be animal, rather than human. It was a dog. A huge, shaggy black dog that followed them, never getting too close, or too far behind. Anabeth found the presence of the dog strangely comforting. As long as he was around she knew that no one else followed her. When she reached the outskirts of Santa Fe, she noticed he was gone.

Jake was still unconscious when they arrived at the back door to Frau Schmidt's boardinghouse, so Anabeth simply cut the travois free from his saddle and left it lying there. She took the two horses to the livery and walked back through the alleys to the boardinghouse. It was just breaking dawn as she slipped in the back door and into her room.

Anabeth yanked her shirt, trousers, and boots off, then stripped off her long johns and stuffed everything in the bottom drawer of the chest. She pulled on a clean chemise and drawers, a shirtwaist and a calico skirt, then donned a voluminous apron to cover it all.

She sat down to roll on stockings and slipped her feet into a pair of high-button shoes Sierra had loaned to her. There wasn't time to do anything with her hair except pin up her braids and cover them with a large white kerchief tied at her nape.

She was halfway out the door to her room when she realized she had forgotten her spectacles. Anabeth quickly retrieved them, but left them perched at the far end of her nose so she would be able to see what she was doing. She skidded to a halt when she reached the kitchen and discovered that Frau Schmidt was there before her.

"Sorry I'm late. I'll get some kindling," Anabeth said, hurrying to the back door. She was so out of breath that it was easy to sound breathless and excited when she opened the door and "discovered" Jake lying there.

"Frau Schmidt!" Anabeth cried. "It's Mr. Kearney. He's been hurt!"

"What?"

Eulalie swooped down like a mother goose who discovers a hawk attacking her gosling. She knelt beside Jake and put a hand to his forehead. "He's burning up with fever." She took a quick look at the wound in his thigh. "Somebody's done some surgery here. I suppose Doc Alton ought to take a look at this.

"Anabeth, go wake up Mr. Struthers and Mr. Oxenfeld. We'll need some help getting Jake upstairs."

Anabeth rushed off to do as she was bidden. As soon as Jake was settled on the bed in his room, Eulalie sent Anabeth off to find the doctor. If Anabeth had been less distraught, she might have paid more attention to where she was going. As it was, she turned a corner and slammed right into one of the Calhoun Gang. It was Whiskey. And he was drunk.

Whiskey grabbed hold of her to keep them both from falling, and Anabeth was paralyzed for a moment with fear. What if he recognized her? She didn't have a weapon of any kind to protect herself. She decided to use the protection her sex ordinarily would have given her.

"Let me go," she said primly. "Please."

Whiskey leered at her. "What's your hurry?"

She had known Whiskey was trouble when he was drunk. But never had she felt so threatened as she did now. "I . . ." She wasn't about to admit the truth. "I have an errand to run."

Whiskey peered into her face. "You look familiar."

Anabeth nearly gagged from the smell of whiskey

that fanned her face when he spoke. Her face bleached white with fear that he would yet recognize her. "We haven't met," she said frantically. "I'd like to go now."

"In a minute," Whiskey said. "First, you have to pay a toll, Missy."

Anabeth was so outraged when Whiskey put a hand on her breast that for a moment she didn't do anything. But even docile Anabeth Smith had to draw the line somewhere. She would cheerfully have shot the drunken outlaw then and there, if she'd only had a gun on her. She had to settle for mauling his toes with the heel of her high-button shoes.

Whiskey howled in pain and limped his way over to the wall. He leaned back and lifted his foot to his hand to inspect the damage.

"That will teach you not to assault young ladies who don't wish to engage your attention," Anabeth said in her best Anabeth Smith voice. But Kid Calhoun couldn't resist adding, "You ill-bred, gully-raking lecher!"

When Whiskey grabbed for Anabeth again, she took off running. She could hear him swearing behind her, but his foot was in no shape for him to come after her.

When Anabeth made the return trip with Doc Alton she kept a sharp eye out for the outlaw. Whiskey had evidently retreated indoors to drown his pain in drink. Anabeth hated Whiskey for what he had done to Booth. She loathed him for what he would have done to an innocent young woman. She wasn't just being vengeful when she voiced the thought that the world would be a better place without him.

The hardest thing Anabeth had to do that day was pretend an indifference to what was happening in Jake Kearney's room. The doctor left soon after he

came, and Anabeth forced herself to wait in the
kitchen until Frau Schmidt came down.

One look at Eulalie's face and Anabeth couldn't
stay silent. "How is he?"

"He'll live."

"Are you sure?"

"As sure as a mortal can be," she said. "He'll be off
his feed a while. He's going to need somebody to keep
an eye on him."

"I'll do it." Anabeth bit her lower lip. That offer
hadn't exactly been in character for shy little Anabeth
Smith. "He . . . uh . . . seemed like a nice man."

Eulalie raised a brow, then smiled and said, "I
think that's a fine idea." Jake wouldn't gladly suffer
Anabeth Smith one moment longer than necessary.
Having the girl nurse him ought to speed his recovery.

Jake surprised Eulalie by being more ill than she
had expected. Anabeth sat by his bed through the day,
soothing his brow with a cool cloth and feeding him
broth when she could get him to take it.

Once Anabeth ran a delicate fingertip across the
scar on Jake's mouth. She was surprised by the softness of his lips. The sheet was turned down to Jake's
waist and she couldn't keep from staring at his body.

To spare her blushes, Frau Schmidt had warned
her that Jake was bare under the sheet. Her curiosity
was hard to contain. At last, she could no longer resist
the urge to look, to touch.

Touching Jake, Anabeth discovered, was not at all
the same as touching Wolf. For one thing, her heart
skipped to her throat when her fingertips grazed his
flesh. Wolf had no body hair, so she was fascinated by
the wedge of black curls on Jake's chest. She tested
its crisp texture and traced the dark curls on his belly
to where they turned to soft down at his navel.

He was also far more muscular than Wolf. His

shoulders were broader, narrowing to lean hips. She lifted the sheet near the foot of the bed. His legs were incredibly long and were also sprinkled with black hair. She wanted to look higher up, at the male part of him, but admitted there was more of bashful Anabeth Smith in her than she realized.

Jake spoke in his delirium, but the disjointed phrases only left her wondering more about him. He mentioned "Claire" and "Sam" and "Sam's gold." She felt the weight of guilt. If she had known where Booth hid the gold, she would have found a way to return it. Unfortunately, the little bit of gold she had saved wouldn't have begun to replace what had been stolen.

And Jake had mentioned his mother. His voice had become guttural, and he had used a lot of hard words to describe the woman.

Once, when Anabeth was bathing Jake's chest, he caught her wrist in a viselike grip and said, "I know where you can put those hands to better use." He had slowly slid her hand—cloth and all—down his body toward his private parts.

She had torn herself from his grasp and backed away the length of the room. Of course he hadn't come after her. He was caught in the throes of his delirium, mumbling and making no sense. Later, she regretted her missishness. If she had let him have his way she would have known once and for all what he felt like—the textures and shapes that made him male to her female.

Fortunately, good sense—not to mention virginal fear—had overcome her curiosity. Anabeth Calhoun had no business examining the private parts of an unconscious man.

At dawn on the second day after he had been shot, Jake opened his eyes to find Anabeth Smith leaning over him. He was thirsty and his leg throbbed with pain. He pinned her with a stare. "What the hell are you doing here?"

Anabeth sat stunned for a moment, then flushed a bright red. "I'll be damned if I know!" She rose and threw the damp cloth down on his bare chest.

Jake had forgotten Miss Smith's penchant for strong speech. He looked at the cloth on his chest, then back to the dark circles under the young woman's eyes. He picked up the cloth and let it plop into the bowl of water beside the bed. Lord knew how long she had been nursing him. Maybe he ought to back up and try again.

She was halfway to the door when he said, "Wait. Don't go."

Jake studied the string of emotions that flickered on Miss Anabeth Smith's face.

Dislike. Distrust. Defiance.

The first two he understood. The third surprised him.

"I don't see much sense in hanging around where I'm not wanted," she muttered.

Jake rubbed the stubble on his jaw. "I guess I owe you an apology. And my thanks." He didn't want to be in Anabeth Smith's debt. It was like opening the door and inviting trouble inside. "How long have I been here?"

"I found you when I went out for firewood yesterday morning. You've been delirious for the past twenty-four hours."

"My leg?"

"Seems to be getting better."

The last thing Jake remembered was seeing an Apache at the mouth of the cave and having Kid Calhoun tell him the Indian was a friend. "How did I get here?"

"Someone left you out back in an Indian travois."

Jake assumed Kid Calhoun was responsible for his return to civilization. But he still had no answer to why the Kid had bothered to help him. More importantly, where was the Kid now?

Jake tried to sit up, but found the effort almost more than he could manage. Anabeth walked over to help, but he shoved her hand away. "I can do it."

"Then I'll be leaving," she said.

He caught her wrist to keep her from going. A crooked grin curled his lips. "Guess I'd better put a rein on my tongue. At least till I'm on my feet again."

Anabeth's eyes narrowed. She ought to leave him now, while she could still get away. The urge to flee was strong, even though she wasn't sure exactly what she was running from. Yet the threat was there—in the form of new and bewildering feelings that flustered and frightened her.

Anabeth raised her chin. During the years she had masqueraded as Kid Calhoun she had learned it was often dangerous to run when she was afraid. It was far better to face her fear and conquer it. "All right. I'll stay. But don't expect me to suffer any more of your sharp tongue. Because I won't."

Jake had a vision of using his tongue on her in a way she might not have minded. The next words were out before he could stop them. "You have very beautiful eyes."

Anabeth stared at Jake for a moment before she realized she could actually *see* him! She yanked her wrist from his grasp and knuckled her spectacles up her nose. There was nothing she could do about the color that streaked to her face. "I'll thank you not to make comments about my . . . my person," she said.

Jake smiled. "Whatever you say, Miss Smith. Now I could use that helping hand you offered."

Anabeth would have given anything to be able to

leave the room, but that would have been the coward's way out. She took two steps closer to Jake and
put an arm around his shoulders to help him into a
sitting position. That put her face only inches from
his. She was aware of his warm breath on her cheek.

An instant later she felt his lips there as well.

Anabeth stood up with a jerk, and Jake's head
smacked against the headboard. "Ow!"

"Serves you right!" she snapped. "I'll thank you
not to touch my person, either!"

Jake rubbed his aching head. "I was paying you a
compliment!" he said. "Skin as smooth as yours—"

"Mr. Kearney!"

Jake grimaced and rubbed his head. "Your point is
taken, Miss Smith."

Fortunately for both of them, Eulalie picked that
moment to visit Jake. "How are you feeling?" she
asked as she crossed to his bed.

"My head hurts like the devil."

"Your head?"

Anabeth rolled her eyes, and Jake relented. "Never
mind," he said. "I'm hungry as a she-bear after a long
winter nap. What have you got to eat?"

"What do you want?" Eulalie asked.

"Steak, potatoes, beans, and coffee."

"I'll fix it," Anabeth volunteered. *Anything to get
out of this room!*

Eulalie sat in the chair beside the bed and watched
Anabeth's hasty departure. "I think that girl might be
sweet on you."

Jake tore his eyes from Anabeth's retreating form.
"What?"

"She's an innocent, Jake. The likes of her is not for
you."

"Hell and the devil, Eulalie. I'd sooner bed down
with a rattlesnake!"

"I hope you mean that, Jake. I saw you kiss the girl."

Jake flushed. "Leftover delirium," he muttered. He didn't have any other explanation for what had come over him. He had been entranced by the girl's blue eyes. He had the uncanny feeling that he had seen them somewhere before. When she had leaned over him, the smell of her, the softness and the smoothness of her skin, had been more than he could resist. So he had kissed her. It didn't mean anything.

"Who shot you, Jake?"

Eulalie's question forced his thoughts from Anabeth, which was just as well. "I ran into the Calhoun Gang."

"Ambush?"

Jake scratched his chin and nodded. "Funny thing was, the man who saved my bacon was none other than Kid Calhoun."

"The Kid on the WANTED poster saved you from the rest of them?"

"I agree it doesn't make much sense, but that's what happened."

"What'll you do now?"

"Get well and go after the gang again." His eyes slipped to the door. "What's keeping my breakfast?"

"I'll go see," Eulalie said.

When she was gone, Jake tried to remember everything he could about the ambush and his rescue. Had there really been an Apache at the cave? Or had he imagined it. He remembered the fierce look in the Kid's blue eyes as he recounted how the Calhoun Gang had murdered his uncle.

The Kid's blue eyes.

That's where he had seen Anabeth Smith's eyes! Kid Calhoun had eyes the same damn color. That was a strange coincidence. Or was it?

Jake's eyes narrowed.

Anabeth *Smith*. Awful damn suspicious last name.
That same, smooth-as-a-brat's-bottom face.

And the most damning evidence of all. He remembered Kid Calhoun speaking in a moment of distress
and heard the same words issuing from Anabeth
Smith's mouth.

Son of a bitch!

He frowned. If he was right, Kid Calhoun wasn't
what he seemed. Neither was Anabeth Smith. Was it
possible they were one and the same person? That
was impossible to believe. Kid Calhoun was known
for his speed with a gun. Clumsy Anabeth Smith
could never . . .

What if all that clumsiness was an act? He remembered holding Anabeth's waist and finding it slim beneath her clothing. He wondered what he would find
under Anabeth Smith's kerchief. And Kid Calhoun's
hat.

He shook his head at such fanciful thoughts. He
was creating something out of nothing. Anabeth
Smith just had a pair of eyes that happened to be the
same color as Kid Calhoun's. He had better concen-
trate on getting himself back on his feet.

Jake slid his legs off the bed. He felt weak as a day-
old baby. He forced himself to walk across the room
to his saddlebags, where he found some clean long
johns and another pair of Levi's. He lacked the
strength to stand and put them on, so he retreated to
the bed and sat there for a moment to rest. He had
managed to drag on the long johns and was just pulling up his Levi's when he was interrupted by a voice
at the door.

"What on earth are you doing?"

Jake looked up to see Anabeth at the door with a
tray of food.

"I'm getting dressed." He methodically buttoned
up the front of the Levi's. He tried to put his weight

on his bad leg, and bit back a groan as it collapsed under him. He swore under his breath, tried again, and failed again. He clenched his teeth in frustration. "Hell and the devil."

Anabeth set the tray of food on a table just inside the door and crossed to help lift Jake's feet back onto the mattress. "You need to be in bed."

Jake noticed she hadn't been the least bit clumsy, and had, in fact, moved with speed and grace. Of course she had those spectacles slid down her nose so she could see over them.

"Why not give yourself a day of rest?" she said, fixing him with a stern look.

"I don't have a day," Jake retorted. He had to find Kid Calhoun and locate Sam's gold. "Bring that tray over here. I'm hungry."

Anabeth glared at him.

Jake stared right back at Anabeth, who quickly shoved her spectacles back up her nose to hide her eyes. He watched her closely and realized that now she couldn't see a thing. She hit the footboard of the bed with her knee on the way past and muttered something he couldn't quite make out.

"Are you all right?" he asked.

"I wish you'd stop asking that!"

"You keep running into things. Are you sure those spectacles are right for you?" He watched closely and was rewarded by the color skating up her cheeks.

"They're fine," she said. But she set the tray down on the edge of his lap instead of the middle. Jake grabbed for it, but his own reflexes weren't in too good shape. He watched in resignation as it slid off the bed and landed on the floor with a crash of crockery.

"Son of a—"

This time Anabeth caught herself, but it was all the confirmation Jake needed for his growing suspicion.

He reached out and snatched the spectacles from her
face. "Maybe you'd be able to see better if you try it
this way for a while."

Anabeth blinked her eyes, amazed at how clear everything had suddenly become. "But I need my spectacles to—"

"Do you?" Jake demanded.

"I . . ."

Jake's eyes narrowed as he examined's Anabeth's
features. Was this the same person he had seen in the
cave? He already knew the eyes were the same. The
height was right, and the lean body, too. Anabeth had
the same hollowed cheeks, the same baby-smooth
face, the small straight nose. He found a wide mouth,
lips not too thin. And the hair, what he could see of it,
was the same crow-wing black. By God, it *was* the
same person!

"You're Kid Calhoun!"

"No!"

"Yes, you are."

Anabeth bolted for the door, but Jake somehow
managed to catch hold of her skirt and held on.

"Let me go!" she hissed.

He slipped his feet off the bed and used her skirt to
reel her in between his legs. Then he grabbed her
around the waist and pulled her back down onto his
lap. "Not before I get some answers, *Kid.*"

Anabeth yelped as she lost her balance and fell
back on top of him. They both lay there on the bed for
a moment stunned. When Anabeth tried to pull free,
Jake rolled her under him and used his greater
weight to hold her down.

Anabeth's one thought was escape. Jake Kearney
was a lawman. She was an outlaw. He would turn
her in for the reward. He would see that she hanged.
She wanted to scream her fury at getting caught. But
she was all too aware of the tenants in the surround-

ing rooms, and of Frau Schmidt downstairs in the kitchen. She was utterly, desperately silent as she hit and bit and kicked at the Ranger in her efforts to win free of him.

Her kerchief came off in the fracas and two thick silky braids fell free. Jake twisted one around his hand to hold her still.

"Settle down!" he hissed. Jake was no more anxious than Anabeth to be discovered. Because it had dawned on him, as he felt her woman's body beneath him, that he didn't want Anabeth Smith to end up at the end of a rope. Which was where Kid Calhoun belonged.

But Jake had learned long ago that sympathy for an outlaw was a misplaced emotion. He reminded himself of the taunts Kid Calhoun had thrown at the outlaw called Grier. Whatever he thought of Anabeth Smith, Kid Calhoun had held a deadly weapon on a man and threatened to shoot him in the knees, crippling him for life.

He had to remember that the soft female in his arms had stood there watching while Sam was murdered.

"Get—off—me!" Anabeth said through gritted teeth.

"This is the only way I can be sure you won't run off," Jake said. "You're not going anywhere, so you might as well stop fighting and answer my questions."

Abruptly, Anabeth relaxed beneath him. He thought he heard her mutter "Son of a bitch." She was panting and her eyes were wide and wary, but she was no longer resisting him.

"That's better. Now, I want some answers. Where's the gold that was stolen from Sam Chandler."

"I don't know!"

"You expect me to believe that? Try again, *Kid*. Where's the gold?"

"I don't know. Booth hid it before he died. I suppose it's somewhere in the valley—"

"What valley?" Jake interrupted.

"Treasure Valley, where my uncle and I lived."

"Where is this valley?"

"None of your business." The valley was her refuge. Once she told a lawman where it was, once its location was no longer a secret, it would be a refuge no more. "I'm sorry about your friend getting killed."

Jake sneered. "It's a little late for regrets. If you're really sorry, you'll tell me where to find Sam's gold."

Anabeth swallowed hard. "I don't know where the gold is."

"You can take me to that valley of yours and help me hunt for it."

"No."

"You don't have much choice, *Kid*. Either you take me there, or I'll turn you over to the law in Santa Fe and you can rot in jail while I find it myself."

"Jail?"

"Until you hang for Sam Chandler's murder."

Anabeth stared up at Jake. The look in his gray eyes was ruthless, determined. She didn't see that she had any choice except to give in to his demands. At least for the moment.

She heaved a sigh of defeat. "All right. I'll take you to the valley."

"And help me hunt for the gold."

"I've already told you I will! Now can I get up?"

"Not quite yet. There are a couple of other things we'd better get settled first."

"Like what?"

When Anabeth looked into Jake's eyes, she realized they had darkened to a smoky gray. His nostrils were flared, and there was a tautness about his mouth. She recognized the signs because she had seen them on Wolf's face. *Desire*. But her reaction to Jake wasn't at all the same as it had been with Wolf. Jake's gaze made her body feel tense all over. There was a sensual stirring in her belly, a tightness laced with pleasure.

"You have to let me up," she said.

"Not quite yet." Jake's hand tightened in her hair. "You're quite a beautiful woman, Anabeth. Or is that an alias, too?"

"It's my name." Anabeth couldn't seem to catch her breath. Her eyelids dropped to conceal her uncertainty.

"I find you very desirable, Anabeth." He had the hard ridge beneath his jeans to prove it.

Anabeth swallowed hard. "Is this going to be part of my punishment for your friend's death?"

"What?"

"Raping me."

"It wouldn't be rape, Anabeth."

"I don't want you."

His hand tightened in her hair. "Don't you?"

Anabeth couldn't turn her head away because of the hold Jake had on her hair, but she closed her eyes to shut out the fierce gray eyes that demanded the shameful truth from her. There was no denying her arousal. She wanted him, all right. But she figured she ought to give him fair warning.

"I'm a virgin," she said.

Jake grimaced. Hell and the devil! He wanted the woman beneath him like a house afire, wanted to thrust inside her hard and deep, until he exorcised the need that churned inside him. But he sure didn't want the complications that came with seducing a virgin. Especially a virgin *outlaw*.

Jake untangled his hand from Anabeth's braid and levered himself to his knees. Slowly, painfully, he got onto his feet, then used the bedpost to keep him steady.

Anabeth sat up on the bed and hugged her knees to her chest, eyeing Jake warily. "Are you turning me in?"

"Eventually."

Anabeth clenched her teeth in an attempt to stop her chin from quivering. "What does that mean?"

Jake limped across the room to the chest where his gunbelt had been left and buckled it on. "It means we're going to stay close enough to use the same toothpick until that gold is found." Jake paused. "If you want to remain a virgin, don't even hint that you want things otherwise."

"Why you—" Anabeth spluttered as she came flying off the bed to stand spread-legged across from him. "*I'm* not the one can't keep his hands to himself!"

"When I woke up you had your hands all over me!"

Anabeth flushed painfully, because while he was exaggerating about that moment, she was nevertheless guilty of touching him. She quickly changed the subject.

"What about the Calhoun Gang? Are you going after them?"

"From what I heard, you're the one who knows where Sam's gold is tucked away."

"Look, the same man who killed your brother-in-law shot my uncle Booth in the back. The rest of the gang each put a bullet in him. I intend to see that they pay for what they did."

Jake noted the ferocity of her voice, the ruthlessness of her expression, and reminded himself that he had better not underestimate the woman standing before him.

He made a vow not to think of her as Anabeth Calhoun. Anabeth was much too soft a name for the woman he had just heard swear vengeance on the

Calhoun Gang. He would have problems being hard-nosed to a woman named Anabeth. It was a lot easier to call her Kid—and treat her like the outlaw she was.

"I'm afraid your days of hunting down the Calhoun Gang are over, Kid. I've got other priorities right now."

"I told you I don't know anything about the gold!"

"Your uncle never said anything to you about it?"

"Nothing!" Unless you counted the two words Booth had spoken as he lay dying. But she didn't even understand what they meant herself, so what use would they be to Jake Kearney?

Jake's mouth thinned. "Maybe it'll come back to you in time. Until I find that gold, you'll stay where I can keep an eye on you. Do you have anything to wear that's better for riding astride than the getup you have on?"

Anabeth looked down at the frumpy clothing that had been meant to conceal her figure. "I have my Levi's."

Jake shook his head. "With the WANTED poster out on Kid Calhoun it'll be less trouble if you stay dressed as a woman. If what you say is true, Wat Rankin will be as anxious to find you—and that gold—as I am. Disguising you as a woman isn't a bad idea. But you need something you can wear to ride a horse. I guess we're going to have to go shopping."

Anabeth could see Jake had just agreed to do something he considered a distasteful labor.

"One more thing," Jake said. "Did I imagine that Apache I saw at the cave?"

"No."

Jake arched a brow. "What is he to you?"

It occurred to Anabeth that Jake's tone of voice had a lot in common with Wolf's when he had asked the same question about Jake. "Wolf is my friend. We met when we were children in the valley where I grew up."

"Any chance your Apache friend will come after us?"

"Wolf? Why would he?"

"You tell me. He's your friend."

Anabeth thought of Wolf's coldness toward her in the cave. He wouldn't come after her. He would be glad she was gone. "Wolf won't bother us."

"All right. It's time we got out of here. You just stay right where you are while I finish getting dressed. I'll leave a note for Eulalie telling her who you really are and where we're headed."

Anabeth frowned, but she didn't argue.

Jake would have welcomed the contest. The Kid wasn't the only one unhappy with the situation. Jake was stuck with the girl until they found the gold. Somewhere along the trail Wat Rankin was bound to be waiting, watching for Kid Calhoun. Jake shuddered to think what would happen to Anabeth if the outlaws, or some bounty hunter with a WANTED poster, got hold of her. He would just have to make sure that didn't happen.

8

Anabeth fingered the Wedgwood blue silk taffeta dress. It was exquisitely soft, and she would have given her eyeteeth to have it.

Jake arched a brow and said, "That wouldn't be very practical on the trail."

"But it's very beautiful, don't you agree," Anabeth said wistfully.

Jake cocked his head and examined the garment displayed in the window of Miss Tuttle's dress shop. He tried to imagine Anabeth in the gown. It was difficult because the dress fit the top half of the mannequin like a second skin, giving it generous breasts and a tiny waist. The bottom half of the dress was gathered and draped to hide as much as the top half revealed.

"I can't see you in it," Jake admitted at last. He knew nothing of Anabeth's upper proportions, though he'd liked what he had seen of her bottom half in jeans. He rather regretted the necessity of putting her into something that would hide everything.

But he had made up his mind that the most practical thing to do was buy Anabeth a split riding skirt, shirtwaist, and boots. Dressing her in anything more feminine would make it necessary for them to travel in a buggy. On the trail, they needed the speed and versatility of riding horseback.

Miss Tuttle left the customer she had been helping and crossed to join Jake and Anabeth. "How can I help you? Oh, I see you admire the silk," she said to Anabeth. "I made it for a tall, elegant woman very like yourself, but she died of cholera, poor lady, before she could claim it. Would you like to try it on?"

"Yes," Anabeth said.

"No," Jake said.

Miss Tuttle had dealt with this situation before. "Why don't you just have a seat here, sir. This won't take any time at all."

Before Jake knew what had happened he was sitting in a comfortable chair with a copy of the Santa Fe paper at his elbow. Anabeth had disappeared through some curtains with Miss Tuttle and the blue silk dress.

Once they were in the back room, Miss Tuttle took over, and Anabeth felt as though she had been picked up by a whirlwind. The dressmaker had Anabeth stripped down to her drawers in no time.

"My goodness, dear," she said. "You're not wearing a corset!"

"I . . . uh . . . Do I need one?"

"Absolutely, my dear. If you wish for the gown to fit properly. Wait just a moment. I'll be right back."

Anabeth stared at herself in the tall oval mirror, searching for the young woman who was trapped inside trying to get out.

But she couldn't find her.

"Here we are," Miss Tuttle said as she whisked back through the curtain a few moments later.

Miss Tuttle had Anabeth raise her arms and slipped the corset on and tightened the laces with practiced expertise. Anabeth found herself struggling to draw breath.

"Does it have to be so tight?"

"Do you want to look your best?" Miss Tuttle asked with an arched brow.

Anabeth figured she needed all the help she could get. She grabbed hold of a nearby ladderback chair and said, "Do your worst."

Miss Tuttle pulled the strings a notch tighter. She added a petticoat before slipping the dress over Anabeth's head. The bodice buttoned up the front, but Miss Tuttle insisted that Anabeth stand still and allow her to do all the work.

When Miss Tuttle was done, she stepped aside and allowed Anabeth to see how she looked.

Anabeth couldn't breathe. But it wasn't the corset causing her shortness of breath. It was the sight of the woman—the *real* woman—in the mirror.

Anabeth suddenly noticed the tiniest ruffle of white lace at each wrist, matched by another frill of lace at her throat. She ran her fingertips over the frog trim at her waist, which was formed in the shape of flowers along either side of the row of cloth-covered buttons. She lifted the toe of her shoe to get a better look at the scalloped overlay to the pleated hem. So much detail!

"One more thing," Miss Tuttle said.

"Oh, this is already perfect," Anabeth said. "What else could you possibly add?"

"How about a ribbon in your hair?" Miss Tuttle said. She was already at work releasing the first of Anabeth's two braids. She brushed Anabeth's hair into silky black waves, letting tendrils curl at her temples and beside her ears. Then she captured it at the nape with a large Wedgwood blue bow that exactly matched the dress.

Miss Tuttle stood back and looked at Anabeth. *"Now* it's perfect. Shall we show your young man how you look?"

Suddenly Anabeth was frightened. Would Jake

Kearney see the woman in the mirror? Or would he see only Kid Calhoun? "I don't think—"

But Miss Tuttle had a firm hand at the small of Anabeth's back. Before she could retreat, she had been pushed through the curtains and was standing before Jake.

Jake had read the front page of the newspaper and most of the advertisements by the time Anabeth reappeared. He lurched to his feet when she stepped through the curtains.

She was absolutely stunning.

"What do you think?" Anabeth asked when Jake said nothing.

"Hell and the devil," he muttered. "You're goddamn beautiful!"

The dress fit Anabeth like it had been made for her. Only, on a living, breathing woman the silk emphasized the softness of her bosom, her hand-span waist. The dress flowed when she walked, giving her a grace he had known she possessed, but which he had never seen displayed to such advantage.

But it wasn't the dress that drew his eye at last. It was the look on Anabeth's face. Her shy smile was enchanting. Her cheeks were flushed so she appeared almost feverish. And her eyes . . . her sapphire blue eyes had the look of someone who has seen heaven.

"Jake?"

She was asking him for the dress. As if he had the kind of money that sort of frivolity cost. As if she had anywhere she could wear such a fancy frock. "Anabeth, I . . ."

Miss Tuttle saw her sale going out the window and stepped into the breach.

"The dress fits as though it were made for her, don't you think? Why, I don't even have to take a tuck. Why don't you come over here and see for yourself."

Reluctantly, Jake crossed the room. Anabeth's lids lowered to cover her eyes, leaving a fringe of dark lashes on petal-smooth cheeks. Jake could feel the warmth of her, see the rise and fall of her bosom, smell the honeysuckle in her luxurious black hair, which fell in a thick tail all the way to her waist.

He wanted to kiss away the tiny bead of moisture at her temple and press his mouth to the pulse at her throat. He wanted to thrust both hands into her hair and let it slide endlessly through his fingers. He wanted to put his hands on her breasts and feel their softness, their fullness. He wanted to unbutton every one of those eighteen buttons from her neck to the point where they ended at her belly and expose the creamy flesh hidden beneath the silky fabric. His fingers reached out to touch the silk and stayed to caress Anabeth's shoulder.

Jake frowned at the direction his thoughts had taken. He had to remember who Anabeth Calhoun was.

Miss Tuttle mistook his expression and said, "I could let you have it at a very good price. There aren't too many tall women who are as slim as this young lady, you see."

She went on to name a price that made Jake choke.

"I'll pay you back," Anabeth said. "I've got some gold—"

"I'll bet you have," Jake said in a hard voice. Anabeth's timely interruption had reminded Jake that the woman standing in front of him was nothing more than an outlaw. She had seen Sam killed, most likely knew were Sam's gold was buried. The only reason they had come into the dress shop was to buy something appropriate for Anabeth to wear on the trail.

"Take off the dress," he said. He turned to Miss Tuttle and said, "She needs a riding skirt and a couple of shirtwaists and maybe a jacket, if you have one.''

Miss Tuttle bowed to the ferocious look on his face. ''As you say, sir. Come, my dear, I'll help you undress.''

Anabeth's chin was trembling. Her eyes were liquid. ''I can do it myself,'' she said. Shoulders back, chin high, she turned and marched back through the curtains.

Jake clamped his back teeth to keep from saying he would buy the gown. It was totally inappropriate. Ridiculous. ''Miss Tuttle,'' he said in a quiet voice.

The dressmaker turned back to him. ''Sir?''

''When she takes off the gown, wrap it up for me. Don't tell her . . . I want it to be a surprise,'' he said.

Miss Tuttle beamed. ''Of course, sir. I'll wrap it up in brown paper while she's trying on the other clothes.''

Jake put a hand to his forehead and wondered what had gotten into him. He was going crazy. And Anabeth Calhoun was driving him there.

Anabeth didn't bother to model the riding clothes. When she reappeared a second time wearing a plain white cotton shirtwaist and a split brown corduroy riding skirt, there was nothing of the softness he had seen in her face before. There was only resignation. And regret.

He opened his mouth to tell her he had bought her the dress, but she cut him off.

''It doesn't matter,'' she said. ''I don't need the stupid dress. It was made for a lady. Which I'm obviously not. We have what we came for. Let's get out of here.''

She never said another word as Jake paid for the clothing and collected the packages.

''I've got one more stop to make in town,'' Jake said.

Anabeth said nothing, just followed him to the post office where he asked if there were any general delivery letters for Jake Kearney.

"There's one, sir," the postmaster said.

Jake took the letter and ripped it open on the spot.

Dear Jake,

   I've had another visit from Will Reardon. He's given me until the end of the month to come up with the money to pay the note.

   I thought maybe if you came and talked to him you could convince him to wait until you locate the gold.

   You'll know what's best.

                                              Love,
                                              Claire

Jake folded the letter back up. "Hell and the devil."

"Bad news?" Anabeth asked.

"We're going to have to make a detour on our way to that valley of yours," Jake said.

"Where are we going?"

"Window Rock."

When Anabeth arched a brow in question, Jake clarified, "Sam Chandler's ranch."

"Is that really necessary?"

Jake nodded. "I think it is." Jake waited for an argument, but it never came.

Anabeth didn't think she could face Claire Chandler, especially since the woman's husband had died in her arms. As they saddled their horses at the livery and headed south toward Window Rock, she relived Sam's death—always with a different ending where, somehow, by some miracle, the rancher survived.

They had been on the trail for a full hour when Jake interrupted her thoughts.

"How did you become an outlaw?" he asked.

"I was sixteen the first time I rode with Booth," Anabeth said bitterly. "I thought it would be fun. I didn't know what I was getting into."

"Why didn't you quit when you found out the truth?"

"I couldn't talk Booth into quitting with me, and it was too hard staying home worrying about him. I started saving a little from each job so we could go to Colorado and start over."

"You should have had enough for that years ago."

Anabeth's lips twisted in disgust. "Booth's tastes were very expensive. I'd offer what I've saved to Mrs. Chandler except it's not much more than a cowboy would earn in a couple of months."

"What are your plans now that your uncle is dead?"

"I haven't made any plans—beyond seeking revenge for Booth's death."

"Have you ever killed a man?"

Anabeth shook her head no.

"What makes you think you can?"

"What makes you think I can't?" Anabeth retorted. "I'm fast on the draw, and I always hit what I aim at."

"I'm not saying you can't. Just that maybe you shouldn't."

"Why not?"

"For one thing, it makes you no better than they are. For another, you might be the one who ends up dead." Which, Jake realized, was a possibility he found surprisingly unpleasant to contemplate.

"Are you saying I should forgive the men who betrayed my uncle and shot him down in cold blood? I can't."

"I suppose not," Jake murmured.

"You've probably killed lots of men," Anabeth accused.

Jake stared Anabeth straight in the eye. "When I wasn't given any other choice, when it was necessary, yes."

Anabeth shivered at the coldness in Jake's eyes, the granite set of his features. The lawman could be just as merciless, she realized, as any outlaw. She wondered what had made him so hard. "How do you know when it's necessary?" she asked at last.

"I made the mistake once of believing an outlaw, a young man, who told me he would go straight if I would just give him another chance. He had tears in his eyes when he begged me to let him go. Bobby Latham wasn't much older than you. I put my gun away because I didn't want to think of a kid his age spending the best years of his life in jail."

"What happened?"

"A month later he murdered an entire family. Eviscerated the father. Raped and stabbed the mother and daughter. Slit the little boy's throat. And threw the baby against the wall."

Anabeth swallowed the gorge that had risen in her throat. "Oh, my God."

When Jake turned to her this time, his eyes were fierce with anger and stark with pain. "I won't make that mistake again."

Anabeth felt a shiver of foreboding. Jake Kearney was telling her that if she gave him a reason, he would kill her like any other outlaw. It was plain now, if it hadn't been before, that the only reason she wasn't already in jail waiting to hang was because he wanted her help finding Sam Chandler's gold.

Anabeth hadn't realized until this moment just how serious her situation was. She was an outlaw in the custody of a lawman. Jake wasn't going to let her go. If she didn't want to find herself at the end of a hangman's rope, she would have to find a way to escape.

They were halfway to Window Rock when they bedded down for the night. Jake chose a spot at the top of a ridge, where he had a view of the surrounding country, but where he was protected by a cover of pine trees. There was no water, but they had enough if they were careful to get them to the next waterhole. If the outlaws came looking for the Kid, Jake wanted to see them before they saw him.

When Jake laid out their bedding, he put Anabeth's next to his own.

Anabeth snatched up her ground sheet and blanket and stalked to the other side of the fire. "I'll feel safer over here."

Jake opened his mouth to argue and snapped it shut again. It was going to be difficult enough getting any sleep when she was even that close. "I'm a light sleeper," he warned. "Don't get any ideas about trying to escape."

Anabeth turned her back on Jake and pulled the blanket up over her shoulder. Tired as she was, she couldn't sleep. She sat up and pulled the makings for a cigarette from her vest. She lit up and took a deep drag, then blew it out.

"I could use a good smoke," Jake said from across the fire.

Anabeth slid her cigarette to the corner of her mouth and said, "I'll roll you one." Her fingers moved swiftly and surely.

Jake walked around the fire and sat down cross-legged beside her. She lit Jake's cigarette from her own, then handed it to him.

Jake took a drag and exhaled with a great sigh. "Now all I need is a whiskey to be a happy man."

Anabeth reached across her saddle to the bedroll and pulled out a flask. "Help yourself."

Jake's brow furrowed. "Is there any bad habit you don't have?"

"I don't cheat at cards."

Jake took a swig of whiskey and wiped his mouth with his sleeve. He didn't start a conversation. He didn't feel like talking. Instead, he closed his eyes and listened. To the wind rustling in the pines. To the hooting of an owl. To the crickets. To the buzz of a mosquito. To the crackling of the fire.

"It's times like this I miss Booth most," Anabeth said in a quiet voice. "Late at night, when my father was asleep, we used to sit by the fire and talk. Booth was a dreamer. He would spin tales about all the places we would go when he finally found that vein of gold in the Two Brothers mine.

"Of course I learned later it was all a lie. He was never working the mine. He was robbing stages. But even when I knew the truth, I didn't stop loving him."

Jake opened his eyes, careful to look out into the darkness instead of at the fire, so the light wouldn't blind him. "Then why do you sound so angry?"

"Because he should have quit robbing stages a long time ago! Because I warned him that Wat Rankin was dangerous, but he wouldn't listen to me!" Anabeth said fiercely. "Now he's dead! And I'm all alone!"

It didn't do any good for Jake to remind himself that Anabeth was Kid Calhoun. All he saw was a young woman scrubbing tears from her eyes with a sleeve. Right now she was just a kid who had lost the last of her family. He flicked the butt of his cigarette into the fire. A second later he had her in his arms.

Anabeth hadn't realized how much she needed the comfort of Jake's arms around her. Or how close her grief was to the surface. Because now she couldn't seem to swallow the lump in her throat. Or stop the tears that streamed from her eyes.

She hid her face against Jake's shirt. "I don't— I can't—"

"Go ahead and cry, Kid," Jake said.

Anabeth fought the sob that threatened until her

chest ached. At last it escaped. She clutched at Jake as she let go of her anger and allowed herself to grieve for her uncle.

Anabeth had no idea how long she cried. She became aware little by little of the feel of Jake's damp shirt against her cheek. Of the feel of his silky hair threaded between her fingers. Of the way her breasts were pressed against his chest. And the fact that she was sitting in his lap.

She lifted her head to look into his eyes. Her throat felt raw from crying and a raspy whisper was all she could manage. "Thank you."

He gently brushed the hair back from her forehead with callused fingertips. "Are you all right now?"

"I guess so." She took a deep breath and let it out. "My chest doesn't ache like it did."

There was an uncomfortable moment when she didn't know what to do. At last she said, "I guess I'd better be getting some shuteye."

But Jake made no move to release her. Instead, his fingers tightened on her shoulder. "Kid . . ."

Anabeth saw the kiss coming. She could have avoided it. But she had wondered what his lips would feel like. Now she would know.

They were soft and pliant.

Their lips clung for a moment before Jake abruptly broke the kiss. Anabeth could feel the tension in his body.

"What's wrong?" she asked.

"This. I can't do this," he said in a hard voice. He practically shoved Anabeth off his lap, and she landed in an undignified heap on the ground.

He rose and stomped back around to the other side of the fire. He yanked his boots off, glared at her, and said, "Go to sleep, Kid."

Anabeth took one look at Jake's face and decided not to argue. He was right. They were playing with fire. And she was the one who would most likely end up burned. Anabeth lay down and pulled the blanket up over her shoulder again, shutting Jake out. But sleep wouldn't come.

Her thoughts weren't at all what she had expected them to be. And the questions that rose in her mind were the kind for which she could find no answers. Because she had no experience in this area at all. At last she whispered, "Jake?"

There was no answer.

"Jake?"

"I'm trying to sleep."

"Have you ever been in love?"

There was a long silence. "What makes you ask?"

"I just wondered if you ever thought about falling in love and getting married."

"Love is for fools! No woman's ever gonna hogtie me."

"What woman would want to?" Anabeth snapped back.

"Plenty have tried."

"So why haven't you married one of them?"

"You might as well ask why I haven't stuck my hand in the fire and let it burn."

Anabeth turned over and leaned up on one elbow to stare at the lawman. Some woman must have hurt him once upon a time, she realized. She couldn't let the subject drop. "Who was she?"

"What?"

"The woman who made you so cynical. Who was she?"

"My mother."

"What did she do that was so horrible?"

"She cheated on my pa so often that he couldn't hold his head up in town. He stayed drunk to avoid facing the truth. Once, when he was sober, I asked him why he didn't leave her. You know what he said?"

Anabeth shook her head.

"He said he *loved* her!" Jake spat. "He finally caught her with one too many men. He shot and killed both my mother and her lover. Only her lover turned out to be the son of somebody important. I was fifteen when my father was hanged for murder. Claire was just eight.

"I won't ever give a woman the chance to do to me what my ma did to my pa."

"All women aren't like your mother."

"My experience says differently."

"I'm not like that," Anabeth said in a quiet voice.

"No, you just carry a gun and rob stages," Jake shot back.

Anabeth dropped back down on the blanket and stared up at the star-strewn sky. At least she had a reason now why Jake had stopped kissing her. Actually, she found his revelation something of a comfort. It wasn't her particularly that Jake didn't trust, it was women—and outlaws—in general. If they spent enough time together, he would see that she was different from those others who had left him feeling betrayed and disillusioned. Although why that was important to her, Anabeth refused to contemplate.

Anabeth wasn't aware she had fallen asleep until she woke with a start. Wolf had taught her that she had no need of eyes to see in the dark. The desert animals would tell her when there was another human being present. Their silence was a warning that should be heeded. In fact, it was the complete absence of natural sounds that had awakened Anabeth. She focused all her senses outward, trying to locate the source of danger.

Her hand slipped to where Booth's guns ought to be, and she remembered that Jake had put them away in his saddlebags. She turned her head slightly and froze. Reed stood at the edge of the light from the fire. His Colt was aimed at her heart. He put a finger to his lips for silence and motioned her to follow him.

Anabeth looked over to where Jake lay sleeping. She debated whether to cry an alarm and realized Reed could shoot her or Jake, or both, before Jake even awoke. She had no choice except to do as Reed bid her. She moved as silently as an Apache to avoid waking the lawman.

Anabeth saw the exact moment when Reed realized she was wearing a skirt, and that her braided hair fell all the way to her waist.

His smile was feral and frightening.

She followed Reed some distance from the camp and down into an arroyo where the sound of their voices wouldn't carry back to the campfire.

"Well, well," Reed said. "Who'd have thought it. Kid Calhoun is a female!"

"How did you find me?" Anabeth asked.

"Pure chance, actually. I never did cotton too much to Rankin. Lately he's been gettin' a little too big and bossy for his britches. I figured I'd head out on my own.

"I was just lookin' for a cup of coffee when I came up to your campfire." His grin widened. "Imagine my surprise when I found you and that other fella. Who is he, by the way?"

"Nobody you'd know. What do you want from me?"

"The gold, of course. And maybe something more. You don't make a bad-looking woman, Kid."

"I don't know where the gold is," Anabeth said flatly. "And I would roast in hell before I let you touch me." It was difficult to see Reed's features in the shadow of his hat, but his broadening smile reflected in the moonlight.

"Now, Kid, you don't expect me to accept that, do you?"

"It's the truth."

Reed cocked his gun. The metal click sounded thunderous in the nighttime silence. "I don't want to put a bullet in you, Kid. But I'll do what's necessary to persuade you I mean business."

"You're getting pretty good at shooting unarmed men," Anabeth taunted. "How does it feel to know you have a yellow streak?" She watched Reed's smile disappear. For a moment, she was certain he would shoot.

"I never did feel right about shooting Booth," he said in a tight voice. "I'm sorry for my part in it, for whatever good that does."

"I can't forgive you, Reed, if that's what you want. I can never forgive what you did."

"I made a mistake, Kid."

"So how do you explain what you're doing now?" Anabeth demanded. "Another mistake?"

She could almost hear Reed's teeth grinding. They were still clenched when he said, "I've never been a patient man, Kid. If you want to live through the night, you'd better start talking, and tell me where that gold is."

"Touch her, and you're a dead man."

Anabeth stood between Reed and the chilling voice. Jake took another step, and it became clear to Reed that the man who had been asleep by the fire had a Colt aimed at his heart.

"Get out of the way, Kid," Jake said.

"Stay where you are, Kid," Reed countered. "You stay right there while I back up out of here. You owe me that for all the years we rode together."

"I don't owe you anything, Reed. You helped kill my uncle."

"You can't blame me for Booth's death, Kid. My bullet didn't kill him."

"You didn't do anything to stop it, either. I'm just going to do what you did, Reed. I'm going to step back and let whatever happens, happen."

"Don't do it, Kid!" Reed shouted.

Anabeth knew there was little Reed could do to stop her. If he shot at her, he wouldn't have time to bring his gun to bear on Jake before the Ranger shot him. She hardened her heart to Reed's plight. An eye for an eye. A death for a death.

She moved suddenly, diving headlong out of the line of fire. She heard two quick, loud shots, and the sound of a body falling. But Anabeth was unprepared for the violent way Jake yanked her to her feet.

"Tell me again how women aren't all the same," he snarled. "What the hell were you doing sneaking around out here with that outlaw?"

"In case you hadn't noticed, I wasn't here by choice," Anabeth yelled back. "He was holding a gun on me. All he wanted was the gold."

"Which you didn't want to share, is that it?"

"You're a fool, Jake Kearney." Anabeth stomped past him and headed back to camp.

Jake figured the less time they spent in the area, the better, since the gunshots would attract attention they didn't want. Anabeth remained stubbornly silent the whole time they were breaking camp and saddling their horses.

Meanwhile, Jake was angry enough to bend horseshoes. It took him a while to figure out why. He had woken at the snick of a gun being cocked. His first reaction at finding Anabeth gone hadn't been anger. It had been fear. Which meant he cared what happened to the woman. Which was something he had sworn he would never do.

When a man started letting his heart control his

head, he was in trouble. Look what had happened when he had let that youthful, innocent-looking outlaw Bobby Latham go free. Look what had happened to his father when he had cared enough for a woman to let her break his heart.

Jake could give a dozen other examples where men had been brought low by letting emotions, instead of logic, govern their actions. So, sure he was angry. It was a way of exorcising those other feelings for Anabeth Calhoun that he had no intention of acknowledging now, or ever.

"You only see what you look for," Anabeth said to Jake as she mounted her dun.

"What's that supposed to mean?"

"You figure it out."

Anabeth was fighting the remorse she felt for Reed's death. She hated herself for feeling sorry that he was dead. Reed had been smiling when he shot her uncle. He had deserved what happened to him. And she was glad he was dead. *Glad.*

Only they hadn't ridden far before Anabeth abruptly stopped her horse and scrambled off a short ways into the darkness to wretch.

Jake came up behind her and handed her his bandanna. "Killing is never easy."

"I didn't kill Reed," Anabeth retorted. She wiped away the vomit and stuffed Jake's bandanna in her trouser pocket.

"Close enough," Jake said. "You let him die."

"He deserved to die."

Jake shrugged. "Probably so."

"He was only twenty-two," Anabeth said in a ragged voice.

Jake wanted more than anything to take a step toward her, to hold her in his arms, to comfort her. He reminded himself who she was. And what she had done. And why he had brought her along on this journey.

"Better get mounted up," he said in a hard voice. "We have a lot of riding to do tonight."

He waited while Anabeth marched past, her head held high, her lips flattened in defiance of him. It took every bit of willpower he had to keep from reaching out for her.

His head knew he was doing the right thing.

His heart sent a message to his body, a pounding, furious pulse, a rush of blood to his groin that left him hard and aching.

Jake's lip curled in a grim smile that twisted the scar at the corner of his mouth. Kid Calhoun was a force to be reckoned with. And damned if he didn't relish the few days he had left in her company. But he would send her to jail. It was where she belonged. He would never compromise on that.

Never.

And if they hanged her, it was no business of his. He was merely doing a job.

Jake felt acid in his throat. Hell and the devil. He just wouldn't think about what Anabeth Calhoun would look like at the end of a rope.

9

As they rode the last few miles to Window Rock, Jake realized he was going to have to think of some way to explain Anabeth Calhoun's presence to Claire. Finally, he decided the truth would work best. At least, part of the truth.

"I'm going to tell my sister that you're Booth's niece, and that you've agreed to help me look for the gold your uncle stole. But I don't want Claire knowing that you rode as part of the gang."

"Why not?"

"Because I'm not sure she'd let you cross her threshold, and I don't fancy spending the few nights I'm visiting Claire sleeping outside with you. That means no smoking around Claire." He reached out and plucked the makings from her vest pocket and put them in his own. "And no drinking or swearing, either."

Anabeth glowered at Jake's highhandedness. His warnings only confirmed her increasing nervousness about meeting Claire Chandler. She just knew she was going to get caught in her charade as a woman. If the truth came out, there was no telling what Claire's reaction would be to having an outlaw under her roof.

On the other hand, Anabeth wished there were some way she could relate Sam Chandler's dying words to his wife. Unfortunately, that was impossible without giving away her true identity to Claire, which Jake had just forbidden her to do.

Anabeth's gaze slipped to the horizon. A familiar sight greeted her there. "Have you seen that dog following us?"

"I've seen him," Jake said.

"I think it's the same animal that followed me to Santa Fe when I brought you there on the travois."

"Might be. That's Dog."

"Dog? That's his name?"

"He doesn't answer to it," Jake said. "But it's what I call him."

Anabeth turned a startled look on Jake. "How come he's walking over there all by himself, instead of joining us?"

"I don't know. And Dog isn't talking."

Anabeth snorted in disgust. "Very funny."

Jake rubbed the itchy healing spots around the wound in his leg.

"How's your leg?"

"It won't bear my weight for long at a time. But it'll do." Jake pointed and said, "There's Window Rock."

Anabeth angled her head to examine the odd rock formation. "It does look like a window, doesn't it?"

"I always thought so. When we get to Claire's place, let me do the talking," he admonished.

Anabeth bristled. "I'm perfectly capable of speaking for myself."

"Just keep your mouth shut, *Kid*."

Anabeth was stung by his use of her outlaw name. It was obvious that although Jake was presenting her to his sister as a young woman, he didn't think much of her as one. Anabeth would have welcomed the opportunity to argue further with Jake, but they had already arrived in front of a one-story white-washed adobe house.

Jake stepped down from his horse and called out to his sister. Anabeth also stepped down, but she stayed where she was rather than follow Jake up the two steps onto the shaded porch. The woman who came out of the house in response to Jake's call seemed tiny for the sister of such a large man.

Claire's eyes brightened when she spied Jake, then widened in concern as she realized he was limping. "Jake, you're hurt! Come inside and let me take a look at you."

Jake resisted Claire's efforts to force him inside. "I'm fine, Claire. It's already been taken care of." He caught her hands and turned her to face Anabeth, who stood at the hitching rail beside her dun.

"This is Anabeth Calhoun." Jake paused and added, "She's the niece of one of the outlaw gang who robbed Sam. She's agreed to do whatever she can to help us recover the gold that was stolen from Sam. She has an idea where we can start looking—a valley where she lived with her uncle."

Claire stared at Anabeth for a moment, apparently uncertain how to greet the young woman.

Jake perceived Claire's growing rigidity and said, "Anabeth saved my life. She was the one who nursed me after I was bushwhacked by the Calhoun Gang."

Maybe that was stretching the truth a bit, but he was willing to do what was necessary to limit Claire's hostility toward Anabeth Calhoun. Jake told himself he did it because things would be easier over the next couple of days with the two women in the same house together. He refused to acknowledge he was acting out of consideration for Anabeth's feelings.

"I'm pleased to meet you, Anabeth," Claire said with genuine warmth. She crossed down the steps to hug the younger woman.

Anabeth found herself being scrutinized by a pair of penetrating hazel eyes. While she watched, the expression in Claire's eyes visibly softened. "I can't thank you enough for taking care of Jake. He means a lot to me."

"It was nothing, really," Anabeth protested.

Claire turned to her brother. "Beautiful . . . and modest, too."

Jake looked at Anabeth. Even flushed with embarrassment and dusty from the trail, she was undeniably lovely. But he responded merely, "If you say so."

Claire laughed. "I do!" She turned back to Anabeth and wrinkled her nose at the sight of Anabeth's dusty clothes. "If I know Jake, you haven't had much rest on the trail." She slipped an arm around Anabeth's waist and began dragging her up the porch steps. "Come on inside. You look like you could do with a nice warm bath."

Anabeth gave one desperate look back at Jake over her shoulder as Claire ushered her inside.

Jake frowned. So maybe Anabeth Calhoun *was* beautiful. What difference did that make? She was still an outlaw. And she was still going to hang. At least now Claire had given him an explanation for why he was so attracted to her. He had only responded to Anabeth Calhoun the same way any man would who had been too long without a woman. He was willing to admit he desired her. But that was the extent of his feelings for her.

In fact, just the thought of having Anabeth's long legs wrapped around him, of sheathing himself deep inside her while she writhed beneath him, made his blood pound. Jake looked down at the hard ridge in his jeans. Damned if that Kid hadn't done it to him again!

Jake walked around for a few moments and thought of awful things until his body was under control, then followed the two women inside. He found Claire in the kitchen pumping water to put on the stove to heat.

"I suppose if you were laid up, you haven't had a chance to start hunting for the gold yet," Claire said when Jake joined them. "But you arrived at a perfect time. Will Reardon is coming for supper tonight. He practically insisted on the invitation, but now I'm glad he did. Surely he'll be more patient about collecting on the note when you explain that Anabeth is going to help you find the gold."

Anabeth turned her face away from Claire so the other woman wouldn't see her frown. Frankly, Anabeth didn't hold out much hope that they would find Sam's gold. She had already looked everywhere in Treasure Valley she thought it might be. The two words Booth had spoken to her as he lay dying might have been a clue. But they meant nothing to her.

"The tub is on the back porch. Would you bring it in please, Jake?" Claire asked.

Jake set up the copper tub. When it was full, Claire shooed Jake out of the kitchen. "Let this young lady have some privacy now. Why don't you go catch up with Shug?"

Jake tried to catch Anabeth's eye, but she avoided looking at him. Finally, he walked over and leaned down so he could whisper in her ear. "Watch what you say. I don't want Claire upset. Don't even think about trying to escape. I'd come after you. And you wouldn't like what I'd do when I found you."

Anabeth's face flamed with humiliation. She didn't need Jake's warning. She wouldn't have purposely hurt Claire Chandler for anything in the world. As for escaping, there would certainly be plenty of opportunities for that once they were gone from Window Rock. Jake had disappeared before Anabeth found a retort that could be repeated in mixed company.

Anabeth, who had never been shy with Wolf, felt awkward disrobing in front of Claire. Claire didn't allow Anabeth's self-consciousness to survive very long.

"Just step in here. That's right. You can scooch down if you like. Here's a cloth to wash with. Just let me get you some soap."

Claire made herself busy in the kitchen, all the while reminiscing about the years she had spent with Sam. It was almost more than Anabeth could bear. She was uncomfortably aware of the ravaged look on Claire's face whenever she mentioned her late husband's name. If a sentence began with "Sam always said," Anabeth could count on Claire's voice being a little sharper, her movements a little jumpier, her body a little stiffer.

Finally Anabeth felt compelled to say, "You must miss him very much."

Claire threaded her hands together and clenched them until the knuckles turned white. "I do. I only wish I'd had a chance to tell him I loved him before he died."

"Surely he must have known."

"That's just it. I . . . I wasn't a very loving wife the last three years we had together."

"I'm sure Sam's last thoughts of you were good ones," Anabeth said. Actually, she knew for sure that Sam had been thinking of Claire.

"Do you think so?"

The desperate look in the other woman's eyes nearly broke Anabeth's heart. "Aren't you remembering only the good times right now?" Anabeth said. "Don't you think Sam must have done the same thing at the end?"

Claire thought about it for a moment. A sweet smile slowly spread on her face. "Yes," she said softly. "I'm sure he must have thought of me kindly. And of Jeff."

"Jeff?"

"Our son." Claire swallowed over the thickness in her throat. "He was killed by Apaches three years ago. Afterward . . . I blamed Sam for Jeff's death."

"It all sounds very sad," Anabeth said.

"It was," Claire said. "It is." She cleared her throat and asked, "How's that water? Still warm enough?"

"It's fine. Wonderful, actually."

"Good. I'll go fix up Jeff's bedroom for you, and leave you alone to finish your bath."

Anabeth laid her head back in the copper tub and relaxed for the first time since Booth had been killed. The hot water in the tub seemed to melt her bones. She felt languorous and serene in a way she hadn't imagined possible.

The same could not be said of Jake.

It had occurred to him as he stood out in the barn explaining his wound to Shug Smith, that he had given Anabeth Calhoun a perfect opportunity to escape—if such was her intention.

Jake ignored the voice that told him she would have given him more trouble on the trail if she had intended to flee at the first opportunity. He told Shug that he had forgotten to tell Claire something and headed for the back door of the house, which led to the kitchen.

Jake listened at the kitchen door for voices, but heard none. Was the Kid already gone? He shoved the door open without knocking and discovered why it was so quiet.

Anabeth Calhoun was sound asleep in the tub. She was also naked.

Her long legs extended over one end of the copper bathtub. Her head lay angled back across the other, a towel under her neck providing a substitute pillow. Everything else from the slope of her breasts downward was hidden beneath the soapy film on the water.

Jake swallowed hard. He started backing away toward the door, determined not to make a fool of himself by getting caught in here with her. Unfortunately, he ran into the straw broom Claire had set beside the door.

The wooden handle of the broom made an awful clatter when it landed on the planked floor. Jake held his breath, hoping against hope that the Kid wouldn't wake up.

But Wolf had done a good job honing Anabeth's survival instincts. She not only woke when the broom hit the floor, she came flying out of the tub and landed on her feet poised to protect herself.

It was woefully apparent within seconds that she had neither weapon to defend herself, nor enemy to defend against. Unless she counted Jake. Which, considering the avid look on his face, wasn't out of the question.

"Oh, it's you," she said.

"For God's sake, cover yourself up!"

With self-defense her only consideration, Anabeth had been totally unaware of her nakedness. Once Jake spoke, she felt the sting of heat in her chest that quickly became red flags in her cheeks. She reached for the towel that had cushioned her neck and quickly wrapped it around herself.

"What are you doing in here?" she demanded, holding the towel closed with both hands.

It seemed stupid to admit that he had been worried she was planning to run away. Why put ideas into her head? "I . . ." He couldn't think of a reasonable excuse why he might have come into the kitchen when he knew she was taking a bath there. So he said, "I thought you'd be done by now."

Anabeth let go of the towel with one hand and

rubbed the back of her neck where it had lain against the tub. "I guess I fell asleep."

Jake watched the towel slipping and resisted the urge to tuck it around her. He was getting not only a good look at the swell of her breasts, but a tantalizing hint of two lovely pink aureoles as well. He was appalled at how quickly his body responded to her. The Kid wasn't the type of female he normally sought out when he needed a woman.

Jake had a firm rule about leaving virgins alone. Let a man get involved with a good woman, and she would soon have him cinched to the last hole. So he had always been careful not to get his spurs tangled in virtuous petticoats. Not that Anabeth was wearing petticoats. But that only made the whole business trickier. Because innocent or not, dressed in petticoats or not, he wanted her.

"Don't you think you'd better get dressed," he said in a husky voice.

Anabeth looked around the room for her clothes. She arched a brow. "I would if I had anything to wear. I think Claire decided the things I had on needed washing."

"Claire!"

Claire came running at Jake's bellow. "What's wrong? What's the matter?" She stopped at the threshold when she saw Anabeth standing there in nothing but a drooping towel. "Jake! What are you doing in here? Scat! Shoo!"

She marched forward and would have thrown him out the kitchen door like a mangy cat except Jake held his ground.

"I'm afraid this is a case of closing the barn door after the horse is gone," he drawled.

Claire looked from Jake to Anabeth's rosy cheeks and back again. "Oh."

"Besides, I'm not interested."

He saw Claire didn't believe him. But Anabeth did, and her relief was almost tangible. Which irritated him. "Where did you put my saddlebags?"

"In Jeff's room."

"There's a package wrapped up in brown paper in one of my bags. Would you get it for me, please?"

The tension hummed between Jake and Anabeth for the few moments it took Claire to leave and return. She handed the package to Jake. "Here it is."

"This is for you," Jake said. He held it out to Anabeth, but she had both hands occupied holding on to the towel.

"Would you open it for me please?"

Jake untied the brown string and the Wedgwood blue silk taffeta dress spilled out, along with a lacy chemise, a corset, and pink-ribboned drawers.

"Oh, Jake!" Anabeth let go of the towel with one hand and reached out to caress the silken fabric. Her eyes glowed as she lifted them from the dress to meet Jake's gaze. "You bought the dress for me. Thank you."

Jake's cheeks burned with heat. "I figured with company coming tonight you could use something a little fancy to wear to supper."

"Thank you," she said. "I'll always treasure it."

"Come back in a little while," Claire said as she shooed Jake out of the kitchen. "Supper will be ready soon."

Jake didn't waste time arguing. When he left the kitchen he headed for the barn, where he saddled up his gelding and took off toward the small graveyard where Sam was buried. He sat on the grass beside Sam's grave and pondered the situation.

He needed to get things settled soon, so he didn't have to spend any more time than necessary in Anabeth Calhoun's company. Because the longer he knew her, the more vulnerable he seemed to be to the woman. All he had done was buy the damn woman a dress, and you would think he had given her the pot of gold at the end of the rainbow.

Speaking of gold, although he didn't want to think it, he had to consider the possibility that Anabeth knew—had known all along—where Sam's gold was hidden. Somehow he had to convince her that she must give it up. Maybe he could make a deal with her. The gold in exchange for letting her go, maybe.

Jake froze. He would get the gold *and* send the Kid to jail. That was the way he did things. No compromise. Ever. No deals. Ever. Not even for Anabeth Calhoun. Especially not for Anabeth Calhoun.

Because he found her too attractive for his peace of mind, Jake had to be firm. He had to stick to his guns. He had past examples to show him he was courting disaster if he let an outlaw go free.

Jake's mind was still churning as he headed back to the ranch house. He saw a man dressed up in a city suit riding toward him in the distance and figured it was probably Claire's company. He headed in Will Reardon's direction. It might not be a bad idea to have a talk in private with the man before supper.

"Howdy," Jake called as he approached the other man on horseback. Reardon looked almost the dandy in his black suit and string tie. He didn't hold a candle to Sam Chandler.

"I'm Jake Kearney, Claire's brother. Am I right in assuming you're Will Reardon?"

"You are. And I am."

Reardon's face turned a chalky white. Jake wondered if Claire had been making threats of violence on his behalf without his knowledge. His sister was nothing, if not resourceful.

"I didn't know you'd be here," Reardon said. It was almost an accusation.

"I just arrived this morning. When I saw you riding

up, I thought I'd take advantage of the opportunity for us to have a little talk in private."

Reardon took his hat off, ran his hand through silky blond hair, then put his hat back on again. "I wish I could give Mrs. Chandler more time to pay," Reardon said, getting right down to business. "But I've got debts of my own to take care of."

"Would it make a difference if I told you I've got a lead on where to find Sam's gold?"

Reardon's odd-colored yellow eyes widened. "You do? Where is it? I mean, how do you know where to find it?"

"I met up with a niece of one of the gang members, Anabeth Calhoun. She seemed to think her uncle might have hidden the gold in the valley where they lived. She's going to take me there and help me hunt for it."

"She is? That's very interesting. A niece, you say? When do you think you might get started?"

"Soon," Jake promised. "Just thought I'd lay up a day or two here and visit my sister. I wanted to ask you whether, in light of this latest information, you might not be able to wait a little longer for payment on the note."

Reardon pulled a handkerchief from his pocket and swiped at his brow. "Yes," he muttered. "Yes, this does change things a bit. If what I think is true . . ."

"So your answer is yes?" Jake prodded.

"Certainly. Certainly I can do a favor for a neighbor, Mr. Kearney. Actually, I only rode over to apologize to Mrs. Chandler and tell her I can't come for supper this evening. I've got some urgent business that's going to take me away from the ranch for a while. Perhaps you'd be willing to extend my apologies to your sister for me?"

"If that's the way you want it." Jake knew Claire would be happy to avoid the rancher if she could.

Reardon tipped his hat. "Then I'll be leaving. Nice meeting you, Mr. Kearney. I wish you luck on your treasure hunt."

"Thanks," Jake said. *I'll need it.*

Jake kicked his horse into a lope and soon arrived back at the house. He called for Claire as he shoved the front door open.

"No need to yell, Jake. I'm right here."

She wasn't the only one there. Anabeth was standing right beside her in front of the fireplace. And she looked radiant. Her face glowed with pleasure. Her hair had been freed from its braids and was caught up high in back with a blue bow.

Claire urged Anabeth a step closer to Jake. "Now tell me she isn't beautiful," she dared Jake.

"She's beautiful," Jake agreed. "About the most beautiful woman I've ever seen."

Claire laughed. "I'm going to let you get away with that because I'm your sister and don't expect such compliments from you," she chided.

Without Reardon's presence, the supper Claire had planned was relaxed and cordial. Or at least as relaxed as it could be for a man sitting across the table from a beautiful virgin who shot bashful looks at him from under long, fluttery lashes.

After supper Jake mentioned to Claire that he wanted to speak with Anabeth alone for a few minutes.

"Why don't you take Anabeth into the parlor," Claire said. "I've got a fire going there, and it's more comfortable."

Anabeth eyed Jake warily as he sat down across from her in one of the two Spanish leather chairs that were situated in front of the stone fireplace. In her Levi's, with her gunbelt at her waist, she would have known how to handle Jake Kearney. But in the silk taffeta dress, she was someone else. Someone less confident of who she was, and what she wanted from the attractive man whose eyes had never left her all evening.

Jake's guts were tied up in knots. From the moment he had walked into the house and seen Anabeth in that dress, he had tried to imagine her behind iron bars. It wasn't a picture he could conjure. What came more readily to mind were pictures of her sleek naked flesh as it had appeared when she stood before him earlier in the kitchen. During supper he had mentally undressed Anabeth Calhoun and made love to her a dozen times.

And he was still hard as a rock.

He cleared his throat, but his voice was still husky with desire when he spoke. "I'd be willing to speak to the judge on your behalf, ask for leniency, in exchange for the gold. All you have to do is take me to it."

"I can't."

"You mean you won't!" Jake retorted. "You stubborn—"

"Can't! Won't! What difference does it make?" Anabeth said. "If I've told you once, I've told you a thousand times, I don't know where it is!"

An instant later she found herself nose to nose with an angry man. Jake had risen and leaned over with his hands braced on the arms of her chair so she was trapped between them. Anabeth could see the fine webbed lines around his eyes and the thin white scar that pulled his mouth down on one side. Right now he looked like he could easily—and happily—wring her neck.

"I'm not going to argue with you about this, Kid. When we leave here in a couple of days, after my leg has time to heal a little more, you're going to lead me to that gold. Understand?"

Anabeth said something in Apache very unflattering to Jake's family tree.

Being an intelligent man, Jake didn't ask her what she had said.

"You can't make me do anything," Anabeth said at last.

"Can't I?" Jake stood and in the same movement grabbed Anabeth's hand and yanked her out of the chair. She came flying toward him, stopped only by contact with his chest. He tunneled his fingers into a handful of her hair and arched her head back at a painful angle so she had no choice except to look at him. His other arm circled her hips, pinning her against his thighs.

Jake felt the heat in his loins and cursed. "You'll do what I say, Kid, or I'll—"

Anabeth opened her mouth to argue and Jake closed it in the most efficient way possible—with his own.

He wasn't sure what he had expected her to do— fight him, maybe, or jerk her head away. Instead, her body melted against him, and her mouth trembled under his, open and vulnerable to his kiss.

Jake felt the blood pound in his veins, felt his whole being slipping away as she surrendered to him. He gentled his mouth on hers, but the effect was no less devastating to his senses. He lifted his head and looked into eyes dark with passion—yet confused and a little frightened, too.

The breath she had been holding shuddered out of her.

He realized he was still pressed against her, that his hand was still fisted in her hair. He released her.

Almost in slow motion she took a step back away from him.

"Look, Kid, I—"

Claire entered the room in what had to be the most

awkward moment of Jake's life. She took one look at Anabeth's frightened face, frowned fiercely at Jake, and said, "I think it's time I showed Anabeth where she'll be sleeping."

Claire led Anabeth to Jeff's room and showed her the nightgown she had laid out for her on the bed. Anabeth's glance slid to Jake's saddlebags in the corner of the room. Those bags contained Booth's guns.

"Are you all right? Do you need any help undressing?" Claire asked.

"I'm fine," Anabeth replied with a stiff smile. "I'll undress myself."

"Good night, Anabeth," Claire said. "Sleep well."

"Good-bye, Claire," Anabeth murmured. As soon as Claire was gone, Anabeth began a search through Jake's saddlebags for Booth's pearl-handled guns. Then she began unbuttoning the eighteen cloth-covered buttons on the silk taffeta dress. She stepped out of the gown and laid it carefully across the bed, smoothing the fabric. Where she was going, she wouldn't need it.

She dressed herself in one of Jake's shirts and a pair of his trousers rolled up in the legs. In the masculine clothes, she felt more like what she was. Kid Calhoun, outlaw. She couldn't afford to have feelings for a lawman. Especially not one as determined, as single-minded, as Jake Kearney.

Unfortunately, Anabeth was afraid it was too late. A shuddery sigh escaped as she conceded that she could very well be falling in love with the Ranger.

The worst of it was, she knew Jake didn't love her. He couldn't love any woman. He only desired her, as Booth had desired Sierra. Anabeth needed more than that. So before she let Jake tempt her to go hunting for gold, instead of revenge, she had to leave this place.

She had no doubt he would pursue her. Not for

herself, of course, but for the gold. She would need all the skills Wolf had taught her to elude him.

Anabeth took one last look at the silk taffeta dress. She hated to leave it behind. But the truth was, it had been made to be worn by a lady—not an outlaw named Kid Calhoun.

Anabeth opened the shuttered window and slipped out into the night.

10

Jake knew he ought to wait until morning to confront Anabeth about what had happened between them, but he had never been a patient man. He had persuaded himself that the stunning kiss they had shared had been more a result of his anger and frustration with her than his desire for her. He wanted to reassure Anabeth that she wouldn't have to worry about him losing control again if—when—they traveled to the valley together.

The moment Claire extinguished the lamp in her bedroom, he rose from Sam's chair in the parlor and headed toward the room where Anabeth had retired earlier in the evening. He knocked softly, but when there was no answer he quietly edged the door open.

"You asleep, Kid?"

No answer. In the moonlight that streamed through the open window, Jake could see the silk taffeta dress had been laid neatly across the foot of the bed. The Kid lay wrapped in a lump of quilts. He crossed the room and sat down on the edge of the bed.

"I thought we ought to talk," he said. "Get some things settled between us without involving Claire."

He put his hand on what he supposed to be Ana-

beth's shoulder. The pillow collapsed beneath the
weight of his hand. Incredulous, Jake yanked the
quilts away. At first he didn't believe what he was
seeing. The truth hit him hard and fast. "Hell and the
devil!"

She was gone.

"Claire!" he bellowed. "Claire!"

Jake was already in the parlor retrieving his gunbelt from the back of Sam's chair by the time Claire
reached the hallway. "What's the matter? What's
wrong?"

"She's gone!"

"Who?"

"Anabeth," Jake snarled. "I should have known
she'd light out first chance she got! I never should
have trusted her!" He buckled on his gunbelt and
headed for the kitchen to pack some food for the trail.

Claire followed him. "Why would she run away?"

Jake turned on her and said, "I should have told
you the whole truth. Anabeth is Booth Calhoun's
niece, but she's also Kid Calhoun. She rode with the
gang that robbed Sam."

Claire's brow furrowed. "She didn't act like an outlaw, Jake. And you didn't treat her like one. Are you
sure she's so bad?"

"I don't know!" Jake said in an agonized voice.
"One minute I think she's lying through her teeth,
and the next I just don't know."

"Where would she go?"

After Booth's outlaw gang. Jake's stomach churned
as he thought of the danger she was courting. He
should have kept a closer eye on her! He would from
now on. He had warned her that he would show no
mercy if she tried to run. Now he intended to make
good on that promise.

Claire laid a hand on Jake's sleeve as he grabbed
the supplies he had tied up in a kitchen towel. She

could see the signs of temper in the racing pulse at his temple, the jerk of the muscle in his jaw. "You won't hurt her, will you, Jake?"

"Oh, I'll be gentle with her," he promised. Jake was already out the kitchen door when Claire heard him mutter, "When I catch up to her, I'm going to gently wring her neck!"

Claire frowned. She hoped for Anabeth's sake that Jake didn't catch up to the girl before he simmered down.

Claire headed toward Jeff's room to see how it had been left after Anabeth's abrupt departure. She seldom went into the room because it held too many memories. She didn't light the lamp. She rearranged Anabeth's dress over the rocker in the corner. As she straightened the sheets and settled the pillows at the head of the iron-frame bed she thought of the hours she had spent here reading to Jeff and listening to his prayers.

She sat on the edge of the bed and traced the embroidery on the pillowcase with her fingertips, then laid her head down for a moment and closed her eyes. The ache in her chest was as strong as it had been the day she learned her son was never coming home. Now Sam was gone, too. She needed the demands of Window Rock to give her life purpose.

"Please, Jake," she whispered. "I'm counting on you to find that gold."

She was so very tired. How many sleepless nights had she spent lately wishing, thinking about what might have been. If she could rest here for a moment, she would have the strength to go to her own bed. Slowly, surely, her eyes drifted closed.

Claire woke abruptly when a heavy hand clamped across her mouth. She stared, confused, at the shadowy specter sitting on the bed beside her. At first she thought it was Jake. A second later, both sight and scent told her it was not.

The scream caught in her throat as the Apache spoke to her in guttural tones. She clawed at his hand, trying to free her mouth, but his hold only tightened. She arched her back, trying to raise her head from the pillow, but he held her captive.

"Do not fight me, Stalking Deer," Wolf said in the Apache tongue. "I have come to take you away from this place. You will be my woman. We will be together always."

The Apache's words fell on foreign ears. Claire scratched and bucked and kicked, fighting for her life.

"So be it," Wolf said, his voice hard. He had hoped Stalking Deer would not fight him, but he had come prepared in case she did. He used a piece of rawhide to silence his struggling captive, forcing her mouth open and tying the gag tightly behind her head. He rolled her into the bedding to still her thrashing, then leaned down and whispered, "You give me no choice. I will not let the white man have you. You are mine."

Wolf hefted the still-struggling body over his shoulder and made his way silently down the hall and out the back door. Moonlight flashed on Wolf's self-satisfied smile as he emerged from the adobe house with his prize. Stalking Deer was his at last—and forever.

Silently, stealthily, he carried his burden up the hill to the spot where he had left his pony. Wolf threw the squirming bundle over the withers of his pony and mounted behind. He nudged the pony into a distance-eating lope. He was miles from the ranch house before he slowed his mount.

He patted what he thought to be Stalking Deer's bottom and said, "If you will lie still, I will free you now."

Claire writhed with humiliation and rage and fear

at the familiarity of the Apache's touch. She grunted angry noises through the gag in response to the Apache's guttural speech.

"So be it," Wolf said, frowning at Stalking Deer's continuing defiance. "You can stay as you are until we reach the end of our journey."

After another half hour, when Stalking Deer lay so still she might have been dead, Wolf reconsidered. He knew it was only Stalking Deer's pride that made her fight him, and he did not want her sick when they arrived at the village. He turned her over and pulled her up into his arms. The pained groan of relief he heard from within the bundle of blankets made him smile. Stalking Deer was often stubborn to a fault. Nevertheless, she would make him a good wife.

Claire had been fighting the urge to vomit for so long she took several gasps of air when she was finally turned upright. She was too sick to resist the Apache as he turned her over and pulled her into his arms. When her head fell against his shoulder, she left it there and closed her eyes trying to recover from the awful nausea caused by her upside-down ride.

The Apache continued speaking to her as though she could understand him. The guttural sounds rumbled low in his chest, and she found them almost soothing. She did not fight him again, afraid to draw his attention to her. She could endure this closeness if it meant avoiding another painful ride over the pony's withers.

As Claire lay in the Apache's arms, she was able to detect his man-scent, a not unpleasant, but definitely foreign, musky smell. She was aware of his strength. Only a thin quilt separated her from a body that was hard as rock.

Claire had no doubt of her fate. She refused to think of it. When the time came, she would find a way to end things quickly.

Wolf was not far from home by the time the sun
began its ascent. He did not wish to bring his bride
into the village in such a way. There would be com-
ment enough when it was known he intended to take
a white woman for his wife. He stopped his pony at
the edge of the pines that led up into the forested
mountains where the camp was located. Taking a
firm hold on his bundle, Wolf slipped off his pony.

"Can you stand, Stalking Deer?"

Evidently not. Her knees buckled. He picked her
back up and carried her over to a fallen log and set
her down on it. The sun broke over the mountains as
he slowly, carefully unwrapped his prize.

Wolf's jaw dropped in shock. The woman staring
back at him, her features rigid, her golden eyes blaz-
ing, was *not* Stalking Deer!

"Who are you?" he demanded, teeth bared.

Claire's eyes went wide as the Apache spoke to her
in perfectly understandable English. Of course there
was no possibility of answering him. She was still
gagged.

The Apache recognized his error and roughly released the gag. He grabbed a handful of her golden
hair and yanked her head back until she thought her
neck would break.

"Who are you?" he asked again. "Where is Stalking
Deer?"

Claire's lips were dry, her mouth sore from having
been gagged. She licked her lips painfully and managed to rasp, "My name is Claire Chandler. I don't
know anyone called Stalking Deer."

"She went into the house with the white man, Jake
Kearney. I saw her lie down in the bed where I found
you."

Claire stared at the Apache, fascinated by his sharp,
angular features, the fierceness of his dark eyes.

"She is also called Anabeth," Wolf said.

"Oh. Anabeth left."

"When? Where did she go?" Wolf was angry with himself for making such a foolish mistake. This woman's size alone should have told him of his mistake. She was not nearly so tall as Stalking Deer. Claire Chandler's head barely reached his chin.

"Anabeth left the house sometime last night. I don't know where she went." Claire didn't volunteer the information that Jake had followed Anabeth.

Abruptly the Apache released her and stalked away, muttering under his breath. He turned back and glared at her. "What am I to do with you?"

"Take me home."

Wolf laughed at the boldness of her response. He was not unaware of the trouble he had created for himself by stealing the white woman. With that silky golden hair and those golden eyes, she was like a tawny cat, fearless, her claws barely sheathed. Yet he had no desire to make her a slave, especially when he planned to bring Stalking Deer to the village as his wife. But how to return his captive? That was another problem entirely. Still, it could be done. If he chose to do it.

"I could more easily kill you than return you to your people," he said.

Wolf expected her to cry and plead for mercy. He saw her shudder, but she never said a word. Those catlike golden eyes of hers remained focused on something in the distance. He couldn't help admiring her courage.

Wolf couldn't know that Claire had already resigned herself to dying. Her only regret was the sorrow she knew Jake would suffer. She was determined to die bravely. She turned to confront the Apache who stood before her. "I'm not afraid to die. Do what you will."

At that instant a jackrabbit flashed past her foot.

Claire yelped in surprise. A moment later three Apache boys came racing over the hill, bows in hand, in pursuit of the hare. When they saw Wolf and the white woman, they stopped in their tracks.

Wolf cursed under his breath. There was no time to hide the white woman from the three youths who stood gawking at the top of the hill. The appearance of the boys complicated things. Once the tribe knew he had take the woman captive, he would have fewer choices what to do with her.

Wolf's abilities as a hunter and as a fierce warrior had won him the respect of the tribe over the years. While they might have welcomed him to their campfires now, he was the one who had kept his distance. In the face of the three boys' curiosity, he almost wished for his former isolation. Almost.

"Wolf! Where have you been? Who is that with you?" one of the boys called as he tumbled headlong down the sheer incline.

Wolf hesitated only an instant before answering, "It is a white woman I have taken captive." He reached out to put a possessive hand on Claire's shoulder.

The Apache youths quickly surrounded her, babbling in excitement. Wolf finally stepped in front of the woman to protect her from their stares and said, "Go back to the village and tell them I am coming."

The boys' shrieks were unearthly, otherworldly, and Claire shivered with fear. Her eyes were drawn to the last dark-haired boy before he turned and hurried after the others. There was something about him that reminded her of Jeffrey. She turned her eyes away. Jeff was dead. It could only bring her pain to see her son's features in the face of an Indian boy.

Wolf turned to his captive. "Come. We must go now."

Claire stood and wrapped the quilt more firmly around her shoulders. "I'm ready."

Wolf mounted his pony and reached a hand down to pull her up before him. He felt her stiffen when he put his arms around her, but she did not struggle. He wondered grimly what he was going to do with her.

It struck him suddenly that he could trade her to the white man for the woman he wanted. All he had to do was make sure his captive didn't escape before he could locate Stalking Deer.

Claire was too caught up in what she was seeing to think about escape. She had never seen an Apache dwelling, but she recognized Wolf's wickiup immediately for what it was. The circular, dome-shaped brush dwelling was several feet taller than a man at the center, and easily as wide as it was tall. It was thatched with bear grass, and there was a cowhide suspended at the entrance on a cross-beam so it could be swung forward or backward.

She knew from the presence of the boys that there must be other Apaches living nearby, but she saw only the single wickiup. "Where is the rest of the village?" she asked.

"We have many enemies," Wolf said. "Our homes are hidden among the hills." He pointed to a spot where the landscape rose slightly. "Beyond that rise my mother lives." One by one he pointed out several wickiups that were concealed by the terrain. "Many of the wickiups cannot be seen from here."

It soon became apparent that the three boys had spread the word of Wolf's return. As Wolf and Claire dismounted before his wickiup, Claire found herself the object of a dozen pairs of eyes.

"Go inside," Wolf ordered.

Claire was glad to escape their curious stares and shoved aside the rawhide opening in order to step inside. On one side of the dwelling she saw a grass bed. There were several baskets and shallow coiled trays. Hanging from the wall she saw a horsetail hair rope and a pitch-covered woven basket, which she assumed could carry water. On the dirt floor, near the fire at the center of the wickiup, she found several gourd cups and wooden dishes and a fire drill for starting the fire.

"All the comforts of home," she murmured.

Outside she heard her captor's voice raised in the guttural Apache sounds she found so foreign. A moment later he entered the wickiup. The space that had seemed large, suddenly shrank.

Claire clutched the quilt to her bosom as she met the Indian's fierce gaze. "What are you going to do with me?" she asked breathlessly.

"I have told them you will be my slave."

"I won't!"

The Apache's lip curled derisively. "I would rather not share you with the others. But if you would rather . . ." He started to leave the wickiup.

"Wait!" Claire laid a hand on his forearm to stop him. "I would rather stay with you." Better the devil she knew . . . than the devil she didn't.

He took the pitch-covered container from the wall and held it out to her. "Go back to the stream we crossed and fetch some water for us."

Claire had trouble holding onto the container and the quilt both, and the quilt fell to the ground. She flushed a fiery red as she stood before the Apache in no more than the simple chambray nightgown she had worn to bed.

Wolf felt a surprising hunger as he stared at the white woman. The tie at the neck of her garment had come undone and revealed a broad expanse of pale skin. He should not have found her attractive. But he did. He marveled at the smoothness of her skin, its whiteness. And he found himself desiring to touch the rounded flesh that showed at the opening to her

gown. Her breasts were large and full and would
have overflowed his hands.

He watched a flush of embarrassment dance upward from her throat to her cheeks, tinting them a
rosy pink. Her skin would be warm where the blood
heated it. He reached out a hand to touch her, but she
shrank from him.

"Be still! I only wish to touch you."

"I don't wish to be touched."

The woman raised her chin and boldly met his
gaze. He saw her fear—and her determination to
overcome it. He dared her to deny him as he reached
out a hand and brushed it against her cheek. Her
body quivered and the color faded from her face as
quickly as it had come. But she did not flinch. Instead, she took a deliberate step backward, out of his
reach.

Her defiance both infuriated and amused him. She
could not escape him. She was totally in his power.
Did she not realize the truth of it?

"Come here to me," he commanded.

"No."

"It will be the worse for you if you do not come,"
he warned.

It was then he discovered that she was not only
courageous, but shrewd. He discovered why she had
taken that step backward when he saw her hand
streak out to grasp a knife that hung in a sheath on
the wall. He barely had time to catch her wrist as the
knife slashed toward his breast. The sharpened tip
left a streak of red down his chest as it seared his
skin.

His arms encircled her as he struggled to wrench
the knife from her fisted hand. He howled when her
teeth sank into his thumb.

Wolf's instincts took over, and he treated her as he
would any enemy. His justice was swift and sure.

Within moments she was lying on her back under him and the knife was at her throat.

"Kill me!" she hissed. "Do it! I would rather die than be a slave to an animal like you! I hate you and all your kind! You killed my son!"

There were tears in her eyes, but she fought him like a wildcat. Her body bucked under his, creating a desire that had not previously been a part of his plans for her. As his body tightened, he used his knees to spread her legs apart and pressed himself against her.

Suddenly she stilled. Her eyes went wide with terror. Her mouth fell open gasping air. Her whole body lay as tense as a taut rope beneath him.

Wolf kept the weight of his hips pressed firmly against her. But he did not move. The danger was as clear to him, as he saw it was to her. It would not take much provocation for him to take what he now desired.

Wolf was confounded by his body's reaction to her. He had no wish to have this woman under him. It was Stalking Deer he desired. Only his body said otherwise.

"Do not move," he said in a quiet voice. "Not a muscle, not a hair."

He saw her swallow, saw the pulse at her throat throbbing heavily where the tip of his knife lay.

"I will have obedience from my slave," he said. "And you *will* be my slave!"

She opened her mouth to speak but hesitated when the tip of his knife pierced the skin at her throat.

"You will do as you are told. You will not argue. And whatever I wish done for me, you will do. Do you understand me?"

Her response was a mere hiss of air. "Yessss."

"Put your hands around my neck," he ordered.

He lifted his body to free her hands, which were pinned between them, and waited to see if she would obey him. Slowly, as though they were leaden, her hands reached up to circle his neck.

He took the knife from her throat and laid it down beside them, easily within her reach. He watched her eyes glance longingly toward the weapon. He threaded his free hand into her golden hair to feel its silky softness. Then he took hold of a handful of it and lifted her face up toward his.

Their lips were a breath apart when she made her grab for the knife. He instantly flattened her beneath him.

Wolf heard her sob of frustration as he easily wrestled the weapon from her and threw it to the edge of the wickiup beyond her reach. "I admire your spirit, my brave little one. But you must also learn obedience."

"I'll never obey you! I'll fight you until my dying day!"

"Which may be sooner than you would like, Little One, if you are not careful." He grinned ruefully. "Come, it is time for us to begin again."

Abruptly he released her and stood up. He reached out a hand to help her up. She ignored it, scrambling to her feet on her own.

"I am called Wolf," he said. "And I will call you—"

"My name is Claire."

"I will call you Little One," he finished. "There is no need for you to fight me, Little One. I do not want you for my woman. There is another I desire for that purpose. But you will be my slave while you are here.

"Someday perhaps I will trade you for Stalking Deer. Until then, you will cook and haul water and take care of my belongings. We will do well together, Little One, no matter what you might think now."

"I'll run away! I won't stay here and be your slave!"

"Do you even know which direction your home

lies?" He saw the panic-stricken look in her eyes.
"When the time is right, when I find Stalking Deer, I
will find a way to return you to the place from which I
took you."

"Take me home now."

His lips thinned. "I cannot."

"Will not," she muttered.

At that moment a small, wizened Apache woman
pushed aside the hide opening of the wickiup. She
spoke to Wolf in the Apache tongue. "Welcome home,
my son. Who is this woman you have brought to your
wickiup?"

"My captive," Wolf said. "You will teach her what
she must know to serve me."

"A white woman is no damn good," the old Apache
woman said. "They cannot work very hard. You are
wasting your time to try and teach her the Apache
ways."

Wolf flushed. "It is not for you to question what I
do."

The old woman rubbed her chin. "You have always
been different. It is what comes of having so many
fathers, I suppose. An elbow from this one. A nose
from that one. The eyes of yet another."

"You talk too much, old woman."

"And took too many men to my blankets, eh, my
son? But all of them lusty from the looks of you," she
said, cackling with glee. "It took many men to sire
such a special one as you, eh?"

Claire cowered at the fierce look on Wolf's face.
What had the old woman said to him?

Abruptly Wolf turned to her and said, "This woman
is called Night Crawling. She will take you to the
stream for water and teach you what it is needful to
know."

"How will I talk to her? I don't understand your
language."

Wolf's grin was feral. "She will speak in gestures you will understand."

"You can't mean for me to go with her now!"

"But I do," Wolf said. He took the blanket from her and held the hide opening of the wickiup aside.

Night Crawling pinched Claire's arm.

"Ouch!"

"She is telling you it is time to go," Wolf said.

"I get the message," Claire muttered, glaring at Wolf.

When Claire stepped out of the wickiup she found herself facing most of the tribe, who had gathered to ogle Wolf's captive.

She backed up a step and found she had run into Wolf. Somehow, the Indian she had found so fearful was now her refuge among the savages. "Wolf?"

"They will not harm you, Little One. They are only curious."

Claire squared her shoulders and stared back into the sea of Apache faces. Eventually, they became individual men and women and children. It was the children whose faces she returned to. One dark-haired boy in particular. One with green eyes.

"Oh my God," Claire whispered. She grasped Wolf's arm, her nails digging into his skin.

"What is it, Little One? What is wrong?"

"That boy. The one with the green eyes . . ."

"He is called White Eagle."

Claire shook her head. "No. His name is Jeffrey. *That's my son!*"

11

Jake had felt a murderous rage when he found Ana-beth gone from Claire's house. It wasn't until several hours later, when he had calmed down, that he realized it was fear for her safety that had provoked his anger. It soon became apparent that his concern for the bare-faced brat was misplaced. As Jake followed her trail he quickly discovered that Anabeth Calhoun could take damned good care of herself.

In fact, Jake wasn't sure when he had ever trailed so skillful an adversary. The Kid left no signs of her passing that would have been seen by the average cowhand. But Jake had spent a lifetime tracking down outlaws. He had two other advantages that made it possible to stay on the Kid's trail. First, he knew she was heading for Santa Fe to find Wat Rankin. And second, Dog had come along.

If it hadn't been for Dog's nose, Jake would have missed the shortcut the Kid took up over the mountains. The narrow path was obviously intended for mountain goats. Jake had several times held his breath when one stirrup brushed rock while the other hung out over a steep cliff. That was when he realized Anabeth Calhoun also had nerves of steel.

Jake felt a grudging respect for the willful brat that

made it all the more satisfying when he finally caught up to her just before dawn. He had to admire the camp she had set up. Whoever had taught the Kid had taught her well. A bed of loose stones would warn her of any approach on three sides and a sheer rock wall rose up behind her. It was nigh impossible for him to reach her without making enough noise to wake her up.

Nigh impossible. But not totally impossible. Jake was determined to teach Anabeth Calhoun a lesson. He had to lower himself by rope over the sheer rock wall to do it. The stamina required, not to mention the danger involved and the pain to his wounded leg, left him tense and irritable when he finally touched ground beside her. But the satisfaction when he clamped a strong hand around her narrow female wrist was worth every second of the effort.

Anabeth was jerked awake—and out of her bedroll —by a towering hunk of furious male. She reached instinctively for her gun, only to have it torn out of her hand. Her free wrist was caught in a powerful grasp and yanked up behind her back, pulling her flush against a muscular male frame.

"Don't waste your time struggling, Kid," a familiar voice snarled. "It won't do you any good."

"Jake? Jake!"

"That's right, it's me, Kid," Jake said with a feral smile. "Now stand still and listen."

Anabeth struggled harder. When she tried to bite Jake his elbow came up reflexively and slammed her in the jaw. She yelped in pain.

"Dammit, Kid. Look what you made me do!" Jake hadn't meant to hit her, but how else was he supposed to keep her from biting the bejesus out of him? "Settle down," he snapped.

Anabeth had to concede she wasn't going to escape from this giant of a man when he had such a good hold on her. He was too big and too strong. She would have to bide her time and wait for the right moment to make her escape. But escape she would! How humiliating to be caught sleeping like a baby!

"All right," she said sullenly. "I'm not going to fight you anymore. You can let me go now."

Jake laughed harshly. "Let you go? Hell, Kid, I just caught you! This time I'm taking no chances you'll get away."

He hauled her over to where he had left his horse hidden and pulled a length of rawhide rope out of his saddlebags.

Anabeth tensed. "What are you planning to do?"

"Make sure we stick together till we get where we're going." Jake proceeded to tie both her wrists together in front of her with one end of the rope. The other end he tied around one of his own wrists, leaving about a six-foot length between them.

"You're crazy!" Anabeth said. "You can't tie yourself to a woman like this!"

"You're right, Kid. If there were a *woman* involved, I wouldn't dream of doing such a thing. But what we're talking about here is a troublemaking brat!"

"But I—but you—" Anabeth's face flushed red with anger and humiliation. She would kill him. The first chance she got. Shoot him right in the—hell, he didn't have a heart! A heartless bastard like him would probably laugh if she tried!

"Are you hungry?" Jake asked. "I could use a cup of coffee and something to eat."

Anabeth sat down cross-legged right where she was. Let him see just how far he could get tied to a *woman* who wasn't going anywhere. "Fire's over there," Anabeth said with a smirk. She gestured with her tied hands back toward the area where she had made camp.

"You coming?" Jake asked, eyeing the lump of stubbornness at the end of the rope.

"Thought I'd rest here awhile," Anabeth said.

"Uh uh," Jake said. "Time for breakfast, brat."

Anabeth shrieked in outrage when Jake simply curled a huge arm around her waist, lifted her onto his hip, and headed for the fire. He was tall enough that both her hands and her feet barely dragged the ground. When they reached the fire he dropped her so she landed hard on hands and knees.

"Don't particularly want to be hauling you around, Kid," he said. "But I'll do what's necessary. Do we understand each other?"

Anabeth glared at him from ice blue eyes. "Yessss," she hissed.

"Now, how about some breakfast?"

"I'm not hungry!"

"Suit yourself," he said. "Now, I want you to point your nose toward that valley of yours and lead the way."

Anabeth sulked for a moment and then had a brilliant idea. Jake had no idea where the valley was. She would take him back to Santa Fe. He couldn't keep her tied up in town without attracting unwanted attention. Once they were no longer tied together, she would somehow manage to escape him again.

"All right," she said at last. "Let's go."

Anabeth had time later in the day to regret her refusal of breakfast. Jake ate dinner in the saddle, and she was too proud to ask him for something to eat in the middle of the afternoon. By suppertime, she was famished—as well as having other needs that had remained unattended. When at last they stopped for the day, the stars were already out.

Jake had found a hollow protected from the wind and with enough piñon trees to diffuse the smoke from their fire.

To Anabeth's surprise, Jake untied the thong from his wrist. But he left her hands tied together.

"I'll give you a few minutes of privacy. Make good use of them. They're all you're going to get till morning."

Jake was grinning when Anabeth returned. "I thought you'd be too smart to run."

"I'm hungry," Anabeth retorted. "I figured I'd eat supper first."

Jake laughed as he tied the end of the rawhide thong back around his wrist. "Too bad, Kid. You'll have to haul me along if you want to leave now."

Anabeth ate ravenously, planning her escape the whole while. "I need to be alone again before we bed down," she said after Jake had banked the fire for the night.

"Uh uh. Not a chance."

"Jake, you have to let me go!" Anabeth pleaded.

"Uh uh," he said again. "Bedtime, Kid." He reeled in the extra rope until Anabeth was standing in front of him. "I have a pretty good idea of your inventiveness, so I think I'll just nip in the bud any ideas you might have about leaving tonight."

As Anabeth watched with incredulous eyes, Jake prepared a blanket for himself and another for her right beside his. There wasn't enough rope for her to escape to the opposite side of the fire.

"I'm not sleeping with you, Jake," she said.

"Suit yourself," he said, lying down and pulling her into his arms. "Awake or asleep, this is where you'll be spending the night."

Anabeth felt her breath catch in her throat when Jake's arm snugged around her waist and pulled her up tight against him. She could feel the heat of him down the entire length of her back. The hard strength of him. The huge maleness of him.

Jake cursed up one side and down the other. His

body had definite ideas about what it would like to do with the woman in his arms. But he would be a fool indeed to lust after an outlaw who didn't give a spit in the wind for an offer of leniency.

"Damn you, Kid! Stop squirming!"

A little voice inside reminded Jake that calling her a kid just didn't make it so.

He felt the weight of her breasts on his arm. The hips pressed into his groin definitely belonged to a woman. And the long silky hair flowing over him like a cloak—that belonged to a woman, too. So, maybe he had better rethink this plan of his.

Jake was on the verge of admitting he had made a dreadful mistake when Anabeth muttered, "If I live to be a hundred I will never forgive you for this!"

"For what? Holding you in my arms?"

"For . . . touching me."

Jake's groin tightened painfully. "Believe me, Kid, this is hurting me as much as it's hurting you."

"It doesn't hurt," she was quick to reassure him. "Exactly."

Jake hesitated, knowing he shouldn't ask. "What do you mean, it doesn't hurt *exactly*."

She took his hand and moved it down to her belly. "There it is again. Kind of a squirrely feeling right *there* when you touch me."

Jake's whole body tensed like a bowstring. "Dammit, Kid. What are you trying to do to me?" He yanked his hand away from her belly and snugged his arm around her midriff once again. And groaned deep in his throat when he felt the soft weight of her breasts against his forearm.

"Something wrong, Jake?"

"As if you didn't know! Go to sleep, Kid."

Jake closed his eyes, but he felt anything but sleepy. A few moments later he heard, "Jake? Are you awake?"

"How can I get any sleep with you making so much noise," he grumbled.

"I can't get comfortable. I always sleep on my other side."

"Turn over then."

She did. And Jake found out what real hell was. Because now they were lined up breast to breast and thigh to thigh. The only place for his arms was around her, surrounding her. She laid her head on his shoulder and snuggled closer.

"You're warm," she said.

Hot was more like it, Jake thought with a sigh of resignation. "Can you sleep now, Kid?"

"I think so, Jake." A pause and then, grudgingly, "Thanks."

It was a grumpy man who rolled out of the blankets early the next morning. Jake had spent the night aware of every move the Kid made. The tips of her breasts brushing against his chest. Her silky hair tickling his chin. Her nose pressed against his neck. Her leg shoved between his thighs. He doubted the Apache could have conceived a worse night of torture.

It soon became apparent to Jake that Anabeth was taking him straight to Santa Fe. Rather than confront her, he remained silent. He was thinking it might not be such a bad idea to go there. At least in Santa Fe he could find a woman upon whom he could ease himself.

"When we get to Santa Fe, I'll remove that rope from around your wrists," Jake said as he saddled his horse. "But I want you to stick close."

When they entered Santa Fe, Jake kept to the back alleys. But it didn't take Anabeth long to figure out where they were headed.

"This way," Jake said, turning down a side street.

Anabeth recognized the two-story building. The

small wooden sign that read "Eulalie Schmidt" was swinging back and forth in the breeze.

Jake knocked on the door, but as usual, didn't wait for an answer before he pushed his way inside. "Eulalie?"

Eulalie was surprised to see Jake back again so soon, especially in the company of the woman he had identified to her as the outlaw, Kid Calhoun.

"What brings you back this way, Jake?" she asked. "Come on in and get comfortable, Anabeth—or should I call you Kid?

"Anabeth, please."

"I must admit you're the first outlaw I ever had working for me, Anabeth."

Eulalie took one look at the dark circles under Anabeth's eyes and said, "Jake, shame on you! What have you been doing traipsing around the country without taking better care of this poor child?"

"What have I—? You've got the shoe on the wrong foot, Eulalie."

By now Eulalie had ushered Anabeth into the kitchen and sat her down at the table. A moment later a cup of coffee appeared in front of both Jake and Anabeth, followed quickly by sauerkraut and sausage.

"Now, what can I do for you?" Eulalie asked.

"I need a safe place to leave Anabeth for a while." He was going to talk to Sierra Starr again. Maybe she would be able to give him a lead to Booth's secret valley. It was plain the Kid wasn't going to help him out. While he was at the saloon he would see if Sierra still indulged herself by occasionally inviting a man upstairs. He had high hopes that taking another woman to bed would ease his discomfort around the brat in britches who was too much on his mind.

"I'll wait while you lock Anabeth in," Jake said.

Eulalie's brows rose, wrinkling her forehead into a river of lines. "Is that really necessary?"

"It is if I expect her to be here when I come back," Jake said flatly.

"Don't leave me locked up here!" Anabeth cried. "I've told you what I have to do and why. Let me go, Jake."

"Forget it, Kid. I've also told you what I have to do and why." Jake followed Anabeth upstairs and ushered her into the corner room he had used the last time he had been here.

The instant the lock clicked, Anabeth ran to the window of the second-story room, searching for a way to escape her prison. There was no tree, no porch, nothing to help her get to the ground. She looked up and realized the roof was not nearly so far. She remembered seeing an outside stairway on at least one side of the building.

Before Jake had limped his way through the bat-wing doors of the Town House Saloon, Anabeth had already reached the roof and was well on her way to escape—and her pursuit of the men who had murdered her uncle. If she checked all the saloons in town, she might very well find Whiskey. And she could count on Whiskey to lead her to the outlaws' camp.

Sierra Starr was dealing at the faro table. She was wearing something red and shiny that attracted the eye and left a lot of flesh exposed. She was even more good-looking than Jake remembered. He sat down in an empty chair and put some money on the table.

"You in, Jake?" Sierra asked.

"I'm in," he replied.

He played faro for an hour, winning some, losing some, and watching Sierra Starr. It was apparent she was selective about bestowing her smiles, and Jake felt privileged to get one. When she passed the box to an older gentleman and left the table, he quickly discovered the smile hadn't been an invitation to anything more.

"I'd like to talk to you," he said when he caught up to her at the bar.

"Buy me a drink."

Jake smiled cynically. Always hustling. He supposed that was how she had gotten where she was, and he admired her more than he blamed her for it. "Sure. What'll you have?"

"Rye."

Jake ordered the same for himself. "Let's find a table."

She followed him to a table at the corner of the room where Jake sat with his back to the wall.

"I was wondering whether you might know where Booth Calhoun's valley is," he asked.

Her eyes hardened into chips of green glass. "He didn't confide in me."

Jake decided she was either telling the truth—or a damned good liar. "Have any of the gang been here asking the same question?"

She lifted her hair from the side of her neck to reveal bruises arrayed in the shape of fingers. "Wat Rankin came by to visit. It took a derringer at his throat to convince him I didn't know anything. If you're going after him, I'll be glad to tell you what I know."

"I'd appreciate that. But there's something else I'd rather give my attention to first."

Sierra raised a brow. "What's that?"

"You."

Sierra met the big man's heavy-lidded gaze and felt a shiver run down her spine at the sensual look of hunger in his gray eyes. She could pick and choose the men she gave her favors to these days. She had been lonely. And Booth was never coming back.

"Come with me." Sierra took the Ranger's hand and led him up the stairs.

Jake's footfalls were barely audible, but they might as well have been drumbeats, for the resounding effect they had on Anabeth Calhoun.

She had made her way to the Town House Saloon in time to watch from a side window as Jake disappeared upstairs with Sierra Starr. She wasn't sure exactly what they were going to do up there, but she felt a churning in her belly at the thought of Sierra putting her hands on Jake. Or Jake's large, callused hands on the other woman.

Anabeth laid a hand on her stomach to try and stop the queasy feeling there. She was a fool to be thinking about Jake Kearney. Sierra Starr was welcome to him! She had more important business to take care of, or she would have marched right upstairs and told him so!

The irony was, not thirty seconds after Jake disappeared upstairs, Whiskey walked into the Town House Saloon. He didn't stay long, just went up to the bar and bought a pint bottle of whiskey and headed out the door.

Anabeth took one last look at the man disappearing up the stairs before turning her back on him. Right now nothing was more important than keeping her vow to avenge her uncle's death.

She slipped away from the window and headed for the livery where she and Jake had left their horses. By the time Jake Kearney found his way out of that woman's bed, she would have exacted her revenge on Wat Rankin and be on her way back to the valley to hide.

Anabeth never saw the odd-colored yellow eyes that followed her as she mounted her horse to ride the vengeance trail.

12

Wat Rankin watched with a smile on his face as Kid Calhoun left the Town House Saloon. If she followed Whiskey long enough she would walk right into the trap he had set for her. Imagine the Kid being female! Wat still couldn't believe Booth had been able to practice such a deceit on the gang.

When the Ranger had started talking about Booth Calhoun's "niece" helping him find the stolen gold, Wat had become suspicious. He had watched the Chandler house, and sure enough, the Kid had left in the middle of the night. Wat hadn't been far behind.

He had been hoping the Kid would lead him straight to the valley. Instead the Ranger had interfered, and they had ended up back in Santa Fe. Well, Jake Kearney had had his chance. Now it was Wat's turn.

Rankin had gathered up what was left of Booth's gang and worked out a plan to capture the Kid. Anabeth Calhoun had become a thorn in his side that needed to be removed—as soon as he had tortured the location of the valley out of her.

Wat figured Treasure Valley was the most logical place for Booth to hide Sam's gold. And he was convinced the Kid knew where in the valley the gold was

hidden. He planned to make very sure that Anabeth
Calhoun told what she knew before she died.

In fact, the trap Wat had laid for Anabeth worked
very well. Her mind was still on Jake, not on the dangers of the trail where it should have been. She had
no one to blame but herself for getting caught. She
was crossing a dry creek bed not two miles south of
Santa Fe when a lasso settled around her shoulders.
An instant later she was yanked from the saddle and
landed hard in the dust. Her hat came off and her
hair spilled down around her.

She heard the shocked intake of air and the foul
curses that revealed the astonishment of the men who
had captured her when they realized she was female.

"You were right again," Snake said to Wat. "Who'd
have thought we had a girl ridin' with us!"

Rough hands grabbed her by the arms and yanked
her to her feet. She stood facing the man she had
sworn to kill, knowing that the chances were good
that she would be the one who didn't leave this place
alive.

Wat lifted a handful of Anabeth's hair and let it
slide through his fingers. "Very pretty."

"To kill a woman, it is a bad thing," Solano said.

Even Wat had to admit that Solano had a point.
Women were so scarce in the West that they were
protected among both honest and dishonest circles
alike. Anyone who harmed a woman would likely be
hunted down and killed himself. Unless there was no
one around to complain.

Who knew Anabeth Calhoun was here? She had
come after them wearing men's clothes and toting a
pair of six-guns. For that matter, who knew this
woman was a woman? The answer was Jake Kearney. It was plain Wat would have to take care of the
Ranger, as well.

Anabeth shuddered as Wat fingered her hair. She

shrank from his smooth-fingered touch as he caressed the pearl handles of Booth's revolvers before removing them from the holsters at her sides.

Finally, Wat loosened the rope that had been used to snatch Anabeth from her mount and began recoiling it. "Hold her," he ordered Snake.

Snake's hands gripped Anabeth's shoulder painfully. "Why you been followin' us?" Snake demanded.

"I saw you kill Booth!" Anabeth spat. "All of you!" She kicked out and caught Snake in the knee. He swore and let go of her, grabbing his injured knee instead.

Anabeth ran. She was fast, but bullets were faster. The gunshot whizzing past her ear was a warning.

"The next one won't miss," Wat said in a perfectly calm voice.

Anabeth came to a screeching halt. It was the voice that stopped her. The fact she was female wasn't going to save her from the likes of Wat Rankin. He didn't have a conscience to be bothered. And dead was dead. If she wanted a chance for the revenge she had come so far to get, she had to stay alive.

"Well, a female with brains," Wat said. "That is a surprise."

Anabeth glared at him.

"Come here," Wat commanded.

Anabeth's footsteps dragged as she returned to stand before the outlaw. She flinched when he grabbed her jaw, but met his strange yellow eyes without turning away.

"Where's the gold?" he asked.

"I don't know."

"She's lyin'!" Snake said.

Wat's fingers tightened on her face. "Well, Kid?"

Anabeth lowered her gaze. "I'm telling you the truth."

"I don't think you are." Wat's hand tightened until Anabeth cried out.

Her eyelids flickered up, revealing the hate and rage she felt toward the outlaw who was responsible for her uncle's death. "I can't tell you what I don't know!"

"Then I'll ask you something you do know. Where's that valley?"

"I'll never tell," she retorted.

"Oh, I think maybe with a little persuasion you might even be willing to take us there."

"Never!"

Wat's hand slipped down from Anabeth's jaw to her throat and squeezed. She choked as she tried to draw breath, but couldn't. Her hands grappled with his wrist, trying to pull it free. Not until things began to go black, did Wat's grip loosen. Anabeth gasped and heaved a lifesaving breath of air.

"I think maybe you'll talk," Wat said with a leering smile. "Because there are other types of persuasion, you know, if plain old violence doesn't work."

Anabeth searched the faces of the other outlaws, looking for compassion, but found none. On the Mexican's face she saw disapproval of her treatment, but also fear of Wat Rankin that far outweighed it. Teague was too dumb to think for himself. He would do what he was told. In the eyes of Whiskey and Snake she saw lust and a primitive animal excitement. It would only take a nod from Rankin to release the savages within.

"Maybe I do know something," Anabeth admitted at last.

Wat smiled broadly. "I'm a reasonable man," he said. "Let's sit down and talk business."

Anabeth shuddered as Wat put an arm around her shoulder and led her back toward a camp that had been set up near the main waterhole along the trail.

Stupid men, she thought. This was the first place Jake would think to come looking for her. He would come looking for her, wouldn't he?

Yes, he would. First, because he would be angry that she had gotten away from him. Second, because he believed she would eventually lead him to Sam Chandler's gold. And third, because there was unfinished personal business between them that had begun when they exchanged that stunning kiss in Claire's parlor.

Anabeth had a feeling Jake was going to be pretty damned mad by the time he found her. Only Jake wouldn't figure to take out his fury on a puny female. Anabeth smiled inwardly. Wat Rankin and his gang had better look out!

Jake lay back on the pillow with an arm behind his head and stared at the ceiling. Every so often he took a drag on the cigarette Sierra had rolled and offered to him after they had finished having sex. He scratched around the pink edges of the gunshot wound on his thigh, which itched where it was healing.

The sweat hadn't dried on his body from the physical exertion of the act, but he felt the need for a woman again. The problem was, he didn't want the woman lying beside him. She had satisfied the desires of his body, but not the needs of his soul.

In the past, whenever Jake had needed a woman, he had found a willing one and taken what he wanted. Not that he hadn't given pleasure in return. Jake wasn't so selfish as that. This time he had sought out a woman to fulfill his need, but his body refused to be satisfied with the intense physical release he had found. It wanted something more. He wanted something more.

Anabeth Calhoun.

There, he had admitted it. He wanted her and only her. There was a fire in his body that sought out an answering flame. An ache in his soul that sought out an answering solace. As much as he wished it were not true, the only woman who could satisfy the burning within him was an enticing young female locked into a second-story room in a boardinghouse on the other side of town.

Jake frowned when he thought of any woman having that sort of power over him—over his happiness. Hadn't he learned his lesson from his mother? He might want Anabeth Calhoun like hell, but that didn't mean he had to succumb to her allure. The sooner he said good-bye to her, the better.

He looked down and realized his body had hardened at just the thought of her, the blood pumping through his shaft, engorging it painfully.

"Hell and the devil."

"You say something, Jake?"

Jake stubbed out his cigarette in a tray on the bedside table, then sat up and began pulling on his jeans. Sierra rolled over in bed to admire the play of sinewy muscles in his back. She reached out a hand to touch him, but let it drop when he stood and moved away from her.

Sierra sat up, letting the covers slide down to her waist, exposing a lush female figure still covered with a faint sheen of perspiration from the lovemaking just past.

"You seem in a godawful hurry, Jake. I must be losing my touch."

Jake threw a wry glance over his shoulder. "Just remembered something I've got to do." He pulled some bills out of his pocket without counting them.

Before he could lay them on the bedside table Sierra said, "Save your money. The pleasure was all mine."

Jake met her gaze and saw the pride there—and the regret. "Thanks, Sierra. I . . ."

How could he explain his desire to leave this room as quickly as possible. His urgent need to see the lithe young woman who had been the bane of his existence since the moment he had first met her. "It's not you, Sierra. I just—"

Sierra smiled and at the same time pulled the sheets up to conceal her body from a gaze that no longer found it the least bit tantalizing. "Don't worry, Jake. I don't have the kind of feelings that can be hurt anymore."

"Dammit, Sierra, I—"

"She must be some kind of woman to tie you up in knots like this. Who is she?"

"A spoiled brat! A troublemaking whelp! I don't know why I bother with her."

She must be some kind of woman to tie you up in knots like this. The sentence replayed in Jake's head. Sam had warned him he would one day meet such a woman. He hadn't believed it. Dammit, he *refused* to believe it.

"She means *nothing* to me," Jake muttered.

"Sounds like you've got it bad," Sierra said.

"I don't need her kind of trouble."

"Don't you?"

Jake felt his groin tighten at the mere thought of doing with Anabeth what he had just done with Sierra.

Sierra saw the blatant evidence of Jake's desire and laughed. "Don't try to fool yourself, Jake. You want her like a house afire."

"She's just a kid," Jake muttered.

"Thirteen? Fourteen?"

"Nineteen."

Sierra's brows rose significantly.

"So maybe she's not a kid, exactly," Jake said. "But she's as innocent as a day-old babe."

"There has to be a first time for every woman."

"Not with me!"

"Is she asking for forever?"

"She isn't asking for anything!"

Sierra's smile was wistful. "But she's going to get it, isn't she, Jake. Oh, to be young and innocent again and to have a man like you walk into my life." She pulled her knees up and wrapped her arms around them. "She's a very lucky lady."

"She's a pain in the ass."

Sierra laughed. "Get out of here and go see her."

Jake bit his lip on the insincere protest he was about to make, stomped his feet down into his boots, buttoned up his shirt, yanked on his buckskin jacket, and left without another word. He thought he heard Sierra sigh as he closed the door behind himself.

Jake didn't exactly hurry back to the boarding-house, but he didn't make any detours either. He stopped to see Eulalie in the kitchen to get the key to the upstairs room where he had left the Kid, then headed up the stairs, two at a time.

He called to Anabeth as he unlocked the door and shoved it open—to find the room empty.

"Kid? You in here?" His eyes quickly searched the room, but there was nowhere for her to hide. He crossed to the window and looked out—then up. There was a thread from his flannel shirt caught on the edge of the windowsill and another on the edge of the roof.

"Damn her to hell!" Jake came down the stairs three at a time. "Eulalie!" he roared. "She's flown the coop again!"

Eulalie came to the kitchen door kneading a handful of bread dough. "What's wrong?"

"She's gone! When did you last see her?"

"Not since you left early this afternoon. I went by the room once and knocked, but she didn't answer, so I figured she was asleep. You say she's gone? I swear I didn't let her out, Jake."

"She went out the window."

"Where would she go?"

Jake was afraid he knew the answer to that question. It made his gut tighten with fear for the imp of Satan who had tied him up in knots—and threatened to steal both his heart and his soul.

He stopped long enough to pick up his saddlebags and say good-bye to Eulalie.

"You leaving already?"

"I have to find her. Don't know when I'll be back."

"Take care of yourself, Jake." She grinned and said, "Bring her back when you can stay longer."

Jake gave the old woman a quick hug, mindful of the yeasty dough in her hands, and hurried out the back door.

Whatever doubts Jake might have had as to whether Anabeth had left Santa Fe were settled when he got to the livery and found her dun missing. It took him a while to find the mustang's tracks outside of town, but once he did, he kicked his buckskin into a lope. Shortly thereafter, Dog joined him.

When Jake reached the spot where Anabeth had been taken by the outlaws, he deciphered the signs as though Anabeth had left a letter behind to tell him what had happened. Jake didn't like what he read. It left him feeling cold inside, with a need to kill.

The gang had waited here. Anabeth had come off the dun and hit the ground in a heap. He looked for blood, but thanked God when he didn't find any. She had tried to run but had turned around and come back. The gang had camped by the waterhole and eaten a meal. After the heat of the day, they had headed south, back the way Jake and Anabeth had come.

She's taking them to the valley.

Jake saw Dog freeze. The beast's nose pointed toward the hill above Jake. Without stopping to think, Jake dropped and rolled. It was all that saved him from the bullet that went winging by him. Reflex took over, and Jake drew his gun and fired before another second passed, pinning the bushwhacker down long enough for Jake to run for cover.

It didn't take much guessing for Jake to figure out that the man who had been waiting for him with a rifle was one of the Calhoun Gang. The question was, how had the outlaws known Jake would be coming after Anabeth? Had she been forced to tell them about him? Or had she volunteered the information? Neither possibility pleased Jake. The big question now was how badly they wanted him dead.

He was going to have to move if he wanted to get out of here alive. But any movement was bound to draw another shot from the outlaw hidden in the rocks above him. He might be able to wait out the bushwhacker and escape in the dark, but every minute he delayed reaching Anabeth Calhoun was another minute she had to face the outlaw gang alone.

Jake was all too aware what her fate would be once the outlaws had the gold they sought. Or what it was liable to be if Anabeth refused to give them what they wanted. Either way, she needed him. He had no choice except to escape from the trap they had set for him.

The bushwhacker would be expecting him to sit tight. He wouldn't be looking for Jake to take the kind of chance that might cost him his life. Which, of course, was exactly what Jake intended to do.

He holstered his gun and began the climb that would take him to his quarry. Jake was rewarded

when he reached the top of the bluff by the sight of
the outlaw laid out on his belly, his Winchester balanced on a rock overlooking the terrain below. He
was drinking from a pint glass bottle.

"Hello, there."

It was all the warning the outlaw got, but it was
enough to bring him around to face Jake.

Whiskey lay frozen for a moment. The pint of rotgut
whiskey occupied one hand. His other hand held a
rifle that had his finger curled around the trigger.

He had been drinking almost constantly since the
Kid had left with the rest of the gang. Before they
rode away she had looked him right in the eye and
said, "You're a drunken son of a bitch, Whiskey. Too
drunk to defend yourself against an armed man. Even
one you're planning to bushwhack. So you just sit
there with your bottle and wait. Because that Texas
Ranger is coming to kill you.

"At least you'll have more time to make peace with
your Maker than you gave Booth. Good-bye, Whiskey.
You're a dead man. We won't be seeing each other
again."

Whiskey was remembering what she had said. And
seeing it all come true. He had missed his first shot,
and somehow the Ranger had managed to sneak up
on him. His heart was pounding. Sweat was stream-
ing down his back. Damned if his hands weren't
trembling! And he had to pee.

The glass bottle shattered on rock, making a sound
as explosive as the two gunshots that followed. Jake's
hand was steady and his aim was true. Whiskey's shot
went wild.

"Damn that Kid Calhoun," Whiskey muttered as
his eyes closed on a star-filled sky. "Damn that Kid
for calling me a dead man."

Jake kept his gun steady on the outlaw as he approached him, waiting to see if the bushwhacker

would reach for the rifle that had fallen a short distance away from him.

"What's your name?" Jake asked.

"They call me Whiskey."

Jake caught a whiff of the dark liquid that had spilled over a nearby rock—and the reek of a body that oozed alcohol from the pores—and didn't have to ask why. Jake probably owed his life to the fact the man's aim had been spoiled by the liquor he had drunk.

"Where have they taken the Kid?" Jake asked.

"Kid's not a kid, he's a girl," Whiskey said.

Jake's gritted his teeth. So Anabeth's luck had finally run out, and the gang knew she was female. Every second counted now. "Where did they go?"

"To find the gold," Whiskey replied. "The Kid said you would come after her. And kill me. Shouldna had that last drink, I s'pose. I'm gonna die, ain't I?"

Jake checked the hole in Whiskey's chest, which was bubbling as his lungs filled with blood. "Looks that way."

"At least the Kid'll get what's comin' to her," he said.

Jake stiffened. "What about the Kid?"

"Gonna kill her, sure."

Jake felt his skin get up and crawl all over him. "Not until they find the gold, though." He said it to convince himself that Anabeth was safe, even though he feared she was in deadly peril.

Whiskey's lips formed a macabre grin. Blood streamed from the side of his mouth. "I'm gonna die. But so is she."

A hissing sigh escaped between the outlaw's teeth, and his eyes began to glaze over. Jake shuddered as he reached over to lower the outlaw's eyelids. There was nothing he could do about the ghastly smile that remained on the outlaw's lips.

Jake didn't take the time to bury the man. He doubted there would be much left of the carcass when the scavengers were done with it. He hadn't any sympathy to spare for the bushwhacker. His every sense was focused on how to get to Anabeth Calhoun in time to prevent her death or debauchery—or both.

The outlaws hadn't bothered to hide their trail, most likely because they had expected Whiskey's ambush to get rid of Jake if he followed them. It was the middle of the night when Jake finally caught up to the men he was following.

They had made camp in the shelter of some rocks. He looked first to find out where the Kid was sleeping. She lay close to the light of the fire. He wasn't surprised that they had tied her up, but he wasn't happy to see the rope that ran from her hands up under Wat Rankin's blanket. Not that he could blame the man. He didn't trust the Kid farther than he could throw her himself.

It wasn't going to be easy stealing her out of there without somebody getting shot. Jake rubbed the bristle on his chin. He might have to follow them for a while and try to take her from them on the trail.

As Jake was contemplating, he saw Anabeth begin to move. It was soon clear that the rope which bound her to Wat Rankin was no longer attached at her end.

Jake held his breath, waiting to see if she would escape on her own. *Run, Kid! Run!*

But she didn't run. As silently, as stealthily as any Apache she headed straight for Wat Rankin.

Jake cursed silently as Anabeth slowly inched the outlaw's gun from the holster that hung from the horn of the saddle he was using for a pillow.

Hurry up, Kid. Get your butt out of there!

She was holding the gun on Rankin now. He could see her trembling even from where he lay hidden. He watched her aim the gun at the sleeping outlaw's heart. But she didn't cock the gun. And she didn't shoot.

You're running out of time, Kid.

The outlaw had begun to turn restlessly on his pallet, forcing the Kid to take a step backward—where she snapped a twig.

The noise was loud in the soundless night. Rankin awakened instantly and reached for a gun that wasn't there on the way to his feet.

Shoot! Dammit, shoot the gun! But Jake shouted it in his head. The Kid never heard him.

Anabeth was frozen, staring into the eyes of the man who had shot her uncle in the back. She wanted desperately to pull the trigger. But she couldn't.

She swallowed hard. Despite her professed ruthlessness, Anabeth hadn't been able to shoot a sleeping man. Now the villain was fully awake, his venomous eyes full of murder and mayhem. Only he was unarmed, defenseless. She could have her revenge for Booth's death, but she would have to commit cold-blooded murder to get it. Jake's words replayed in her head. *It makes you no better than they are.*

"You ain't gonna shoot, Kid, so put that gun down before you get hurt."

"Stay back! I will shoot!" Anabeth warned.

Wat took a step forward. Nothing happened.

Except the gun began visibly shaking in Anabeth's hand.

Wat took another step. His lips pulled back to expose a ghoulish grin. "Go ahead and shoot her, Teague."

Anabeth heard the *snick* behind her and knew Teague had cocked his gun. She turned and fired at the same moment.

Teague looked from her horrified eyes to the hole in

his belly. "You shot me!" he said. "Goddamn if you didn't kill me!"

"You've always done what you were told, Teague," Anabeth said in a raspy voice. "You even shot Booth because someone told you to do it. This time you should have stayed out of it."

By now the other outlaws were also awake, but none of them dared to reach for their guns while Anabeth held a weapon aimed at Wat. Things were at a dangerous stalemate, and someone besides Teague was surely going to die.

Finally, Jake conceded that if he didn't do something, the Kid was going to get herself killed.

"You're outnumbered," Wat said, reaching for the gun in Anabeth's hand. "Hold it right where you are—"

"No, you hold it right where you are," Jake said.

When Rankin whirled to search out the voice in the darkness, the outlaws dove for cover.

And Anabeth ran like hell on wheels.

Jake kept the outlaws pinned down with gunfire while Anabeth escaped into the night.

When the shooting stopped a few minutes later, the outlaws realized they were alone. Their prisoner and whoever had called out to her from the darkness were both long gone.

13

Claire had been Wolf's captive for a week. She still hadn't gotten over the shock of finding her son among the savages.

She had stared at the small boy backed up against an Apache brave and known it was Jeffrey. She had been sure of it. The boy's eyes were as green as the leaves on the trees. Surely no Apache had green eyes! His banded hair had been slicked down with some kind of animal grease that made it considerably darker than the blond it had been three years ago. His nine-year-old body was lithe with muscle it had never had and tanned nearly as dark as the copper shade of the Apache boy beside him.

"That's my son!" she had cried, pointing at the buckskin-clad boy.

Wolf had put his arms around her to restrain her. "Come away from here, Little One. This boy's parents are known to me. He is not your son."

Claire had struggled to be free. "You don't understand. That boy is my son!"

Wolf looked at the child Claire had pointed out. "That is the son of Broken Foot. He is called White Eagle."

"His name is Jeffrey," Claire insisted. "I thought he

was dead. Sam told me—oh, Sam!" She choked on a sob of frustration. "You lied to me! Jeff wasn't killed. He was *stolen*!"

Claire's throat was swollen with joy and with pain. To find Jeffrey was a miracle she couldn't have imagined. She wanted to ask her son about everything he had been doing for the three years they had been separated. Most of all she wanted to hold him in her arms, to feel his heart beat next to her own.

The boy Claire had pointed out turned around and said something to the Indians behind him, who laughed.

Claire turned her eyes up to Wolf. "What did he say?"

Wolf frowned. "You do not want to know."

"I do! What did he say?"

"He was making fun of you—of your size. He said you would barely make a mouthful for the camp dogs."

Claire turned wounded golden eyes on the boy and saw the disdain and defiance in his eyes. She felt a twisting stab in her belly as the truth dawned on her. *This boy was Jeffrey, but he was no longer her son.* The child who stared back at her with such dislike and scorn must have no memory of what they had shared together. It wasn't possible that he could remember her and yet treat her so cruelly, was it?

She thought of the Tripley boy, who had been returned to his parents after spending four years with the Apache. James Tripley had ruthlessly murdered his white family. It occurred to Claire that perhaps Jeffrey had purposely chosen not to acknowledge her.

It was like losing him all over again.

Claire looked down at the pitch-covered water basket she held. The ache in her chest was as strong a week later as it had been the day she had stumbled past the crowd of dark-eyed strangers toward the stream she and Wolf had crossed to reach the village. She headed there again.

Claire dropped to her knees beside the stream and stared with unseeing eyes into the water that rippled by her. In the past week her life had been turned upside down. She needed to put the jumbled pieces of her life back together in a way that made some sense.

Why had Sam lied to her about Jeffrey's death? How had he faced her every day knowing the awful secret he had harbored? She tried to imagine what might have caused him to tell her Jeffrey was dead. The obvious answer was that he had wanted to spare her the pain of knowing her son was perhaps alive and living among the savages. Sam had also seen the carnage left by the Tripley boy. *But, Sam,* she cried to the heavens above her, *at least I would have been able to hope!*

Mightn't that have been worse? Look at the truth she had discovered. How long had it taken Jeff to learn to hate her and Sam? How long had it taken him to become truly a savage? What if they had found him like this and tried to bring him back to the white world. Would Jeff have been able to learn to live as though his captivity had never happened? Not if the Tripley boy was any example.

Claire closed her eyes in acceptance of the awful truth. Jeff's life among the Indians—who taught their children the arts of thievery and merciless killing—might have changed him forever. She doubted that her son's life among the Indians could ever have been erased from his memory.

But if that were true, wasn't it equally true that Jeff must retain some memory of his life with her and Sam? Claire had confronted her son that first day in a way that had made it impossible for him to acknowledge her without having to deal with the reactions of all those other Indians. Maybe if she had approached him alone he would have run into her arms.

Well, perhaps that was hoping for too much. But surely in only three years Jeff had not forgotten all the English he had learned as a child. Surely she would at least be able to talk to him, to find out if he was happy, if he had ever thought of her and Sam, if he had ever hoped for rescue and despaired when it did not come. Surely there was some hope that she could find a way to reach her son.

Hope. What a powerful word it was! It gave Claire the courage to survive her primitive surroundings, to face the challenges that were constantly thrown in her path. And to have a reason to conquer them.

The woman Wolf had called Night Crawling tugged on the sleeve of the fringed buckskin clothing she had been given to wear. Night Crawling pointed at the stream, at the basket Claire stilled hugged against her, and then back at the water again. Even without words, her meaning wasn't difficult to understand.

"All right," Claire said. "I'm filling the pitcher." When she had it full of water and stood again, the old woman started pulling her toward Wolf's lodging. Claire followed, noticing for the first time since she had arrived in the village the sharp rocks and dew-damp grass beneath her moccasined feet.

Suddenly everything around her was vivid, as though someone had enhanced all the colors, all the smells, all the textures. Her eyes sought out the Apache children laughing and playing with a hoop nearby. It startled her, somehow, to discover that such a savage people also began life as children playing games.

Claire breathed deeply, catching the tangy scent of venison cooking and a breeze redolent with manure from the herd of horses she knew must be picketed

somewhere among the pungent juniper and pines. All
were familiar smells, and yet slightly foreign.

She cocked her head for the soft, guttural sounds of
a group of Apache women talking as they pounded
seeds in stone bowls. Gossiping, she supposed, as
women everywhere spoke of home and family and
hopes and dreams.

Claire looked up at the fluffy clouds drifting by in a
sky so blue and bright it hurt her eyes. Was the sky so
big, so brilliant at home? She thought it must be, only
she had not seen it for so long it seemed brand new.

The stones pressed into the arches of her feet, making her more careful where she stepped. The small
hurts surprised Claire because she had not felt—anything—in so long that she actually welcomed the pain
as a sign that she was once again among the living. In
fact, Claire had not felt so alive in the three years
since she had first learned that her son had been
killed by Apaches.

She followed Night Crawling back to Wolf's lodging. There the old woman showed her where to put
the water.

Claire had never considered what the life of an
Apache woman was like, but over the past week she
had been getting a rugged introduction. Every day
she learned something new. Night Crawling handed
Claire a large burden basket and gestured for her to
come along.

Claire recognized the narrow-leafed yucca plant
when the old woman pointed it out, but had no idea
what she was supposed to do. The old woman broke
off the slender green central stem, which was still
without blossoms, and put it in the large basket they
had brought along.

Once they had a number of stems in the basket they
headed back to camp, where the woman instructed
Claire how to peel the pieces of stalk and cut them up.

They carried the yucca to a wide, deep hole that contained heated stones that made it into an oven. The prepared yucca was placed on the heated stones and covered with dampened grass. Then the hole was covered with earth to bake the plants inside.

That was only the beginning of the workday. Claire went with the old woman to gather wild onions and helped her strip bark from the yellow pine and scrape off the sweet insides. When that was done, they gathered wood.

Night Crawling tied the short pieces of brush and sticks together in a bundle at either end with a hide rope, leaving a loop in the middle. Then she showed Claire how to put the loop over her head and across her chest to support the load of wood on her back.

Claire was indignant at the thought of becoming a beast of burden, until she saw the old woman do the same thing herself with another load of firewood.

Once back at camp, Claire was given the disgusting job of skinning several wood rats and a couple of prairie dogs. Not that she found the skinning difficult. It was the thought of eating the animals later on that made her stomach queasy. She was relieved to see there was also venison cooking.

Later in the afternoon, Claire was shown how to replace the soles of a pair of buckskin moccasins which she felt sure belonged to Wolf. While she removed the worn-out soles from the decorated upper part of the moccasin she wondered for the first time where Wolf had spent the day. Over the past week, she hadn't had a spare moment to think about him. She had rarely even seen him.

Claire might not have seen Wolf, but the same was not true of the reverse. In fact, Wolf had checked often to see how his captive was faring. But he did not interfere with the woman's work his mother had

set her to do. Once again, the white woman had
amazed him with her strength and fortitude.

They met again for the first time in a week face to
face over the campfire at the evening meal. They were
sitting cross-legged outside on the ground. As Wolf
chewed on a piece of venison he asked, "How was
your day?"

"Hard."

"It is good that you learn to do a woman's work."

"Why?"

Wolf was stymied for a moment. It was easier to
answer the question with a question. "Why should
you not?"

"Since you plan to trade me for Anabeth, I won't be
here long enough for it to matter."

Wolf's lips flattened. "Perhaps." Before any trade
could be made, he had to find Stalking Deer. That
was not proving an easy task.

"While I'm here there is something I want," Claire
said.

"What is that?"

"To learn your language. Will you teach me?"

Now it was Wolf's turn to ask, "Why?"

"I want to be able to speak to my son." *And perhaps
persuade him to escape this place with me.*

Wolf put down his venison and wiped the grease
from his fingers onto his thighs. It was a custom every
Apache followed, to thus feed his legs, to keep them
strong for running. "I have spoken to Broken Foot.
He says there was no woman near the canyon where
he found White Eagle."

"I was at home. My son was with my husband."

"You have no man to share your blankets."

Claire's head turned sharply. "How do you know
that?"

"I looked into each window of the house by the big
rock to find Stalking Deer. You slept alone."

"My husband was recently killed by outlaws."

"So you have no man to hunt for you, to protect you from your enemies?"

Claire took a deep breath. "No. I have no man. All I have left is the land where I lived with my husband. And now my son."

"You have no son," Wolf said in a hard voice. "White Eagle has a new mother and father now."

"But he's my son!" Claire cried.

"Enough! He is Apache. He cannot go back to live among the white man."

"Then I must learn Apache! You will teach me."

Wolf's eyes narrowed. Even Stalking Deer did not dare so much. An Apache brave took orders from no man—or woman.

"If I have to stay here, it will be easier if I can speak the language," Claire reasoned. "Please."

Wolf hesitated. To grant her request would make it necessary for him to spend time with her. The thought of sitting next to her, of looking into her golden cat's eyes as he taught her the Apache words that described his world, caused a tautness in his body. The temptation was there to deny her, to avoid the situation entirely because he was not comfortable with it. But to deny her, he would have to acknowledge to himself the strange power she had over him. And that he refused to do.

"It shall be as you ask, Little One," he said at last. "I will teach you the words."

Claire clasped her hands together between her knees to keep from clapping them. There was a chance now that she could reach Jeffrey. Once she knew the words . . .

"When can we start?" she asked.

"Let me eat in peace, woman."

Claire dropped her eyes, unwilling to allow him to see her triumph. She forced herself to eat some venison and even some of the baked yucca she had helped to make, which wasn't the best-tasting vegetable she had ever eaten, but not the worst either.

They had almost finished eating when they heard shrieks and shouting, followed by more shrieks. It sounded like the commotion was headed in their direction. Claire searched the gathering darkness for some sign of what had caused the excitement. She got her answer in the form of a black-and-white-striped animal that scurried practically across her toes.

"Don't—"

Whatever warning Wolf was about to give was lost in Claire's startled cry. "Skunk!" She jumped up, frightening the animal, who turned tail and let go. In the shadows someone stopped short, not bothering to chase the skunk any farther, because the animal had left the best part of himself behind. As a gift for Claire.

Claire was gasping at the pungent perfume that covered her from head to toe.

"He Makes Trouble!"

"A *lot* of trouble," Claire rasped. She couldn't seem to catch a breath of air that didn't choke her.

"He Makes Trouble!" Wolf said again.

Suddenly a boy of about six appeared before Wolf, his face split by a wide grin. "Did you call for me?"

"This is nothing to smile about!" Wolf chastised. "Did you set that animal loose in camp?"

The grin disappeared, replaced by a rebellious look. "It was only a little skunk."

Wolf's nose pinched as he caught a whiff of the reek coming from the white woman. "It was big enough," he muttered.

"Am I hearing you right?" Claire held her clothes away from her body—as though that would help keep the awful smell from sinking into her skin. "Did that child purposely chase that skunk in my direction?"

Wolf sighed. He Makes Trouble had earned his name. For a child so young he had provided more than his share of chaos in the camp. "Go away, He Makes Trouble. You are not wanted here."

Furious as she was at the child for what had happened, Claire couldn't help noticing how the boy stiffened when Wolf ordered him to go away. But there was no remorse in the uptilted chin, the pugnacious jut of the boy's jaw as he faced Wolf, then turned and ran off into the darkness.

"Come, I will take you down to the river so you can wash yourself. The smell will not completely disappear, but at least we will be able to breathe again."

Claire followed him gratefully to the stream. She couldn't help asking, "Where are that boy's parents? Can't they keep him from doing things like this?"

"His mother is dead. His father . . . He is like me. He has no father."

"His father is dead?"

Wolf shook his head. "His mother slept with many men. He Makes Trouble has many fathers."

Claire was confused. "I don't understand. How can a boy without a father have many fathers?"

"Each man who shared the blankets with He Makes Trouble's mother helped to create him. Some part of each man can be found in the boy. He has my eyes," Wolf said.

"Your eyes? *You* slept with his mother, too?"

Wolf nodded. "I am but one of his fathers. There are many who claim a part of making him."

Claire recollected what she had seen of the boy's dark brown eyes. They were not quite as black as Wolf's, nor as widely spaced. But certainly the look in them had been the same as Wolf's—fierce and defiant.

"Who does He Makes Trouble live with? Who takes care of him?" Claire demanded.

Wolf shrugged. "He eats where there is extra food. He sleeps in a wickiup at the edge of the village."

"You mean no one wants anything to do with the boy himself—only his parts," Claire accused. Then she realized Wolf had said the boy was like him. "Was it like that for you? Did you grow up all alone like that?"

"I had a mother."

Claire tried to imagine whether that would make a difference, and if so, how much of a difference. She looked at Wolf with new eyes. Had he been an outcast like this child, forced to pull pranks to be noticed at all? Proud and disdainful when the only attention he got was a cry to "Go away and leave us alone!"

Her heart went out to He Makes Trouble. And to Wolf. Even though they were Apache. Even though these people had stolen her son. It was hard to keep hating all Apaches when they had become individuals. Like Night Crawling. And He Makes Trouble. And Wolf. And her own son, White Eagle.

"You can undress over there," Wolf said. "Your clothes will have to be buried later."

Claire slipped behind the bushes Wolf had indicated and gratefully pulled off the buckskin clothing. This was no time for false modesty. Claire couldn't wait to get out of the stinking clothes. The night was dark. It was cloak enough for her.

Besides, Wolf had said he did not desire her.

Those were his words, but Claire remembered his body had said otherwise. Still, she did not think the threat was great. He could have had her naked at any time this past week simply by demanding it. He hadn't. He had left her alone to do the work of a woman. Nor had she been beaten or tortured or even mistreated.

Claire smiled ruefully. With the way she smelled

now, it was unlikely any man would want to be near her—for a few days, at least.

When she had stripped down she stepped from behind the bushes, slipped into the frigid stream, and ducked her head underwater. When she came up, she could breathe easily again.

It was so dark that Wolf's voice seemed to come out of nowhere. "Rub yourself with sand," he advised. "It will help get rid of the smell."

Claire reached down and grabbed a handful of sand and began to rub it gently against her skin.

"I will be back in a little while."

"Wait! Where are you going?" But he was already gone. Claire laughed. She was stark naked in the middle of an Apache Indian village, and the only clothes she had to put on reeked of polecat perfume. She took advantage of Wolf's absence to clean herself as thoroughly as she could. By the time she was done, her whole body felt raw, sensitized by the cold and the rough sand.

She began to shiver. She supposed Wolf had gone to find her something to wear. What was taking him so long?

"You are very beautiful."

Claire froze. She had gotten out of the water because the air was warmer, and she stood now pressed up against one of the cottonwoods that lined the stream. Gradually she made out the silhouette of the Apache standing several feet from her. Gooseflesh rose on her arms. It wasn't the cold. It was . . .

Anticipation. Fear. Excitement. The myriad emotions assaulting her senses left Claire feeling breathless. "Did you bring something for me to wear?"

"Yes. I brought something else as well. Something I think might help." He took a step toward her.

"Don't come any closer."

He took another step.

There was nowhere she could go, no way to escape. Claire's heart pounded. Her stomach did a strange flipflop.

"Do not be afraid, Little One. I will not hurt you."

His words were soothing, his voice a low, mellow sound. But he continued stalking her.

The moon had risen and Claire could see his eyes glittering in the darkness. He stood in front of her without touching her for a moment. Claire could feel the heat of him. She flinched when he reached out a hand. Instead of his fingertips she felt something cool and smooth against her skin. He began to rub it across her shoulder, past her collarbone and down across her breasts.

"What is that?" she managed to ask.

"Sage."

It was nearly as strong a scent as the other smell that had soaked into her skin, but much more pleasant. Claire put her hand on Wolf's to stop the motion that was causing such disturbing sensations.

Wolf dropped the sage in his hands and took more from a pouch he wore at his belt. He crushed the leaves in his powerful hands, then divided the pungent greenery into two handfuls.

He began again at her shoulders, pressing hard enough to force the sage to release its scent onto her skin. From her shoulders his hands turned inward, down over her breasts. When he reached her belly his hands slid in opposite directions, each seeking a hip bone, and then turned downward just to the nest of curls at the apex of her thighs.

Claire held her breath. She thought he held his, too.

Instead of going any lower, Wolf's palms slid around to her flanks and finally to her buttocks. His arms completely surrounded her now, and Claire had never experienced the sort of tension she was feeling now.

She was aware of Wolf's every move. His body was taut. A muscle in his jaw jerked. Though the night was cool, a thin sheen of moisture caused the moonlight to reflect off his skin. His dark eyes were hooded, his nostrils flared.

Claire recognized the slow, careful movements of an animal that has cornered its prey and must decide when to make the leap that will result in the ultimate conclusion of the hunt.

Claire had to take a breath or die. It was an appalling thing to admit, but she was as aroused as the man standing before her. The awful thing was, she was certain his intention when he had begun to apply the sage to her body had not been to seduce her. That had been the result all the same.

She saw the moment when he acknowledged the truth of the situation. She let the air sough out of her lungs, then reached out and placed her fingertips on his chest to stop him. Or so she thought.

The warmth of his flesh, the softness of skin over corded sinew and muscle drew her, so that her hand moved across his chest in much the same slow caress as his had. She skimmed across a male nipple that tightened to a hard bud, and then down over a washboard belly that involuntarily jerked at her touch.

Claire trembled at the wave of need that washed over her, threatening to buckle her knees. She didn't know what magic web he had woven, didn't understand how she could desire a man who had kidnapped her, and who held her captive.

But she did.

She did not try to understand what was happening. She did not fight it. If the Apache wanted her, she was his. All that remained to be seen was whether he would accept the gift she offered him.

"Wolf?"

She felt him shudder under her hand. His eyes were heavy-lidded, his breathing harsh. Whatever fire burned in her had not left him unscathed.

He dragged the sage up her back, pulling their bodies close together. The feel of his smooth, hot flesh against her breasts was a sensation so exquisite as to be almost unbearable.

"Wolf?"

Abruptly he stepped back from her, chest heaving, body taut. He whirled and stalked a few paces away, then returned with buckskins that he threw at her. "Put these on."

Claire felt a myriad of emotions at Wolf's rejection of her. Humiliation. Anger. Relief. Regret. Then anger again. Had Wolf been playing some subtle game with her? One look at the pulse throbbing in his temple, at the tautness in shoulders and thighs, convinced her that he had shared in the madness that had overtaken her.

Claire stepped into the fringed skirt and tied the thongs at her waist, then pulled the shirt over her head and laced it up in front. She could tell even in the dark that the buckskins were exquisitely made. Her fingertips lingered on the intricate workmanship of the porcupine quill decoration.

She could feel his eyes on her, caressing her, even as her hands smoothed the soft skins over her body.

Wolf muttered something she couldn't understand. "What did you say?"

For a moment she thought he wouldn't tell her. He repeated the Apache words slowly. "What does it mean?" she asked.

"It is your first lesson," he said. "One should not wish for what one cannot have."

He turned and walked away, leaving her standing there.

It took a moment for Claire to realize the import of what Wolf had said. She quickly saw the flaw in it. There was no one stopping Wolf from taking what he wanted. Except himself.

Where are you, Jake? she wondered. *Do you know yet that I'm gone from home? Are you searching for me? Find me soon. Please, find me soon!*

14

Jake was searching for a woman, but it wasn't Claire. Anabeth had slipped away in the dark, and it took him nearly half an hour to find her, even though he was riding and she was on foot. When he caught up to Anabeth, Jake slipped out of the saddle and walked beside her, leading his horse.

Wat's gun still hung from her hand. He reached down and took it from her and threw it away as far as he could. She was his prisoner again.

"You're crazy, you know that, Kid?"

Anabeth glowered at the persistent man who had tracked her down. "You mean because I couldn't kill an unarmed man? I lost my nerve."

"You're just not a cold-blooded killer, Kid. That's nothing to be ashamed of." Jake put an absolutely brotherly hand on her shoulder—and was immediately aware of the softness of the flesh beneath his fingertips.

His touch might be brotherly, but his feelings, unfortunately, were not. But there wasn't time to think about anything right now except putting miles between them and the outlaws Jake was sure would follow them.

"Rankin and those other two are going to catch up

to us pretty soon. If that valley of yours is as well hidden as you say it is, I'd suggest we head in that direction."

"I prefer to go alone."

Jake's voice hardened. "That isn't a choice. There's the small matter of Sam's gold to be resolved."

Anabeth flashed a look at him. The distant sound of hoofbeats interrupted what she would have said to him.

Jake threw himself onto the buckskin and held out a hand to Anabeth. "Come on, Kid. We've got to get out of here."

Anabeth reached out and took his hand, and he pulled her up behind him.

"Hold on tight. We'll have to make a run for it."

Anabeth grasped Jake around the waist and held on for dear life as the buckskin bolted into a gallop. They ran for several miles, then slowed to a trot, then ran again, always in the direction of the valley. The outlaws stayed on their trail through the night.

Anabeth considered pulling Jake's gun from his holster and demanding her freedom. What stopped her was the unsettling realization that if she left him in this dry land without a horse or weapon he would either die of thirst or be killed by the outlaws chasing them. So she rode through the night with him, torn by the knowledge that her feelings for the Ranger had caused her to put his welfare before her own.

Forced together as they were on horseback, Anabeth was aware of Jake in ways she would rather not have been. His belly, where she had her hands clasped, was hard with muscle. She laid her cheek against his back and felt the flex and shift of sinew and bone.

Their constant closeness caused a strange tension deep in her belly, one that grew worse as the hours passed. Her breasts felt full and tight, and only by pressing against Jake could she ease the curious ache in them.

Jake finally stopped toward dawn, after a night when he thought he would burst with needing the woman who rubbed herself against him. He threw his leg over the horse's neck to dismount, then reached up to help the Kid get down. He should have held her at arm's distance, but instead he slid her down the entire length of him.

Which turned out to be a big mistake.

Startled, she looked down at him, at the blatant evidence of his arousal, and then met his gaze with wide blue eyes that seemed both too innocent and too aware.

"You should think twice, Kid, before you look at a man like that," he said in a ragged voice.

"Do you feel it too?"

"Feel what?"

"Sort of an ache. Here." She reached down to place her palm over her womb.

Jake half-laughed, half-groaned. "I've got a fire in me ready to burn you up, Kid."

A small gasp escaped Anabeth when Jake took her hand and placed it on the hard length that signaled his desire.

"Does it ache? Like I do?" she asked.

Jake couldn't imagine the kind of innocence that could ask such a question. But he couldn't resist it either. "Would you like me to make the ache go away?"

"Can you?"

A harsh laugh escaped Jake. "Ask me again when we're not running for our lives, Kid." He knew it was a mistake, but he couldn't let her go without touching her once. He laid a hand on her belly and watched her eyes drift closed as he slid his fingers down toward the cleft between her legs.

Jake felt his pulse leap when she spread her legs to make room for him. She reached out to grasp his forearms to keep her balance as she arched her whole body into his hand.

The soft, murmurous sound she made as his palm rubbed against her caused a corresponding tightness in his groin. He slid his hands across her belly and around to cup her buttocks, then pulled her tight against him.

The kittenish sound she made as his hardness pressed against her softness tore a corresponding groan from his throat. "Kid, you're going to get us both killed."

"Is this dangerous?" she asked.

"Only because it means we're not putting distance between us and the outlaws on our trail. We have to stop, Kid."

"But it feels good," Anabeth protested. Her hands slid up Jake's arms all the way to his shoulders, then found their way into the hair at his nape.

Jake shuddered at his body's powerful reaction to her touch. He looked down into blue eyes that were dark with desire and lips he found impossible to resist.

"Kid."

Anabeth's whole body quivered with anticipation as Jake lowered his head. His lips were wet and warm. She felt bereft when he started to lift his head, but a moment later he was back for more. This time he kissed only her upper lip, and then the lower one. Finally his tongue ran along the seam between them, and when she gasped with the pleasure of it, slipped inside.

Anabeth had never imagined the joining of mouths and tongues that allowed for Jake to taste her, and for her to taste him in return. His tongue slid in and out of her mouth, teasing her, taunting, leaving her wanting more. His hands held their hips together and Anabeth met his gentle thrusts as she reacted to the urgent need of her body to be closer than she was.

The attack came without warning.

Strong arms tore Jake away from Anabeth and latched around his throat. Jake tripped his attacker and the two of them fell to the ground, each grappling for a stranglehold on the other. The two men grunted with the effort of attacking one another and choked on the dust they churned up between them.

In the gray predawn light it took Anabeth a moment to realize who was fighting with Jake. "Wolf! Oh no, Wolf! Stop!"

Oblivious to her presence, the two men were locked in a fight to the death. Fists pummeled. Fingers gouged. Heads knocked. When the knife appeared in Wolf's hand, Anabeth knew she had to do something to keep them from killing each other.

When the shots sounded over their heads, both men froze, then looked up at the woman who held Jake's rifle pointed at them. "Get up, both of you," she ordered in an icy voice.

The two men disentangled themselves and stood, legs spread, shoulders squared, facing each other on balanced feet, ready to resume the battle when this lesser threat had been disposed of.

"Why are you with this man?" Wolf demanded in the Apache tongue. "You are mine!"

Anabeth bristled. She answered in the same tongue. "I do not belong to you! Or to him! He saved me from those who wished to kill me."

"So you let him take you in his arms?" he raged.

There was nothing Anabeth could do to stop the revealing flush that pinkened her cheeks. Nor was there anything she could say that would satisfy Wolf, as angry as he was. So she remained silent.

"You will come with me," Wolf ordered in English.

When he reached for her, Jake's arm clamped down on his wrist.

"Don't touch her."

"She belongs to me," Wolf said through clenched teeth. "I will return the woman called Claire to you."

Jake's heart stopped. "What? You have Claire?"

Wolf sneered and jerked his arm free. "I left her sleeping in my wickiup. You may have her in exchange for Stalking Deer."

A muscle jerked in Jake's jaw as he ground his teeth. The choice the Apache had given him was no choice at all.

"How did you get Jake's sister?" Anabeth demanded. "What is she doing in your village?"

"I came to the white man's house to get you—and took her by mistake," he said.

"You would have taken me against my will?" Anabeth was incredulous.

"You do not belong with the white man. You are mine," Wolf said, as though that explained everything. As far as he was concerned, it did.

"What if I don't want to belong to you?" she asked. "What if I would rather be with him?" Anabeth nodded her head toward Jake.

"Then I will kill him. And take you with me," Wolf said.

"She's not going anywhere she doesn't want to go," Jake said.

Wolf turned fierce eyes on the white man. "Then you will never see your sister again."

"You touch my sister, and if it takes me the rest of my life I'll hunt you down," Jake said. "I want Claire back. Unharmed."

"Then you will have to persuade Stalking Deer to come with me," Wolf said.

"I won't—"

Gunshots cut Jake off. He pivoted and saw that the

outlaws had caught up to them. He swore under his breath. When he turned back the Apache was gone. And Anabeth had gone with him.

Or so he thought. As Jake mounted the buckskin and spurred it away, he realized their tracks soon parted and went in two different directions. He followed the Kid's trail, anxious to catch up to her before the outlaws—or the Apache—did.

In fact, Wolf had grabbed Anabeth and pulled her along with him for some distance. She had yanked herself free and railed at him, "I will not be your woman, Wolf." They were running full tilt by then, and her voice was breathless as she warned, "If you try to take me to your village, I will only run away."

"Come with me—"

"No! Go away from me! I do not want you."

Wolf's face paled. But he did not argue further. He turned in a different direction and moments later had blended into the terrain.

Anabeth kept running. She knew Jake would come after her. She didn't intend to make it hard for him to find her. Indeed, it was only minutes before Jake rode up behind her, leaned down, and pulled her up and across his lap.

"I'll take the rifle, now."

Anabeth handed it over, and Jake put it back in the boot on his saddle.

"Will he hurt Claire?" Jake asked.

"Apaches don't make war on women and children."

"They killed Claire's son."

"Sometimes there are accidents. But I don't believe Claire will be mistreated. It's only the men who get—" Anabeth stopped.

"—tortured to death? Is that what you wanted to say?"

"The Apache learned what they know of torture

from the Spaniards. And the Mexicans. And the Americans." She put her hand on Jake's forearm, a gesture of comfort. "Claire will be all right."

"Will he let her go?"

"I can't answer that."

"Will he—" Jake swallowed hard. "Will he rape her?"

Anabeth turned stark eyes on Jake. "I don't know. If he decides he wants her . . ."

"But he would rather have you."

"Wolf and I grew up together. We were like brother and sister. I don't feel for him . . . what I feel for you."

She felt Jake's thighs tauten beneath her. She waited for him to ask her what it was she felt for him.

Jake held her tight, but said nothing, just spurred the buckskin into a lope again. The sky was beginning to lighten with pinks and yellows, a beautiful dawn breaking over the horizon.

They rode for most of the day with no sounds of pursuit. At last Anabeth asked, "Do you think we've lost them?"

"I doubt it."

"We're not far from the valley now. You can let me down here."

His arms tightened for a moment before he released her so she could slide to the ground. She headed directly for what appeared to be a solid rock wall. She picked up a piece of brush and began to wipe away their trail in the sand.

"What are you doing?" Jake asked.

"We've already passed by the entrance to the valley once. When we double back, I'm going to make sure there are no tracks for the gang to follow."

Jake turned and looked back at the high canyon wall. He saw nothing that looked like an opening. No wonder the valley had remained hidden. Jake turned and rode the buckskin back in the direction from which they had come, looking for the entrance to the valley. Still he saw nothing. He stopped the buckskin and waited for Anabeth to wipe out the tracks he had left.

She pointed to a slight vertical shadow along the wall. "There."

It was not until Jake was at the opening that he realized the stone overlapped a deeper wall and that it was possible to ride into the crevice.

"Stop there," Anabeth warned as she followed him inside. "This tunnel goes on for a while before you reach the valley. There are several booby traps to discourage unwanted visitors."

The tunnel narrowed in places so that Jake's stirrups scraped against the walls. At one point Anabeth showed Jake where a rockslide had been rigged. A small rope stretched across the narrow tunnel at ground level where it could be tripped by man or animal.

"What happens if someone triggers that slide?"

"We won't be leaving the valley again this way," she said.

"Is there another way out?"

Anabeth opened her mouth to tell Jake the truth, then shut it again. He was still a lawman determined to bring her to justice. She might need the advantage of being the only one to know the one other way out of the valley. She avoided answering his question by saying, "Don't worry. They're not going to find the opening. No one ever has. No one ever will."

"I hope you're right," Jake muttered. He saw the light at the end of the tunnel and slowed to let Anabeth lead the way into the valley. He was amazed at the size of it—the sheer cliffs on all sides, the acres of grassy valley that stretched out before him.

Sometime, aeons ago, a volcano had erupted and

mounds of molten lava had split and flowed around
this island of land. The lava had cooled, leaving a
pristine valley captured within its towering grasp. He
saw the stone house backed up against the wall near
the entrance to the valley, a fortress against intrud-
ers.

"You can stable your horse behind the house," Anabeth said. "There's a cave back there that has a seep
of water."

Jake began to appreciate the planning that had
gone into the placement of the house, with its protected water source. This must have been a perfect
hideout for someone like Booth Calhoun. A tunnel
that was hard to find unless you were right on top of
it. Booby traps to catch interlopers. And a fortress to
fight off anyone who managed to get past that first
line of defense.

"Come into the house, and I'll make us some coffee." Anabeth busied herself with making a fire in the
fireplace while Jake seated himself at the head of the
table. Here he was in the valley at last, but finding
Sam's gold suddenly didn't seem so important anymore. Finding Claire did.

"Can you take me to the village where that Apache
is holding Claire captive?"

Anabeth paused in what she was doing to look at
Jake with bleak eyes. "Even if I knew where it was, I
wouldn't take you there."

"Why not?"

"Because you would kill Wolf. Or he would kill
you."

"I can't just leave her there!"

"Wolf knows how to get here. He'll come to see me
again. When he does, I'll talk to him. Once he realizes
I'm not going to change my mind, he'll surely let
Claire go."

"What am I supposed to do, meanwhile? Just sit here and wait?"

She gestured to a book on the table. "You could read that. Maybe you can find a clue in there that tells where Booth hid your friend's gold."

"What is it?"

"Booth kept a journal. I've read it, but it doesn't tell any secrets."

Jake grimaced. It was better than doing nothing. Jake read through the day, looking for some clue, some hint where Booth Calhoun might have put the gold he had stolen from Sam. According to the journal, Booth had little to show for his life of crime. What Jake found in the journal were drawings of astonishing beauty.

Of Anabeth. Of the valley. Of Sierra Starr. It gave him an entirely different picture of the outlaw who was Anabeth's uncle. And explained in part why she wasn't the hardened outlaw she might have been.

While Jake was reading, Anabeth went out to walk the length of the valley by herself. What was Wolf doing now? she wondered. What would he do if he came to the valley and found Jake here? What words could she use to convince him that Claire must be returned to her home?

Anabeth was gone most of the afternoon. When she returned to the house, she found Jake outside. He had picketed the buckskin gelding where it could crop grass while he brushed its coat to a glossy gold.

Anabeth found a comfortable spot in the grass and sat down cross-legged to watch him work. "Did you find out anything from Booth's journal?" she asked.

"Nope."

"What will you do now?"

"Go on a treasure hunt, I suppose."

Anabeth pulled some clover and sucked on the

sweet juices at the end of the stem. "That sounds like it could take a while."

"However long it takes, I'm going to find that gold."

Anabeth twirled the stem between her fingers. "What about Claire?"

Jake's lips flattened. "Wolf will be coming here— for you. When he does, I'll be waiting for him."

"Jake—"

"Don't waste your time worrying, Kid. You be thinking about whether Booth ever said anything that might give a clue to the whereabouts of that gold."

It seemed urgent now to help Jake find the gold and get him out of the valley before Wolf returned. Perhaps it was time to reveal the words Booth had whispered as he lay dying. Maybe Jake would understand them. "Booth did say something about the gold before he died."

Jake's hand paused in mid-stroke. "What?"

"Just two words."

Jake dropped the brush and marched over to sink down on one knee beside her. "What two words?"

"I would have told you before, except they didn't make any sense to me, so I didn't see how it could make—"

Jake put his fingertips on her lips to quiet her nervous chatter. "Just tell me what he said."

"Back door."

"That's all? Just back door?"

Anabeth shrugged. "See what I mean? It doesn't make sense. There isn't a back door to the house, only a front door and a side door that leads to the cave. I can't imagine what he was referring to if it wasn't the house."

"What about a back way into the valley? Does such a trail exist?"

Anabeth lowered her eyes so Jake couldn't see them when she lied. "Not that I know of."

"What about that cave behind the house?" Jake asked. "How far does it go? Does it have a back way out?"

Anabeth's brow furrowed. "It's only as deep as it looks. We can look at it together, if you like."

"We? Does that mean you plan to help me search for the gold?" Jake asked.

"The sooner you find what you're looking for, the sooner this will all be over."

Jake felt a rush of irritation. "Then what, Kid? You have your Apache friend bushwhack me?"

"I'm not going to march willingly to the gallows, if that's what you're asking!" Anabeth retorted.

The argument might have become more heated, but it was interrupted suddenly by the sound of falling rock at the entrance to the valley.

Someone in the tunnel had tripped a booby trap.

Wat would never have found the entrance to the valley if it hadn't been for the dog. He and the Mexican and Snake had been up and down the length of the stone wall without finding anything remotely resembling an entrance to any secret hideout.

Just as they were riding away, a huge black dog had showed up. It had simply disappeared into the rock as though it were walking through the wall. Wat had rubbed his eyes and looked again, but the dog had disappeared.

"Let's get back down there," he said to the other two men.

"No, señor," the Mexican said. "I do not go down there."

"You go down there, or you don't get your share of the gold."

"A dead man cannot spend gold, señor."

"Suit yourself," Wat said. "Let's go, Snake."

The two outlaws rode down to the spot where the dog had disappeared. Even knowing that the opening was there, it was still difficult to find. Neither man was happy when they saw how dark and narrow the tunnel was that led inside.

"You go first," Wat said to the other man.

"Why don't you go first?"

"I'm boss here. I give the orders," Wat said.

Snake hesitated for a moment. Then, because he was afraid to say no, he did as he was told. He was careful. He moved slowly. He looked for the trap that he was sure was there. When he found it—a loaded gun on a trip wire—he dismantled it, then remounted and headed farther into the tunnel, confident that he could handle whatever he encountered.

Wat followed behind the other outlaw, keeping well back in case he should have to make a run for it. He heard Snake's cry of distress and then the cacophonous rumble of rock falling. He looked around at the walls and ceiling of the tunnel. Would the landslide ahead cause these walls to cave in and bury him?

Wat panicked. He couldn't turn his horse in the space he had, but he frantically backed the animal out of the cavelike tunnel. The animal was spraying stone with its hooves by the time Wat finally felt sunshine on his back again.

He was trembling and looked around to make sure there was no one around to see how scared he was. He used his bandanna to wipe the sweat from his face, then dismounted and stepped up to the tunnel opening.

"Snake!" He waited for an answer and called again. "Snake!" There was no answer, only the eerie echo of his voice coming back to him again. It was plain no one was getting into Booth's hideout this way. But that meant no one was getting out this way, either.

Solano heard the shouting and rode down to join Wat. "Where is Snake, señor?"

"It was a trap," Wat said. "Snake's dead." He gestured toward the rock wall. "Can you find another way to get inside there?"

The Mexican looked up at the towering cliffs. "Perhaps there is another way inside. But to climb this wall—it would be a difficult thing."

"Find me a way in," Wat said. "You do, and half the gold is yours."

"If the gold is there," the Mexican said quietly.

"It's there," Wat said. "Where else could it be? That girl is in there, too. You can bet on it. Once we get into that valley she'll tell us where the gold is, all right. I'm good at persuading people to tell me what I want to know."

Solano didn't doubt it. He would do his part and find a way into the valley. And leave it to the other man to take care of the girl. He was an old man. It would be nice to take his share of the gold and go back to Mexico.

If Rankin let him live.

The Mexican had no illusions about the true nature of the fiend who had arranged for the Calhoun Gang to brutally murder the man who had been their leader for many years. Look what had come of it. Of the six outlaws who had ridden in Booth's gang before Wat Rankin showed up, he was the only one left. He didn't trust Rankin, but he figured he was safe until they found the gold.

Once that happened, he would have to watch his back.

When Jake saw Dog crossing the floor of the valley he let go with a string of profanity. Dog must have shown the outlaws the entrance to the valley. "Apparently one of the outlaws tripped the booby trap at the end of the tunnel," he said.

"Do you think any of them got through?" Anabeth asked.

"Whether they got in this time or not, now they know for sure where the valley is." It was only a matter of time before they found a way inside. Which meant that he was racing against time to find the gold and get himself and the Kid out of here.

"There's Dog. He must have sniffed out the entrance to the valley!" Anabeth headed for the animal on the run.

"Don't touch him," Jake warned. "You go near him, and he'll take your hand off."

"He doesn't look vicious to me," Anabeth said. But she slowed her approach to the huge dog.

"Looks can be deceiving. You stay here. I'm going to see who found his way into the tunnel." And whether he had come out alive on the other side.

"I'm coming with you."

"Look, Kid—"

"I know more about this place than you do, Jake. I can help."

He stopped arguing with her and headed for the tunnel on the run. He stopped where he still had cover and checked to see if anything had been visibly disturbed around the entrance to the valley. There were stones blocking the entrance to the tunnel.

"It looks like we're not going back out that way," Jake said.

Anabeth was hanging over Jake's shoulder. "Do you see anyone?"

"No. But that doesn't mean someone isn't hidden nearby. You wait here, and I'll go take a look."

Jake might as well have been talking to a wall. Anabeth didn't stay put two seconds before she was right behind him again.

"Look, Kid. When I told you to stay put, it was for your own good. What if someone's down there with a gun?"

"You can be shot just as easily as I can." She stared at his wounded leg. "More easily," she said with an arched brow.

Jake gritted his teeth and kept on walking—make that limping—toward the valley entrance.

The gruesome sight they found made it clear no one had gotten out alive. A hand extended out of the stone —nothing more.

Anabeth pointed to a ring on one of the exposed fingers. "I recognize that ring. Snake wore it." Another of her uncle's murderers was dead. "It seems fitting somehow that he ended up buried like this."

"How so?" Jake asked.

"Because snakes are always hiding under a rock." Anabeth picked up a flat stone and finished the job of burying Snake's exposed hand. "Rankin knows we're here now, doesn't he?" she asked.

Jake looked sharply at Anabeth. "Yes. Unless he got caught in the slide, too."

"The slide wasn't rigged to catch more than one man," Anabeth said.

"Then he'll be looking for another way to get into the valley. Will he find it?"

"It's there," Anabeth admitted in a quiet voice.

"Will you show me where it is?"

"So you can stick me in jail and come back here to look for the gold on your own? No, Jake, I'm not that crazy. You're welcome to try finding it for yourself."

Jake grabbed her by the shoulders and turned her to face him. "It's not safe for you here anymore."

"This is my home. It's where my father and my uncle are buried. It's where I'm going to stay."

"What happens when Rankin comes after you? And he will."

"I'll be waiting for him."

He saw in her the determination of the outlaw, Kid Calhoun, for revenge. He had to finish his business here and get her out of the valley.

Jake grabbed her hand and dragged Anabeth after him. "Let's go find that gold."

15

Go away from me! I do not want you.

Stalking Deer's words rang in Wolf's ears. He was furious at the fact she had sent him away. But it wasn't only anger he felt. The sting of rejection had taken him by surprise. Not since he was a very young boy had he allowed himself to care what another human being thought of him. He had learned his lessons well as a son of many fathers. Or so he thought. He had not realized he could still be hurt.

When Stalking Deer had seemed unconscious of what Wolf wanted from her, it had been easy to convince himself that once she knew how he felt, she would change her mind and come to him willingly. It had been a shock to discover that she desired another. It had been an even bigger shock to realize on the journey home that when he tried to picture Stalking Deer beneath him, another woman took her place. A woman with golden eyes and tawny hair.

What he had felt when he saw Stalking Deer with the white man was not the result of jealousy so much as it was wounded pride. She had chosen another man over him. On the other hand, he realized that if another man had touched Little One, he would have killed him. Wolf did not know when his desire for

Stalking Deer had died. He only knew that what he
felt for her now was not the same as what he had felt
before he met Little One.

The closer he got to home, the more eagerly he
looked forward to the sight of his captive. He remembered Little One as she had been in the moonlight
when he had caressed her body with sage. He remembered her sleeping on a bed of animal skins in his
wickiup, where he had left her the next morning. He
could not understand why he found her so attractive.
But he was aware that he was not nearly so anxious
to force an unwilling Stalking Deer to come away
with him now that he held the golden-eyed white
woman captive.

Her brother wanted her back.

Wolf's lips curved in a feral smile. The white man
had Stalking Deer. It was only fair that Wolf should
keep the woman he had taken in exchange.

It was nearly dark by the time he reached the village. Wolf tried to imagine what Little One would be
doing when he saw her again. He pictured her sitting
at the fire before his wickiup preparing his supper.
Thus, when he arrived at his lodge to find there was
no fire, nor any sign of his captive at all, the anger
Wolf had thought under control, erupted again.

He strode through the village, nodding to those
who greeted him from their fires, but refusing to stop.
He did not ask if any knew where his captive could be
found because he did not want them to know he was
seeking her out. It would have told them more than
he wanted them to know about his interest in her.

When he had been through the entire village without finding any trace of her, he sought out his
mother's wickiup. He pushed aside the hide covering
and without even stopping to greet her asked,
"Where is she?"

"Welcome, my son. Who is it you seek?"

"You know who I mean. The white woman. Where is she?"

The old woman cackled. "You are eager for your woman, eh?"

Wolf scowled. "If you know where she is, tell me."

Night Crawling pulled the blanket tighter around her shoulders. "Maybe she sought out the blanket of another."

Wolf's eyes narrowed to slits. His mouth flattened. He knew she was taunting him, but he felt a tightness in his gut. "She does not like the Apache. She would not do such a thing."

The old woman cackled again. "Perhaps she does not like The People. But she has a softness in her heart for a small Apache boy."

Wolf frowned. "White Eagle?"

"No. He will have nothing to do with her. It is He Makes Trouble she has taken under her wing."

Wolf left his mother's lodging and headed for the small wickiup where He Makes Trouble spent his nights. It was isolated on the edge of the camp. A fire burned in front of the tiny brush lodging and the woman he sought was seated there cross-legged, stirring a pot of stew.

"What are you doing here?" Wolf demanded. "You should be at my wickiup waiting to serve me."

The smile that had started to appear on Claire's face froze half-formed. "I'm cooking supper for a small boy who would otherwise go hungry," she retorted.

"Where is He Makes Trouble?"

"He went to fetch some water for me," Claire said. "Did you find Anabeth?"

"Yes."

Claire's hand stopped in the act of stirring. "Was she with anyone?"

"Your brother."

Claire's head snapped up. She looked into Wolf's eyes. "Did you—? Is he—?"

"Your brother is with Stalking Deer. She chose to stay with him rather than to come with me." He paused and said, "So I will keep you—as my woman."

"What?" Claire dropped the spoon and stared at him. She wrapped her arms around herself protectively. "You can't mean that!"

"I do not say what I do not mean!" Wolf retorted.

"You can't—"

At that moment He Makes Trouble returned with a basket of water and set it down beside Claire.

"We will speak more of this later," Claire said.

"There is nothing more to say."

"Hello, Wolf." The six-year-old seemed to sense the tension between the two adults and sought a way to diffuse it. "Little One has cooked some food. Will you share a meal with us?"

Wolf saw the longing in the boy's eyes, the wary way he held himself to absorb the refusal of his offer that he was certain would follow.

But Wolf had walked too many miles in this boy's moccasins. "I will be pleased to join you at your campfire."

The boy's smile was jubilant. That alone would have been reward enough for Wolf. But the warm look of approval the white woman gave him caused a flush of pleasure to crawl up his throat and singe his cheeks. He tried to pretend that he was doing nothing special, but Little One's surreptitious looks, her pleased smile, made it clear she knew otherwise.

He Makes Trouble served Wolf the best parts of the stew, and split the rest with Claire. Wolf was pleasantly surprised at how good the food was.

"What have you put in here to make it taste so good?" he asked.

Claire muttered something he didn't hear.

"What did you say?"

"Sage." She glanced up with eyes that were luminous with the memory of what had happened between them.

Wolf's pulse leaped.

Before he could pursue the matter He Makes Trouble said, "I am teaching Little One how to speak with Apache words." The child beamed on his adult pupil and said, "Show Wolf what you have learned."

Claire dutifully recited the Apache words for all the items around the campfire as He Makes Trouble pointed them out. She mispronounced the word for "fire" so badly that both Wolf and He Makes Trouble laughed at her.

Claire smiled when she looked into the happy face of the tiny Indian boy. What a difference from the rebellious look he had borne when Wolf had called him to task for chasing the skunk through camp.

When the laughter died, Wolf grasped Claire's wrist and drew her to her feet. "It is time for us to go now."

"We can't leave He Makes Trouble here alone," Claire protested.

"It is where he sleeps."

"But he's too little to be here all by himself."

"I am not afraid," He Makes Trouble said, puffing out his tiny chest.

Claire realized she had touched the boy's pride. "I am sure you do not mind staying here," she said. "But what if Wolf invited you to his wickiup. Would you come?"

Claire glanced sharply at Wolf, daring him to rescind the invitation, then met the hopeful glance of the child.

The Apache boy obviously knew who had the final authority over such a suggestion. His eyes left Claire and sought out Wolf.

Wolf found himself in a quandary. He felt no responsibility for He Makes Trouble other than as a member of the tribe. If the boy asked him for food, he provided it. If the boy caused trouble—which was often—he chastised him for it. Wolf sympathized with He Makes Trouble's plight, for it had been his own. But he had never gone so far as to invite the six-year-old to share his lodging.

The white woman had. Wolf waited for her to plead with him to take the boy. She said nothing, merely looked at him with her wide, golden eyes. It was enough. Her eyes spoke words that needed no voice.

"He Makes Trouble," Wolf said at last. "I ask you to come to my wickiup."

The boy grinned. "I accept your invitation."

Claire laid her hand on Wolf's forearm, then leaned over to whisper in his ear, "That was a wonderful thing to do." She let go of him before he was ready to be parted from her, and bustled around banking the fire and putting things away to help get He Makes Trouble ready to go with them.

As they were leaving, she reached out to the child and Wolf was astonished to see the Indian boy slip his small hand into hers. Usually He Makes Trouble had nothing to do with anyone. Wolf was surprised at the boy's willingness to accept the closeness offered by the white woman. It dawned on him that the reason he had never seen the boy with another was because no one else had ever made the effort.

Wolf couldn't help frowning as he thought of the noise and inconvenience of having a small boy in his wickiup. What would the wagging tongues of the village have to say when they discovered what he had done?

Do you care what they say?

Wolf realized the white woman's approval meant more to him than the rest of the village combined.

Which made him uneasy. He must make it plain to her that she could not be inviting every stray she found to join them in their wickiup. It was already plenty crowded with the three of them.

The child was so excited it took him a long time to settle down. Finally, Claire lay down beside He Makes Trouble and put an arm around the boy to hold him still.

Wolf stared, unaware of the envy in his eyes. He wanted to be that boy. He wanted this woman to take him in her arms. To keep her from seeing his need he said, "I will go for a walk until the boy sleeps. Then I will return."

He saw the flash of fear in her eyes, quickly hidden. He made a sound of disgust that caused her to flinch. A moment later he was gone.

Claire refused to contemplate what would happen when Wolf returned to the wickiup. Instead she held the Apache boy in her arms and thought of her son. She hoped Jeff's Indian mother had found a way to ease the fears he must have felt when he was stolen from her three years ago.

She had tried again while Wolf was away from the village to reach Jeff, to speak with him. Her son had ignored the English words she spoke to him and taunted her in Apache. When she had tried to touch him, he had pulled a knife and threatened her away.

The Apache boy in her arms grunted and Claire realized she was holding him too tight. But he didn't try to free himself, and in fact snuggled closer. Claire couldn't help but see the irony in the situation. She was mothering an Apache boy while her own son refused to acknowledge her.

When He Makes Trouble had been asleep for a while and Wolf still hadn't returned, Claire separated herself carefully from the child and left the wickiup for a walk in the night air. She almost tripped over

Wolf as she stepped outside. He was sitting there in the dark.

She hesitated, then sat down beside him and asked, "Why didn't you come inside?"

"It was too noisy in there," he said disgustedly.

"He Makes Trouble never breathed a word once you asked him to be quiet."

"That won't last. Before long he'll be chattering like a jay."

"Good," Claire said. "Children should always be talking, asking questions, learning."

"An Apache child learns early to be quiet. To watch and to listen."

Claire grimaced. "I suppose that's a good lesson to know when there's danger around."

"There is always danger for an Apache these days," Wolf said.

"I never see him laughing and playing with the other children."

"I have told you the reason for that."

"Isn't there any way to change the situation?"

Wolf rubbed his chin thoughtfully. "If some family adopted him. Then perhaps—"

"Why don't you?" she interrupted.

Wolf was annoyed at Little One's habit of speaking her mind whenever she felt like it. No Apache woman would dare to interrupt. And what she had suggested —it was ridiculous.

"Why would I want to adopt He Makes Trouble?" His lips turned up wryly. "Believe me, he has earned his name."

"You should do it because he has your eyes. Because he is a part of you. Because it would be a good thing to do," Claire said in a rush.

Wolf's eyes narrowed as he looked at her. "And because you miss your own son, and want another child to care for?"

"No one can replace Jeffrey! I only thought—"

"No," Wolf said flatly. "I do not want a child to sleep between us."

"He wouldn't be between us," Claire argued.

Wolf met her eyes and waited for them to drop under his regard. She continued staring defiantly at him. He saw a way he could have what he wanted—at a small price. "I will take you at your word, Little One. The child may stay, but when we sleep, you will be by my side. The boy will sleep alone."

Claire had resigned herself to endure whatever was necessary during her captivity in the Indian village because she had hopes of someday reaching Jeff. She had let herself believe that she would not be forced into intimacy with Wolf. She realized now how naive she had been.

But if he was going to have her anyway, wouldn't it be better if some good came of it? At least this way, if she was ever able to escape this place, the Apache boy would still have a home. "All right," Claire said at last. "I agree to your terms."

"Go inside now," Wolf said. "I will join you in a little while."

Claire didn't hesitate, didn't argue, simply rose and shoved aside the hide opening and entered the wickiup. She arranged her grass bed on the opposite side of the spacious dwelling from the sleeping boy. She had no clothes to change into, so she lay down in the buckskins she had been wearing since the night Wolf had given them to her at the stream.

Claire heard the soft footfalls that signaled Wolf's return to the wickiup. She held her breath, lying perfectly still in the darkness. Unerringly, he walked toward her, stopping near her head. He sat down on the ground beside her and slipped off his knee-high moccasins.

He reached out in the dark and laid a hand on her

shoulder. His touch was gentle. "Are you asleep, Little One?"

"No."

His callused fingertips slipped between the thongs that tied at the shoulder. "Your skin is very soft," he said.

Wolf's hand slid up her shoulder to her throat, where her pulse throbbed. He felt her whole body quiver beneath his touch. He lay down next to her and pulled her back against him. But she remained stiff in his arms.

"There is no need to be afraid, Little One."

"I . . . this is the first time I've lain with another man besides my husband. I . . . it's too soon," she blurted.

Wolf remained silent for almost a minute. At last he said, "I am in no hurry, Little One. I can wait until you desire me as I desire you."

Claire half-laughed, half-sobbed. "You'll have a long wait!"

Wolf traced his hand down her throat and felt her shiver. He smiled with satisfaction in the darkness. "I do not think so."

Claire felt the color creeping up her neck. She was humiliated by her body's reaction to the Apache's touch. He was the enemy. She had to remember that so she would be able to leave here when the time came. She couldn't let herself admire him . . . or care for him . . . or desire him.

The thought that she could even consider coupling with him should have horrified her. It did not. In fact, she had stiffened in his arms because her body had been all too receptive to his touch. Claire felt confused by the feelings she was experiencing for a man she knew to be a savage.

She closed her eyes and clenched her teeth and tried very hard to hate him.

It was a long time before Wolf felt the woman in his arms relax. At last he heard the slow, steady breathing that told him she was asleep. He pulled her into the curve of his body and stared into the darkness.

He heard rustling on the other side of the wickiup. "He Makes Trouble?"

"I woke up and did not know where I was," the little boy said in a frightened voice.

"You are in my wickiup. You are safe here," Wolf said.

"Where is Little One?"

"She is here with me."

"Oh."

Wolf knew what the boy wanted, and that the child would not ask for it. He felt a strange tightness in his chest. He opened his mouth to invite He Makes Trouble to join them, then snapped it shut again. It was better not to raise the boy's hopes that his situation was changed merely because he had been invited to spend one night in Wolf's wickiup.

Among the Apache a bastard was not mistreated. But because he was different, he lived his life separate from the rest of the tribe. Wolf understood exactly what that involved. It was hard enough to survive the nomadic life of an Apache. A bastard had the additional burden of making it on his own. Wolf could not change He Makes Trouble's fate. It was far better if the boy accepted the truth about who he was and learned to live with it.

"Good night, boy," he said.

"Good night, Wolf."

Wolf closed his eyes and waited until he heard the boy settle before he succumbed to sleep.

In the morning, Wolf tried to turn over but couldn't because there was something in the way. Something warm. Something with arms and legs.

"He Makes Trouble!"

The child sat bolt upright. His smile was sheepish as he disentangled himself from Wolf.

Wolf scowled ferociously, but He Makes Trouble seemed unconcerned. A cuff was little enough payment for a night spent unafraid. Only Wolf did not hit him, and the scowl soon disappeared to be replaced by a different look entirely as Wolf watched the woman in his arms stretch and waken. He Makes Trouble took advantage of Wolf's distraction to escape outside.

Claire was still half asleep, but she was aware of a hard male body fitted against her as she stretched. A male hand caressed the length of her from shoulder to hip, then slid down to cover her womb and pull her back into the niche created by his hips. She could feel his arousal, and a corresponding heat deep in her belly where his hand lay against her.

"Sam?"

Wolf froze.

"Sam?"

Claire reached back to lay a hand on Sam's thigh. Only instead of long johns, the skin she touched was bare. Her eyes flickered open. It took a moment to orient herself.

She was not in her bed at Window Rock; she lay upon a grass pallet on the ground. It was not coffee, but the smoke of a campfire she smelled. And it was not Sam who lay beside her. Sam was dead.

Claire groaned, a ragged sound of despair.

The Apache brave pulled her more tightly against him. "I am Wolf. I am Apache. You are my woman," he whispered in her ear. "What came before must be forgotten."

"I can't forget!" Claire cried.

"You must."

"I had a husband. *I have a son*. And nothing you say can change that!"

Claire struggled to be free of Wolf's hold, but he easily turned her under him. He caught both of her hands in one of his. The sheer weight of him was enough to keep her captive beneath him.

"Be still," he said.

Claire was fighting the frustration of the situation as much as she was the man who had created it. She bucked under him and had the awful—arousing—experience of feeling his hardness pressed against her softness.

The husky sound she made in her throat caused Wolf's body to tense. His voice was harsh as he said, "Your husband is dead. Your son has a new family. Nothing you say or do can change that."

Claire swallowed hard. She felt the tears welling in her eyes and closed them. One slid out and rolled down the side of her face. Suddenly her hands were released and she felt herself pulled into Wolf's embrace. She resisted only briefly before she succumbed to the solace to be found in his arms.

Wolf didn't know what to make of the feelings roiling through him. He knew he was responsible for Little One's distress in part. But even returning her to the place from which he had taken her would not bring back her husband. Or her son. He had never held a crying woman. He wanted to take the pain away so that she would smile again.

His lips barely touched her brow, a gesture of comfort. His hands smoothed the tawny hair away from her face, and he brushed away her tears with the pad of his thumb. He murmured words in Apache, words he would not have imagined himself saying to any woman. Words of comfort. Words that told of his need to keep her safe. To protect her from harm. To take all the hurt away.

At last her tears stopped. She hiccuped, and the sound surprised a smile from him.

Claire sat up and eased herself from Wolf's arms. She wiped at her eyes and dabbed at her nose with her sleeve. "I don't know what came over me. I—"

A ruckus outside had Wolf on his feet and running before Claire could finish her sentence. She jumped up and followed him outside. It quickly became clear that He Makes Trouble had been hard at work earning his name. He was surrounded by at least four older boys who were taunting him with their bows and arrows.

"What is happening here?" Wolf demanded.

The four boys turned wide eyes toward the Apache brave. Clearly they hadn't expected any interference on He Makes Trouble's behalf.

"He wanted to come hunting with us," one of the boys said.

"But he has no bow—"

"—nor any arrows."

Wolf looked from the boys to the small nuisance who had been planted in his wickiup by the white woman. "Is this true?" he demanded of He Makes Trouble. "Have you no bow or arrows?"

The small boy's moccasin traced a circle in the dirt. The chin that nearly rested on his chest bobbed slightly.

"So . . ." Wolf turned his fierce, dark eyes on the other boys. "We will have to make you a bow and arrows."

The four boys stood stunned at Wolf's pronouncement.

"But—"

"Enough!" Wolf said. "Be gone now."

The four boys departed in different directions, like shifting winds. Wolf stood there feeling awkward, not sure why he had offered to do something that would require him to spend even more time in He Makes Trouble's company. Making a boy's first bow and arrows was a task that would ordinarily fall on a member of his family—his father or his uncle.

The boy's toe deepened the circle it was making in the dirt. "Did you mean it?" he asked.

"I do not say what I do not mean."

He Makes Trouble looked up, his eyes full of admiration for his new hero. Wolf felt his spirits lift. "After breakfast we will go look together for the wood from a mulberry to make your bow and some ocean spray or mock orange to make your arrows. Then you can hunt for feathers from the red-tailed hawk. For now, go and get some water for Little One."

He Makes Trouble shrieked a childish war cry and headed into the wickiup to get something in which to carry water.

Wolf turned to share a look with the white woman and saw her eyes still followed one of the boys as he ran away.

White Eagle.

Wolf might not have been paying attention to which boys were teasing He Makes Trouble. But Claire had been very much aware that Jeffrey was among them. She had caught her son's eye once, but he had quickly turned away. Even that small glance was enough to tell her that Jeff wasn't as unaware of her as he wanted her to think.

This incident pointed out to her another of the changes in her son. The child she had been raising would not have been so cruel as to tease a younger boy. Or if he had, she would have soon shown him the error of his ways. But Apache boys learned in a more ruthless school.

Claire had not been so focused on Jeff that she hadn't been aware of what Wolf had offered to do for He Makes Trouble. She met the Apache's dark-eyed gaze and smiled at him. "That was a wonderful thing you did."

"It is not the boy's fault that he does not have the weapons of a warrior."

"Now he will," Claire said.

Wolf grunted. It had begun to dawn on him that by agreeing to help He Makes Trouble he had put himself in the role of father to the boy. The last thing he had intended was to commit himself to the troublesome child in such a way. Only he had to admit he had felt good when the boy looked up to him. And he had basked in Little One's approval. He was startled from his reverie when Little One spoke.

"How do you say 'I love you' in Apache?"

Wolf told her the words and repeated them with her until she had them right. Finally he asked, "Why do you need to know these words?"

She kept her golden eyes lowered as she answered, "You never know when you may need them."

Then she turned and walked away, leaving him standing there. Wolf felt the band tighten in his chest. The woman and the boy were slipping past barriers he had erected years ago to keep himself safe. He did not know what to do to keep them at a distance. Most worrisome of all was the fact that he was not sure he wanted to.

Because he had realized as he taught his white captive how to say "I love you" that he wanted her to say the words to him.

16

It rapidly dawned on Jake that he was stranded in this godforsaken valley with a woman who irritated and infuriated him—and whom he desired with a violence he kept tethered on a short leash.

"Let's get a few things straight," he said to Anabeth their first evening in the valley. "I need you to tell me where to start hunting for the gold, but we won't be needing to spend much time together."

"I couldn't agree with you more!"

Jake threw his arm wide. "It's a big valley," he said. "There's no reason our paths have to cross any more than necessary."

"That suits me just fine!"

"You stay out of my way, and things will be fine around here."

"I'll be invisible," she assured him. "You go hunt for Sam's gold your way and I'll go hunt for it in mine."

Her eyes had darkened with every lash of his tongue, so that by the time he was through with his tirade they were almost violet.

"So we're agreed?" He wanted an argument from her. It wasn't like her to go along with him. He didn't care at all for the wounded look in her eyes.

But he hadn't underestimated her after all, because she seemed to visibly straighten as he stared at her— shoulders back, chin up, stance widened for battle.

All she said was, "I'm not about to hang around where I'm not wanted." Then she turned and marched away from him.

Jake had known he had to keep her away from him, but he felt a sense of loss as he watched her leave. He was torn by the contrast between the dangerous, destructive emotion he had perceived love to be as a child, and the protective, possessive instincts he felt for Anabeth as a man. He wanted to believe that it was possible to care for a woman and not end up being destroyed by the relationship. But with Anabeth, things were complicated.

Anabeth Calhoun wasn't just any woman. She was an outlaw who had sworn to take vengeance on other outlaws. She was a female brought up without the chance to behave as a woman. But whether she approached him as Anabeth or Kid Calhoun, he found himself attracted to her.

So he had taken the safer course. He had told Anabeth to keep her distance. And meant it. All the while wishing for something he felt sure he could never have.

Anabeth stayed away from Jake as he asked. But she found another challenge. At first she tried to get close to Dog simply because Jake had told her it couldn't be done. As the weeks passed and Dog remained aloof, she began to think that if she could just reach Dog on some level she would also be able to somehow, someday reach Jake as well.

They were two of a kind, the dog and the man, loners, not needing anyone or anything to survive. She was determined to prove Dog could be reached because that would mean Jake's stone wall could also be breached. Anabeth wasn't sure why that was so important to her. She only knew it was.

Anabeth never missed a chance to speak to the black beast. She would sit a half a field away from him and croon words that meant nothing. Dog never gave her so much as a glance. She would have despaired except his ears stayed cocked in her direction, and he lingered to listen.

She began to leave gifts of food for him. At first they remained uneaten until they rotted—or the crows got them. But she caught him once, sniffing the rock where the food had been. When he suddenly looked up to find her standing nearby he stared at her with his dark eyes for a full minute before he turned and trotted away.

Jake wasn't unaware of Anabeth's efforts.

"I don't want you to bother Dog anymore," he told her.

She murmured something noncommittal and ignored him.

What he had really wanted to say was that he didn't want her bothering him. But there was nothing she did overtly that he could complain about. She was simply there. Smelling like the green grass on a summer day. With eyes that seemed to have the whole damn sky in their depths. And flesh that looked like honey, so warm that he was dying to taste its sweetness.

But he had laid down the rules, and now he was forced to follow them. He was determined to keep his distance from her, and in order to do that he had to keep temptation from his path. Not that he had to worry. She never came near him unless she had to.

Unfortunately, she was never far from his thoughts.

Jake had watched her with Dog and felt the roots of a deeper feeling growing within him. Tendrils of need

twined around his heart, threatening the stone walls
that protected it from harm.

Jake knew he was in trouble when he saw Dog take
a slab of bacon right from the Kid's hand. Of course
Dog had immediately trotted away to eat it all by himself, but Jake knew Dog would be back. As he had
come back again and again for the sight of her. For
the scent of her. For the accidental touch of her hand
on his skin.

Anabeth had begun to feel a shred of hope that she
would succeed in taming Dog. It had taken her every
bit of three weeks, hour after hour, day after persistent day, before the huge beast would stand still long
enough for her to touch him. Dog had swallowed the
bacon she offered him whole, but he hadn't run from
her. He had stood there . . . waiting.

She had suddenly been afraid to reach out to him,
afraid that despite her patience, he would bite. Her
hand trembled as it settled on sleek black fur.

Dog shuddered, but he stayed where he was, black
eyes watching her steadily, muscles tensed for escape.

She slid her hand down the length of his back,
smoothing raised hackles. But when she lifted her
hand and tried to touch his head, he jerked and
bounded away.

"I never thought I'd live to see that," Jake said.

Anabeth stumbled getting to her feet, and Jake
reached out to break her fall.

"Let go of me!" she cried.

Jake let her go and watched with sucked up breath
while she somehow managed to regain her balance.

Anabeth's skin felt seared where Jake had touched
it. "Don't touch me! That was our agreement. You
keep your distance. And I leave you alone!"

She left him standing there by himself. Alone.

Jake had been slowly going crazy over the past

three weeks, watching her with Dog, watching her search for gold, watching her . . . when she didn't even notice he was alive.

Well, he was damned sick and tired of it! Let her act like a sulky child. He didn't have to.

That night he joined her for supper. He didn't say anything, but neither did she—just shared the bacon and beans she had cooked and took his dish away to clean afterward. She didn't acknowledge him in any way. She was as damned invisible as she had promised she would be.

Anabeth was more aware of Jake than he suspected, but she wasn't about to let him know it. When he wasn't looking she smiled to herself and thought how the mighty had fallen. A lonesome dog. And a lonesome man.

That evening Jake looked in through the glass windows from where he was spreading his blankets outside and discovered Anabeth was playing solitaire at the kitchen table. She had a glass of whiskey in front of her and a cigarette stuck in the corner of her mouth. There was nothing feminine about the pose, but he felt himself harden at the sight of her.

He walked inside and asked, "Where do you keep the whiskey?"

"Top shelf of the cupboard. There's a cup below."

Jake helped himself, then pulled out the ladderback chair across from Anabeth, turned it around and straddled it. "Mind if I sit here for a while?"

Anabeth just grunted and ignored him.

He watched for a while, noting how the single lantern on the table outlined her face in shadows of light and dark. He waited for Anabeth to invite him to join her. But she didn't.

At last he said, "How about a hand of poker?"

She looked up, surprised. "You want to play cards with me?"

Jake stood, turned his chair back around, and sat down facing her across the table. "A game of poker."

"What stakes?"

"Matchsticks?"

Anabeth laughed. "Oh, I think we should play for something more serious than that."

"Your cooperation finding the gold, then," Jake said. "If I have more matchsticks than you by, say, dawn, then you'll work with me to locate Sam's gold."

"And if I win?" Anabeth asked.

Jake grinned crookedly. "You name it."

"If I win, you'll tell me about yourself. I mean, answer any questions I want to ask about your life."

Jake sat stunned for a moment. Those were high stakes indeed. He eyed Anabeth and tried to gauge whether she could be any good at poker. Surely a face that open and innocent would reveal what cards were held by its owner. Jake took a gamble and said, "Three questions."

"What?"

"If you win, I'll answer three questions about myself."

Anabeth grinned. "Done."

Several hours later, Jake was having second thoughts. He stared into a female face so blank, so absent of emotion that he would have sworn there was no brain behind the eyes. In fact, the girl was shrewd beyond telling. Most of the matchsticks were already sitting in front of her. And she had done it by trickery.

In the first few hands her face had been animated with delight or despair—neither having anything to do with the cards in her hand, he had discovered to his chagrin. She might be smiling and have only a pair of deuces, and chewing on her thumbnail with a full house.

Once Jake realized her tactics, he tried to antici-
pate whether Anabeth was lying with her face or her
bet. But he wasn't much good at guessing. He lost
more often than not. It seemed like it was going to be
a short evening when he noticed a flaw in the Kid's
otherwise flawless bluffing.

When she had a good hand, Anabeth held her cigarette between two fingers while she bet. When she
had nothing, she kept the cigarette in the corner of
her mouth and squinted through the smoke. In an
embarrassingly short time, all the matchsticks were
sitting in front of him.

"I don't understand it," Anabeth muttered. "It was
as though you could see what I held in my hand." Her
eyes narrowed and she turned to look behind her for
a shiny surface that might have reflected her cards
back to Jake. But there was nothing. "How the hell
did you do it?"

"Superior play," he said with a rakish grin.

Anabeth gave a very unladylike snort. "All right. I
give up. How did I give myself away?"

"Depending on the cards you held, I could count
on your cigarette being held in your hand, or the corner of your mouth."

Anabeth disgustedly stubbed out her cigarette in a
tray on the table. "Damn! I'll have to give up smoking
when I'm playing, I suppose."

"You ought to give it up altogether. Along with
poker. And swearing. And drinking, too, for that matter. How can one woman have so many vices?"

"You have all the same vices," Anabeth retorted.
"I'll give them up when you give them up!"

"It's different for me."

"How?"

"I'm a man."

"So what?"

"The rules for women are different than the rules for men."

"Then I'll just follow the men's rules."

Jake laughed. "That won't work."

"Why not? So far I've been doing just fine."

Jake raked all ten fingers through his hair, leaving it standing on end. "So far you've been living your life as a man. What happens when you want to live it as a woman?"

"Why would I want to do that?"

"You tell me," Jake retorted, his patience at an end. If she couldn't see her proper role in life, he wasn't going to be the one to point it out to her.

After a long, uncomfortable silence, during which Anabeth shuffled and reshuffled the cards, she said, "I only know what I was taught by my father and my uncle. I don't know how to act like a woman acts, Jake. I'm more comfortable the way I am.

"Not that I haven't thought about becoming a lady," Anabeth said. "I felt like a real woman for the first time when I tried on the dress you bought for me. It made me feel . . . like the person I might have been if I hadn't grown up in Treasure Valley.

"But I enjoy riding astride. And smoking. And a glass of whiskey now and then. And I especially enjoy a good game of poker. Do I really have to give all those things up to be considered a woman? Isn't it enough to be just what I am?"

Jake swallowed hard. The appeal in Anabeth's voice was difficult to deny. "Sure, Kid. What you are is fine."

What you are is enough woman to drive me crazy.

"Thanks, Jake. I needed to hear that." She set the cards aside and said, "What time do you want to start hunting gold in the morning?"

"What?" Hunting gold was the last thing on Jake's mind.

"I don't cheat at cards, and I don't welsh on a bet. I'll be up whenever you want to go gold-hunting tomorrow."

"Early," Jake said. He wasn't going to get much sleep anyway, thinking about her, so they might as well get an early start.

"All right. I'll meet you out front in the morning. Good night, Jake."

Jake realized he had been dismissed. As a lady might dismiss a gentleman from her parlor. Only he was being sent outside to sleep under the stars. He rose and stretched, but his eyes never left Anabeth.

He watched her remove their whiskey glasses from the table and set them on the sideboard. Then she put the cards away in a box and put them in a drawer of the sideboard.

She turned suddenly and realized Jake was still in the room. "Jake? Is there something you want before you go to bed?"

She shouldn't have asked, Jake thought. Because he knew she wasn't going to like his answer. "You," he said.

Anabeth laughed nervously. "I don't understand."

"I want you."

Jake took a step forward and Anabeth retreated. "Just a minute," she said, holding a hand palm outward, as though that could stop his advance. "You told me to stay out of your way. Are you saying you've changed your mind?"

"Yes."

"I just want to be sure I've got this right. Are you saying you care for me?"

Jake was startled by the words she had chosen to attach to feelings he preferred to keep regarding as purely physical. "No, I don't think I'm saying that."

"So, what you want from me is what you can get

from a woman like Sierra Starr, is that it?" Anabeth clarified.

Jake could see the trap and walked into it anyway. "I suppose so, yes."

"I'm not interested. Good night, Jake." Anabeth turned and walked away from him to her bedroom door. She stopped and with the door against her cheek said, "I think maybe it's better if we stick with your rules from now on—except when we're hunting for Sam's gold. I'll see you tomorrow morning."

Jake came to relish the time they spent together over the days that followed. They searched the house, and he found the collection of wooden animals that Booth had carved for Anabeth, including a burro she said was her favorite. They searched the cave behind the house, and he found a collections of pretty stones that Anabeth had hidden there as a child. They searched the stream bed and the whole area around the pond, and Jake found Anabeth's breechclout.

Anabeth grabbed for it and said, "That's mine!"

"It looks Indian to me."

"It's an Apache breechclout. Wolf gave it to me."

Jake's brows rose nearly to his hairline when he saw how little there was to the garment. "What's it doing here by the pond?"

"I wear it when I go swimming."

"When you're alone?"

"Sometimes Wolf is here."

"Where's the shirt that goes with this?" he demanded.

"Hidden in the house."

Jake thought about it a moment and came to a conclusion that put a scowl on his face. "You wore this" —he shook the breechclout at her—"and only this— when you went swimming with that Apache buck?"

Anabeth nodded.

"He's seen you half-naked?" Jake was having trouble accepting that degree of intimacy between Anabeth and any other man—much less the Apache.

Anabeth put her hands on her hips and tapped her toe as though she were dealing with a not particularly bright child. "The first time I met Wolf I was six and swimming half-naked in this pond. What was there to hide later?"

"You sure are damned modest around me," Jake roared.

"I don't know you the way I know Wolf!"

"And whose fault is that?" Jake demanded.

"Yours," Anabeth retorted. "You asked me to leave you alone. And I have."

"Maybe I'll just change my mind."

"You do that!" Anabeth shouted.

Jake threw the breechclout down and marched off in high dudgeon. But he couldn't forget what Anabeth had said. Maybe it was time to admit—at least to himself—that he cared for her. Because, dammit, he did.

Shortly after their argument over the breechclout, Anabeth caught him swimming naked in the pond.

"I see you like swimming without even a breechclout!" she shouted as she scampered away with every stitch of his clothing, including his boots.

Chagrined to be caught with his pants down, so to speak, Jake stalked, stark naked, back to the other end of the valley to confront Anabeth and demand their return.

He had the satisfaction of seeing her flush to the roots of her hair before she flung his clothes in his face.

But by then his body had already shown her, in no uncertain terms, how much he desired her.

Two days later, she put a snake in his bedroll. He nearly had heart failure when his toe made contact with the reptile. He had already scrambled out of his blankets by the time he realized it was only a grass snake, and not something poisonous. When he looked up, he found Anabeth standing in the doorway of the house laughing like a hyena.

"You think it's funny now, Kid. But just wait. Your day is coming."

"Good night, Jake. Sleep tight. Don't let the bed bugs bite."

She was sound asleep the next morning when he lifted the covers and laid that selfsame snake on her belly. He leaned back against the stone wall, crossed his arms and waited for the fun to start.

It took about twenty seconds.

Anabeth's eyes flew open and she let out a shriek that would have done an Apache proud. The snake came flying out of bed first, and Anabeth soon followed.

Only, this time she was the one who was naked.

"Don't play games, Kid," Jake warned as his eyes drank their fill. "Because I always play to win."

His warning was wasted. A week later he took a bite of beans only to have his mouth catch fire.

Hot peppers!

"Water!" he gasped.

She held her hands wide and shrugged. "I've run plumb out," she said with a grin.

"Then maybe we better go get some," he replied in an ominous voice.

Jake yanked Anabeth from her chair and dragged her all the way to the pond. He didn't even hesitate, just picked her up and tossed her in.

"How does it feel to cool off?" he shouted down at her.

Anabeth came up spluttering and howling, but he was the one who suffered. Her wet shirt clung to her like a second skin, revealing rounded breasts and nipples turned to stiff peaks by the icy water.

He whirled and left her to climb out on her own, not trusting his self control.

Jake stopped sleeping near the house, unable to bear being so close and yet unable—unwilling—to risk touching her. There was no question he was walking the edge of restraint. The moment finally came when she pushed him over.

Jake was tossing restlessly in his bedroll. He had been worrying lately about Claire. Where was she? How was she? Why hadn't Wolf returned to the valley as Anabeth had promised he would?

But whenever he thought of leaving Anabeth here alone to go after Claire, he knew that even if he found the way out of the valley now he wouldn't leave. The Kid wasn't safe here. It was only a matter of time before the outlaws discovered a way into the valley. But he felt torn between needing to go and needing to stay.

Finally, he left his bedroll and headed for the pond at the far end of the valley.

He and the Kid had criss-crossed the valley together for the better part of a month now in search of Sam's gold. All to no avail. This was one of the last days of Indian summer, and Jake knew they were running out of time. If the outlaws didn't find them soon, winter would. He didn't plan to spend the winter alone in this godforsaken valley with a woman who turned his insides out every time he looked at her.

The moon was up and he could see as though it were daylight. He stripped quickly when he reached the pond and slipped quietly into the water. Which was when he realized he wasn't alone.

"Kid? Is that you?"

Jake's senses came alive when there was no answer. He had grown lax over the past weeks of isolation in the valley. He had brought no weapon with him to the pond. A quick search of the surface of the pond revealed nothing. His glance skipped to the area surrounding the pond, but he found nothing threatening there, either.

The hairs on the back of Jake's neck prickled, giving him a second's warning before a tempest erupted behind him. Water sprayed everywhere as two hands clamped onto his shoulders, forcing him underwater.

Jake's reaction was instant and instinctive. He whirled underwater and reached for whoever had attacked him. His huge hands grasped the neck of—

Jake kicked hard to reach the surface, bringing his assailant with him. He broke the water in a lunge that carried both him and his prisoner high in the air.

"Damn you, Kid!" he roared.

Before Anabeth could say anything they plunged back into the water. Jake grabbed Anabeth around the chest and swam to the edge of the pond. He hauled himself out onto the rock and dragged her out after him.

Anabeth coughed and gagged and coughed again trying to get rid of the water she had swallowed. She gasped air to fill starving lungs.

"You little idiot! You demented brat! What the hell did you think you were doing?"

Anabeth put a hand to her bruised neck. "Playing," she grated out.

"*Playing?* I nearly killed you!" he ranted. "I could have broken your neck!"

She managed a grin. "Pretty funny, huh?"

"Like a funeral," he snarled.

Anabeth didn't try to get out from under Jake. She simply lay where she was. Her eyes never left his face, so she saw the moment when he realized that naked flesh met naked flesh in all the places where their bodies touched.

He sucked in his stomach, but that only caused his

chest to press against her breasts. The hair on his chest brushed against her nipples causing them to peak. Anabeth heard Jake's husky groan as his body reacted to the changes in hers.

Jake's hands were braced on either side of Anabeth. Her lips were parted, her breath coming short and fast. Jake's body tautened as her tongue reached out to catch a drop of water on her lower lip. As though drawn by some unseen force, he leaned down and claimed her lips with his, sipping at her mouth, tasting her.

He loved the feel of her, the sweet, sweet taste of her. Too much. Jake recognized the danger. And sought to save himself. He started to lift himself away from her, but she clutched at his arms, holding him where he was.

"Wait," she whispered. "Make the ache go away, Jake. *Here.*" She touched her breasts. The tips had hardened into tight pink buds.

"And here." Her fingertips skated across her belly, flat and taut.

"And here." Her fingertips slipped down to the nest of coal black curls between her legs.

Her blue eyes were dark with a passionate need that Jake was helpless to deny.

"You want my hand here, Kid?" Jake claimed her breast and tugged rhythmically on the swollen crest.

Anabeth twisted beneath him as the pleasure streaked from breast to belly. She shivered uncontrollably as his hands slid down to search out her hipbones.

"And you want me here?"

Anabeth took a shuddering breath as a rush of pleasure shimmered through her.

Jake made a husky sound in his throat when she arched upward under his hand.

Her head fell back as she offered herself up for his gentle torment.

"What do you feel, Kid?"

"It . . . hurts," she whispered in a ragged voice.

"Shall I kiss it to make it better?"

"Yes, Jake. Yes!" She gave a tiny, wild cry as his lips claimed her flesh.

Anabeth's shaking hands clutched at Jake's hair as she succumbed to his slow, teasing touch. Her body bucked beneath his hand. Voice trembling with need she begged, "Please, Jake."

She didn't know what she wanted, but Jake did.

"You want me here, sweetheart?"

He captured her moan of pleasure with his mouth, and bit lips already swollen with passion.

"You taste so sweet, girl." He made a thick sound as he claimed her mouth.

Anabeth took a shivery breath as his tongue thrust deeply, penetrating her mouth, just as his finger penetrated her below.

She cried out in sensual surprise, and Jake absorbed the sound with his mouth. Anabeth shivered uncontrollably, and her hips sought out the cradle of his thighs.

Jake's breath came in sharply as she reached down to touch the shape of him, hard and throbbing in her hand.

Anabeth whimpered softly as she realized the violence of his need. Her hips moved sinuously upward, and Jake made a thick sound of pleasure.

"Don't, sweetheart. Stop."

"Why, Jake? I want you. I . . ."

Anabeth caught herself before she said the words. Jake didn't want to hear that she loved him. Nothing was more likely to make him leave her. "I need you," she whispered instead.

The harsh groan seemed torn from Jake's throat.

His gray eyes glittered in the moonlight. He shifted his muscular weight so that he could touch her, but she couldn't touch him, settling a heavy thigh across her legs to hold her captive for his hungry mouth, his slow, loving hands.

He drank in her sudden gasp as he slipped two fingers inside her.

"God, sweetheart, you're so small!" But she was slick and wet and ready for him. Jake sought out the small bud of pleasure with his thumb.

Anabeth made a breathless sound of protest that was taken by Jake's mouth as it claimed hers.

"That's right, Kid," Jake murmured. "Come with me."

Anabeth arched wildly beneath his tormenting hands. She gripped the bunched strength in his shoulders and whimpered softly as his mouth forayed to her ear and then down her throat.

"Jake, I want—I need—"

Eyes dark as smoke found hers in the moonlight. "What do you need, Kid? Tell me."

"I need . . . you . . . here."

She reached down between them and covered his powerful hand with trembling fingers.

Jake took a shuddering breath. Her sensual honesty made his pulse leap dangerously.

"Please, Jake."

A deep, animal sound escaped Jake's throat. He slipped his fingers out of her and lifted himself over her, pressing against the feminine portal with the tip of his shaft.

Anabeth gasped as he sheathed himself within her.

Jake drank in her sudden cry of pain as he broke through her maidenhead. Once he was seated completely, deep inside her, he held himself perfectly still.

"Are you all right?" he whispered huskily.

Anabeth felt full, but the ache was still there, unsatisfied. She threaded her hands in his hair and pulled his mouth down for her kiss. She found the scar on the side of his mouth and lightly traced it with her tongue. Then she slid her tongue along the seam of his lips and slipped it inside his mouth. The moment her tongue touched his, her body arched against him.

Jake made a thick sound of pleasure and grabbed her hips to hold her still. "Don't move, Kid."

But Anabeth's body arched under him as his warm flesh rubbed against her mound, creating a feeling of pleasure so intense it was almost pain. Her fingernails dug crescents in his shoulders as her body thrust upward, seeking the pleasure that was beyond her grasp.

Anabeth's sensual thrusts made Jake's pulse thrum. He found a nipple and suckled hard, feeling her body arch with desire. He began to thrust slowly, steadily, holding the bucking woman beneath him, tasting her flesh with a hungry mouth, drinking in her animal cries and coming back for more.

Anabeth's body tightened as she sought desperately for the satisfaction that eluded her.

"Jake . . . I need . . ."

"What do you need, Kid?" he grated.

"I don't know!" she cried.

But Jake knew. Slow, hot, hungry, his body thrust into hers. His hands caressed the woman, shaking and wild beneath him. He thrust his tongue in rhythm with the joining of their two bodies.

Jake felt her body clenching around him, felt the tension building in her until it exploded in a series of volcanic shudders, wringing cries of pleasure from her throat.

Jake's body thrust powerfully within her until at last he spilled his seed, claiming her for his own.

Jake heard Anabeth's shuddering sigh as her

clenched muscles relaxed, totally exhausted by the violent coupling.

He slipped to her side and pulled her close, wanting to feel her warmth. He kissed the heavy fringe of dark lashes feathered on her cheeks, causing her to make a soft, murmurous sound of pleasure.

His throat was thick with feeling, and he had to clear it to speak. "I . . ." Jake was reluctant to speak the words of love that described his feelings. But he would not deny himself the pleasure of touching her, of holding her, of joining himself to her—for however long they were together.

Anabeth's hand slid across Jake's sweat-slick body to his hip. "That was . . ." She sighed. "I can't describe it. Beautiful. Amazing. Incredible. Unbelievable."

"You liked it, huh?"

Anabeth's breath puffed across Jake as she released a throaty chuckle.

The pad of Jake's thumb slid across her kiss-swollen lower lip. "A man doesn't want to talk at a time like this," he said in a husky voice.

"What does he want to do?" Anabeth asked in an equally husky voice.

"He wants to . . ." But sleep wasn't at all what Jake wanted to do right now.

His lips sought hers. A gentle taste, a softly passionate claiming.

Anabeth whimpered softly. "Jake."

His name sounded like a prayer. He took a shuddering breath. "You'll be sore," he said bluntly. "We have to stop this right now."

"I don't hurt, Jake. But I ache. Here." She took his hand and laid it low on her belly.

Jake groaned and slid a finger into her. She was wet and ready. He felt every beat of his heart pumping blood to his extremities, making him pulse with need.

Anabeth reached out to touch Jake tentatively, innocently. He jerked as her trembling fingertips caressed him.

"So soft," she said in a breathless voice. "And so hard."

Jake's throat released a low, very masculine laugh. "You're crazy, Kid."

She grinned impishly up at him. "Crazy for you," she teased.

He saw the wary look in her eyes, as though she had said too much. He dragged her into his arms and held her tight.

"We're both crazy," he said. "But somehow I don't want to be sane right now."

His mouth found hers again. He felt her body tremble with need, felt his own body's shuddering response.

This time he joined them quickly. His body thrust into hers hard and fast and deep. His mouth claimed an already swollen nipple and he bit and soothed the hurt, suckled hard and strong with all the need he felt to swallow her whole, to make her a part of himself so she could never go away and leave him alone.

He made a raw sound as his body climaxed within her. He was aware suddenly that her legs surrounded his hips, that her heels dug into his buttocks, forcing him more tightly against her, keeping his pumping body buried inside her as she arched upward.

He caught her hoarse cry of pleasure with his mouth as his body emptied itself deep within her.

Neither of them had the energy to move, but Jake knew the cool night air would chill them unless they sought shelter. He picked her up and carried her the length of the valley.

When they arrived at the stone house he joined her in the big brass bed that had been hers alone.

With his woman in his arms, with no thoughts of Claire or gold or dangerous outlaws, Jake fell deeply, soundly asleep.

17

Jake woke the next morning with a frown etching his brow. He had a vague feeling of unease, but he couldn't identify its source. He rolled over and realized he lay sprawled across Anabeth Calhoun's bed. He remembered that he had made love to her twice by the pond and once in this bed in the middle of the night. Now he was alone.

"Kid?"

She didn't answer. He swore under his breath when he realized he had left his clothing by the pond. He sought out his saddlebags for more long johns, some jeans, and a wool shirt. He had also left his boots at the pond, so he pulled a pair of moccasins from his saddlebags as well.

The instant he stepped outside the door he spotted Dog.

"What are you doing here? You're supposed to be keeping an eye on her."

Dog howled. It was an awful sound, full of pain and aching with loneliness.

Jake felt the hairs stand up on his arms. "What's wrong, boy?" Jake searched the horizon for the danger he could feel all around them. "Where's the Kid? What's happened to her?"

Then he saw the sheen of blood on the dark fur. At the same moment, Dog swayed and collapsed.

Jake was beside the animal in an instant. He smoothed his hands over Dog's fur and found several knife wounds in his side. It was the first time he had ever touched the animal.

Dog whined and licked his hand.

Jake felt a well of tears in his eyes. "Dammit, no! You can't die, you mangy animal!"

He wasn't sure Dog would even let him help without turning vicious. But he had to try. He picked up the animal, but instead of biting him Dog lay quiet in his arms. Jake carried Dog into the house and laid him gently on the floor. He grabbed one of his shirts from his saddlebag and tore it into strips.

"No time for stitches now, but this ought to keep the wounds closed and stop the bleeding. You'll have to wait for the rest, boy, until I find the Kid."

Jake performed his makeshift surgery as quickly as he could, knowing that he had to leave Dog and go find Anabeth. He felt a killing rage by the time he left the stone house wearing his gunbelt.

Jake searched the length of the valley with narrowed eyes. The outlaw gang was here somewhere. He had known he and the Kid were living on borrowed time. That time had run out.

Jake knew the only reason Dog would have approached any human close enough to get stabbed was if he had been protecting Anabeth. Which meant that she was in deadly peril. He followed the trail of blood Dog had left, keeping to the shadows of the cliffs.

Jake moved slowly, sniffing the wind, listening for the echo of the slightest sound that didn't belong to the valley. He reached the other end of the valley without finding the Kid, knowing somehow deep in his gut that she wasn't there.

He found the spot where she had been stolen. There

was blood on the ground and signs of a violent struggle. But was it all Dog's blood? Had the Kid been hurt? Jake felt his insides clench. Cold gray eyes searched the rim of the valley. He knew Rankin was up there somewhere, waiting for him.

Jake followed a narrow deer trail he soon realized led up out of the valley. He had nearly reached the top of the cliff when a voice he recognized called out to him across the valley.

"I've got the girl, Kearney. I'm willing to trade her for the gold. She won't tell me where it is. But I figure if you want to see her alive again, you will."

"You lay a hand on her, Rankin—"

"Don't waste your breath with threats. The gold for the girl, Kearney. That's the only deal I'm going to make."

"Jaaaake!"

Anabeth's cry of pain made Jake roar with rage. "Rankin! Leave her be! You'll get the gold! Just tell me where you want me to take it!"

"You bring it out of that valley, hear? You bring it right to me!"

"Where? Damn you, where?" Jake shouted.

Rankin stood on the rim of the valley, too far for Jake's handgun to do any good. "Over here, Jake."

"I want to see her, Rankin. Before I do anything, show me she's all right."

Rankin turned to look over his shoulder and a moment later Solano appeared with Anabeth. Her hands were tied, but otherwise she looked fine. Jake saw the bloody rag tied around Solano's arm and realized Dog had gotten in a few licks of his own.

Rankin grabbed Anabeth by the hair and said, "Here she is, Kearney. You have a piece of this yet?" He ran an insulting hand down across her breasts all the way to her belly. "Better-lookin' than your average whore, eh, Kearney?"

Jake gritted his teeth, refusing to be baited into responding. Rankin wasn't going to hurt the Kid—yet.
Jake would make sure the outlaw paid for every
bruise on Anabeth Calhoun's body.

"I see her, Rankin. You just make sure you're waiting for me when I get there with the gold."

"I'll be here," Rankin said, "till sundown. Then I
think maybe I'll have to get some sleep. I bet the girl
can warm up a man's blankets pretty good. What do
you think, Kearney?"

Wat Rankin waited for the big man to answer, but
he was met with silence. He slipped back off the rim
out of sight. No telling how quickly Kearney could get
to a rifle. Wat turned to Solano and said, "Take her
back down by the horses and tie her up. Be watching
for a double-cross. I don't trust Kearney."

"Jake will kill you," Anabeth hissed.

Rankin laughed. "Better men have tried, Kid."

Anabeth jerked her head away as he chucked her
under the chin. "Don't touch me! You vermin! You
vulture! You back-shooter!"

Rankin froze and turned to stare at Anabeth.
"What's that you say?"

"I saw you shoot my uncle in the back, you yellow-
bellied coward!"

"Bring her here, Solano," Rankin said.

"But, señor, I should take her down below and—"

"Bring her here," Rankin repeated in a menacing
voice.

The Mexican put a hand on the woman's elbow and
escorted her over to Rankin. "I will wait below, señor."

Anabeth glared at the long-haired outlaw. "You're
going to pay for what you did to my uncle."

Wat grinned. "Looks like you're the one who's
gonna pay, Kid. With all that gold." He laughed and

grabbed her chin with a dirty hand. "Maybe you'd like to share it with me," he said suggestively.

"I'd rather die!"

He sneered. "That can be arranged, too." His hand slid down to her throat. "After I'm finished with you."

"You're finished right now!" Jake said.

Rankin whirled with his arm around Anabeth's throat, planning to use her as a shield. Her hands were tied in front of her, but her feet were unbound. Anabeth found Rankin's kneecap with her heel and kicked him as hard as she could.

Rankin cried out in pain. He slung Anabeth away as he lost his balance and fell, keeping his face averted so Jake couldn't later identify him as Will Reardon. Anabeth went careening toward the edge of the plateau at the top of the cliff.

Jake got off a shot, but Rankin quickly disappeared over the opposite side of the slope where he and So-lano had left their horses. Without a clear target, Jake held his fire. He heard the clatter of hooves as the outlaws made good their escape.

"Jaaake!"

A look back at Anabeth had Jake's heart in his throat. She was teetering on the edge of the cliff, hanging on by her fingernails. He quickly holstered his gun and ran to help.

"Hold on, Kid!" he shouted. "I'm coming!"

"Hurry! I'm falling!"

Jake grabbed for Anabeth's tied hands just as she let go. Her feet dangled over fifty feet of nothing.

"Hang on, Kid. I've got you!"

Anabeth didn't have breath to answer. She simply pedaled her legs trying to find some toehold that would help her get back up on the rim.

Anabeth had underestimated Jake's immense strength. His shoulders bulged as he leaned back, dug in his heels, and slowly but surely pulled her up.

And right into his arms.

Anabeth felt his heart pounding in his chest, felt his body trembling.

"You're safe now," he murmured. "That was too close, Kid. Too damn close!"

At first Jake kissed her on the forehead, then on the temple. He kissed her eyes closed and finally made a low, shuddering sound when he found her mouth with his.

He tore his mouth away to demand, "Where the hell were you that you got yourself caught?"

Anabeth shoved herself upright with still-shaking hands. "I was out walking."

"Walking?"

"Along the rim. I was on my way back down into the valley when Rankin caught me."

"What were you doing up here by yourself?"

"Thinking."

He didn't ask about what. After what had happened between them last night he wouldn't have minded some time alone to think himself. "You know we have to leave here now. Rankin will be back. Next time he's liable to bring reinforcements."

"Dog—"

"He's back at the house," Jake said. "I did what I could for him but . . . I don't know if he's going to make it, Kid."

Anabeth clutched at Jake. Her eyes filled and her throat swelled closed. "Jake . . ."

"I know, Kid."

Anabeth hid her face in Jake's shoulder. "Dog was trying to save me from the Mexican when he was stabbed," she murmured.

"I thought something like that must have happened."

She lifted her head and looked into Jake's somber

gray eyes. "If I hadn't tried to tame him, he might not
have been hurt," she choked out.

"All you did was love Dog. And he loved you back.
I'd say it was a pretty good trade." Jake realized how
natural it seemed for the beast to trust the girl. He
wondered when he had begun to feel the same way.
Because he did trust Anabeth. Enough to give her his
heart. Enough to take the risk of loving her himself.

He felt vulnerable. Too much so to admit to the girl
how he felt. He wanted to savor the knowledge for a
while before he shared it with her. But the thought
was there. He just wasn't sure what he wanted to do
about it.

Anabeth laid her head back on Jake's shoulder and
said, "Why did you tell Rankin you had the gold?
Have you found it?"

Jake shook his head. "I was stalling for time so I
could save your troublesome hide." He rubbed his
hand down her back and felt her shiver. He tried to
think of a good reason not to kiss her again. And
couldn't.

He slid his fingers into her hair and angled her
head back so he could claim her mouth.

Jake's lips were gentle at first. Anabeth slipped her
tongue out to taste the seam of his lips. When he
gasped, she thrust it inside his mouth.

Jake groaned softly as he felt her tongue come seeking the soft underside of his upper lip, the serrated
edge of his teeth, the taste of him. She slipped her
bound hands over his head and threaded her fingers
into the hair at his nape.

"Jake," she whispered. "I thought I'd be killed. I
thought I'd never see you again."

He tightened his arms around her. "I couldn't bear
to lose you, Kid."

Both seemed to realize suddenly what they had
said. And what it might mean. A lawman and an out-

law admitting that they cared about each other. It was a situation full of pitfalls. And one neither was ready yet to acknowledge or confront.

Jake reacted by sliding out from under her arms. "We'd better be on our way." He pulled his knife and slit the rope that had held her wrists together. But he didn't let her go without checking the burns left by the hemp, soothing the raw skin with his lips.

"Are you all right? Are you hurt anywhere else? I saw blood—"

"It was Dog's." Anabeth saw concern in Jake's gray eyes, but nothing more. He was letting her know that what had happened last night belonged in the past. That he hadn't forgotten who he was, or who she was.

"I'm fine," she murmured.

"Then let's get Dog and get out of here," Jake said.

Anabeth suggested they rig a travois for Dog and lead the horses up the deer trail that led out of the valley.

"Is that the trail I was looking for and never found?"

Anabeth nodded.

Jake shook his head. Now that he knew where it was the trail seemed perfectly obvious. He wondered how much of his failure to find it was due to not wanting to leave Anabeth Calhoun behind.

"Let's go, Kid." Jake stood and grabbed Anabeth's arm to pull her upright. When she cried out he immediately shifted his hold on her. "I thought you said you weren't hurt anywhere else?"

Anabeth put a hand on her tender shoulder. "It's just a bruise where Rankin grabbed me."

Jake's eyes looked dangerous as he scanned the horizon for the outlaw who had hurt Anabeth. *His woman*. He didn't know where the thought had come from, and he was damned uncomfortable with it, but he didn't deny it. Anabeth Calhoun belonged to him in the most elemental way a woman could belong to a man. He didn't dare think ahead to what he was going to do about it.

When they arrived back at the stone house, Anabeth knelt beside Dog and spoke softly to him, calling his name. "You're going to be all right, Dog. I'm going to take care of you and make sure you get well."

Dog rewarded her with a soft whine and a thump of his tail.

Anabeth carefully unwrapped Jake's makeshift bandages. "He needs to be stitched. Do you think he'd lie still while I do it?"

"I'll hold him for you, if that's what it takes."

Anabeth raced to her bedroom and found her sewing basket. She was trembling so much she had to try twice before she could thread the needle. Then she hurried back into the other room and sat on the floor beside Dog.

Jake joined her there, kneeling at Dog's head. He gently laid his hand on Dog's neck. He was ready, if necessary, to use more pressure to hold the animal still. "Go ahead," he said to Anabeth.

Anabeth saw the trust and encouragement in Jake's eyes, but was still reluctant to start.

"If you can cut a bullet out of me, you can stitch Dog up just fine," he said.

Anabeth smiled. "At least he won't be able to complain later about my work." She took a deep breath and poked the needle through a flap of torn flesh.

Dog flinched, but Jake held him down and spoke soothingly to him. "You're going to be fine, boy. Anabeth will have you on your feet in no time."

Anabeth's hands were slippery with sweat by the time she had stitched the deeper of Dog's two knife wounds. "I think the other cut will be fine if I just wrap it up tight." She sacrificed the rest of Jake's shirt and soon had Dog bandaged. "There. I'm done."

"He looks like a mummy," Jake muttered.

"I was worried that he might start bleeding again while we're traveling."

They worked together to rig a small travois and attached it to one of Anabeth's horses. Then Jake carefully lifted the wounded animal and carried him outside. Anabeth was ready with another blanket to cover Dog.

They walked the length of the grassy valley one last time, leading their horses past the plot where Anabeth had raised vegetables, past the pond, and up the deer trail that led them finally over the rim and down onto the malpais, the volcanic wasteland that surrounded the valley.

"Where are we going?" Anabeth asked.

"South," Jake said. "To Window Rock."

Anabeth sighed inwardly with relief. She had yet another reprieve from jail. And the hangman's noose.

Jake's eyes were constantly trained on the hills, watching for an ambush. Apparently Wat Rankin didn't like his chances when his opponent was armed and expecting him, because they didn't see hide nor hair of him the entire distance to Window Rock.

It was quite a homecoming when Jake showed up at the ranch house with Anabeth.

"Claire's gone!" Shug said the minute he saw Jake.

"I know," Jake said.

"You know? Do you know where she is? Is she all right?"

"Let me get Dog settled inside, and I'll explain everything." Jake was appalled at how empty the house felt. He moved quickly through the parlor to Jeff's bedroom and laid Dog on the rug beside the bed.

"I just want to make sure he's comfortable," Anabeth said. "Then I'll join you."

Jake headed back through the house to the kitchen, where he found Shug pouring three cups of coffee.

Shug handed Jake a cup, then took one himself and said, "I'm all ears. Where is she?"

Before Jake could answer, Anabeth joined them. Jake gestured her to a seat at the table. He took a sip of coffee, swallowed it and said, "She was stolen by an Apache."

Shug's face blanched. "Merciful heaven help her. We have to find her, Jake. We can't leave her to those heathen savages."

"She wasn't taken by a savage," Anabeth said.

"What?"

"Anabeth knows the man who kidnapped Claire," Jake said. "He's a friend of hers."

"You're the first I've known to call an Apache friend," Shug said. "I say let's saddle up and go hunting."

Anabeth turned stricken eyes to Jake.

"Let it be, Shug," Jake warned. "I'll get Claire back in my own way. I don't want a lot of innocent people getting killed."

"I don't like it," Shug said.

"I'm doing what I think is best for Claire's safety," Jake said. "Let it be."

Shug's mouth twisted in disgust, but he didn't argue further. "I've got work to do. Let me know what you decide." He left by the back door.

In the silence that followed Anabeth asked, "What are we going to do now?"

"I go looking for Claire. Alone."

Anabeth's eyes were haunted. "You won't find her."

"Not if I don't try."

"I'm going with you."

"No! You stay here until I get back. Shug will make sure you have everything you need."

"I can't stay here, Jake. Have you forgotten I'm wanted by the law."

Jake felt as though he had been punched in the gut.

She had just reminded him with a vengeance that he was in love with an outlaw. One he had sworn he would send to jail. One who was destined to hang. Even if he was willing to pretend that things were different, she was not.

"All right," he said. "We'll leave after we pick up supplies and get some shuteye."

Anabeth slipped a hand around Jake's nape to draw his mouth down for her kiss. Her lips were as soft as butterfly wings against his.

Jake tore his mouth away from hers. "What was that for?"

"For taking me with you."

His eyes were bleak, his voice harsh. "You didn't give me a helluva lot of choice."

Jake picked her up and carried her to the bedroom. If they were going to be bound together by this unholy alliance, then he was damn well going to take what he wanted—what he needed—from her while he could.

18

With the threat of winter not far off, Claire spent most of her days gathering ripe chokecherries, mulberries, and wood sorrel. But she watched closely as Wolf began the training that would mold He Makes Trouble into a fierce Apache warrior.

She had been relieved that although Wolf made a real bow for He Makes Trouble, he had given the child small willow arrows with wooden points to practice with. She heard him tell He Makes Trouble, "You can hunt birds or squirrel or any small animals you find. You may have to crawl on your belly to sneak up on a wild thing, because it will see you as soon as you see it. Thus you will move as the wild animal who must be silent to survive. These things a warrior learns."

For a long time He Makes Trouble did not bring home anything for the dinner pot. Claire noticed the child was impatient and often scared the animals away before he could release the arrow from his bow. At last the day came when He Makes Trouble shot a quail. He brought it directly to Wolf, who told him, "A hunter must eat whole the raw heart of his first kill to ensure that he will always be skillful with his bow."

Claire's eyes went wide with horror at the thought,

but one look from Wolf stilled any protest she might
have made. She couldn't watch as He Makes Trouble
did as he was instructed by the Apache brave. Claire
reminded herself that the Apache ate raw meat as a
matter of course. Only she had to think of something
else to keep from gagging when He Makes Trouble
turned to smile at her with his blood-rimmed mouth.

Claire felt her heart leap when Wolf put a hand on
the boy's shoulder to praise him. It was plain from
the reverent look in He Makes Trouble's eyes that the
Indian boy would have lain down and died for Wolf.
To be commended by his idol was a great moment in
his life.

It was only the first of many such moments. There
was the day Wolf demanded that He Makes Trouble
run from the village to a far mountain and back again
without stopping for water.

At first Claire thought what Wolf was demanding
was cruel beyond belief. "You can't make that child
run all the way to that far mountain and back again
without any water. He'll die of thirst!"

"He will have a pebble to put in his mouth. It will
keep him from feeling thirsty."

"What if he swallows it?" Claire demanded.

Wolf smiled. "Then he will have a heavy belly."

"You can't allow this!"

Wolf had taken her by the shoulders and stared
down at her with his dark eyes. "In the land of the
Apache a man must be able to travel great distances
without water."

"He's just a boy!"

"He goes a boy's distance. When he is a man he
will journey much farther."

Claire had pleaded with Wolf, but he had remained
obdurate. She had stood stoically in the dawn light as
He Makes Trouble began his sojourn. She was standing there waiting for him when he arrived back after

dark that same night. His lips were parched and he was staggering, but he had done it.

She had offered him water, but he had refused it saying he must see Wolf first. When the Apache put a hand on the boy's shoulder, Claire saw the child's fatigue fall away from him.

"It was well done," Wolf said. "You will get better with practice."

Claire had swallowed the lump in her throat and watched as Wolf offered the boy water from his own gourd.

The greatest day in He Makes Trouble's life came when Wolf brought a spotted pony to the door of the wickiup and called the boy out to him.

"He Makes Trouble, here is some work for you. Here is a pony for you to take care of."

The boy's chin dropped in amazement. "For me?"

"He is called Wind Rider."

When Claire saw the joy on He Makes Trouble's face it brought tears to her eyes. She quickly dabbed them away and watched in astonishment as the tiny Indian boy put his foot on the horse's leg, got hold of the mane, and crawled up onto the animal's back. He Makes Trouble grabbed the rawhide reins and kicked the horse into a gallop.

"When did he learn to do that?" she asked in an awed voice.

Wolf shrugged and said, "All Apache boys spend time playing with the herd where it is hobbled in the woods."

Claire's admiration for Wolf had slowly but surely grown over the summer and fall as He Makes Trouble had grown in self-confidence like a tree bud unfurling. When the boy had become less troublesome he had been shooed away less often by the rest of the tribe. Soon he was actually invited to join games with

the other boys. Which was when he came into contact
with White Eagle.

To her despair, Claire had made no progress with
her own son. Jeff stubbornly refused to talk with her,
or even allow her to speak to him. Finally she had
spoken to White Eagle's Apache father, Broken Foot.

She caught him sitting in the shade of a cotton-
wood making arrows. She sat down nearby and
waited patiently for him to acknowledge her. At last
he did.

"You have words you wish to say?"

Claire's command of the Apache language was
good enough to make herself understood as she said,
"I want to know why you stole my son from me."

The Indian kept right on working. He split the arrow shaft of carrizo and inserted a flint arrowhead,
then began wrapping the shaft tightly with moistened
sinew. At last he said, "It is not a good thing to speak
of the dead. It brings only sorrow. But I will tell you
my story, so that you will understand.

"I had another son," he began. "He went to hunt
one day. When he did not come home, I went to look
for him. And I found him."

With a sharp stone, Broken Foot scratched three
channels on the shaft in line with the three hawk
feathers. He laid the arrow aside and took another
piece of carrizo from the stack beside him.

He continued speaking as though he had never
paused. "One Who Was My Son said the soldiers
caught him. They laughed as they dragged him behind their ponies.

"I took him home to his mother. But she could not
make him well. The shaman could not cure him, either."

He looked off into the distance. "I was proud of
him. He did not cry out from the pain. One Who Was
My Son died bravely."

He busied himself again with the arrow in his lap. "My son's mother cut off all her hair. She cut her arms. She cried for many moons. I could no longer look at the tears of my wife. So I decided to get her another son.

"The white man took my son from me, so I took a son back from the white man. Now my wife smiles again, and she is happy."

Claire was silent. What words could ever apologize for such a travesty? "I am sorry to hear the story of your son. But surely you can understand my loss. The boy called White Eagle, the one you stole, he is *my* son."

Broken Foot looked up sharply. "Do not speak so foolishly, woman. White Eagle is Apache. You have no son in this village. Your son is gone."

He rose abruptly and left her.

Claire was chagrined to discover later that Broken Foot had gone directly to Wolf and complained. Wolf had fiercely scolded Claire to leave both Broken Foot —and White Eagle—in peace.

As a result, her battle for her son had become a thing of subtleties. When the boys went to the river to swim, she went there also to wash clothes. When White Eagle shot at a target of twisted grass thrown into the air, she gathered a bundle of wood from the ground nearby. When he played hide-and-seek or tag, had foot races, played tug-of-war, or wrestled, she was always there.

And she listened. As Claire's grasp of the Apache tongue improved, she began to understand exactly what her son said—especially his ridicule of Wolf's woman. But there was never a time when he made reference to his life before he came to the Indian camp.

She was relieved to discover that Broken Foot was not an unkind father, and that Jeff's Indian mother,

Cries Aloud, was a friendly woman. But it was small comfort when what she wanted was to be a mother to her own son.

She began to despair of ever reaching him. So one day when White Eagle went hunting by himself, she followed him. It was a sign of how well trained the boy was that he discovered her presence right away.

He turned and spoke to her in Apache. "Stay away from me. I do not want to talk the white man's words with you."

She spoke in Apache, hoping that would make him stay and listen. Her speech was halting because she was constantly searching for the Apache words for what she wanted to say. "Do you remember a time when you did not live with The People?"

White Eagle stared warily at her. "My true life began when Broken Foot brought me here to be his son."

"You had another father. Do you remember him?"

White Eagle nodded abruptly.

"He is dead now," Claire said. She watched closely for some sign of the tremendous loss she knew this would have been to a small boy named Jeffrey. This boy's features remained stony. "I am the mother who bore you," she continued doggedly. "I thought you had been killed by The People. I did not know you were alive, or I would have searched for you until I found you."

There was a slight trembling in the boy's chin, but he tightened his jaw to stop it. It was the first sign Claire had seen that Jeff had any feelings at all about the tragedy that had occurred—that her son had any regrets about the fact that savages had dragged him from two loving parents and thrust him into a harsh foreign world.

He does remember me! He did wish for us to find him!

"My white parents did not want me anymore," White Eagle said.

"Who told you that?"

"Broken Foot said that if you had wanted me you would have come for me."

"And you believed him?" Claire asked incredulously. "The only reason I never came after you was because I thought you were dead!"

"Your son *is* dead," White Eagle said with finality. "Only the son of Broken Foot lives. Go away Wolf's woman. Do not bother me again."

With that, White Eagle turned and ran off toward the village.

Claire knew it was useless to follow him. She had already been warned to stay away from him, and she was certain to be punished if she was seen chasing him. Claire wasn't altogether sure he wouldn't tell his Indian father and mother what had happened here anyway.

She didn't care if they punished her for talking to him. If they beat her maybe she would be able to weep the tears she couldn't seem to shed for her son. But how could she cry when he was well and whole and happy?

I want him back. He's my son! I bore him and nursed him at my breast. I held his tiny hands when he took his first steps. I want the chance to watch him grow into a man. I want to hold my grandchildren on my knee.

When Claire felt the hand on her shoulder she whirled to knock it off. How could anyone dare to offer her comfort? There was no comfort to be had for the calamity that had torn her only child from her bosom.

Claire fought Wolf with fisted hands as he grabbed her by the shoulders and forced her to her feet.

"Let me go! I hate you! Why did you bring me here

to see my son day after day and know he wants nothing to do with me?"

"You know why you are here," Wolf said.

She sneered in his face. "To be your woman? That's a joke! I know all about The People now, Wolf. I know that no self-respecting Apache would take a white woman for his wife. Why can't you leave me alone to grieve in peace?"

Wolf shook her hard. "It is time for you to leave the past behind. I will give you another child to suckle at your breast. You will be too busy then to weep for one that needs you not."

"What?" Claire froze, stunned by what Wolf had said.

"When the sun leaves the sky I will come to you, and we will make a child between us."

He left her standing there and stalked away.

Claire's mouth remained rounded in an O of surprise. Her hands remained paralyzed in mid-air. Her breath was stuck in her throat. Had Wolf meant what he said? Of course he had. He never said anything he didn't mean.

A baby. Another child to hold in her arms. A baby to love as she had loved Jeffrey.

Her first thoughts were euphoric. Oh, to hold a tiny, sweet-smelling baby in her arms again! To feel its petal-soft skin, to feel a tiny hand clasped around her finger, to have that small mouth suckle at her breast. It was an idyllic picture that made her ache with longing.

A baby whose father would be Apache. A child who would be raised as an Apache warrior if he were male or who, if female, could look forward to working from dawn to dusk to make a home for her Indian family.

She would not do it! She could not do it! It would mean living the rest of her life among the Apache, or taking a half-breed to live among the whites if Jake was ever able to rescue her. Or, God forbid, leaving yet another child behind to live his life among the savages.

Only they weren't savages, Claire had learned. The Indians laughed and played and loved as much as any white family. They hunted and gathered food, rather than planting it. Yes, they were vicious to their enemies, but so were the whites.

Claire could not escape, and there was no one to say Wolf nay. She could fight him, but there was no doubt who would win such a battle. Tonight he would come to her. Claire felt a frisson of fear—or was it anticipation?—run down her spine. Wolf was a virile man. He would bed her until he got her with child. She had no doubt of it.

God help her, it was what she had waited for—wished for—every day over the long hot summer and into the cool fall. She didn't understand her desire for the Apache, she only knew it burned within her. But it had seemed wrong to turn into his arms at night. His people had stolen her son. He had stolen her and made her his slave. And she had not yet been widowed a year.

Claire could deny to Wolf what she felt, but that didn't mean the feelings weren't there. Now he had told her they would couple not because he desired her, or she desired him, but to make a child to replace the one she had lost. She wanted Wolf. And she wanted the child. But to have them both she must give up the hope of returning to the world she had left behind.

For the first time, Claire allowed herself to imagine what it would be like to live among the Indians for the rest of her life. Only it wouldn't be the rest of her life. It was only a matter of time before the soldiers forced the Apache onto a reservation. The wild savages would not be allowed to raid and pillage the increasing numbers of white homesteads in *Apachería*.

Soon Wolf's way of life would be coming to an end. What would happen to her then? What would happen to White Eagle and He Makes Trouble—and her own half-breed children if she had them?

We could go to Window Rock.

But she was going to lose Window Rock. Unless Jake had found the gold that had been stolen from Sam. Or maybe Jake had figured out a way to keep the ranch without the gold. She knew Jake would welcome her back, but would he also welcome an Apache husband and half-breed children?

Nightfall came too quickly. Claire considered running away, but knew she wouldn't get far before Wolf overtook her. She must face her fate. She would not beg for mercy. But she would not give herself freely either.

Claire knew when she entered the wickiup after they had eaten the evening meal that Wolf had not changed his mind. He had sent He Makes Trouble to stay with Night Crawling. They were alone in the wickiup with the entire night before them.

"Have you thought about what I said this morning?" Wolf asked.

"I've thought of nothing else," Claire said in a quiet voice. She suddenly noticed the sheen of perspiration on Wolf's upper lip, the pulse throbbing in his throat. He looked pale. This was not at all the conquering warrior she had been expecting. It made him seem more approachable.

"Are you sure you want to do this?" Claire asked.

In an instant all vulnerability was erased from his countenance. An Apache warrior stood where only a moment before she had seen an ordinary uncertain man. Wolf's muscles flexed, his eyes narrowed. "I do not say what I do not mean."

Claire searched his face for some sign of yielding. "Have you never changed your mind? Have you never made a mistake?"

"I am not wrong about this."

"You've never asked how I feel about your decision."

"Your feelings do not matter to me."

"Even though I would be the one to bear your child?"

"It will be your child as well. There has been too much talking already. Come here to me."

"No." Claire lifted her chin and stared back at eyes as black as night. She could not deny even to herself that she desired him. But she would not willingly take the steps that might bind her to him forever.

"Come here," Wolf said in a soft voice filled with warning.

Claire waited with bated breath, knowing that she was testing the Apache's patience. If she had thought he would back down, she was sadly mistaken. However, Wolf didn't do what she expected, either.

He took a step toward her, then angled his path slightly so he walked in a close circle around her. His shoulder brushed hers as he passed by her. He stopped behind her. She could feel him there, feel his breath on her neck, the heat of him along her back from shoulders to heels.

Her eyes fell closed as he traced a hand across her shoulder and under the golden hair that fell to her waist. His fingers threaded up into the silken strands at her nape and tightened into a fist. He used his hold to turn her slowly, inexorably to face him.

He slid his other hand around her waist to the small of her back and pulled their hips close. Then he tugged her head back, tilting her face up to his.

"Open your eyes, Little One," he murmured in a husky voice.

When Claire opened her eyes Wolf's face was directly above her. His dark eyes were heavy-lidded, his lips full, his nostrils flared for the scent of her.

"You are my woman now."

Wolf had wanted her for a long time. He had lain beside her through the summer, feeling her warmth next to his. But he had not taken her, waiting to see if she would come to him on her own. She had not. But not because she did not desire him. He had seen her watching him when she thought he was not looking.

His waiting was at an end.

Wolf's hunger was great, but long before an Apache reached manhood he learned patience. He took his time. His mouth lowered ever so slowly to capture hers. His body clenched at the soft sound she made in her throat.

Wolf wanted to touch her flesh without the hindrance of clothing between them. He freed the ties on her buckskin shirt and her fringed skirt and let them drop at her feet. He saw the color streak from her throat to her high cheekbones.

"You are more beautiful than the sunrise on the mountains," he said as his hand cupped her chin and kissed the flags of color on her face.

"Your skin is softer than the grass that grows in the spring." His hand inched its way up her spine, fingers spread to touch as much flesh as possible.

He caught her soft cries with his mouth, tasting her for the first time. She was sweet like honey, and he supped at her lips like a man dying of hunger.

Claire had been prepared to meet force with force, but she had no defense against Wolf's gentleness. He stole her breath as he had stolen her heart. Her body betrayed her, her breasts swelling with need, her belly curling with desire, her knees refusing to hold her upright.

"Wolf," she murmured.

He lifted her into his arms and carried her over to his pallet where he laid her down. Before he joined her he rid himself of his buckskin shirt, breechclout, and leggings. He pulled her back into the curve of his body and held her there, relishing the feel of his bare skin next to hers.

"I was wrong," he said.

"That's quite a confession," Claire said breathlessly. "What were you wrong about?"

"Your skin," he murmured huskily. "It's even softer than the grass in spring, as soft as the petals of a mountain rose."

He caressed her as he spoke, and Claire's whole body quivered in response. She knew he was aroused, and yet he seemed satisfied with touching alone. He filled his hands with her breasts, teasing the nipples until they were taut buds. Then he slid his hands down to her belly and the thatch of blond curls at the apex of her thighs.

"There is honey here, too," he said as his fingers slid between the golden curls.

Claire gasped as he slid a finger inside her. He put his other hand on her belly, pulling her into the curve of his thighs as his fingers played between her legs.

She whimpered softly. "Wolf, I can't . . . I don't . . ."

His mouth found her nape and sucked lightly. Then he bit her shoulder and soothed the flesh.

Hunger. Wolf didn't know when he had ever wanted a woman more. *Desire.* He wanted her more with each moment that passed. But he forced himself to let her go. He dragged his hands up her body so that only his fingertips at her waist held her close.

"Come to me. Be my woman," he urged in a ragged voice.

Claire could feel Wolf trembling. *Need.* She had never known such need for a man. *Passion.* Never had she felt such desire for a man—any man. Something that felt so right could not be wrong. With a shuddering breath, she turned to face him and found herself enveloped in his arms.

"Mine. My woman," he murmured.

He twisted her quickly beneath him and spread her legs with his knees, settling himself in the cradle of her thighs.

Claire shivered uncontrollably. "Please . . . Wolf."

He sheathed himself inside her with one swift stroke. *Tight. Hot. Wet.*

Claire clasped his hips with her legs to hold him inside her. *Wonderful.* She didn't want him to move, but she knew that he must if he was to ease the ache inside her. "Wolf . . ."

He made an animal sound deep in his throat as he began to thrust, slowly, steadily, deeply. His mouth found hers and his tongue mimicked the action of their bodies, tasting lips and teeth and tongue.

Claire arched into him, seeking the satisfaction that was just beyond her reach. She bit his shoulder hard as her body clenched around him. "Wolf!"

He was not far behind her. Wolf cried her name as with one powerful, sinuous move he spilled his seed inside her, claiming her at last.

As her breathing eased Claire waited for the guilt to come. But she didn't feel sorry for what she had done. She only felt the pleasure of having shared a precious moment with the man who held her in his arms, and the anticipation of loving him again and again until they made a child together.

She reached out a hand and caressed a small mark on his shoulder. "I must have bitten you."

He kissed the tip of her nose. "I did not feel it."

Her hand slid across copper skin. "I had forgotten how it feels to touch a man." She felt him tremble beneath her hands as she caressed him. There was no turning back now. She belonged to him . . . and he belonged to her.

She gave his shoulder a nudge and forced him onto his back, settling herself on top of him.

"What are you doing?" he asked.

"I . . ." *Love you. Need you.* "I desire you," she said at last. "And I am claiming you, the way you claimed me."

Claire laughed softly at the stunned surprise in Wolf's dark eyes. She put a hand around each of his wrists and pinned them to the ground above his head. That put her breasts near his mouth, and he lifted his head and suckled her.

Claire gasped and her hips arched into him, causing him to groan with pleasure. She lifted herself slightly and impaled herself upon him.

"Now you are mine," she whispered in his ear.

Wolf answered with a hoarse groan as his body thrust upward into her. Wolf's whole body shuddered as Claire's muscles clenched around him. He had never been held captive before, and though he could easily have overwhelmed Claire, he allowed her to keep his hands bound as she made love to him.

She drove him mad with her mouth as she kissed and licked and suckled his skin. At last he could stand it no longer. He grasped her at the waist and turned her under him. It took only a few thrusts before he heard her cry of satisfaction and spilled himself yet again.

It took longer this time for him to catch his breath. He tucked her head beneath his chin and spooned her into his body. He was nearly asleep when he heard her whisper, "Wolf?"

"Hmmm." It was the most discouraging response he could think to make. This was not a time to talk.

"Wolf?" she whispered again.

Perhaps he must tell her what he wished of her. "Be quiet. I want to sleep."

She was quiet, but he could feel her body moving restlessly in his arms. He sighed and said, "What is it you want to say, Little One?"

"Will you take me to see my brother?"

Wolf frowned. "This is your home now. Why would you want to go to him?"

"You never had any brothers or sisters, but if you had you'd know that it's a very close relationship. Jake will worry about me until he knows I'm all right. I just want to see him and tell him . . ."

"Tell him what?"

"That everything's fine. That I'm . . . all right. That he doesn't have to worry about me anymore."

Wolf was silent for so long that Claire thought he wasn't going to speak at all.

Wolf was leery of allowing Claire to leave the camp. He did not want to take the chance of Jake Kearney stealing her back. Then he thought of how she had made love to him the second time. He did not want to believe she would run away. But he would watch her to make sure she did not try to escape. Even if she was not truly bound to him, she would not want to leave White Eagle. Or He Makes Trouble.

"Perhaps we will go in the spring," he said at last. By then he hoped she would have his seed growing inside her. By then he hoped she would no longer wish to leave him.

"Thank you," Claire whispered. Her body melted into his, and she pressed her lips against his shoulder.

Wolf felt an ache in his throat. He wanted more than her thanks. He wanted her love. But he would not ask for it. Ever. He could only hope that someday she would freely offer it to him.

19

When they first began the search for the Apache encampment Jake took the lead. Anabeth didn't offer her help tracking because Jake didn't seem to want it. Jake didn't even have the advantage of Dog's nose to help him, because the animal still wasn't well enough to travel any distance. Eventually, as the weeks passed and Jake got more frustrated, he asked for Anabeth's opinion of the signs he found.

Often Jake found moccasin tracks, but they inevitably disappeared onto rocky ground. They heard a wolf howl once, and Anabeth explained it was a signal used by members of a scattered party to contact each other. They rode toward it, but again the tracks disappeared into the rocks.

Jake was excited the day they saw smoke signals, but Anabeth explained that the distance to the signals was so great that the Apaches would be long gone before they got there.

"Can you tell what they're saying?" Jake asked.

"If the smoke comes from a mountaintop like this does, it usually signals that strangers are around," Anabeth said.

"Do they mean us?"

Anabeth watched the smoke. A second fire was lit

to the right of the other. "They're asking who we are," she said. "Whether we're friend or foe."

Jake pulled his hat off his head and shoved a hand through his hair. "Can we answer them?"

"What would you answer? Are you friend . . . or foe?"

"Neither," Jake muttered.

"Then it would be better not to answer," Anabeth said.

"We're never going to find Claire," Jake said disgustedly.

"Not if Wolf doesn't want her to be found," Anabeth replied in a quiet voice.

"I'm not giving up."

"I didn't ask you to."

"Let's go."

"Where?" Anabeth asked. "The last tracks we were following disappeared up into the mountains."

"To the source of that smoke signal."

"There won't be anyone there."

"There'll be a sign," Jake snarled. "Someone's going to make a mistake sometime, and I'm going to be there to see it."

Anabeth didn't argue further, just mounted up and followed after him. They made it to the far mountain by dusk. There was too little light for Jake to see whatever trail might have been left. The air was cool, but not cold. And it was quiet. Too quiet.

Jake searched the countryside with wary eyes. The hair prickled on his neck. Someone was out there. Not too close, but close enough. "We'll camp here tonight," he said.

"All right." Anabeth was exhausted. It had been a long day, but she had endured longer days over the past few weeks they had been on the trail without feeling so tired. She wasn't about to admit her weakness to Jake and give him the excuse he needed to take her back to the ranch.

"I'll gather some wood," she said.

Jake unsaddled the horses, rubbed them down, and picketed them close in. Anabeth hadn't yet returned, so he made a circle of stones for the fire and set out ground sheets and blankets for bedding. When she still hadn't returned, he went searching for her.

Jake found Anabeth unconscious, an armful of firewood by her side.

"Kid? Anabeth?" He shook her, but her eyes remained closed. His heart skipped to his throat. He looked quickly around for evidence that someone had attacked her, but there were no moccasin prints on the sandy ground. He scooped her up into his arms and hurried back to camp, where he laid her down on one of the pallets he had prepared. He left her long enough to dampen his bandanna with water from the canteen, then returned and pressed it to her brow.

When that had no result he picked her up and rocked her in his arms. "What's wrong, Kid?" he whispered. "What happened?" Her face was pale, lifeless, her pulse thready.

He thought then of snakebite. He looked her over from top to booted toe, looking for some sort of wound that would explain what had happened to her. He wet the bandanna again and pressed it to her lips, forcing her to swallow a few drops of water.

Finally her eyelids flickered. She shook her head from side to side, and her hands came up to push away the cloth he was once again using to cool her brow.

"Jake?"

He stared into eyes that were confused and a little frightened. "I found you unconscious. What happened, Kid? Did you fall? Were you attacked?"

"No . . . I . . ." She had bent over to pick up a

piece of wood and had gotten dizzy and then . . .
she must have passed out.

"Kid?" Jake's voice was impatient, anxious. "What
happened?"

"I . . . must have fainted," she admitted.

"Why? Did something frighten you?"

Anabeth tried to rise, tried to get away from Jake's
perceptive gaze, but he held her captive in his arms.

"I want an explanation, Kid."

"I don't know!" she said. "I leaned over and I felt
dizzy and I fainted."

Jake's eyes narrowed. "Are you sick? You look awful pale to me."

"A little upset stomach," Anabeth said. "It must
have been something I ate."

That seemed to satisfy Jake, and he heaved a sigh as
he loosened his hold on her. "Be careful what you eat
from now on," he said gruffly. "Are you hungry
now?"

Anabeth felt famished. "Yes. I'll help make supper."

"You'll sit and take it easy," Jake ordered, easing
her out of his arms and into a sitting position on the
blankets.

"I most certainly will not—" Anabeth tried to stand
too quickly and almost fainted again.

Jake was at her side in an instant. "Dammit, Kid."
He shoved her head between her knees. "I want you
well enough to ride tomorrow, so you'll do what I say
and rest tonight."

Anabeth's answer was muffled because her mouth
was hugging her knees.

Jake pulled her upright by the scruff of her neck.
"What did you say?"

"I said all right!"

Jake kept a close eye on Anabeth while he cooked
some venison and beans for supper. To his amaze-

ment she ate a huge helping and asked for more. Apparently whatever had caused her upset stomach wasn't bothering her anymore.

Anabeth insisted on helping with the cleanup after supper. "I'm fine now, really."

Jake gave her a good looking over, but all he saw was a young woman in the peak of health. Her cheeks were like roses, her eyes sparkled, and she was wearing a beguiling smile. He couldn't help feeling relieved.

And aroused.

"Time to get some shuteye," he said. He turned away from her, hiding the proof of the effect she had on him—had been having on him ever since they had left Window Rock. It was hard to stay angry with her when she kept him so . . . hard.

He had kept his distance from her on the trail, but the need he felt hadn't abated one whit. His body ached for her morning, noon, and night.

"Jake?"

He kept his back to her. "What?"

"Thanks for coming after me—for caring." She came up behind him and put her arms around his waist and hugged him.

"Kid . . ." Jake could feel his self-control slipping.

"Ummm. You're so warm."

He was warm, all right. Hot to the core. "Kid . . ." He put his hands over hers, intending to loosen her grasp. Instead he slowly shoved them down across the hard length of him.

Jake made an animal sound as he felt her hands moving under his. He spread his legs to give her better access to him, then reached around to grasp her buttocks in his palms and pull her snug against him.

Anabeth loved having the freedom to touch Jake as she pleased. She felt her body tighten when she heard his guttural groan of pleasure. He was thick and hard beneath her hands. She reached for his belt buckle.

"Don't start anything you don't plan to finish," Jake grated out.

By then she had his belt unbuckled. Her hands were trembling as she reached for the buttons on his trousers. Jake's whole body tightened as she released the buttons one at a time. She made a V with the flaps of denim and reached her hands down inside his long johns to touch bare flesh.

A harsh groan broke from Jake's throat. "Kid, I can't stand much more of this."

"You don't like it?" Anabeth whispered.

"Don't you dare stop," he said with a soft male laugh. He was willing to endure this heavenly torture for as long as she was willing to punish him.

Anabeth relished Jake's sudden gasps, his sensual moans as she explored the feel of his hard male shaft, the crisp thatch of hair and the softness of the sac below.

Finally Jake couldn't take any more. He freed himself from her touch and exchanged places so that she was in front, and he had his hands around her. "Turn about's fair play," he murmured in her ear.

Anabeth made a soft noise in her throat as Jake cupped her breasts in his hands, fondling her tender nipples through cloth until they became hardened buds.

Jake hadn't the patience to unbutton her shirt. He grabbed a bunch of flannel in each fist and yanked until the buttons popped free. He rubbed his hips against her at the same time he caressed her naked flesh with his palms. His body tautened as her breath sucked in sharply.

"Your turn, Kid," he said as he slid the buttons on her trousers free.

"Jake, I—" Anabeth cried out as Jake spread her

legs wide with his hands. She angled her head back to
look up into his eyes. They were lambent with desire.
"Jake—"

Jake's mouth found Anabeth's, and he swallowed
her groan as he slid his hands down inside her long
johns. He teased her with his fingers until she was
writhing with pleasure in his arms.

"Jake, please," Anabeth pleaded.

Jake felt her delicate shivers as he eased his hands
back up the length of her. He lifted her into his arms
and carried her to the pallet he had made for them.
He stripped her of boots and jeans, then did the same
for himself before mantling her body against the cool
night air.

Anabeth made a thick sound of pleasure when Jake
thrust inside her. Her hands threaded into the dark
curls on his chest, and her fingernails scraped across
his warm skin as she arched her hips into his.

Jake found her mouth with his, tasting her with his
tongue, thrusting in rhythm with the movements of
his hips.

Anabeth knew now what she was seeking, knew
what was happening when her body tightened like a
bowstring. She grasped her lower lip in her teeth, but
it wasn't enough to hold back the whimpers of pleasure being wrenched from her throat.

"Come with me, Kid," Jake murmured. "Come on.
It's all right. Trust me, Kid."

Anabeth stopped fighting the waves of pleasure
rolling over her. She pressed her face hard against
Jake's throat as her body erupted in waves of ecstasy.

Jake was not far behind. His climax was so powerful it left him gasping. He dropped his forehead onto
hers for a moment, then slipped to Anabeth's side and
pulled her into his embrace.

He couldn't understand what it was about this
woman that made him want her—need her—so

badly. He didn't understand why he felt whole with her. He only knew he did.

Anabeth kissed Jake's mouth lightly, then kissed his half-lidded eyes closed. "Rest now," she said. She brushed her fingertips across his furrowed brow. "Don't think. Sleep."

Jake heaved a tremendous sigh that evidenced both his confusion and his satisfaction. Moments later he was sound asleep.

As tired as she had been all day, Anabeth was now wide awake. How she loved the man who held her in his arms! She longed to tell him how she felt, but felt certain if she did that he would run like a deer in flight. But if he was going to turn her over to the law in Santa Fe anyway, why not tell him? At least then he would know. At least then there might be a chance . . .

Maybe tomorrow she would tell him.

Anabeth was lying there trying unsuccessfully to sleep when she heard her name being called. Her Apache name. Jake grunted as she slipped out of his embrace, but he didn't wake.

A moment later Anabeth had pulled on her jeans and boots and tied her torn shirt into a knot that half-way hid her breasts. She headed away from the fire in the direction of the voice in the darkness.

"Wolf? Where are you?"

"Here." He appeared right in front of her.

Anabeth crossed her arms over her chest when she saw the way his eyes raked over her.

"I see you have chosen a mate, Stalking Deer," he said with a sardonic curl of his lip.

She lifted her chin. "I have," she replied in a steady voice. "How are you, Wolf? And how is Claire?"

"What right have you to ask?"

"Are we not still friends?" Anabeth asked.

The tension seemed to drain out of Wolf. "I had

once hoped to be more than your friend, Stalking Deer."

"But you do not desire me anymore." She stated it as a fact, and he didn't deny it. In fact, she watched two interesting flags of color appear on his cheeks. Anabeth smiled. "So you have found a mate as well, my friend?"

"I have," he said.

"And you will return Claire to her brother now?"

"No."

"Why not?"

"Because I have taken the white woman as my mate," Wolf said. "She is the woman I desire."

Anabeth looked into Wolf's dark eyes and saw a flicker of unease. "Why did you seek me out, Wolf?"

"I wished to speak about . . . about . . ."

"About Claire?"

He nodded curtly. Stalking Deer had been his friend when others had turned aside from him. He had not realized how much he would miss the closeness they had shared. He had sought her out because his heart was full, and because he did not know where else to turn for the answers to his questions.

"I'm listening," Anabeth said.

"Do you think . . . is it possible the white woman can come to care for me?"

"Oh, Wolf . . ." How could she answer him? She didn't know herself why she loved Jake or even how she had fallen in love with him. How could she offer hope that Claire would come to love Wolf, when the emotions she felt herself seemed to have so little rhyme or reason? She didn't think Wolf could make Claire love him. For Claire to love Wolf, she would have to see in him the man of her dreams. And really, what were the chances of that?

Anabeth took a step toward Wolf, then another that took her into his strong arms. It was an embrace of long friendship. They both sought comfort and gave it freely. But there was no desire between them. Their hearts had been given by each of them to another.

"Did you ever dream when we were children of what our futures might be?" Anabeth murmured against his chest.

Wolf snorted. "The white woman I pictured in my wickiup was you, Stalking Deer."

"Isn't it strange how things turn out?"

"Are you happy, Stalking Deer?" Wolf asked. "Do you want to come away with me now to my village—as my friend?"

"I don't think that would work," Anabeth said in a strained voice. "I wouldn't make a good Apache woman, Wolf. I would always want to be doing what you're doing."

"But—"

Anabeth put her fingertips to his lips. "I'm glad you have Claire, Wolf. I hope you'll both be happy. I'll try to make Jake understand—"

"What is it you're going to make me understand, Kid?" Jake said in a dangerous voice.

"Jake!" Anabeth tore herself guiltily from Wolf's embrace.

"This is cozy," Jake said.

"It's not what you think!" Anabeth protested. She put herself between Wolf and the Colt Jake had aimed at the Apache's belly.

"Get out of the way, Kid."

Anabeth saw a killing rage in Jake's cold gray eyes. "Let me explain!" she cried.

"I've got eyes, Kid. I can see what's right in front of me."

"You saw two old friends hugging each other. That's all it was. Wolf is my *friend*. Nothing more."

"Not because he wouldn't like to be more," Jake said.

"That's not true. Wolf—" Anabeth stopped herself because she had been about to say that Claire had taken her place.

Jake read between the lines. His eyes narrowed and a muscle worked in his jaw. "Wolf has another woman. Is that what you were going to say? Who is it, Kid? Is it Claire?"

Anabeth looked over her shoulder at Wolf's stony face. Did she dare tell Jake the truth? Would her lover then kill her best friend? "I—"

"I have taken your sister for my woman," Wolf said.

Anabeth knew in that moment that if she hadn't been standing between them, Jake would have pulled the trigger. She felt the tension in both men, the barely leashed fury in Jake, the hate for all white men seething in Wolf.

"Jake, don't!" Anabeth pleaded. "What if Claire loves him? What if she wants him—the same way I want you? If you kill Wolf you might break your sister's heart!"

She could tell Jake was torn.

"Claire wouldn't love an Indian," he said at last.

"Why not?"

"Because of what happened to Jeff. Does Claire love you?" Jake demanded of Wolf. "Does she want to be with you?"

Wolf avoided answering Jake's questions. He said instead, "She wishes to stay among The People."

"Why?"

"Because her son lives among The People."

"Jeff is dead."

"Claire says the Apache boy called White Eagle is her son."

"Jeff is alive? He's living in your village?"

"He was taken by Broken Foot in a raid three harvests ago. He is Apache now."

Jake swore under his breath. "No wonder Claire wants to stay with you!"

"You have to let Wolf go, Jake," Anabeth said. "You can't kill him." Her voice was barely a whisper when she said, "He loves Claire."

Jake's lips pursed. He had heard no confession from the Apache, however, that Claire loved him. If he let Wolf go, the chances were slim, with winter coming on, that he would be able to find Claire before spring. He looked into the fierce eyes of the Apache, but found no answers to his dilemma there.

Then he looked at Anabeth, and realized that he would have died himself rather than hurt her. And killing Wolf would hurt her.

He holstered his gun. "Get the hell out of here," he said brusquely.

Anabeth put a hand on Wolf's forearm to stay the Indian's fraying temper. "Good-bye, Wolf."

"Where will you go now, Stalking Deer?"

Anabeth looked to Jake for an answer.

His eyes were bleak as he answered, "Home. To Window Rock."

"Will you bring Claire to visit us?" Anabeth asked Wolf. Her glance skipped from one man to the other. There was no love lost between them.

"Perhaps. In the spring," Wolf said, never taking his eyes off Jake.

"Take care of her," Jake warned.

"I would give my life for her," Wolf said. "She will be the mother of my children."

Jake's features hardened. "Till spring," he said.

The Apache said no more, simply turned and disappeared into the hills.

Once Wolf was gone, Jake grabbed Anabeth by the wrist and headed back to camp. When he got there he shoved her down onto his blanket and stripped her, then sat down beside her and stripped himself. He lay down and pulled her into his arms, spooning their bodies together.

"Go to sleep," he ordered. "We'll get an early start in the morning."

Anabeth lay beside him, aware of the tension that radiated the length of him. "Jake?" she whispered.

"What?"

"What's going to happen now?"

"I don't know what you mean."

"To us. What's going to happen to us? Are you going to turn me in to the law in Santa Fe?"

"No."

"Then will you let me go?"

"No." Jake's arm tightened around her waist. "You're going to stay with me, Kid."

"As your prisoner?"

"If that's the way it has to be," he snarled. "At least through the winter." By then he would have figured some way out of the tangle his life had become.

"What happens in the spring?"

"Let's take one day at a time, Kid. We have a lot of cold days ahead of us yet."

But thoughts of the cold were far away as Anabeth fell asleep in the warmth of Jake's embrace. It was easy to dream that everything would work out fine.

If only she had known . . .

20

In the first days after they arrived back at Window Rock Anabeth didn't see much of Jake. She did all the ranch chores that would have fallen to Claire. He worked from dawn to dusk rounding up cattle and making an inventory of the stock left on the range.

Dog had completely recovered and followed Anabeth around like a shadow. One night at dinner, Anabeth announced, "I've decided on a name for Dog. I'm going to call him Blackie from now on."

"Blackie?"

Dog thumped his tail.

"See, he likes it," Anabeth said.

"Why does he need another name? I thought Dog suited him just fine."

"Dog isn't a name. It's a . . . a label. Blackie's not just any old dog. He special. He belongs to us."

Jake caught Anabeth's gaze, and she flushed. "There is no *us*, Kid. Don't forget that."

Jake abruptly left the table, and Anabeth sank down off her chair onto the floor and hugged Dog. "But I wish there were an *us*, Blackie."

Dog whined and licked Anabeth's face.

"At least I've got you now," she said. "I won't be alone anymore."

One of the things Jake did early on was make a visit to Will Reardon's ranch to tell him the status of the hunt for Sam's gold. But Reardon's foreman said his boss was gone on business, and he didn't know when Reardon would be back.

Jake couldn't be sorry for it. He was beginning to get attached to Window Rock, and he didn't want to think what he would do, where he would go, if the ranch was lost for want of the gold to pay Will Reardon's note.

Jake sent a wire to his Ranger captain in Texas, explaining the circumstances that required him to take an indefinite leave of absence. But he knew the day was coming when choices would have to be made.

Each night after supper, Shug joined Jake and Anabeth at the kitchen table, and they talked about what it would take to keep Window Rock afloat without the gold that had been stolen from Sam. Anabeth had sent Jake to the valley to collect her small cache, which was her contribution to keeping the ranch solvent. In the absence of Will Reardon, the biggest decision to be made was whether to move another herd to market or feed the stock through the winter.

"I've got enough between my own money and the Kid's gold to buy feed," Jake said. "Let's wait until spring to send more beef to the Colorado market."

Shug agreed, and Anabeth couldn't help feeling relieved, since that meant Jake wouldn't be leaving her alone for the long drive north.

Anabeth talked Jake into playing poker with her again one night, only this time, she didn't smoke. "Same stakes as before," she said.

Jake grinned. "Three questions?"

"Right." Anabeth reached down and whispered to Dog, "Don't you go giving away my cards, Blackie."

Dog's tail thumped, and Jake quipped, "Thump once if she's bluffing, twice if she's got the cards."

Dog's tail thumped once and Jake laughed.

"So, you're bluffing," he said to Anabeth. Jake bet big.

Without the telltale cigarette to reveal when Anabeth was bluffing, Jake didn't laugh for long. He lost steadily, and before long Anabeth had all the matchsticks sitting in front of her.

Anabeth grinned. "Three questions," she said.

Jake threaded his fingers and laid his hands in front of him on the kitchen table. "Go ahead."

"First question. Why did you become a Ranger?"

"The bank took my father's ranch when he was hanged for murder. The bastard who got my father hanged made sure nobody would hire me on to work cattle. I had to support Claire, so I joined the Rangers."

"Shug told me Sam and Claire invited you to come work here. Why didn't you?" Anabeth asked.

"Window Rock belonged to Sam. I needed a place to call my own."

"Then why haven't you gotten a place of your own?"

Jake shrugged. "I like my work. And I never had a reason to settle down. No wife. No family."

"But if you had a family—"

"That's four questions," Jake said. He rose and said, "I'll take Blackie out for a walk."

He had to call Dog to make him leave Anabeth's side. Jake was late coming in that evening, and he was quiet when he did. But as usual, he undressed, slipped into bed beside Anabeth, and pulled her into his arms.

"Jake?"

"Ummm?"

"If you had a family—"

"I don't want to talk about it, Anabeth."

They had both gone to sleep unsatisfied.

Anabeth hid from Jake the fact that she still felt less than her usual self. Nausea plagued her in the mornings. Though she hadn't fainted again, she had learned not to move too fast to avoid feeling dizzy. That wasn't always possible. She was in the corral one morning when she had to duck quickly to avoid getting kicked by a fractious mare.

Shug caught her just before she fainted.

When Anabeth recovered her senses she was lying in the big four-poster in Claire's bedroom. The elderly foreman was sitting in a ladderback chair beside the bed.

"How you feelin', young'un?" Shug asked.

Anabeth sat up too quickly and had to lie back down again. She put a hand to her head. "I think maybe I'm sick," Anabeth admitted. "Lately I haven't been feeling so well."

Shug had his own suspicions as to what was wrong with the girl. "You been havin' a sick stomach in the mornin'?"

"Sometimes," Anabeth confessed.

"You been feelin' tired?"

Anabeth grimaced. "I can barely keep my eyes open in the afternoon."

"That's what I figured."

"What have I got?" Anabeth was worried because Shug wouldn't meet her eyes. "Is it serious?"

"Nothing that won't work itself out in about nine months," he said with the hint of a smile.

Anabeth continued to look puzzled, and Shug swore under his breath. "Old man like me ought not to have to be tellin' such things to a young girl like you."

"What's wrong with me?" Anabeth demanded.

Shug put a hand on her shoulder. "Nothin's wrong, Kid. You're just gonna be a momma."

"What!"

Shug flushed a bright red. "Bein' sick and feelin' tired—those're things a woman feels when she's gonna have a baby."

"I'm going to have Jake's baby?"

"Looks that way to me. When you gonna tell that boy the good news?"

"I have to get used to the idea myself first."

"Don't wait too long," Shug warned.

"Just promise you'll let me be the one to tell him," Anabeth said.

Shug scratched the bald spot at the top of his head. "All right, young'un. Just so's you tell him soon."

After Shug left, Anabeth smoothed a hand over her abdomen, still in awe of the older man's revelation. A baby. Jake's baby. Anabeth drew her knees up to her chest and hugged herself. She tried to imagine Jake's reaction when he found out.

But she had no idea what he would think. He had refused to answer when she had asked whether a family was reason enough for him to settle down. And he liked being a Ranger. Anabeth desperately wanted Jake to want the baby. And was desperately afraid that he wouldn't.

Since returning to Window Rock, they had made love every night. Jake had held her close and murmured love words in her ear. But he had never mentioned marriage. He had never mentioned forever. She even knew why. She had heard the story of his faithless mother and his drunken father. Jake's fear of repeating his father's mistakes wasn't going to disappear because she was pregnant.

She knew how Jake would see things. A baby meant staying in one place. A baby meant settling down with one woman. A baby meant he would have to come to terms with what had happened between his parents.

He should realize by now that I'm different from his mother. That he's different from his father. That our relationship is different, Anabeth thought angrily.

She was going to have to tell him about the baby. But not right away. Not until she couldn't keep it a secret any longer. Because Anabeth was certain it was going to change everything.

Meanwhile, she was going to have to find a way to convince him that they could succeed where his parents had failed.

Jake had been so absorbed in the ranch that he hadn't focused much on Anabeth. He knew she kept busy doing chores around the house, and that she usually had something to contribute in the discussions he had with Shug about how to make the ranch succeed. By the end of each day he was exhausted. But not too exhausted to make love to Anabeth.

It always amazed Jake that the moment Anabeth pressed her naked body to his in bed his whole being surged to life. Only lately he had been noticing changes in her. A tenderness in her breasts and a taut roundness to her belly that hadn't been there before. He had been denying to himself what those signs meant.

Today he had caught Anabeth sleeping in the middle of the afternoon. When he had confronted Shug for working the girl too hard, the foreman had lost his temper.

"When you gonna make an honest woman of that girl and marry her?" Shug had demanded.

Jake was caught off guard. "Marry her?"

"Why not?"

"She's an outlaw."

"Bullshit."

"I . . . I'm a wandering man."

"Not since you inherited this ranch you ain't," Shug snapped back.

"Claire—"

"You told me yerself Claire's got her an Apache buck. She ain't comin' back here. Window Rock is yours now, Jake. Your travelin' days is over."

Jake rubbed a hand across his bristly chin. He hadn't shaved last night because Anabeth had wanted to feel his beard against her skin. Later he had found a cool cloth and soothed the redness on her breasts and belly, her throat and chin. She had only laughed and enticed him to leave more of those same marks on her inner thighs. Just thinking about it made his groin tighten.

"That girl deserves to know you ain't gonna run out on her," Shug said, still ranting.

"No female is going to throw a rope on me," Jake retorted.

It was the vow he had made to Sam, and he realized as he said it that it was already too late. He was hogtied good and tight.

Anabeth hadn't meant to eavesdrop. And she was sorry now she had. She had tried to convince herself that because she cared for Jake, he would learn to care for her. But he had just made it woefully plain he was never going to let go of the past.

Jake heard a small gasp behind him and turned to find Anabeth standing there, her face bleached white, her eyes two deep pools of pain.

"Don't worry, Jake," she said bitterly. "I won't tie you down. When spring comes you won't have to worry about me holding you here. I'll be gone."

"You can't take that baby away from his pa!" Shug said.

"Shug, you promised not to tell!" Anabeth's stricken eyes searched out Jake's face to see his reaction to the news he was going to be a father.

He looked horrified.

Jake turned fierce eyes on the foreman. "What the hell are you two talking about?"

"That girl's gonna have your baby, that's what!"

"Not his—mine!" Anabeth said.

Jake's gaze swung back to Anabeth like a baited bear torn between two attacks and not sure which one to defend against first. He felt trapped by the circumstances. Because Shug had forced him to see the truth about something he had suspected, but avoided facing. Because he had hurt Anabeth by refusing to admit the depth of his feelings for her. And because she was an outlaw wanted for murder, and he had sworn to bring her to justice. What the hell was he supposed to do now?

Jake grabbed Anabeth by the shoulders and shook her hard. "You listen to me, *Kid*. And listen good. You're not going anywhere."

"I'll go where I damn well please! And you can bet it'll be somewhere the law will never find me."

Jake saw the tears welling in her eyes. It tore him up inside. "Go on back to the house," he said in a voice laced with anger at himself and frustration with her. "We'll talk more about this later, when I can think straight again."

"I won't change my mind, Jake."

When she was gone Jake propped his elbows on a stall door and dropped his head into his hands. "How the hell did this happen?"

"What you been doin' in that big bed every night?" Shug asked.

Jake groaned. "I should have known better than to get involved with a woman who rides on the wrong side of the law."

"What's that yer sayin'?" Shug asked. "That girl loves you to death. She'd walk through fire for you.

She ain't the one shovin' you away. Seems to me it's t'other way around."

"How can I get her to stay?"

"Tell her you love her," Shug said flatly.

"I can't do that."

"Why not?"

Because he was afraid to admit just how much in love with her he really was. Because she had him tied up in knots. Because he loved her enough to compromise everything he had ever believed to make an outlaw his wife. But he'd be damned if he let her leave him!

Because Jake had ordered her there, Anabeth purposely avoided going back to the house.

"Come on, Blackie," she said. "Let's go for a walk."

She headed for the giant willow that overlay the stream at the bottom end of the valley. She had found it to be a cocoon of peace in what had become her hectic life. The leaves were nearly all gone, and it wouldn't be long before the tree was bare. But for now, there was still some shade, the rustle of the leaves above, the crackle of the leaves below, and the burble of the water not far away.

Anabeth pulled her knees to her chest—as best she could with the bulge in her stomach—then laid her cheek on her knees and stared at nothing. The tears dripped sideways across her face and off her nose. Dog whined and licked the salty wetness off her face.

Anabeth hid her face in her skirt. She couldn't even wear her Levi's anymore, since they didn't fit around her waist. "What am I going to do, Blackie?" she asked. "What am I going to do?"

She heard Dog's growl, and when she reached out, she felt the hackles on his neck standing straight up. She raised her head and found herself looking straight into the eyes of Wat Rankin. And the bore of a Colt .45.

"What are you doing here?" she demanded.

"I've been watchin' this place. Where's Claire Chandler?"

"None of your business."

"You're talkin' mighty big for an outlaw with a reward on her head."

Anabeth's eyes went wide as Rankin pulled a WANTED poster from his pocket and shook it out in front of her.

"I figure if you don't lead me to that gold, I can always shoot you dead and turn you in for that thousand-dollar reward."

Anabeth blanched.

"I see I've got your attention now. You and me are goin' on a little trip, Kid."

"I'm not going anywhere with you."

Dog growled and bared his teeth.

"Call off your dog, or this time I'll kill him," Wat warned.

"Your gun is making him nervous," Anabeth said.

Rankin slipped his gun into the leather holster. "I won't be needin' a gun, will I, Kid?" He folded the poster and put it back in his coat pocket.

"It's all right, Blackie," Anabeth said. Dog sat down beside her, but he never took his eyes off Rankin.

"I was real surprised when you didn't tell that Ranger where to find the gold," Wat said.

"I didn't tell him because I don't know where it is."

"I don't believe for a second that your uncle didn't tell you where he put that gold. Now you're goin' to come with me—"

"Where was it you had in mind to take Anabeth, Mr. Reardon?" Jake asked.

Rankin turned stunned eyes toward the Ranger,

who had appeared without warning. Wat had no idea
how much of the conversation Jake Kearney had
heard, but he took the chance that it wasn't much. He
threw a warning glance at Anabeth and said, "I was
just invitin' Miss Calhoun to come for a ride with
me."

"Anabeth isn't going to be doing much riding.
She's expecting a child. My child."

"My congratulations," Rankin said.

"If you've come about the note—"

"What note?" Anabeth asked.

"Mr. Reardon loaned Sam some money. Claire
hasn't been able to pay the note because Sam's gold
was stolen by the Calhoun Gang."

"Where is Mrs. Chandler?" Rankin asked.

"She's visiting friends down in Texas," Jake replied
smoothly.

Rankin frowned. "I understand there's been some
delay locatin' the gold. I suppose seein' as how we're
neighbors I'd be willin' to let things slide till spring."

"That's mighty generous of you, Mr. Reardon,"
Jake said.

"Call me Will, please. I'm not goin' to be around
much till then—spring, I mean. I'll be leavin' now."
He turned to Anabeth and said, "Trust I'll see you
again soon."

Anabeth stayed mute until Rankin had ridden
away. To do otherwise was to provoke a confronta-
tion when Wat Rankin knew his enemy and Jake
Kearney did not.

As soon as Rankin was gone, Anabeth jumped up
and threw herself into Jake's arms. "That was him!"

"Who?"

"Rankin. Wat Rankin. That was him."

Jake grabbed Anabeth's shoulders and forced her
to arm's length so he could see her face. "Will Reardon—"

"—is Wat Rankin!"

"Son of a bitch," Jake said.

"My thoughts exactly," Anabeth said vehemently.

"Why didn't you say something? Why did you let him get away?"

"By the time I got the words out of my mouth, he would have drawn his gun and killed you."

Jake grabbed her by the wrist and began marching back toward the ranch house. "You don't leave the house anymore without me knowing where you are," Jake said. "And you keep Blackie with you at all times, understand?" He shoved her inside the front door, kissed her hard, and turned to leave.

"Where are you going?" she asked.

"I'm going after that bastard, Rankin."

"What about me?"

"You wait here until I get back."

"I want to go with you."

Jake came back and pulled her into his arms and hugged her tight. "You can't, Kid. Don't you see. You have someone else to think about now." He curved his palm over her rounded belly. "Promise me you'll be here waiting for me when I get back."

"You'd believe the word of an outlaw?" Anabeth asked.

"I'd believe you."

Anabeth's heart missed a thump. "All right, Jake. I'll be here. But you be careful."

"I'll watch my back, Kid. You just take care of yourself and the baby."

He kissed her hard once more, and then he was gone.

Jake tracked Wat Rankin/Will Reardon as far as Santa Fe. There the trail disappeared. He stopped at the Town House to ask questions and saw Sierra Starr. When she invited him upstairs, he declined.

"So she did hogtie you," Sierra said with a chuckle. "Was it as bad as you thought it would be?"

Jake managed a chagrined smile. "It's not at all bad," he confessed. "I'm going to be a father."

"Congratulations," Sierra said. She gave him a kiss on the mouth, then leaned back and looked at him. "You're hogtied, all right. Look, you're not going to find Rankin before winter sets in. Why don't you go home where you belong?"

Sierra's suggestion made a lot of sense. Jake missed Anabeth. And Rankin wouldn't go far. He would stay where he could keep an eye on Kid Calhoun. Which was another good reason for Jake to stay close to home.

"Good-bye, Sierra," Jake said.

"You're leaving now?"

"Yeah. I'm going home."

As the weather turned colder and the foliage clothed itself in yellow and gold, Claire acknowledged that her life was full of good things. A boy who needed her. A man who wanted her. But like all humans, she wanted what she didn't have. She wanted White Eagle to acknowledge her as his mother.

It wasn't going to happen.

She tried to tell herself it didn't matter. That it was enough to know Jeff was all right. But it wasn't enough. There was a constant ache in her throat, a powerful constriction that made it difficult to swallow whenever she saw him playing with the other Apache boys.

She tried to hide how she felt from Wolf, but he knew. Whenever he saw her watching White Eagle he would find something for her to do—a buckskin shirt that had hardened in one spot and needed to be softened with a rough rock, or a basket that needed to be repaired with pitch from a piñon tree. But he never asked her to stop caring. He seemed to understand that she could not.

The day came when the Apache moved their village down out of the high mountains to escape the harsh cold and deep snows of winter. They rebuilt their homes in the lowlands, taking care to make sure they were concealed as well as possible among the hills and rocky habitat.

Claire was surprised to discover that White Eagle's family had selected a site for their wickiup not more than two hundred paces from her own front door. Now she came into contact with her son every day. He Makes Trouble began to spend more time with White Eagle and his friends.

The boys didn't harass He Makes Trouble, although Claire kept a close eye on them for fear they would. She soon relaxed her vigil as the days wore on and nothing more serious happened to He Makes Trouble in his play with the older boys than a skinned knee. It never occurred to her that anything was amiss when the older boys—eight-, nine-, and ten-year-olds—decided to go swimming and invited He Makes Trouble to come along.

Claire was occupied collecting the mesquite beans that were now ripe in the lowlands and merely waved as He Makes Trouble trotted away toward the spring-fed pond. She had learned from Night Crawling how to grind the beans into flour using a mano and metate, a sort of stone mortar and pestle. The flour was then made into something that looked like a pancake. Or the beans were cooked and mashed into a kind of mushy gruel. Or the whole beans could simply be cooked and eaten with seared meat—only it was necessary to spit out the seed coat when the bean was eaten.

Her mind had quickly wandered from He Makes Trouble to thoughts of her nights with Wolf. He came to her every night that he was not away from the village. Because he had to hunt and because he went on raids, he was often gone for a week at a time. When he returned, he sought her out—whatever time of night or day—and took her to his pallet.

Claire had begun to look forward to those moments when he took her into his arms. She tried not to think of Sam, tried not to feel as though she was betraying his memory. Sam would have wanted her to be happy. And she was happy, more so than she could ever have dreamed possible. Because she was in love.

She wasn't sure when it had happened. She only knew that her feelings of admiration for the Apache had become something considerably more. And she fell more in love with him every day. She worried about him every time he left the camp, especially after Wolf told her one night about his fight with a soldier. The Blueleg had fisted his hand in Wolf's hair so tightly that the Apache couldn't get it loose.

"I thought I would have to cut it all off to get free!" Then he winked, as though it was a huge joke.

Only Claire didn't find the thought of Wolf in such danger at all funny. The story had made her blood curdle, and she gave him the sharp side of her tongue.

He had gotten angry then. "I am a warrior and must fight my enemies," he said. "I will not be made a coward by a woman's fears."

"Go ahead and get yourself killed, then!" she had ranted. "I don't care. But be sure to tell your people what is to become of me when you are gone. I won't be some other Apache buck's woman! I couldn't bear it!"

Wolf had taken her then and laid her under him and thrust himself inside her. "You are *my* woman," he had said fiercely. "If another man touches you I will kill him!"

Claire was panting as she arched her body into his and fisted her hands in his long black hair. "Be careful, Wolf. I don't want to lose you." It was as close as she had come to telling him that she cared for him.

Wolf had filled her with his seed and held her tight against him throughout the night. He hadn't made any promises about being careful, and he had dared her to say anything when he rode out the next morning on another raid. She had looked up into his eyes as he left her and let him see the love she felt for him. He had simply turned away from her and kicked his pony into a gallop.

Deep in thought, Claire wandered toward the pond. As she became aware of her surroundings, she heard the sounds of water splashing and children shrieking. Only she realized it wasn't children—it was one child. And he was shrieking in terror.

Claire dropped the basket of mesquite beans and raced for the pond. What she saw when she arrived confirmed her worst fears. He Makes Trouble was thrashing in the water, clearly unable to keep himself afloat. The other boys were standing by watching.

She was tempted to jump in after him, but she had no idea how deep the water was, and she couldn't swim. "Help him!" she cried.

The Apache boys looked back at her with disdain. They continued hurling jeers and insults at the struggling child.

Apparently this was some sort of test, only if He Makes Trouble flunked, it was going to mean his life. Claire couldn't stand by and do nothing. She began searching for a branch to hold out for the boy to grab onto. But there was nothing long enough.

At last she turned to her son and cried, "Jeffrey, please. You can't let him drown!"

White Eagle turned his back on her. But he said to

the other boys, "Perhaps He Makes Trouble is too young to learn this. We will let him grow a little, eh?"

The other boys looked at each other. None had been willing to admit they had made a mistake, but now that White Eagle had suggested it, they all seemed more than willing to consider rescuing He Makes Trouble. Only when they looked at the thrashing boy, the idea of jumping into the water with him seemed more dangerous than they had bargained for.

Claire was on the verge of leaping into the frigid water herself when Wolf suddenly appeared. He took stock of the situation, and a moment later He Makes Trouble was standing beside her choking and gasping as he tried to rid himself of the water he had swallowed. Wolf only had to give the other boys a look before they scattered without a word, leaving Claire and He Makes Trouble alone with him on the bank of the pond.

"They would have let him drown!" Claire said to Wolf. "They wouldn't have lifted a finger to save him!"

"An Apache boy must learn to do many things," Wolf said. "Swimming is but one of them."

"But surely he doesn't have to learn so young!"

Wolf shrugged. "A boy is usually older," Wolf said. "But the lessons are the same."

"Aha!" Claire said. "So there are *lessons* involved. What were those boys thinking to just throw him in there?"

"They were only playing," Wolf said, his voice becoming harder as Claire continued her tirade. "And He Makes Trouble has learned a lesson."

"What lesson?" Claire demanded.

Wolf looked down at the soaking-wet child. He put a finger under He Makes Trouble's chin and lifted it until the boy was forced to meet his gaze. "What did you learn today, He Makes Trouble?"

The Apache child blinked the water from his eyelashes and said, "Not to stand too close to the water. To kick my feet to stay afloat. And not to trust anyone."

Wolf turned to meet Claire's stricken eyes. "See. He has learned many good lessons."

"Not to trust—"

"It is a good lesson," Wolf said in a harsh voice. "So also did I learn."

Claire shook her head in disbelief. No wonder Wolf had never said anything about his feelings for her. He would never trust her enough to give her his heart. She felt a sinking feeling in her chest. "Come, He Makes Trouble, I will find something for you to do while you dry off."

She walked away and left Wolf standing there.

Later, when she thought about it, Claire realized that something good had come from the afternoon's events. White Eagle hadn't acknowledged her existence, but he had made the effort to turn the other boys from their ridicule of He Makes Trouble. He had heard her. And he had responded to her.

Hope. She had thought she had given up on her son. But now she realized she hadn't. That she never would. Someday Jeffrey would come to her, and they would speak together of the past. And perhaps then she could put it behind her.

Wolf came to her that night without apology for what he had revealed to her about himself earlier in the day. He could not allow himself to trust her—or anyone. Trust would only bring pain.

It was better to take each day as it came. To bury himself deep inside her, to take pleasure from her body and give it in return. He had learned not to depend on someone else for his happiness. He did not think he could survive it if this woman offered happiness only to snatch it away later.

The long winter nights passed slowly. Two lonely people found surcease from pain in each other's arms. But it was stolen pleasure, because at any moment, both of them expected it to melt away like the snows in spring.

It was a spring that came before either of them was ready for it. Even if they hadn't been expecting the worst, neither of them could have foreseen the events that would finally tear them apart.

21

Spring came too soon for Wolf. He had hoped that Claire would be with child. She was not. Though he had kept her in his blanket through the long winter nights, his seed had not found fertile ground. He could not look at her without wanting her. He had learned to admire her good sense, her willingness to work, and her sharp tongue when she saw some wrong she hoped to right. He had been careful to say nothing of his feelings for her. They were so strong that they frightened him.

He thought perhaps she cared for him a little. One night over the winter she had become so aroused that during their lovemaking she had cried out the Apache words for "I love you!"

She had not said them again. He was afraid to let himself believe it, lest it be not true. She had the power to destroy him, if she only knew it. He was loathe to offer her a part of himself for fear it would not be enough. He had vowed as a young man to always walk his path alone. Now he did not know how to go any other way.

He kept thinking Little One would suddenly come to her senses and see what others had seen all his life. *That he was not worthy of the love and attention that she had bestowed upon him.* So he pretended he had not heard her say the words of caring. He had kept his soul apart from her. He had remained safe. And though he had not been alone, he had felt a desolation of the spirit that made him want to howl like the lone wolf he was named for.

The camp was still mostly asleep when Wolf left his wickiup to escape the heartstrings that bound him to the woman and small boy asleep inside. It was getting harder to say even to himself that he did not care. It was time to admit, at last, that he loved them both.

He had not gone very far from the wickiup when he noticed how quiet it was. He searched the terrain for signs of an enemy, but saw none. Neither did he see the Apache lookout who should have been on the far ridge. Wolf froze where he was and turned his face to the wind.

And smelled death.

"Soldiers." He could smell the stink of their unwashed bodies, the sweat dried on their horses' flanks, and the fear in their hearts.

He walked quickly, but without running, from one wickiup to another. In this case the distance between each dwelling was a severe disadvantage. As he awoke each warrior, they also went to wake others. Soon the whole village was aroused, and yet the attack had not come. Once everyone was alerted, Wolf returned to his wickiup to wake Little One and He Makes Trouble.

Claire immediately sensed the tension in Wolf when he roughly shook her awake. As he began collecting his weapons—his war club, his bow and arrows, and his knife, she knew something was very wrong.

"Are we being attacked?"

"Soldiers. Take He Makes Trouble and go up into the hills and hide. You will be safe there."

"Surely they wouldn't harm me," she protested.

He gave her a piercing look. "They would take you away from here. Is that what you want?"

There it was. The moment of truth and no time to think what was right or wrong.

"Go!" Wolf said, allowing her no time to answer. "I will find you when the battle is over."

"Be careful!" she whispered as she helped him slip his quiver over his shoulder.

Wolf stopped long enough to kiss her hard. "You are precious to me," he said. "Run fast, Little One. Take care of yourself and He Makes Trouble."

When he released her they both realized at the same moment that He Makes Trouble was no longer in the wickiup.

"Ahagake!"

Claire had never heard Wolf use that Apache expression, but she knew what it meant well enough. Wolf had taken as much as he could stand. The boy was incorrigible.

"Don't worry about He Makes Trouble," Claire said. "I'll find him, and we'll go hide in the hills. Go now. Go!"

Wolf seemed torn, but at last he turned away from her. A moment later he had disappeared into the rocky terrain.

Claire heard a pepper of shots, the screams of wounded men, and the bloodcurdling yells of attacking Indians. Then, suddenly, everything was bedlam. Blue-coated soldiers were riding pell mell through the village, shooting at anything that moved—women and children included.

"Stop shooting!" Claire shouted at them in English. "You're killing women and children!"

The soldiers ignored her. Whether from fear or bloodlust, they ransacked the village, setting fire to the wickiups and skewering or shooting any Indians they could find.

Frantic, Claire searched the melee for He Makes Trouble—and found him standing beside Wolf, his tiny bow drawn with a wooden arrow nocked in it. Then, before her horrified eyes, a blossom of red appeared at Wolf's temple. A second later she saw He Makes Trouble clubbed to the ground with the butt of a rifle.

"Nooooo!" She staggered in the direction of their fallen bodies, but she hadn't gone four steps when two small hands grabbed her buckskin skirt and dragged her to a standstill.

"Come with me!"

It was Jeff. He had spoken to her in English. He let go of her skirt and grabbed her arm, pulling her in the direction of the hills and safety.

"The horses are not far from here. Come with me."

"But Wolf . . . and He Makes Trouble."

White Eagle looked over to where the two lay motionless on the ground. "You cannot help them now. We must escape or be killed. Come!"

"But, Jeff—"

"My name is White Eagle," he said fiercely. "My father is fighting the white soldiers. My mother has fled to the hills to hide until it is safe to come back here. I have come only to help you leave this place unharmed."

Jeff had come to save her, even though he still denied being her son. Dazed, Claire followed where Jeff led, ran until her side ached, until her legs protested and threatened to buckle. At last they reached the isolated canyon where the horses were hidden. He quickly bridled two ponies, helped her up onto the back of one and easily mounted the other.

"Where are we going?" Claire asked.

"I will take you back to your people," White Eagle said. "I will take you back where you belong."

"Do you know how to get there?"

"I journeyed there once with Broken Foot. He showed me where I came from."

"You can find your way back—could have found your way back at any time?" Claire asked incredulously.

"I have known the way for many moons," he answered ruthlessly.

Claire was numb through most of the long ride back to Window Rock. Her son had known how to come home, and yet he had stayed among the Apache.

"Why?" she asked finally. "Why didn't you come home when you could? Why did you deny me when I came to the village?"

"My other life is behind me," he said quietly. "I am of The People now. I was afraid you would try to take me away from my mother and father. I would not be happy living among the white man now. I would rather be Apache."

It was a tragic ending to all her hopes. Her son had made his choice. Claire could perhaps force him to stay with her, but she didn't have the heart to do it. She wondered if there was anything she could have done differently. In truth, she didn't think so. This was a tragedy that had started long before Claire had come to New Mexico. A tragedy that had begun when the white man settled on lands that had once belonged to the Indian.

How long ago had the chain of events been set in motion that had resulted in the loss of her son? Had there ever been a way she could have escaped it? If she hadn't met Sam? If she hadn't married him? If she hadn't moved to New Mexico? If Sam hadn't taken Jeff with him that long-ago day?

She would never know. It hardly mattered. She had to accept what she couldn't change, or she would go mad with sorrow. Jeff must have some fond memories of her, or he wouldn't have undertaken this journey. She would have to be satisfied with that crumb, because she simply wasn't going to get the whole loaf.

It was hard to say who was more surprised when the front door of the ranch house at Window Rock opened and Claire found herself staring at a very pregnant woman.

"How did you get here?" Anabeth asked Claire. "Is Wolf with you?"

Claire looked for Jeffrey in the darkness that had fallen, but her son—no, the Apache White Eagle—had already gone. "It's a long story. May I come inside?"

"Of course. Jake!" she called. "It's Claire!"

Jake came on the run and scooped his sister up into his arms, exuberantly swinging her around in a circle. "I can't believe it! How did you get here?"

As soon as Jake set Claire down he knew something awful had happened. Her golden eyes welled with tears that spilled over as she choked out, "Wolf is dead. Killed by soldiers. They attacked at dawn. They shot him . . . shot him in the head . . ."

Jake lifted Claire into his arms as she collapsed and carried her to the bedroom she had shared with Sam —the bedroom he had been sharing with Anabeth over the long winter months. Jake sat down beside Claire and saw the ravages of grief on her face in the shadows of light thrown by the lantern beside the bed.

Jake brushed several wayward strands of hair from her face. It was all he could think to do. How could he comfort her? He had hated the Apache for taking Claire away. But he hadn't wanted Wolf dead this way. Jake wanted to ease Claire's pain, but he didn't know what to say, what to do.

He turned to Anabeth and asked, "How did she get here? Did someone bring her?"

"I don't know," Anabeth said.

Jake put a hand on Claire's shoulder. "Claire?"

She had curled up in a fetal ball, shutting him out, shutting out the world.

"Stay with her," Jake said. "I want to take a look outside."

Jake found tracks from two unshod ponies. Someone had come with Claire, someone lighter than her from the looks of the hoofprints. Whoever it was had gone away again, taking the second horse with him.

When Jake went looking for Claire again he discovered that she had moved into Jeff's bedroom. She lay on the bed, her face hidden against a pillow that muffled her sobs. She had curled back into that fetal position again, her knees drawn up to her chest.

Anabeth was sitting beside Claire, her hand on Claire's shoulder. She looked up at Jake with tears in her eyes. "She's hurting so badly. Isn't there something we can do?"

He shook his head helplessly.

Anabeth held out a hand to him, and he took it and sat down beside her on the small bed. When Claire moved toward Jake, he pulled her up onto his lap. He slipped his free arm around Anabeth and pulled her tight against him. He sat there for a long time with an arm around each woman, holding them close.

Jake tried to imagine how he would feel if Anabeth had been killed, and knew he wouldn't be able to bear it. Death was so final. It took away second chances. He pulled Claire tighter against him, wanting to take her pain and bear it himself.

Anabeth had a lump in her throat so big it was choking her. How awful to have the one you love torn from you by tragedy! How much worse to willingly leave a loved one behind. Anabeth had been waiting for spring to come so she could leave Jake and go back to the valley. She saw now she could never do it. Life would be too empty without him.

She lifted her head from Jake's shoulder and looked up to find his eyes somber, his features strained. She leaned over and kissed his mouth. Then she took a deep breath, let it out and said, "I love you, Jake."

He released a shuddering breath. Did he dare believe her? Did he dare speak the words back to her? Would she stay with him if he did? Jake pulled her close. But said nothing.

Eventually Claire's sobs slowed and finally stopped. She was quiet for a long time on Jake's lap. At last her hand came up and she played with the flannel at the neck of his shirt. "Jake?"

"Yes, Claire?"

"Jeff brought me home."

"Why didn't he stay?"

"He prefers the life of an Apache."

Jake tightened his hold. "I'm so sorry, Claire."

Her eyes welled with tears, but she was smiling. "He's happy, Jake. More than I ever could have imagined."

"So you're giving him up?"

"My son died the day he was taken by Apaches. I met an Apache boy named White Eagle who looked a lot like him."

There was nothing Jake could say to comfort her.

"At least I have something of Wolf left to me," Claire said.

"What is that?"

"His child."

"You're pregnant?" Anabeth blurted.

Claire's lips tilted upward in a secret smile. "The baby will be born in the fall." The smile disappeared as she continued, "I never had a chance to tell Wolf he was going to be a father." Her voice was a mere whisper when she said, "He died without knowing."

Over the next several days Claire stayed in Jeff's

room. She didn't say much, but she didn't cry much either. Jake and Anabeth clung to each other, sobered by Claire's tragedy into realizing what they had each been about to lose.

When they came together that first night after Anabeth had told Jake she loved him, Jake felt unaccountably shy about facing her. He tucked her head under his chin to keep from having to look her in the eye. Anabeth was willing enough to hide her face in his broad shoulder.

"I should have said it sooner," Anabeth said in a rush. "That I love you, I mean. I've felt it for a long time."

"I wish I could believe everything will work out all right," Jake confessed in a quiet voice.

"But you don't?"

"I'm starting to. I know I don't want to lose you, Kid." He paused and said, "I love you, too."

"You aren't just saying that because I did? Or because of the baby, are you, Jake?"

He shook his head. "The baby has nothing to do with how I feel about you." Jake put his hand on her belly, which was round with their child. "I can't promise what kind of father I'll be. I worry sometimes that I won't know what to do."

"Me, too," Anabeth said. "Other people always seem to manage somehow. So can we."

"Sometimes people don't do a very good job," Jake said.

"Like your mother?"

"I've tried to understand why she did what she did. I don't think I ever will."

"She's been dead a long time, Jake. Don't you think it's time you buried her once and for all? She can't hurt you any more. And I never will."

She turned her face up to him and said, "Tell me you love me, Jake. I want to hear it again and again.

And I'll say the words to you as often as you want, so you'll know I mean them, that I'll never stop meaning them. I love you, Jake.''

He kissed her with all the tenderness he was feeling. ''I love you, Kid.''

''I'm still wanted by the law, you know.''

''I haven't forgotten.'' But Jake had used the winter to think about that problem. And he had found, in his heart and mind, what he thought was the solution to it. ''Actually, Kid Calhoun is the one wanted by the law,'' he said. ''The only person I see in this room is a beautiful woman named Anabeth.''

''Wat Rankin knows that Anabeth and the Kid are the same person, and Solano is out there somewhere, too.''

''I'll deal with Wat Rankin and with Solano if it comes to that. Any more problems you need solved, Kid?''

''Just one. I have an ache. Right here.'' Anabeth's hand slid from her breasts, to her burgeoning belly, to the cleft between her thighs, so it wasn't quite clear exactly where the ache might be.

Jake was happy to ease it no matter where it was.

He started by brushing a tendril of hair from Anabeth's brow. He treated her as though she were fragile enough to break, removing her clothing one piece at a time, increasing the tension between them as he exposed her no-longer-slender body to his gaze.

''You are so beautiful,'' Jake murmured as he caressed her rounded belly.

''You make me feel beautiful, Jake.''

He suckled her as their child would suckle and Anabeth felt her body tighten with pleasure. He kissed his way down across her belly to the nest of curls below. When he kissed her there, Anabeth nearly came off the bed.

''Jake! What are you doing?''

"Loving you. Kissing you."

His lips and tongue touched her in intimate ways that sent frissons of pleasure through her. A low groan escaped from her throat. He lifted her up to his mouth and loved her until she was shivering with passion, until her body tightened like a bowstring and then erupted in a series of shuddering releases.

"Jake!" she cried. "Jake, I want . . ."

"What do you want, Kid?" he murmured.

"I want you."

He kissed his way up her body. When he finally reached her mouth she could taste herself on his lips. "I love you, Jake."

Jake liked hearing the words. He had been slow and gentle undressing Anabeth, but he was all haste as he practically tore his own clothes off. When he was naked he spooned his body around Anabeth, and angled one of her legs back over his. Then he held her belly with both hands as he entered her from behind.

Anabeth leaned back into Jake's body, anxious because the only part of him she could reach was his thighs. She found the crease along his inner thigh and had the satisfaction of hearing Jake gasp.

Jake's hands roamed her body, stroking her breasts, her belly, and finally the tiny nubbin hidden in the crisp hair at the apex of her thighs.

Anabeth felt the tension building as Jake slowly, gently thrust inside her. The breath wedged in her throat as she tried to tell him how much she liked what he was doing.

His mouth found her nape and bit her, then soothed the hurt with his lips and tongue. Her ears also got their share of attention, as he teased the lobe with his teeth. His moist breath in her ear sent shivers down her spine.

Her shuddering release caught her by surprise. Her

whole body tightened and she heard Jake's cry as he climaxed within her.

Jake stayed inside her. Anabeth relaxed against him, feeling the strength of his sweat-slick body, secure in the knowledge that she loved him and he loved her and that now they would be able to live happily ever after.

Only things have a way of turning out differently from the way people plan. As Claire had learned. As Jake and Anabeth would find out all too soon.

22

"Claire and I are going on a picnic," Anabeth announced one morning a few days later.

"Fine. As long as you have it on the front porch," Jake said.

"I thought we'd go down to the willow by the stream."

"It's not safe."

"Why don't you come along and keep an eye on us?" Anabeth asked. She gave him a come-hither look from beneath lowered lashes.

"I've got too much work to do."

"Then send someone else to watch over us," Anabeth insisted.

"Please, Jake," Claire said.

Jake looked from Anabeth to Claire and back again. "All right. I can't fight both of you."

"Thanks, Jake!" Anabeth gave him a quick hug. "Blackie will be along to warn us if Rankin comes around."

When Anabeth would have let him go, Jake held on and hugged her back. "Take care of yourself," he murmured in her ear. "Watch out for Rankin."

Anabeth and Claire walked, carrying the picnic

basket between them. Dog padded along behind Anabeth.

"I can't believe the difference in that black dog from the first time I saw him," Claire said. "Or the difference in Jake," she added.

"I don't know what you mean."

"They were both . . . alone. Now they're not."

"So was I," Anabeth said in a quiet voice. "Now I'm not."

The willow already had spring leaves, and once the two of them ducked inside the canopy of branches they were virtually invisible to the outside world.

"I had forgotten how wonderful this is!" Claire said.

Anabeth settled on the ground, and Dog quickly found a comfortable spot and curled up beside her. "This is my favorite place on Window Rock," she said.

"Jeff used to come here," Claire said. "After the Apaches took him, I never came back."

"How is Jeff, really?"

"He's fine, really. I just wish . . ."

Dog stood and stared out beyond the canopy of leaves. His neck fur hackled. A low rumble began in his throat.

Anabeth and Claire exchanged glances. Someone was out there.

"It's Rankin," Anabeth mouthed. "I'd bet on it."

"What do we do?" Claire whispered.

Anabeth put a hand on Dog's neck. She knew he would attack if she didn't hold on to him. And this time Rankin would kill him.

Anabeth leaned over to whisper in Claire's ear. "Here's what we're going to do. . . ."

Jake shielded his eyes and looked down the valley. He could swear he saw a black dot moving down there. Dog? Why was Dog coming back alone? Where was the woman he normally shadowed. *Where was Anabeth*?

"I have come for my woman. You will tell me where to find her *now*!"

Jake had been so focused on the movement in the valley, that the Apache caught him completely by surprise. Jake stared in disbelief at the painted warrior on horseback who had appeared before him to bar his way.

"Wolf? We thought you were dead!" Jake saw the barely healed wound on the Apache's temple where a bullet had cut into his scalp.

Wolf's nostrils flared and his lips flattened. "I have looked for my woman in the white man's house. I did not find her there. What have you done with her?"

Jake felt his neck hairs hackle at the Apache's demanding tone of voice. He reminded himself that Claire loved this man. He thought of how happy she would be to see Wolf alive and tried to ignore the fighting instinct that rose in him when he met the Apache's insolent stare.

"Claire and Anabeth are picnicking under that big willow down by the river," Jake said. "I'll ride with you, and we'll find them together."

Wolf didn't wait for Jake. He kicked his pony into a gallop and headed toward the stream that ran along the bottom slope of the valley.

"Hell and the devil!" Jake kicked his buckskin gelding into a hard gallop and soon caught up to the Indian. The closer they got, the more certain Jake became that the movement he had seen was Dog. He forced himself to remain calm. There was probably some simple explanation for why Dog wasn't with Anabeth. He wasn't going to panic over nothing.

Besides, he had sent a man to guard the two

women. Surely there would have been a signal if anyone had intruded on Window Rock land.

Jake glanced over at the Apache and realized that
he wouldn't want to be the man who touched Claire
against her will. The Indian's dark eyes were frightening to behold. Bleak. Merciless. Jake was glad he
was not an enemy.

Wolf couldn't explain to the white man the empti-
ness he had felt inside when he had woken two days
after the battle with the white soldiers to discover that
Little One was gone. When he had confronted White
Eagle, the boy had stood undaunted before his wrath.
White Eagle would say only that Wolf's woman had
wanted to go home, so he had taken her there.

Wolf was devastated to think that Little One would
leave him. It had taken him another day of brooding
to realize that he was not willing to live his life without her. He was going after her, and he wasn't coming back to the village alone.

As Wolf was leaving the village He Makes Trouble
had come running up to him. The tiny child had
tugged on Wolf's leggings to get his attention and
said, "Take me with you! I want to help find my
mother."

Wolf had not denied He Makes Trouble the right to
call the white woman mother. But the boy was too
young to come on such a journey. "You wait here, and
I will bring her back to you."

"If you say so, Father," He Makes Trouble had answered solemnly.

Wolf had opened his mouth to deny the kinship but
said nothing. He Makes Trouble would be a good son
—once some of the mischief had been lessoned out of
him. "Wait here," Wolf said. "And do not think to be
coming after me," he called over his shoulder. With
He Makes Trouble, you could not repeat a thing too
often.

Now the moment of truth was at hand. Could Wolf force Little One to come back to him against her will? Would it be necessary? Jake had said they thought him dead. Was that why Little One had fled the village? Was that why she hadn't gone to hide in the hills as the other women had done?

Jake saw the brooding look on the Apache's sharp-boned face and wondered what Claire saw in the taciturn man. He wasn't allowed much time to think about it, because the feeling struck him suddenly that something was wrong. They were no more than half-way to the site of the picnic when Jake realized what had made him so anxious.

"The lookout!"

"Where?" Wolf asked. "I see no one."

"That's just it," Jake said in a steely voice. "I sent a cowhand with a rifle along to guard the women and make sure nothing happened to them. He's not where he's supposed to be."

Jake made a slight detour to check on the man he had sent to keep an eye on Anabeth and Claire. His worst fears were confirmed when he pulled his horse up beside the pine where the man had been posted.

"He is dead," Wolf said after one look at the bloody body lying sprawled on the ground.

Jake slipped off his horse to see how the cowhand had been killed. "Stabbed." He mounted again and spurred his buckskin toward the willow.

"I never should have let her out of my sight," Jake muttered.

Halfway to the willow, they met Dog. He barked frantically and raced back toward the willow, then toward Jake again.

"Hell and the devil." Jake realized suddenly that Anabeth had sent the dog back on purpose. She had saved the damned dog instead of letting him protect her!

The two men galloped the rest of the way to the willow. They read the story left in the women's wake as though it were written in a book.

"Four, maybe five white men were here," Wolf said. "The one who killed your sentry joined the others when they left this place."

"They brought an extra horse, so this was planned in advance," Jake added. But Rankin hadn't been expecting to find Claire here because Jake had said she was visiting friends in Texas. So one of them had ridden double.

Jake recalled that Rankin—Reardon—had wanted to marry Claire. Was that why Rankin had killed Sam during the holdup? So Claire would become a widow?

Jake felt his stomach pitch. His flinty gray eyes met Wolf's gaze. "They'll kill the women when they're done with them."

"Why have they been taken? Do you have an enemy among the whites?"

"Wat Rankin," Jake said flatly. "He's hunting for stolen gold, and he thinks Anabeth knows where it is. And I think he had plans once upon a time to make Claire his wife."

"Will they go to the white man's town?"

"No. They'll go to the valley."

"Why?"

"Because that's where the gold is supposed to be hidden."

"Let us go," Wolf said. "I have a need to spill my enemy's blood this day."

The two men rode side by side toward the valley. Dog followed, but along the ridges, at a distance from them.

But Wat Rankin had anticipated pursuit. Jake and Wolf were still some distance from the valley when

they were ambushed, pinned down by a single gun-
man who was guarding the only way into the valley.

Jake pulled his rifle from the boot on his saddle and
returned the outlaw's fire. "I'll keep him busy if you'd
like to go pay him a visit," he said to Wolf.

The Apache's eyes narrowed. "It shall be as you
say." Wolf had spent a lifetime moving across the
rocky terrain without a sound, without leaving even
so much as a stem of grass bent to show that he had
passed. It was child's play to sneak up on the white
man who lay prone with his gun aimed down the canyon that led to the valley.

Wolf gave no warning, and the outlaw who had
been recruited by Wat in Santa Fe for a few dollars in
gold made no sound as he died with his throat slit
from ear to ear.

Wolf waved to Jake, who quickly scrambled up the
trail to join him.

There was no mercy in Jake's eyes when he looked
down at the dead outlaw. "I want Rankin. Leave him
for me."

"Which one is Rankin?" Wolf asked.

"He has long blond hair. The kind that makes a
showy scalp. You can't miss him."

Anabeth glared at Rankin, who was knotting the
rope that held both her and Claire tied to a wooden
stake planted in front of the stone house. "Jake will
kill you for this," she said.

"I expect he'll be comin' after you, all right,"
Rankin said. "But you see, Kid, we'll be waitin' for
him."

Anabeth exchanged a look with Claire, who was
tied with her back to Anabeth on the other side of the
stake. Both of them knew Rankin was right. Jake
would be coming. And with the way Rankin had them
tied to this post, there was no way Jake could save

them without exposing himself to the outlaws concealed nearby.

"Now if you was to tell me where that gold is, Kid, maybe we could make us a deal," Rankin said.

"I've told you I don't know where it is!"

"Maybe a few hours in the hot sun will refresh your memory," Wat said.

Anabeth looked up at a spring sun that felt a whole lot more like summertime. Already her mouth felt dry. She wasn't so much worried for herself and Claire as for what effect such a deprivation might have on the children they carried inside them.

When Rankin left them and moved into the shade of the house Claire asked, "Are you all right?"

"I'm fine. But your face . . ."

"It's nothing."

By turning her head Anabeth got a good look at the huge purple and pink bruise on Claire's cheek. "You shouldn't have tried to fight them," Anabeth said. "You should have just let them take me."

"I couldn't do that, Anabeth. All I could think was, what if it had been me they were after? You wouldn't have stood there doing nothing."

"I'm sorry I got you involved in this," Anabeth said.

"I still can't believe that Will Reardon is also an outlaw called Wat Rankin."

"Rankin was the man who shot and killed Sam," Anabeth said.

"Oh my God," Claire said. "Dear God. Does Jake know?"

"He knows."

"And Rankin wants you," Claire deduced, "because you can lead him to Sam's gold."

"I swear to you, Claire, that I don't know where it is. You have to believe me. If I knew, I'd have returned it long ago. Please don't hate me, Claire. I'm so sorry about what happened to Sam."

"I don't blame you, Anabeth."

"But I was there, Claire! I was on my knees beside Sam when he died. And his last words . . . He said he loved you, Claire. And that he was sorry about Jeff."

"Oh, Anabeth. So much tragedy . . ."

Both women were quiet for a while, each caught up in her own memories. Finally Claire said, "How many men do you think Jake will bring with him?"

"Shug won't stay behind. And surely he'll bring along a couple of the hands.

"They won't be able to do much with us being held hostage like this, will they?"

"Jake will figure something out."

Jake swore vehemently when he saw the two women staked out in front of the stone house. "How are we supposed to get them out of there?"

"We will have to wait until darkness falls," Wolf said.

"We can't leave them in that hot sun all day!"

"It is a small price to pay for their safe rescue," Wolf said.

Jake sighed heavily. "Anabeth is carrying my child."

"I have seen an Apache woman go a long time without water and bear a healthy child. So it will be with Stalking Deer. You will see."

"I hope you're right," Jake muttered.

"You are a fortunate man," Wolf said. "I have tried to make a child with my woman, but it has not happened."

Jake grinned. "Now there you're wrong."

"What?"

"Claire told us she's going to have your child in the fall."

"Why did she not tell me?"

"I gather there wasn't time."

But Wolf knew it was because she had planned to leave him. She had known he would never let her go if she told him she carried his seed. His dark eyes took on a dangerous look as they turned to search the valley. He would kill the men who had threatened his woman. Then he would take her home where she belonged. No one was going to stop him. Not her brother. Not even Little One herself.

"I'm going to take a look around," Jake said, "to make sure Rankin didn't plant some extra men here before he went after Anabeth."

"I will look also," Wolf said. "We will meet here when the sun sets to do what must be done."

The instant the two men left the hill two small heads bobbed up.

"I do not know why I let you talk me into this," White Eagle said.

"It was for her sake, and you know it," He Makes Trouble replied. "We cannot let our mother be taken captive and do nothing to save her."

"Wolf will make sure she comes safely away from this place."

"He may need our help."

White Eagle eyed the smaller boy askance. He knew better than to disobey, and yet he had allowed himself to be swayed by He Makes Trouble. Likely the boy would one day be a leader of the tribe, he talked so smoothly. But they were here now, and it was up to him to see that He Makes Trouble did not make things worse instead of better. It was always possible that the younger boy was right. If they remained hidden, there was the chance that they might be of some use later, when help was needed.

"Come with me," White Eagle said. "Let us move closer so we can hear what is being said."

"Do you remember the white words?" He Makes Trouble asked.

White Eagle frowned. "Most of them."

"I do not understand how you could have a mother like Little One and be willing to give her up," He Makes Trouble mused.

"I did not give her up," White Eagle retorted. "I was stolen from her."

"Did you not miss her?"

"In the beginning. I was only as old as you are now when Broken Foot brought me to the village. I was afraid. I cried for my mother. But she did not come to get me."

"Why not?"

White Eagle tugged on his lower lip with his teeth. "I thought it was because she did not care. I got very angry with her and with my white father. I hated them for abandoning me.

"But Cries Aloud was a good mother. Soon I was too busy doing things—things I had never been allowed to do before—to think about my white parents." He shrugged. "I forgot about them."

"Little One never forgot about you."

White Eagle frowned. "No. She remembered me for a long time."

"Do you still hate her?" He Makes Trouble asked.

"No. I . . . There are memories of our times together that fill my heart with joy. I was only afraid she would try to take me away from Broken Foot and Cries Aloud. Now . . . I do not want her to be hurt."

"Well, that is why we are here," He Makes Trouble said. "With both of us to watch over her, surely she will come back home safe."

The two boys inched their way down into the valley, using skills that were still new. So new, that they made mistakes. Which was how they found themselves facing the barrel of a shotgun with a one-eyed white man holding the trigger.

"Hold it right there, you little Injun bastards!"

There was only an instant to react, but it was enough for White Eagle to shove He Makes Trouble aside. The blast of the shotgun roared in their ears, but only a few pellets found flesh.

The burly outlaw made the mistake of thinking that two Apache kids were all the danger he faced. He stood up to fire the second barrel, which was when Dog ripped the man's throat out. The second blast went off into the ground as the outlaw crumpled to the ground, his scream caught in his ragged flesh.

Jake was there almost instantly to call off Dog. He wasn't sure he wouldn't be bitten himself, but as soon as Jake spoke to the animal, Dog calmly sat down beside the dead outlaw and licked the blood from his jowls.

Wolf's face was fierce to behold, but his hands were gentle as he reached out to run them over the two boys. "How bad is your wound?" he asked White Eagle.

"My shoulder hurts a little," the child replied.

Wolf turned his savage look on He Makes Trouble, whose eyes were still wide with fright. Before Wolf could say anything, Jake joined the Apache.

The Ranger's brow arched when he realized Wolf was nursemaiding two Indian boys. The oldest one couldn't have been more than nine or ten. "What are they doing here?"

"We came to help our mother," White Eagle said in English.

"Jeff?" The boy's hair was darker than Jeff's had been, but his green eyes—Sam's eyes—remained steady on Jake. Then Jake recognized Sam's nose and mouth and chin. "Is it really you?"

"I am called White Eagle," the boy said.

Jake could see Jeffrey was about to faint from shock as a result of his wound. He turned to Wolf and said, "We'd better get them out of here. Rankin will be sending someone up here to see what happened."

"Come, He Makes Trouble," Wolf said.

White Eagle had risen and started to walk on his own when Jake scooped him off his feet.

"I can walk," the boy protested.

"Just indulge your uncle Jake, boy. We have to move fast, and this way we won't leave a trail of blood for them to follow."

White Eagle couldn't argue with that. In fact, he wasn't feeling well enough to protest too much. He laid his head on his uncle's shoulder and let his eyes drift closed.

The two men made their way with the two boys to the far end of the valley where the pond was located. Dog followed them at a distance.

At the pond they encountered yet another newly recruited outlaw. They hid in the bushes while they tried to decide the best way to approach him.

"We can't afford to let him get off a shot," Jake said. "We don't want to alert Rankin that we've come to this end of the valley."

"Leave this to me," Wolf said.

This time it was Wolf who took a misstep. A stone rolled, alerting the outlaw.

"Who's there? Speak, damn you, or I'll shoot!"

Wolf was in plain sight, but he remained perfectly still. He saw the outlaw's eyes pass him by, then come back and light on him. "Dirty Injun!"

Jake had been watching the drama play out in front of him, but he still held Jeffrey in his arms. It was He Makes Trouble who provided the distraction that saved Wolf's life.

The boy stood and shouted, *"Ahagake!"* Then he put his thumbs in his ears and waggled his fingers at the

white man. "Come and get me!" he yelled in Apache.
"Your mother was a coyote bitch! Come and get me,
you coyote pup!"

The outlaw was so startled that he made the mistake of shifting his gunsight off Wolf. The Indian's arrow sang true, catching the outlaw in the heart. He dropped like a stone.

When Jake and the boys joined Wolf, He Makes Trouble kept his eyes aimed down. Once again he had disobeyed.

Wolf put a hand on the boy's shoulder and said, "That was a warrior's deed—to draw an enemy's fire to save another. I am thankful for your courage, He Makes Trouble."

"You are not angry with me?"

"I did not say that," Wolf said with a sardonic smile. "You could as easily have been killed. I would have been sorry for that."

He Makes Trouble beamed up at Wolf. "I will remember your words, Father. And try to do better."

Wolf felt a thickness in his throat. It was pride in the boy. And love for him. And the hope that he would always be worthy of the boy's adulation.

The sun was leaving the sky, which meant it was time for the two men to make their way back to the stone house. Jake had rigged a sling to keep Jeffrey's shoulder immobile. The gunshot pellets still had to be removed, but that could be done later. For now, the bleeding had stopped.

"I want you to watch over White Eagle," Wolf instructed He Makes Trouble. "You will stay here. In this you will *not* disobey me."

"Do not worry, Father. I will do as I am told."

Jake left Dog to guard the two boys while he and Wolf headed down the valley to rescue the women they loved.

* * *

Wat Rankin was furious. "How the hell did they manage to get into the valley without Fredericks seeing them?" he ranted. He had heard the shotgun blast and sent the Mexican to investigate.

"I do not know, señor," Solano said. "But the one-eyed man is dead. I checked the entrance to the valley, and that man, he is dead also."

"What about Pritzel? Is he all right?" Wat asked.

"I did not go to the pond, señor. I thought I would come here first."

Wat's eyes narrowed. The Mexican was right. If that Ranger had been in the valley most of the afternoon there was a good chance Pritzel was dead, too. There was no sense getting Solano killed by sending him into some trap.

"You'll stay here with me," Wat said. He looked around the stone house that he had thought a veritable fortress the first time he had seen it. In light of what he knew about the Ranger, he was beginning to think it could be more of a deathtrap.

Only he had his ace in the hole. The two women tied up outside were his ticket to freedom if anything went wrong. He planned to use them to find out where the gold was hidden. He had already ransacked the house searching for it, and he had searched the cave behind the house as well. But he had found nothing.

Night was falling. In the dark the Ranger would surely try to sneak up on him. Unless he could somehow make sure it was lighter outside than inside.

Wat turned to Solano and said, "I want you to gather up all the firewood you can find. I want to make a bonfire so big it'll light up this whole end of the valley."

"Sí, señor."

Wat Rankin had done things the easy way all his life. It had seemed easier to find the gold that had already been stolen than to rob another stage. It had seemed easier to kill Sam Chandler and take his wife than to find a wife of his own. Now it appeared the stakes were a lot higher than he had thought. There was a chance—a slight one—that he might not make it out of this valley alive.

Maybe he should have stayed an "honest" rancher. At the time, his plan had seemed so simple and so certain to succeed. Now it appeared he had lost not only the gold, but his chance to have Claire and Window Rock as well.

He looked at the two women tied up in front of the house. He might as well enjoy them while he had the chance. He took a knife from his belt and headed outside to cut them free.

Solano went about collecting wood and building the bonfire just as he had been told. When he had the fire burning brightly, he slipped away. That Rankin, he was *loco*. The deaths of the outlaws who had joined them weighed heavily on the Mexican. He did not like the odds of his leaving the valley alive.

Solano decided to improve them by leaving now. He would be waiting for whoever came out of the valley. And he would help himself to the gold if it had been found. He would survive where others had died. The Mexican did not worry about his betrayal of Wat Rankin. An outlaw learned to think of himself first, last, and always.

Solano was quiet as he made his escape. Silent as he had learned to be over the years as a wanted man. Silent as daybreak.

There was another, even more silent, who shadowed him.

23

Anabeth's chin sagged onto her chest. Her tongue felt thick and dry. She was suffering desperately from thirst. "Why hasn't Jake come to rescue us?"

Claire had no saliva to swallow with. "He's probably waiting for it to get dark."

"It is dark."

"Not quite. There's still some pink showing on the rim of the valley."

A fire flared up in front of the stone house.

"Now what?" Anabeth asked.

"I'm afraid we're going to find out soon enough."

Wat had his gun out of the holster when he came to untie the women. "Don't make any sudden moves. Take it slow and easy, and I won't have to shoot."

Wat hadn't counted on how much the lack of water or freedom of movement would affect the two women. When he released the ropes, Anabeth sank to the ground. Claire knelt beside her.

"Get up!" Wat ordered. "Both of you!"

Claire snapped back, "She can't get up, you fool! Can't you see she's exhausted. She needs water."

"There's water inside," Rankin said. "You get her on her feet, or I'll drag her by the hair. Take your choice."

Claire could see that he meant it. She put Anabeth's arm around her shoulder and struggled to her feet. She half-carried the younger woman into the house and sat her down at a chair by the kitchen table.

"Where's the water?" Claire demanded.

Rankin gestured with his gun toward a barrel of water inside the door. "You can get her a dipper from there."

Anabeth guzzled the water greedily, feeling stronger as her body absorbed the life-giving liquid.

"What are you going to do with us now?" Anabeth rasped.

Rankin looked at her burgeoning belly and wondered what it would be like to do it with a woman who had one in the basket. Would he feel the child when he thrust inside her?

He gestured with the gun toward the bedroom and then toward Anabeth. "You go on in there and wait for me."

"No."

He had hold of her hair so fast she didn't have time to escape his grasp. He yanked her head backward, the gun at her throat. "When I say move, you move!"

Claire jumped to her feet. "Leave her alone!"

"You come a step closer, and I'll shoot her dead," he said to Claire.

"Rankin! I know you're in there! This is Jake Kearney. I want to talk."

Wat gave a shove that sent Anabeth flying toward Claire. When she landed, both of them lost their balance and fell in a tangle of arms and legs.

"Don't move!" Wat ordered. He went to stand beside the window. He searched the edges of light outside the stone house trying to find Kearney. "Show yourself, Kearney."

"I'm not that much of a fool, Rankin."

"Where's the gold, Kearney?"

"Let the women go, and I'll take you to it."

"I'm not that much of a fool, Kearney," Wat said with a raucous laugh. "You better start talkin' or I might just—"

"Wait! What if I trade myself for the women? How about it, Rankin?"

"You come out where I can see you with your hands up and maybe we can talk."

"Don't do it, Jake!" Anabeth shouted.

"Shut up!" Rankin backhanded her, but Anabeth came up spitting and fighting. Claire joined the fray. One of them grabbed Wat's hair and yanked hard, the other clawed at his gunhand. For a moment it seemed as though they would overwhelm him. Then the gun went off.

Jake's heart stopped when he heard the gunshot inside the house. "Kid! Claire!"

Then he heard a woman's scream.

There was no thought to his own safety in Jake's headlong rush toward the stone house. He had his gun drawn when he kicked the door open.

Jake froze where he was. Wat Rankin had his arm around Anabeth's throat, his gun aimed at her head.

"Drop it," Rankin said.

Jake dropped his gun.

"Kick it over here," Rankin ordered.

Jake did as he was told. Rankin moved a couple of steps with Anabeth and kicked the gun into the next room.

"Where's Claire?"

Rankin gestured with his chin to the corner.

Jake's jaw tightened when he saw the huddled mass lying there. Blood ran down Claire's face. "Is she dead?"

"Naw. Just knocked her out with the butt of my gun. She'll have a little headache, but she'll be just fine. You, on the other hand, are not long for this world. Unless you start talkin'—fast."

"The gold's not in the valley," Jake said.

"What kind of crap are you tryin' to hand me?" Rankin snarled. "This is the perfect damned hidin' place. That gold is here. I can feel it in my teeth."

"It's not here," Jake repeated.

"Where is it, then?"

"Booth left a clue to the location of the gold when he died," Jake said.

"What is it?"

"Back door."

"That's it? What's it mean?"

Jake shrugged. "You're welcome to try to figure it out on your own. Or you can let the women go, and I'll tell you."

Wat repeated the clue several times to himself, frowning all the while. The two words made no sense. Unless they had something to do with the hideout. Maybe Booth had left the gold at the back door to the shack before he had ridden around to the front. That must be it!

Unless the "clue" was just a bunch of hogwash concocted by the Ranger to throw him off the trail. He cocked the gun he held to Anabeth's head. "I don't trust you."

"He's telling the truth," Anabeth said. "I swear it!"

Rankin's eyes shifted from Jake to the Kid and back again. "If she knows where the gold is, there's no reason to keep you alive is there, lawman?"

It only took a second for Wat to turn the gun from Anabeth to Jake. Everything moved in slow motion for Anabeth as she threw her full weight at the outlaw. She felt herself falling as the gun went off.

Things speeded up again as Jake launched himself across the room. The two men rolled around the wooden-planked floor, first one on top and then the other, writhing, kicking, punching, so that it was hard to see who was winning the battle.

Anabeth lay where she had fallen, her legs pulled up to protect her swollen belly from the pain that seared her like a knife. She made a keening sound, afraid of what the pain in her belly might mean.

"Claire," she whispered. "Claire!"

Claire's eyelids fluttered. She lifted a hand to her bloody head, and tentatively touched the swollen flesh there.

"Can you move?" Anabeth whispered. "Can you reach Wat's gun?"

Anabeth nodded with her chin toward the gun that had flown from Rankin's hand when he had hit the floor. It was halfway across the room.

"I can try," Claire said. She pulled herself along the floor with her elbows and knees, always with an eye to the fight going on between the two men.

Just as she reached the gun, Rankin kicked it away with his boot. "Get away from that, bitch."

Claire met Anabeth's terrified eyes and once again started crawling toward the outlaw's gun.

Jake finally got the hold he wanted on Rankin's neck. "If you have anything you want to say to your Maker, say it now, you bastard."

"I wish to hell I'd taken that gold when I shot the sonofabitch who was carryin' it," Rankin gasped.

Jake froze.

Claire stared with loathing at the yellow-haired outlaw who had killed Sam. "You're an animal," she said in a soft voice. "You deserve to die for killing Sam."

"And for killing Booth," Anabeth whispered.

Jake cut off Rankin's air, and the two women watched with merciless eyes as the outlaw thrashed in Jake's grasp.

The knife appeared so suddenly and was used with

such effect that it took a moment for Anabeth and Claire to realize what had happened.

When the blade stabbed into Jake's forearm, he let go of the outlaw. He howled in pain when Rankin turned and yanked the knife back out again.

Rankin surged to his feet, the knife in his hand still dripping Jake's blood. His triumphant gaze leaped from Jake's cold gray eyes, to Anabeth's dark blue ones, to Claire's golden topaz orbs.

"I'm going to slit your throat, Kearney. But not before I rape your woman. And your sister. I'm going to—"

Rankin looked down at his chest in surprise. There, sticking out from the fourth rib, was a feathered shaft. He looked up again, and his eyes went wide when he saw the Apache standing there.

"I'll be damned. Killed by an Injun." He laughed, but the sound caught in his throat. Blood streamed through his fingers where he clutched his wound.

"I'm gonna miss having me them two women—"

Rankin never had a chance to finish his grisly requiem. Jake broke his neck first.

There was a sudden babble of voices as each of the four people in the room made sure that their respective loved ones were safe.

Anabeth appropriated Jake's bandanna and wrapped it several times around the knife wound in his forearm. She tied it tightly to stem the flow of blood.

"That probably needs stitches," she said.

"Later," Jake said. "Are all the outlaws accounted for?"

"The one who tried to leave the valley, the Mexican, he will trouble you no more," Wolf said.

"Solano," Anabeth murmured to herself. All those who had taken part in Booth's murder had paid for their treachery with their lives. Now, at last, Kid Calhoun could rest in peace. And a young woman named Anabeth was free to think about the future.

Wolf knelt beside Claire and brushed a gentle finger against the bruise on her face. "I wish he were alive, that I might kill him again," he said savagely.

"Wolf! Oh my God, Wolf!" Claire said in a voice filled with wonder and with joy. She clutched Wolf tightly as he sat down and pulled her into his arms.

"Why did you leave the village, Little One?" he murmured in her ear.

"I thought you'd been killed by the soldiers! When White Eagle said he would take me home, there was no reason for me to stay."

He fingered her golden hair, which had been cut off at the shoulder. "You mourned for me in the Apache way?"

"The man who won my heart was Apache," she answered.

"Then you did not wish to leave me?"

"Oh no! I . . . I love you, Wolf. I thought I would never have a chance to say that. I want you to know now in case . . . I want you to know."

Wolf held one of her hands in his, rubbing the knuckles with his thumb. "When I thought you wanted to leave me, I was angry. I came after you intending to take you back whether you wished to come or not. Now . . ."

His dark eyes searched her face. "Now I ask you to come with me. To be my woman. To be my wife."

Claire's heart soared on wings. The smile on her face felt silly—and wonderful. "Do you mean it, Wolf?"

"I never say what I do not mean."

She laughed. "Then, yes. Oh yes!"

He kissed her once hard, a kiss to seal their future. A promise of forever that he had never thought to make.

Across the room, Anabeth felt tears sting her eyes as she listened to Wolf's tender confession of love. The sharp pains in her belly hadn't stopped completely, but they came less frequently, and they were less strong. She relaxed back into Jake's arms. "Booth is avenged now, and the Calhoun Gang is no more."

"Kid Calhoun is dead and buried," Jake said.

"Jake?" Anabeth whispered.

"Yeah, Kid?" he murmured huskily.

"Are you going to marry me?"

"What?"

She punched him in the shoulder. "You heard me."

"Is that a proposal?"

"The man is supposed to do the asking," she said in an aggrieved voice.

Jake grinned. "Will you marry me, Kid?"

"Why should I?" she retorted.

"Because I adore you. Because I want to spend my life loving you."

Anabeth searched Jake's face and found there the truth in his words. "All right, Jake. I'll marry you."

Jake swallowed over the thickness in his throat. His hand scraped across the floor as he tried to lift it to Anabeth's cheek. He looked down and stared at what he saw. "Kid?"

"What?"

"Could what you heard Booth say be 'trap door' instead of 'back door'?"

Anabeth frowned. "I don't know. Why do you ask?"

Jake's fingers traced the wooden floor, feeling for rough edges. Where the floor met the wall he found a small metal loop. Jake stuck his finger in it and pulled. A section of the floor lifted up and out.

There lay Sam's money belt, stained brown with his blood. Jake carefully hoisted it out and laid it on the floor beside him. He looked over at Claire. "There it is, Claire."

Wolf stiffened. He knew as well as any of them the significance of the gold. He looked at Claire, but she was already shaking her head.

"You keep it, Jake."

"If you ever need a place to come, a refuge," Jake said, including Wolf in his gaze, "Window Rock will be there."

"I know," Claire said. "Maybe . . . someday . . . I'll be able to go back there. But not now. I—"

Everyone froze at the sound of footsteps outside the stone house.

"Get the gun!" Anabeth mouthed to Claire, who was closest to it.

The panic ceased abruptly when they realized it was only He Makes Trouble who had arrived in the doorway.

"If I am lucky, the Gray One will come with a basket some night to carry you away," Wolf said in a severe voice.

"I had to come," the Apache boy said. His eyes were wide and frightened, but he held a knife clutched in his hand. "I was worried when you did not return." *And scared.* But He Makes Trouble did not say that. He wanted his father to be proud of him. It was worth the tongue-lashing to know his newfound parents had survived and that he was not going to be an orphan again.

Claire opened her arms, and the Apache boy snuggled into them. "I am glad to see you, Mother."

"And I'm glad to see you," Claire said, smoothing the Indian boy's hair back from his face.

"Where is White Eagle?" Wolf asked.

"He is waiting outside."

Wolf called the boy's name, and Jeffrey appeared in the doorway.

"I did not want to disobey you," White Eagle said,

"but He Makes Trouble would have come alone if I had not come with him."

"He can be very persuasive," Wolf agreed.

Dog stuck his nose in the doorway. He sat down and thumped his tail once.

"Blackie," Anabeth cried. The dog crossed to Anabeth and licked her face. "I sent him to find you," Anabeth told Jake.

"And he did," Jake said.

Jeffrey lingered in the doorway. Wolf called to him. "Come inside and greet your mother, White Eagle."

Claire's eyes widened at the title Wolf had given her. And softened when Jeffrey stepped farther into the room.

"Greetings, White Eagle," she said.

"I am glad you are safe," White Eagle said. He stood before her, feet shuffling. "Broken Foot said I must come to you."

Claire's brow furrowed. "When? Why?"

"He was killed by the white soldiers, and Cries Aloud with him. With his last breath, Broken Foot said I should go live with my aunt's son."

"Your cousin?" Claire asked, confused.

"Wolf."

"Wolf is your cousin? And now your father?"

White Eagle nodded, but kept his eyes on his feet.

"And I am to be your mother?" Claire tried to keep her voice even, but it trembled with emotion.

Again, White Eagle nodded.

"I am honored," she said quietly. "I'll try to be a good Apache mother."

Jeffrey's green eyes flashed up at her. "And I will try to be a good son."

"Then come and embrace me, as a son should greet his mother," she said in a trembling voice.

Anabeth felt the tears welling as Jeffrey crossed the room. She looked up at Jake to share the moment with him. His gray eyes were warm with love, liquid with emotion.

When Claire had her son back in her arms for the first time in nearly four years, she looked up at Wolf. Everything she felt was there for him to see in her eyes.

The Apache pulled He Makes Trouble tight against his side. He did not turn away from Claire when a tear slipped from his eye. He did not wish to hide his joy.

Anabeth shrieked as something slimy landed on her hand.

Jake and Wolf were instantly alert. "What is it? What's wrong?"

"It's . . . it's . . ." Anabeth looked down and laughed.

"What?" Jake asked, irritated that he wasn't in on the joke—especially since his heart was still in his throat.

"It is my frog," He Makes Trouble volunteered. "I wondered where he had gone. I had him in my hand when I was waiting outside, but he got away." He walked over and recovered the bullfrog and held it up for their inspection. "See?"

A smile curved Claire's lips. Jake shook his head and chuckled. Wolf tried not to laugh, but couldn't help himself.

The four adults looked from one to another. They were no longer four people facing life alone. They were a family, with ties that would last a lifetime. And love that would last forever.

Wolf took Claire's hand in his. "Let us go home," he said.

Jake knelt beside Anabeth. "What do you say, Kid?"

Anabeth looked into Jake's warm gray eyes and smiled. "Oh yes, Jake. Let's go home."

Author's Note

Among the Apache, children were taught not to use a person's name to his face, because when a person was called by his name he was compelled to respond to whatever request was made of him. If an Apache was angry and wanted to provoke a fight, he could call a man by his name. Thus, few Apaches told white men their real names.

To avoid using names, the Apache resorted to referring to people in terms of their relationship to others, such as the father of someone or the uncle of someone, by their age, by nicknames, or simply by pointing.

The Apache names we are familiar with were given by white men to the Indians, and many have Spanish origins—Geronimo, Mangas Coloradas, Delgadito, Ponce, Cochise, Kayitah, Juh, Alchise, Benito, and Nana, to name a few. Among themselves, the Apache had names such as Stepping on Water, Thin Old Woman, Coyote Has Sores, Going About with Head Bent Down, Not Quite Enough, Yellow Eyelids, Buckskin Shaker, and so forth. Unless the name itself referred to a sex, such as Red Boy, names were not indicative of the bearer's sex.

For purposes of this book, I have taken the liberty of using what would have been the Apache names for characters. I have allowed them to address each other by name without the consequences that would have ordinarily ensued according to Apache manners and customs.

LETTER TO READERS

Dear Readers,

In response to the tremendous number of letters I received from you asking for a sequel to *The Barefoot Bride* that would tell Patch and Ethan's story, I have written *Outlaw's Bride*. You'll find the first chapter of the sequel following this note. Believe me, there are lots of humorous, hair-raising adventures in store for Patch and Ethan before they find true love with each other.

I always appreciate hearing your opinions and find inspiration from your questions, comments, and suggestions. It would be fun to know more about you—your age, what you do for a living, and where you usually find my books—whether new or used.

For those of you who may be interested, I also write contemporary Westerns. You can look for Hawk's Way Trilogy in April, May, and June 1993, from Silhouette Desire. The series includes *The Rancher and the Runaway Bride*, *The Cowboy and the Princess*, and *The Wrangler and the Rich Girl*.

I've also written a wonderful historical Western novella entitled "One Simple Wish" for the Harlequin anthology *Untamed! Tales of the West*, which is scheduled for publication in July 1993.

Please write to me at P. O. Box 8531, Pembroke Pines, FL 33084 and enclose a self-addressed, stamped envelope so I can respond. I personally read and answer all my mail,

though as some of you know, a reply might be delayed if
I have a writing deadline.

Take care and keep reading!

Happy trails,
Joan Johnston
March 1993

OUTLAW'S BRIDE
by
Joan Johnston

1

She was a lady. Ethan recognized the breed, though it had been a long time since he had seen one quite so fresh from finishing school—feathers in her hat, gloves on her hands, and a steel rod running down her spine. He was hidden from view in a high-backed chair in the lobby of the Oakville Hotel. Waiting. Every so often his green eyes flicked to the dusty street outside. Watching.

His eyes were drawn back to the lady. The soft complexion of peaches and cream and a short, up-tilted nose contrasted with a strong, determined chin. His lip curled cynically. A lady used to getting her own way, he amended. She looked up at the hotel clerk from under long, feathery lashes that concealed big blue—not quite innocent, he thought—eyes. Her voice was melodious, not demanding, but not demure, either.

"I'd like a room please," she said.

"For how long?" the clerk asked.

Ethan watched the lady's brow furrow. Her black-gloved hand reached up to smooth already perfect golden tresses bound up in a very ladylike bun at her nape. "I don't know," she said. "I'm looking for someone who—" She cut herself off.

Ethan was distracted by something on the registration desk. The lady's velvet drawstring purse, which exactly matched her rose red dress, seemed to be moving of its own accord. A moment later a pointed pink nose and long whiskers appeared at the center of the drawstring opening. Ethan grinned. Somehow a field mouse had gotten into the lady's purse.

He started to call a warning, but looked out the plate-glass window first. He didn't want to let them know where he was any sooner than necessary. Instead of speaking, he leaned back into the comfortable winged chair and waited for the fun to start.

To his amazement, elegant gloved hands surreptitiously poked the mouse back into the purse and once again drew the strings tight. Ethan's brow arched in speculation. She wasn't quite what she seemed, then. No lady in his experience had ever carried a mouse around in her purse.

"I don't know how long I'll be here," the lady repeated. "I would love to have a bath sent up to my room. It's been a long trip."

From where? Ethan wondered. And who had she come to find in Oakville, Texas? Lucky man. Because besides being a lady, she was also a woman. Full breasts that would overflow a man's hands, a tiny waist—unfortunately corseted—and long legs that he could imagine wrapped tight around him while he thrust deep inside her.

Ethan felt his body respond, felt the heavy pulse in his throat, the tightness in his groin. He reminded himself that the steel rod down a lady's back didn't usually unbend for the finer pleasures in life. Besides, he thought bitterly, no *lady* was going to want anything to do with him—ever again.

"Hawk! Ethan Hawk! We know you're in there. Come on out!"

Ethan rose slowly from the high-backed chair. He

saw the stunned look on the lady's face as she turned to stare at him. He grinned and tipped his Stetson to her. From the corner of his eye he saw the flash of sunlight on blue steel out on the street. He launched himself at the lady and yelled to the clerk, "Duck, Gilley!"

Ethan twisted in mid-air, trying to keep the lady from being crushed beneath him as he snatched her out of harm's way. Several bullets crashed through the hotel window, sending glass flying. He landed on his shoulder and rolled several times away from the splintering glass.

The lady was a lovely package, but enough to knock the wind from him. He knew every second counted, but he lay frozen for a moment, infinitely aware of the curves lying beneath him. Her hat had come off, and her hair had come loose from its tight bun. A stray curl was tickling his nose, which was pressed against her throat. He blew it away, and felt her shiver.

Ethan lifted his head and looked into big blue eyes that seemed to swallow him in their depths. Her hair lay like a golden nimbus around a heart-shaped face. She had her lower lip caught in straight white teeth. He surveyed that perfect complexion—now pale with fright—and realized that powder half-hid a dozen freckles across her nose. So, he had exposed another of the lady's secrets. He wished he had time to discover them all. But there were men waiting outside for him. Dangerous men.

He reached across her for his Stetson, which lay amid scattered glass on the Aubusson carpet, and settled it back on his head. He was aware of her femininity as firm breasts cushioned his chest. His body naturally slipped into the cradle of her thighs. He swore at his instantaneous reaction to such intimate contact. From the way her eyes widened and darkened, she felt it, too.

She struggled to get up, but he put a hand to her shoulder to hold her down. "Stay here," he warned. "Don't move!"

He started to slide off her, but stopped when she said his name.

"Ethan?"

Her eyes searched his face and for a moment he thought she looked familiar. Especially with those freckles and a strand of that glorious golden hair falling over one eye. "Do I know you?"

Her eyes showed pain, as though a shard of glass had cut her deep. "Are you all right?" he asked. His hands quickly roamed her body searching for some wound.

That perked her up. Her face got that indignant look he might have expected from a lady not used to having a man handle her like a woman. She opened her mouth to speak, but before she could, there was another cry from the street.

"Hawk! Come on out, Hawk!"

He grinned and touched the brim of his hat to her. "Sorry I can't stay to get better acquainted. If you're smart, darlin', you'll get out of Oakville while there's still some starch in your drawers."

She gasped but his attention was already focused on the men out in the street, hired killers who wanted him dead so they could collect their blood money from Jefferson Trahern. Ethan had learned that he couldn't expect help from the sheriff. Careless Lachlan owed his livelihood to the town council. And the town council was owned by the richest rancher in Oak County, Texas—Jefferson Trahern.

Ethan realized the lady was trying to wriggle out from under him. "Keep your head down!" he snapped, grabbing a handful of those golden tresses to hold her still.

"Ethan, it's me! It's Patch!" she hissed at him, her head bobbing up again. "Patch Kendrick."

He stared with dawning horror at the once-impeccably groomed lady lying beneath him, the beautiful stranger who had stirred his lusts. He released her hair and rolled off her as though she had become a bed of angry ants.

"Don't move! Not an inch! Your pa will kill me if anything happens to you!"

He crawled quickly toward the side window and slithered out into the dark alley before another call came from the street.

What the devil was Seth Kendrick's tomboy daughter doing in Oak County, Texas? And when, by God, had she become a *lady*? Ethan stood in the shadows of the alley near the front of the hotel and waited for the hired guns to make their move. And remembered.

The last time he had seen Patch Kendrick was eight years ago in Fort Benton, Montana. She had been a pugnacious twelve-year-old brat with elfin features, budding breasts—and the crazy idea that she was in love with him! He had been twenty-five, her father's best friend—and on the run from the law.

Jefferson Trahern had been hunting him even then. Ethan had ridden hard and fast out of Fort Benton to avoid the detectives Trahern constantly had trailing him. He hadn't been caught—not for another year, anyway. Then . . .

What was it Patch had made him promise her when he had left Fort Benton eight years ago? That he would marry her when she was grown up? No, he wouldn't have—couldn't have—promised that! Not, leastways, to a kid who spent more time sporting a black eye than any three prize fighters, who collected wild animals like marbles, and who swore like a bullwhacker who had been to Sunday meeting. He could hear her ranting now with her *garns* and *durns*. Danged if he didn't!

Ethan smiled at the memory of the precocious child she had been. So what had he promised that rumpled hoyden—now elegant lady—the last time he had seen her? She had made him cross his heart, he remembered that. He frowned, trying to dredge up the memory of that long ago conversation.

But he couldn't recall it. She had just been a kid with romantic notions. He hadn't paid much attention to exactly what he had said to her, something about returning to Fort Benton when she was all grown up, as best he could remember. His mouth flattened and his eyes narrowed as he thought of the reason why he hadn't gone back to see her again.

Otherwise, he had promised her . . . nothing. Which was a damned good thing, considering the fact that no decent woman would have anything to do with him now. Whatever she might once have been, now Patch Kendrick was one helluva lady.

Ethan couldn't believe the carnal thoughts he'd had about her. And the way he had touched her! Ethan felt the heat in his face. How was he ever going to look Seth Kendrick in the eye? Ethan grimaced. Reluctant as he was to admit it, Patch Kendrick was about the most arousing piece of femininity he had ever held in his arms. Even thinking about her had his body thrumming with desire.

Unfortunately, if Seth ever got wind of the thoughts Ethan was having about his daughter, Ethan wouldn't have to wait for Trahern's vengeance to put him six feet under. Seth would kill him first!

"Come out and get what's comin' to ya, Hawk!"

Ethan pulled his Colt and fanned the hammer as he charged out of the alley, spraying bullets at the five men who converged on him from all sides of Main Street.

He saw one go down near the horse trough. Another fell on the wooden porch of the mercantile. A third dropped where he stood in the center of the rutted street. The fourth dove for cover behind the livery. The fifth got off one shot before he pitched headlong through the plate-glass window of the Silver Buckle Saloon.

By then, even with his awkward gait—long step, halting step, long step, halting step—Ethan had reached his horse. He launched himself into the saddle and spurred the big black stallion. The animal hit his stride long before the mass confusion Ethan had left behind him cleared enough for anyone to grab a rifle.

"Ethan! Ethan Hawk!"

He heard Patch Kendrick calling him from the front porch of the hotel and reined his horse to an abrupt stop at the end of the short main street. The urge to answer her was strong. But she could have no idea of the trouble he was in. And he wasn't about to let her get involved. The instant Trahern found out Ethan cared anything about her, Patch would become a target for the old man's revenge.

He pulled off his hat, letting his sun-streaked blond hair blow in the wind and gave her a gentleman's bow from the saddle. Then he spurred the black stud and raced out of town, disappearing in a cloud of Texas dust.

Patricia Wallis Kendrick had watched the gunfight unfold with a mixture of terror and awe. She had traveled all the way from Fort Benton, Montana, to find the man who had just ridden hell-bent-for-leather out of this godforsaken South Texas town. She had an old debt to settle with Ethan Hawk. Years ago he had promised to return when she was a grown woman to court her—and to marry her. Patch was here to hold him to his promise.

She angled her hat in a rakish tilt over her brow and tucked a stray blond curl back into the mass of hair she had repinned into a stylish bun. Then she marched down the front steps of the hotel toward the man who had arrived on the scene—well after the gunfight—wearing a badge on his brown leather vest. There was no need to elbow her way through the crowd of gawkers who had converged on the street, because it parted like the Red Sea before her.

"Are you the sheriff?" she demanded.

Sheriff Careless Lachlan was bent over Johnny Two Toes, who was deader than a doornail. He looked up over his shoulder. Startled by the imposing dignity of the woman behind him, he snapped up like a bent willow branch and yanked his hat off his head.

"I'm Sheriff Lachlan." He smiled, exposing tobacco-stained teeth. "What can I do for you, ma'am?"

"Why didn't you stop this gunfight before it started?"

"Why, uh . . ." He scratched his balding pate and said, "Someone mighta got hurt."

She stared down at the dead man at her feet, then toward the other three men who lay sprawled in various postures on the street, her pointed gaze finally landing on the broken window of the Silver Buckle Saloon. "It seems to me someone did get hurt, Sheriff."

His face turned beet red. "Only this riffraff, ma'am." He frowned and muttered, "I told Mr. Trahern this wasn't a good idea."

"You *knew* these men were hired killers and yet you did nothing to stop them?"

The sheriff pulled at the neck of his shirt and loosened a string tie that was already half undone. "Now

I wouldn't exactly say that, ma'am. I did warn the boy they was after him," he said. "Told Ethan he oughta get outta town and go back to that ranch of his'n. But Hawk, he insisted on stayin' in town, facin' 'em down." Careless shrugged in a characteristic way that showed how little he cared, which was, in fact, what had gotten him his name. "You see how it turned out."

"What if Mr. Hawk had been hurt?" Patch asked.

"Nobody can kill that son of satan," the sheriff muttered. "Not that they ain't been tryin' more years than I can count. Ever since—"

"Ever since what?" Patch asked.

"That's history now. The boy's paid for what he done."

"What do you mean?" Patch asked. "How has he paid? And for what?"

"Why, for killing Jefferson Trahern's boy, Dorne. Claimed it was self-defense, Ethan did. Only thing that kept him from gettin' hung was Boyd spoke up for him."

"Boyd?"

"Boyd Stuckey. Old friend of Ethan's from when they was kids. Boyd's near rich as Trahern these days. Anyway, that Hawk boy finally got out of prison 'bout a month ago. Been there nigh onto seven years. I say he's paid his debt. Oughta be able to walk the streets like a free man. Only . . ." He frowned up at the sun and put his hat back on—lady or no—to keep off the noonday heat.

"Only what?" Patch asked, impatient to hear the rest.

"Only Trahern don't figure it that way."

"So Trahern hired these men to kill Ethan—because Ethan killed his son? Even though Ethan has paid his debt to society by spending seven years in prison?"

"Jefferson Trahern don't forgive nor forget."

"How can I get to Ethan's ranch from town?" Patch asked.

"Head southeast 'bout five miles, you'll find it right along the Neuces. But you don't want to go there, ma'am."

Patch arched her most intimidating brow. "Why not?"

"Ain't safe."

"Why not?"

The sheriff grimaced. "Lady like you has no business bein' 'round a fella like him. Convicted murderer and all."

Patch squared her shoulders and lifted her chin. "I'll have you know that Ethan Hawk is—" Patch cut herself off. She couldn't call Ethan her fiancé, not without stretching the truth. Nothing had been settled that day eight years ago when Ethan had said goodbye.

Patch had waited as long as she could for Ethan to return to Fort Benton. Both her father and stepmother had advised her to keep on waiting. "He'll come back when the time is right," her pa had said. But Patch hadn't been satisfied with that. Finally, in the middle of the night, she had simply packed her bags and left.

She had come to this small South Texas town because Ethan had once told her he was born and raised in Oakville, Texas. It was where she had planned to start her search. Darned if she hadn't found him!

Only her journey wasn't quite over yet.

"Can you tell me where I might purchase some gentleman's clothing?"

Sheriff Lachlan pulled the scruffy hairs on his chin. "Suppose you could check at the Oakville Mercantile, ma'am. Only, why you wantin' men's duds?"

"Why, for myself, of course," Patch said. "I could hardly ride five miles cross country dressed like this." She turned her back on the sheriff, stepped up onto the shaded boardwalk, and marched straight into the Oakville Hotel.

Knowing Ethan was an ex-convict didn't change Patch's intentions toward him one whit. She had known he was on the run from the law when she first fell in love with him. Ethan had once told Patch's stepmother, Molly, that he'd had a good reason for killing the man he had killed. Patch wasn't about to pass judgment until she heard Ethan's reasons herself. Assuming Ethan didn't throw her out before she had a chance to ask for them.

Patch felt the color skating up her throat as she remembered what had happened in the Oakville Hotel. She wasn't very experienced in such matters, but it seemed to her Ethan found her at least a little bit attractive. She was ready now to approach him as a woman rather than a child. Surely he would give her the chance to convince him they belonged together.

As Patch entered the hotel lobby, the clerk Ethan had called Gilley said, "You'll have to wait for that bath until I get this glass swept up."

"That's all right," Patch said. "I have some other errands to do first." The first thing she did was to retrieve her purse from the registration desk. She gave it a little pat and was relieved to discover that Max was still inside. She had rescued the mouse from a hungry cat at the stage depot in Three Rivers. As soon as she found a catless barn she planned to release him.

"I'd like to write a letter. Do you have stationery and a pen I can use?" Patch asked.

"You can sit over there at that table," Gilley said. "You should find everything you need."

Patch made her way to the table and chair in the

corner Gilley had indicated. She found pen, paper, and ink and sat down to let her parents know she had arrived safely in Oakville, and most importantly, that she had found Ethan Hawk.

She laid her purse carefully on the polished cherry surface, then placed a piece of paper in front of her and took pen in hand. She smiled as she thought how much she owed to her stepmother, Molly Gallagher Kendrick. If Molly hadn't come into her life she would still be wearing scruffy shirts and torn jeans and fighting everyone in town to prove her father wasn't a coward. Instead she was a lady close to realizing a childhood dream.

Dear Ma and Pa,
    You don't need to worry about me. Everything is fine. You're never going to believe what happened. I arrived safely in Oakville, Texas, today—and found Ethan!
    I was right. There was a very good reason why he didn't keep his promise to me. He was in prison!
    Ethan has a ranch not far from here. I'll be going there early tomorrow morning. You can write to me care of the Oakville post office.

All my love,
Patch

P.S. Please give my love to Nessie and little Jeremy. Be sure to include my regards in your next letter to Whit. When is his ship due back in port?
P.P.S. I'll write again soon! *Don't worry about me!*
P.P.P.S. I think Ethan was a little surprised to see me, but I know everything will work out just fine.

Love and brown sugar kisses,
Patch

Patch folded the letter and found an envelope, which she addressed to her father and stepmother. She put everything away and retrieved her purse as she stood and turned to the clerk. "Can you direct me to the post office?"

"It's at the end of Main Street," Gilley said. "In the rear of the Oakville Mercantile."

"I'll be back soon."

"I'll have that bath ready," Gilley promised.

Patch stepped out into the sunlight once more and headed toward the mercantile. She walked as though she had an egg in each hand and a stack of books on her head—the way they had taught her at the fancy school she had attended in Boston. What she didn't realize was that her natural physical grace made her body sway in a way that had every cowhand up and down the boardwalk gawking at her.

Patch had learned a lot of rules in Boston, most of which began with *A Lady Never* . . . Patch figured she had broken about ten of them in the past twenty minutes. She found it difficult to always act like a lady, but she was determined that for Ethan's sake she would epitomize that feminine ideal. No matter how hard it was, she would follow the rules—except when it was absolutely necessary to break them.

Patch politely nodded her head to the local ladies and kept her eyes straight ahead when she passed the cowboys on her way to the mercantile. She didn't care to be accosted by any of them. It was a little harder to ignore the trickle of sweat that snaked down her back. But she was a lady now, and that meant enduring certain discomforts.

Oakville's main street wasn't very long and consisted of two saloons, two hotels, the livery, several eateries, and the mercantile. Patch welcomed the cool difference in the temperature when she stepped inside the oak-shaded one-story wood-frame building that Gilley had told her housed the Oakville Post Office. She introduced herself to Mr. Felber, the postmaster, and was assured that her letter would be on its way to Montana on the next stage.

"I'd also like to buy a few things," she said.

"Help yourself, Miss Kendrick," Mr. Felber said. "Help yourself."

As Patch discovered, Mr. Felber never came out from behind the counter. When he said "help yourself" it was because he couldn't be bothered. While she searched out a pair of Levi's, a chambray shirt, socks, and boots, she watched Mr. Felber sit on his stool and play solitaire. He stopped only long enough to take payment from a lady who bought pins and another who bought peaches.

Patch's attention was drawn to the door when the bell rang to announce another customer, mainly because Mr. Felber got up off his stool and walked all the way to the end of the counter. Apparently, whoever was entering the mercantile was a person of some importance.

The tiny young woman who stepped inside had hair as black as coal, dark brown eyes, and the face of an angel. She was dressed every bit as modishly as Patch herself. Patch had never in her life seen such a beautiful woman. She knew she was staring, but she couldn't help herself.

Patch was chagrined when the woman not only noticed her stare, but smiled and walked right up to her.

"Hello," the beauty said. "My name is Merielle. What's yours?"

"Patch—Patricia Kendrick."

"I haven't seen you before," Merielle said.

"I just got into town today."

"Would you like to come to my house to play?"

"To play?" Patch was confused by the invitation, which made no sense. To play what?

"Merielle!"

The tiny woman jumped at the shout from the door. She turned and her smile widened as she hurried up to the sun-browned cowboy standing in the doorway, his hat in his hand, his black hair awry. "Frank! I've found a new friend. Come and meet her."

Merielle took the cowboy's hand and drew him into the store. Patch stared again, because the cowboy was as tall and handsome as the woman was tiny and beautiful. He also had black hair, but his eyes were gray. There were lines beside his eyes and around his mouth, but Patch didn't think he had gotten them smiling.

"Howdy, ma'am," the cowboy said, nodding his head in a jerky motion. He turned his attention to the young woman. "I've been looking everywhere for you, Merielle. I wish you wouldn't run off like that."

Patch frowned as she listened to the way the cowboy was speaking to the woman—as though she were a child. Merielle was tiny, but she had a woman's body. However, as Patch watched the man and the woman together, it became increasingly apparent that Merielle had a child's mind.

"Can Miss Kendrick come home and play with me?"

Patch saw the cowboy's jaw harden, saw his lids drop to cover the melancholy in his eyes.

"Maybe we could get together another time," Patch said to Merielle, hoping to smooth things over.

The cowboy slanted Patch a grateful look before he focused his eyes on Merielle. His features were troubled. "I don't think that's a good idea."

"But we could have fun. I just know it!" Merielle said.

Patch set her purchases on the counter, then reached out and took both of Merielle's hands in her own. "I promise I'll come visit soon," she said. "You go with Frank now."

"You promise?" Merielle asked worriedly.

Patch wondered why Merielle didn't also have a child's trust. She smiled at the other woman. "I promise."

Merielle's whole face brightened. "All right. I'll see you soon." She turned and linked her arm through Frank's. He nodded to Patch, then slipped his hat on. Patch noticed that he leaned down to listen earnestly to Merielle as he led her from the store.

When Patch turned around to pick up her purchases again she found Mr. Felber shaking his head and *tsk*ing.

"Such a shame," he said. "Poor Trahern."

That name struck a strident chord with Patch. "Trahern?"

"That was Merielle Trahern. Jefferson Trahern's daughter. I don't know how Frank can stand to see her like that day after day."

"What is Frank's relationship to her?"

"He's Trahern's foreman. He and Merielle used to be sweethearts a long time ago. Whole town knew those two kids were in love. Wasn't ever going to come to anything, though."

"Why not?"

Mr. Felber played a red nine on a black ten. "Frank Meade was dirt poor. Trahern would never have let his daughter marry a sod farmer's son."

Patch told herself she wasn't going to ask, but the words were out before she could stop them. "Has she always been like that? Childlike, I mean?"

"Nope. And that's the shame of it."

Patch felt the gooseflesh on her arms, but forced herself to ask anyway. "What happened? What made her like that?"

"Poor girl lost her mind when Ethan Hawk raped her."

Joan Johnston is the bestselling, award-winning author of fifteen historical romances and twenty-one contemporary romance novels. She received a master of arts degree in theater from the University of Illinois and was graduated with honors from the University of Texas School of Law at Austin. She is currently a full-time writer who lives in South Florida.